BLUE JAY

A. ZUKOWSKI

Beaten Track
www.beatentrackpublishing.com

Blue Jay

Published 2019 by Beaten Track Publishing
Copyright © 2019 A. Zukowski

ISBN: 978 1 78645 368 6

Cover design: A. Zukowski

Beaten Track Publishing,
Burscough, Lancashire.
www.beatentrackpublishing.com

*This title contains material some may find
objectionable or trigger-inducing.
However, reading the following triggers may cause spoilers:*

*Brief mature content, depressive illnesses, drug use,
child abuse, sexual violence; references to past abuse,
transphobic violence and rape, miscarriage*

ACKNOWLEDGEMENTS

Special thanks to Emily Alter and Laura Zakanych for their beta-reading. The reviewers of Critiques Circle and Skye gave me helpful feedback for the opening chapter of the story. But I am solely responsible for the errors.

Massive thanks to Debbie McGowan, A.M. Leibowitz, Jor Barrie and Paul Iasevoli at Beaten Track. As always, you have all my admiration.

I think my floating gender pronouns capture well the refusal to resolve my gender ambiguity, which itself has become a kind of identity for me. ~ Jack Halberstam, *Trans**

Some days Chris is only pretending, passing between the gender boundaries, desperate for a comfortable position.

Chris Neeser is one of a kind; they got under my skin until I had to create a character easy to fall in love with. They are genderqueer but their daily life isn't an exercise in political provocation. If I were writing a rhetorical piece about queerness, I would have been more forceful, but *Blue Jay* is a story. Chris's gender and sexuality are rooted in lived experiences. They don't always challenge others when they call them names and attack them; they appear more feminine as they interact with Alex because genders are embodied, performed and reiterated. They have to survive in a heteronormative binary culture. All the pronouns they/them/he/him/she/her are used to refer to Chris throughout the book. I struggled to write Chris more than I'd imagined, but the creative process also brought out the gender variance within me. The novel shows my struggles and my refusal to conform as much as that of the protagonists.

Alex learns about himself, too, and about who he and Chris are as he journeys through the narrative. His revelation is incremental. Readers may decide he is a slow learner but please bear with him. Chris and Alex are also the products of their socioeconomic backgrounds, and Alex has mental health issues. As always, the creation of a novel makes me become aware of a range of emotions, sometimes painful. In subtle ways, I hope Chris and Alex complicate some preconceived ideas about who we are and who we can be. That's all.

CONTENTS

BLUE JAY

CHAPTER 1
TANGO

THE CHEAP LANDLORD has set the timer on the landing lights, so Chris can't get to the next level without being plunged into complete darkness. The musty scent of the old apartment block hits them as they touch the bare wall to get their bearings. The cold concrete surface reflects the neglect it has suffered over the years.

All they can hear is the whisper of their own breaths. They hate this place with a passion. If they had a legitimate job, they could have references and move to a better apartment instead of staying in a cramped, shared flat. They are not short of money, however. In fact, they give some to their mum every month and save the rest in a bank account. A secret account for their retirement fund. *Laugh out loud.* Everyone assumes they're stupid. Oh, no. They have a brain behind the pretty face, so they must be a masochist to punish themself by staying in this dump.

Chris has returned from the hotel after a quick wash. These days, they can't get away from the appointments fast enough. Even luxurious hotel rooms hold little appeal.

Washed up. That's what they are. They sigh silently.

For an escort who works late a lot, this lighting arrangement is highly inconvenient. Chris curses and walks up the stairs as fast as they can, almost running.

Forward step in a tango. *Cruzada.* An Argentine cross.

Bang! They bump into someone massive at the first turn. The impact knocks them back down several steps.

"Hey, you okay?" says a gruff voice.

"Shit." Chris stops and feels their way around the walls to find the light switch.

It's gone one in the fucking morning. Who is standing in the stupid stairway, blocking my way? When their hand touches the other person's, they recoil. Long and strong fingers connect with theirs, sending a shot of electricity through them.

Chris finds the switch; they and the stranger are bathed in the bright light from the bare bulb once more. They squint, uncomfortable with the glare of the yellow hue. They really should get their eyes tested—if there was anything they could actually read.

"What the—" Chris exclaims.

The guy must be about six feet six and built like Hercules. He shoulders a large black holdall. Chris is stunned silent by the bulging biceps and arms, and exposed flesh covered by tattoos. The physique of the stranger contrasts with Chris, who's tall and slim like a catwalk model.

Crap. The man had better not be a burglar.

Chris stops a shudder, not wanting to betray weakness. They weigh up their limited options. They highly doubt they can take on the hulk in the middle of the night. Summoning their best act of caution and confidence, their hand reaches for the pepper spray in their trouser pocket. Out of necessity, self-preservation has become part of their routine.

"Where are you going?" they ask, praying the man has a legitimate reason to be in the building.

"I'm looking for Flat Five."

Holy shit. What does he want in my flat?

"It's on the third floor. Who do you want?" Chris's suspicious eyes run up and down the other's body. He is probably visiting Chris's Russian flatmate, Dmitri, the part-time drug dealer. It's not that unusual to have strange drug fiends turning up all hours of the day, but this late and someone who looks like a thug? Chris makes a mental note to have a go at Dmitri again. Give him shit for putting them all in danger by inviting desperate addicts to the flat to trade.

Before the guy can answer, they are in pitch-darkness again.

"Fuck! Can you go up?" Chris orders. "I'll find the switch."

They move with caution, and as Chris is feeling the wall for the next light source, their head is whacked by the man's bag and they're knocked back down a few steps again.

Caida. A fall.

"Shit, will you be careful with your fucking possessions?" Chris's fear turns to annoyance. They can't help it.

"Sorry."

Phew. A burglar or murderer wouldn't apologise in these circumstances, would he? The apartment block does house some unsavoury characters.

In this inopportune moment, Chris also notices how deep the man's voice is, gravelly without sounding like he smokes forty a day. The stranger must have found the light because he is now staring down at Chris with a frown, his brows knitted close, adding to the seriousness of his face. Chris wonders for a second what the other man sees and whether they might get their arse kicked for the way they look. It wouldn't be the first time.

Chris is wearing a kind of work uniform: tight dress shirt and skinny jeans. They like to think their gender-fluidity flows through the garments and aligns with the surface. *Nuh-uh.* Wish it were that simple. Clothes are a shell that has little to do with the insides, and the insides have little to do with the anatomy. Most days, Chris is passing—performing roles back and forth and never still—a dear price they pay for living in a binary world.

Their hold on the pepper spray tightens.

"I'm moving in. Flat Five."

"Okay, can you go up to the third without turning around or hitting my face with your bag? Can you do that?"

Calesita. Carousel.

The man twirls, taking care in the narrow staircase, and proceeds.

Both hurry up the last flight while the light remains. Chris pulls out their keys and hits the switch by the door.

The keys. The spray. Weapons of little consequence.

"I can't let you in, mate. I've never seen you before." Chris uses their most threatening voice, pushing their chest out for extra effect. *Who am I kidding?* Chris's appearance is the complete opposite of their hardened attitude.

"You mean you live here, too?" The man's frown deepens. Something unreadable shifts in his face, amidst the dark stubble. Deep, soulful eyes. Chris never aspires to that kind of masculinity but they *could* fall for it.

Shadows. Great. The light has gone out again, so Chris conveniently hides the pink flush on their face.

Cuarta. The finale.

They have performed a dance, antagonistic and graceful like a tango in the dusk. The two bodies swing in the narrow space, his *yang* complementing their *ying*.

"No, I am pretending I have a key and I'm about to go into my accommodation," Chris retorts, sarcasm dripping off them like overloaded syrup. Their eye-roll in the dark is wasted on the giant, though. "I'm not opening the door unless you have proof you live here, mate."

They turn the light on once more.

The big man schools his face to an unintelligible expression. "I'm...moving in. Proof..." He sighs.

"At one in the fucking morning?" Chris arches their right eyebrow.

"I got delayed." A man of few words. Chris doesn't mind that. They have to talk to too many clients as it is.

"Let me see your keys." Chris is rather pleased they sound authoritative to their own ears, while they hold their palm up.

The big guy exhales again and rummages in his pockets until he finds his set. Ignoring their outstretched hand and gesturing Chris to move aside, he asks, "May I?"

Chris watches him as he inserts the right key and turns the lock. They heave a sigh of relief. A couple of rooms have been vacant since their friend Liam, who used to work as an escort as well, 'retired' and moved in with his boyfriend Ali. Another flatmate left a couple of months ago. Even though the residents of the flat are usually eccentric, the middle of the night is still a stupid time to move to a new place. Chris scowls at the back of the guy as they follow him in.

The man stands in the sitting room and looks around. A corridor leads to three rooms, and off to the side of the lounge are Chris and Liam's adjacent bedrooms.

Chris reluctantly plays host and gestures to the short corridor. "Well, the room next to mine's free. Or you can have the one over there. This one here is a little bit bigger." Chris indicates their neighbouring room with a twirl of their smooth hand, their slender wrist rolling in mid-air.

The space in question isn't bigger by much. Apart from Chris's room, they all have single beds like prison cells with the bare minimum of functional furniture. As Chris has lived here the longest, they have replaced the bed with a double so they can bring hookups home.

The man takes a peep in Liam's old room. "This will do." He puts down his bag on the narrow bed.

Chris stares at the strong back; the guy's muscles stretch, seeming far too bulky for his T-shirt.

"Well, good night." Their new flatmate disappears behind the door.

A challenge.

An ill-mannered but intriguing bastard will fit in well with the other occupiers of the dingy flat. Chris is now wide awake after the impromptu tango of the night. She has no appointment until later tomorrow—or today—so she'll sleep in. She goes into her room and smokes a joint.

When Chris has done smoking, she grabs her towel and shower gel. Dressed in a faded T-shirt and briefs, she opens the door to use the bathroom.

Crash!

"What the—" In the dusk of the lounge, her new flatmate has also emerged. Chris has run headlong into the giant by the bedroom door. The new tenant is making their apartment appear far too crowded all of a sudden.

You will meet someone new and alluring.

It must be her destiny. Chris laughs at how that sounds like her horoscope for the day.

She turns the light on once more. She's so aghast by the sight, she has to stop herself from gasping. The man wears only a pair of black boxers, revealing his huge back covered by two wild animals and a sundial.

He turns to bare a large eagle with wings that spread from his shoulder to his chest. One of his arms is tattooed with an intricate pattern; two snakes grace the other, where the word 'Sam' is inked among the animals. Chris wonders who the name belongs to. She swallows and is lost for words because she does have a thing for people with tattoos. Tattoos or not, she all too often falls for some unbearably nasty bastards. With women, she likes them with long hair and sweet smiles. The femme to her butch.

She's surprised she's horny; after all, she had come in the client's arse an hour ago.

"Ah, you want a shower? Why don't you go first?" That rich tone reaches out to her.

The last thing she wants is to sport an erection with the new tenant. She tries to drop her towel serendipitously to cover herself up. "Oh, no. You go ahead. I'm used to staying up anyway."

Chris runs back to her room and sits on the edge of her bed to wait for her racing heart to calm down.

When was the last time she blushed seeing a hot-blooded naked torso? Maybe never. Annette's body parts. Limbs and flesh. She fails to remember anything before that.

It must have been about fifteen minutes when a knock on her door wakes her from her wandering mind. She opens to see the man, now clad only in a small white towel around his waist. Tiny beads of water cling to his skin. Her reflex might have been to jump her new neighbour, except she's unsure of the other's sexual orientation and he has a few inches and about a hundred pounds on her.

"Shower's free. Thanks, hmm, for your help tonight." He scratches his head. "Name's Alex."

He extends his hand, which is huge, matching the size of the rest of him, the rough and warm skin touching Chris's. Closer now, she notices the slight kink of his strong nose. A broken nose usually matches a *his-story*. He's a gangster, a fighter or a boxer. Dark-brown hair and deep-set black eyes. The man is made up of hard edges and sharp planes, and definitely not conventionally attractive.

Her-story. She's an escort, a cynic and stuck in a rut.

"Chris." She wants to say more, but she closes her mouth, afraid of the kind of rubbish that usually falls out.

"All right, good night."

In the bathroom, when she considers her reflection in the steamed-up mirror and contemplates her face and body, Chris wishes she'd burst open and let everything out. She leans in and scowls at the image of someone whose pretty surface hides nothing but shattered pieces underneath.

~~~

Four and a half fucking years in jail. Alex wouldn't say he'd been looking forward to being out. Standing in front of the gate all alone, he thought about the prospect of life outside but couldn't summon up any enthusiasm.

Still, the smell of freedom was fresh, even though nothing could lift his spirit inside or outside the prison walls. Like a cliché, he sniffed as he emerged from HMP Pentonville, and found it only marginally better than the air in the jail yard.

Alex was less than pleased to see his older brother Gary picking him up this morning. Alex had fallen from grace at the height of his career. So what did he expect? An entourage? A welcome-home party?

"Hey, don't look so glum. I'm afraid your cronies forgot about you the minute you left the ring. Just me." Gary gave Alex a crooked grin and pulled him into a bear hug. "Anyhoo, freedom at last. Let's go and celebrate, bro."

Drinking was the last thing Alex wanted to do, but he knew perfectly well Gary wouldn't have celebrated in any other way.

"I've got to report to probation, and they've already arranged a bedsit for me in London. I'm not supposed to hang around Essex, Gary. It's one of my parole conditions."

"Visiting your folks is fine, right? Come on, man. Fuck probation."

How can Gary be so irresponsible at his age?

"No, G. Bro, if I don't report and do as my probation officer tells me to during my licence, I'm back in the nick. You got that?"

Gary knew all about probation and the criminal system, having had his fair share of troubles when he was younger.

"Kill-fucking-joy. All right. I'll take you to report, then home to the 'rents. They're desperate to see you."

Gary patted Alex's muscly arm. One thing he could say about prison: he was able to stay fit. Most days there was work and little else to do but exercise in the gym. Some of the inmates were in awe of him. Despite what he'd done, the other prisoners still pitched him high up in the pecking order. With a build like his, no one dared to touch him.

Alex wondered why his parents even wanted to see him. He was their golden egg for ten, fifteen years, but they didn't exactly come visit him in prison, or not often. In fact, he'd rarely received regular visits other than Coach. His parents and Gary came once every four months or so even though they didn't live that far from the jail. They were too busy drinking and getting up to no good to visit their son and sibling. He couldn't pretend he looked forward to seeing his folks and being back in Essex.

The probation officer treated him with professional coldness, explaining the terms of his licence and the reporting expectations. Alex received the keys to the flat he'd be sharing with a few other guys. Though not all the flatmates have criminal records, it is a kind of halfway house for probationers and parolees. It can't be any worse than prison. Alex is going to keep his head down and do the time.

The accommodation is near Finsbury Park in North London, away from Sam's family and the extended network of acquaintances from his previous life. Through Coach's connections and approved by his PO, there's already a job interview lined up. The probation officer lifted the curfew for his licence because this is a security job and he'll be covering overnight shifts. It's a start. Alex grew up poor, and his boxing training taught him hard work. He can do this.

On the way to Essex, he stared at the passing scenery, trying to find something familiar to focus on but failing. His connection to this part of the world is permanently broken.

Gary drove him to their parents' large house, bought with Alex's money when he was doing great about ten years ago. At twenty-three, the boxing world had tipped him to be the next big thing, and Alex won quite a few national and international championships. By twenty-six, he ranked among the top twenty heavyweights worldwide.

The mansion stands on the coastline of Southend-on-Sea. As he got out of the car, he noticed the extensive front garden was overgrown, and the building had fallen into disrepair. It had not been painted for as long as he'd been away, and some cracks had appeared on the external walls, like the fault lines in Alex's life. Well, there's nothing he can do for his parents now. Considering his dad was a builder before drinking got the better of him and Alex started to win fights, he should have maintained the house better.

Gary opened the front door. At thirty-five, he's still living at home and sponging off his folks. Alex followed Gary into the dusky hall. The curtains were drawn even though it was almost lunchtime.

"Mum! Dad!" Gary shouted in the direction of the first floor.

Mum appeared in a dressing gown at the top of the ornate stairs. "Shit. Alex. I forgot you're coming out today." Slurring her words, she seemed worse for wear, and it was only late morning. She flew down the stairs in an entrance that would have made Scarlett O'Hara proud, and Alex hugged her. She had gained more weight since he last saw her. Alex's family members are all big-boned and solid, and he's taller than Gary by a couple of inches.

Dad came out of the sitting room. "Hey, son. Good to see ye."

"Good to see you too," Alex replied, unsure whether he meant it.

Gary ushered Alex into the lounge, and he enthused about having some mates over and going to get booze to celebrate his brother's release. Alex felt a dull pain in his head. All he wanted was to go to his flat and collapse in bed, spend his first day as a free man without enduring his family and their drunken acquaintances.

"Oh, come on. Why don't we go and get some beers, maybe a bottle of cava? To celebrate." Gary was totally oblivious to Alex's predicament.

"Gary. I'm not drinking." Frustration infused his words because since that day five years ago, Alex has not touched a drop. Alcohol, unlike love, is easy to give up.

"It's my parole condition." Alex would still be abstinent even if it wasn't a requirement.

"We'll drink on your behalf, then."

As if he needs an excuse to do that.

~~~

Gary dragged Alex out again and bought a bunch of supplies from the boozer, using the allowance given to him upon release. Despite Alex's protests all day, Gary, his mum and dad and their friends continued drinking. Alex should have called a cab, but he was too numb and tired to think straight. Eventually, one of the family friends took pity on him and gave him a lift to the train station.

Since Alex used to get taxis or was driven around London in flash cars, he doesn't know his way around the city, especially the north side. By the time he had eaten dinner and worked out how to reach the flat near the Arsenal football ground, it was gone midnight. Navigating the public transport system is another thing he'll have to learn in his life outside.

~~~

Chris, his new flatmate, is stunning. Probably in his early twenties, he's smart-mouthed and fearless and has the height for modelling because he can talk to Alex without looking up like most people. His ash-blonde hair is cut close to his scalp, and delicate silver jewellery adorns his neck and narrow wrist. Under the bright glow in the stairwell, Chris is close enough for Alex to see his perfectly balanced face, punctuated only by piercings, the tiniest studs: one in his left ear and one under his bottom lip. Alex has seen plenty of pretty people in his life, but the elegant face and clear aquamarine eyes have an intensity so bright they eclipse the artificial light and blind him.

Chris's sultry and honeyed voice, too, draws him in, powering an attraction beyond reason. When he was boxing, Alex would never have let himself notice someone like Chris no matter how much he'd wanted to on occasion. But prison has stripped him of the macho-boxer identity that was potent as much as constraining.

Chris is beautiful and way more alluring than the women who used to hang around the boxing scene. Most of them would thrust their body to draw Alex's attention because he was successful and therefore powerful. He'd hooked up with his fair share of models and starlets then, even though he was married to his childhood sweetheart. No more. After his crime, Alex decided he would never behave like that again, and he hasn't felt horny for a while, anyway. Sometimes he took care of himself in his prison cell, but he didn't think about actual sex that much during the sentence.

As a boxer, he couldn't risk acting on his attraction to the same gender. He had to protect his brand, his image—his manager kept on about those as if he wasn't an athlete but a celebrity with no discernible sporting skill. Now he is no longer in the limelight or married—*what a relief!*—his suppressed interest in more than women has come back with a vengeance. He wonders if the dry spell in prison has played havoc with his sensibility.

Chris's nails are painted with dark-blue glitter, and a subtle shade of turquoise shadow enhances his eye colour. Alex wonders about the make-up. *Chris. Kristy. Christopher.* Could someone be all three? His family would call anyone dressed like that a nancy boy. This is London, though, not back home, and Chris doesn't give a shit about what anyone else thinks. That much is clear.

Chris is gutsy in the way he stands up to Alex. Few people dare to challenge him like that because of his size. Alex even likes the way Chris frowns, creasing his otherwise smooth face, and he's frowning a lot tonight, revealing two deep dimples.

It's understandable Chris is aloof and annoyed—who wouldn't be to find their flatmate moving in so late at night?—and Alex is secretly pleased Chris doesn't recognise him. Before he was released, they'd warned him about the possible media attention. His case was high profile and sensational. Media covered the court proceedings extensively, notwithstanding some reporting restrictions. He wasn't looking forward to the public scrutiny—another reason why he was happy to move to his new accommodation so late at night. The new Alex has replaced the limelight with shadows.

Alex stares at the ceiling in the darkness of his room. Imagining Chris's eyes and the star-like silver studs he wore makes his skin tingle, a warmth building inside of him, reminding him of a long-forgotten sensation. He ponders the shades of London on the bare walls, unable to fall asleep and afraid of the darkness of his nightmares.

His first night of freedom after four and a half years.

~~~

Fifty fucking thousand. Alex reads through the mini statement he's printed from the ATM again and goes home to call Tony, his ex-manager.

"What? Who is this?"

"It's me." He's bought a pay-as-you-go phone—the cheapest you can get—and a SIM card, which is why Tony doesn't recognise the number.

"And who the fuck—"

"Alex." He wants to add 'you idiot' but thinks better of it.

"Blue!" Tony changes to the smarmy businessman in a split second. "When did you come out?"

"Don't call me that, Tone." Alex might not be very good with his money, but he isn't stupid. Tony is good at getting him the deal while always looking out for number one. Alex wanted nothing to do with him when he came out of prison, but he can't ignore the fact that Tony was ripping him off through his personal crisis and jail time.

I can do this.

"Okay, Alex. What can I do for you, son?" Now the wizard turns into the paternally concerned ex-manager.

Alex gets straight to the point. "I wanna know how come there's only fifty grand in my account."

"Alex, you wouldn't believe how many outgoings there've been. Barristers, court costs, compensation. Severance—"

"Is that what you call the hundred thousand you paid yourself? Severance?" Alex drums his finger on the table as he talks.

Silence for a beat. "Alex, don't be like that. I was with you for ten years. I've got my family to consider."

Alex can almost hear Tony's brain calculating before he changes the subject. "Listen, if you want to do some comeback matches, you'll build a nest egg in no time. There will be a lot of interest. I'd say you could buy a nice house in the countryside after a match or two."

A nice fucking house in Essex. Fights that will be televised worldwide. The constriction in Alex's throat threatens to choke him. He can't face the media attention, and it will all rub salt in the wound for Samantha's parents. Samuel Taylor is not a man to cross. Even though Alex found his father-in-law reasonable, the East End hard man has a reputation to uphold. Alex is expecting retaliation anytime although he made a decision while serving his sentence that he was not going to run away. He will face the music when the time comes because he deserves every punishment.

"I'll think about it." Alex rings off and immediately contacts the bank to change his account access in case Tony sucks him completely dry. His old manager will lose interest in him soon enough because he's no longer a cash cow ready for milking. Freedom sometimes comes in the form of poverty.

~~~

Thursday is Jeff's day. Every week in the afternoon, Chris makes her way across town to the older man's apartment in Westbourne Park. The ex-investment banker has taken early retirement and lives alone in a beautiful flat.

Jeff opens the door with a wide smile. Chris steps in and they give each other a friendly peck.

"How's it going, my love?" Jeff gestures for Chris to sit on the plump sofa.

"Same old." Chris shrugs.

Jeff pours Chris a whiskey. "Sorry about last week. I felt a bit under the weather, and they had to check it out. I didn't feel like a visitation."

"Hey, it's fine. Your health is far more important." Chris kicks her shoes off and takes a sip of the offered whiskey.

"What's happening in your life? I'm sure it's a bit more interesting than talking about ART." Jeff sits too and takes a sip of his water. "How's Elena, the Spanish lassie?"

"Huh? Elena and I broke up, like, two months ago!" Chris smiles because it's not the man's fault that her love affairs are all rather short-lived and most of the break-ups have been clusterfucks. The verbal abuse she gets when her lovers quit is always colourful. She should collect it in a compendium: *How Not to Finish With Your Lovers for Dummies.*

"You know what your problem is, Chris?" her last boyfriend had asked her when he broke up with her. She stared at him but couldn't summon any strong emotions. There lay the problem.

He called her a cold-hearted whore and left. *Well, that's that then. Trashy bastard.*

Once, she was chatting up this guy in a bar only to learn that she'd already gone out with him about five years ago and they'd split after a couple of weeks. Chris was embarrassed about not remembering the man at all. Her disastrous love-affair history plays like a dating show. Chris gets voted out early in the series every time.

"Well, I'm single again, anyway." Chris rolls a joint. Jeff used to smoke but gave it up after being diagnosed positive. Now, he thinks *to hell with it* and enjoys passive smoking when Chris is around.

"So, nothing much to tell about boring Chris. Some guy moved into my flat, taking Liam's old room."

Her friend Liam occasionally used to service Jeff when Chris wasn't available. That's why Chris justifies serving up the information about Alex. Nothing to do with how she's been trying to bump into her new flatmate some more over the past week.

"Oh, is he a nutjob like the rest of you?" Jeff teases.

"Thanks. I love you too!" Chris rolls her eyes and grins. "I have no idea. His name's Alex. He's enormous and looks like a bouncer. That's all I know. We've hardly exchanged info."

Chris has told Jeff a lot of things she wouldn't tell anyone else. Chris's own sorry excuse of a mother has never acted like a parent, so Jeff has become an older confidante over the six years they've known each other. Jeff was in a monogamous relationship with a partner for twenty years. They were supposed to be exclusive until this boyfriend had an affair and infected both of them with HIV. When Jeff first told Chris about his past, she'd felt the familiar anger about all the injustices in the world. Jeff was resigned to it. He shrugged it off and said, "Such is life. Let's live the best we can, whether we have a day or fifty more years."

His treatment has been going well, so there is no reason he won't live for decades yet. In fact, he made so much money, he could relax and enjoy his life in early retirement. He sings in a gay men's choir, views exhibitions and attends theatre performances all the time. A man of leisure.

"Look at the glint in your eyes," Jeff coos. "Enormous and bouncer-like sounds your type, no?"

"I'm pretty sure he's straight unless he wants me for a girlfriend." Chris chuckles.

Jeff nods. "You need to tell him you can be his girl, darling."

"He's got a hundred pounds on me. You should see his massive biceps. I'd rather not get my arse kicked."

Chris's face darkens for a second while she takes a toke of her joint before schooling her expression to neutral and changing the subject.

"Now, I love chatting to you, but let me give you a good time, yeah? That's why I'm here."

"Yeah, all right." Jeff laughs. "I like talking to you, though. You don't need to think of me as a client and work for your keep."

Chris only smiles and moves to kiss him. When she first met Jeff, she offered to give him a blow job or perform full sex with a condom, but Jeff rejected the idea. 'Condoms can leak' was his reason even though Chris takes non-prescription PrEp anyway as a precaution. Jeff insists he's happy with Chris's almost-platonic visits.

Chris can't do more than kiss, caress and jerk him off. She feels bad that Jeff always gives her a hundred quid plus a generous tip. Since they have become close, Jeff insists on paying her to make sure she's not there because she pities him.

Pride. Everyone needs a bit of that. Chris will come to see Jeff anyway, whether being compensated or not, because she respects the older man. But if anyone tries to tell her she's a tart with a heart, Chris will rip their head off.

CHAPTER 2
BLUE

T HE ENTIRE JOHNSON household hug Alex, leaving him with a neck-ache because some of them are small, like three-year-old Shona, so he needs to keep bending down. He wonders if the women have left a scattergraph of lipstick marks all around his face and neck. Eventually, Coach ushers them all into the sitting room.

"Come on, give Alex some space, will ya?"

Once in the sitting room, Alex touches his head and stands to one side, trying to make himself less visible, but it's impossible with his stature.

Paula hollers from the kitchen, "What do you want to drink?"

"Diet Coke, if you have it, or water. Please."

Attempting to blend in, Alex sits in an armchair. Shona comes forward and stands in front of him, staring, as though she's trying to work out if the giant is harmless. "Are you grandda's student?"

"Yes."

Coach sweeps the little girl up in one muscular arm and deposits her in her parent's lap. "Let me speak to Uncle Alex first, okay?"

Two of Coach's children are around, as well as their partners, so there are eight for Sunday lunch. By the standard of the Johnson family, that's a pretty small gathering. Coach has avoided too many faces today, to give Alex a chance to acclimatise. He's considerate like that.

The older man puts a hand on Alex's shoulder. "Do you want to come with me out back? We can have a chat away from the riff-raff."

His eldest son Dael shouts, "Hey, speak for yourself, Dad!"

Coach chuckles and leads Alex to the backyard where they sit on a couple of rickety wooden chairs. The space is a little wild and overgrown, but like the rest of the house, it's a welcoming space for Coach's favourite student.

"How are you feeling, son?" Coach asks. For over twenty years, Dex Johnson has been more of a dad to Alex than his real father. Alex never wanted to leave Dex's training school, but he didn't have a choice when he went pro aged seventeen. Coach has always been there, acting as his mentor and emotional support whether Alex trained with him or not. Dex is also the one person who did not abandon Alex when he went to prison.

Alex puts his hands between his thighs. "Okay, I guess, given the circumstances. It's good to be out."

"How's the new job? I know it's not your ideal career." Coach lined Alex up for the security job with his cousin's company. Dex's cousin is fine, but Alex's direct manager is an asshole who takes pleasure in ordering the great Alex Whale around. It's not Coach's problem, though, and Alex is grateful for the introduction nonetheless.

"It's a start, Dex. Thanks." Alex can't hide the darkness in him, no matter how he tries. He wishes he could be more positive and had good news to tell Coach.

Dex encourages Alex as always. "I'm sure you'll find something better soon. What about boxing? Have you thought about your career?"

My career. Alex flinches with the words since all his troubles started when his boxing career was everything. He left his roots, listened to managers and trainers who only wanted to exploit him. Sam changed. His parents and brother tried to squeeze as much out of him as possible. Alex shakes his head, but the memory is embedded so deeply in him that even the words 'boxing career' hurt.

Now, the shackles of fame and fortune have disappeared, leaving him poor and empty, but he's not fighting off people who want to suck him dry. Even the darkest sky has a silver lining.

Has he still got the passion for boxing? He has tried not to think about it for the past few years.

"I don't know. Tony asked me about comeback fights the other day." Alex stares at Dex's garden, not focusing on anything in particular.

Dex tuts. "Tony would, wouldn't he? I never liked the little weasel. What about you? Do you want to do that?"

"No way!" Alex hasn't considered Tony's suggestion seriously because he's not desperate for money. His family will have to look after themselves like everyone else. He made the decision in jail that he is going to live for himself and not try to be the Alex Whale that other people rely on. Easier said than done.

"The prison and probation have kept my release secret as much as they can. I don't know what Sam's family would do if I made a high-profile public appearance. I'm surprised a death squad hasn't got wind of me being out yet." He chuckles.

"It's not funny, Alex. You take care of yourself, all right?" Dex sighs. "I wish they'd understand you've been punished enough. Losing everything overnight like that. Killing or hurting you is not going to bring Sam back."

The mention of Sam not being here anymore makes Alex want to cry, but it's not something he can do in front of anyone, even though Coach has practically brought him up and seen him at his worst. Like the last few times Alex has felt tears prick at the back of his eyes, he clenches his jaw to stop himself.

Dex looks at him intently. "Our club would love to have you. It's not going to be enough as a full-time job. I can barely make a living out of it now, with the few after-school and Saturday classes for kids, plus some adult sessions. But if you like, you can help me train the youngsters. We'll share the fees. I'm getting a bit long in the tooth now, y'know. My children keep telling me to retire."

Alex nods. He has noticed the sprinkles of white in Dex's black curls. "I'll think about it and let you know. I'm taking one step at a time. I've never taught people to box before, though."

"Well, you've got skills and you're patient. I'm sure the kids will like you." Coach smiles, his eyes sparkling with joy. "Do you know which class I love to teach most?"

"The pay-what-you-can session?" Alex answers without thinking. He remembers the first day he met Coach like it was yesterday. His twelve-year-old self knew boxing was what he wanted to do after watching Mike Tyson and Lennox Lewis on the telly. He was lithe and fit, less bulky than the man he'd grown up to be. He'd heard about Dex's club; the Tuesday night class was basically free, and anyone under eighteen could turn up.

Alex was so nervous when he took the train into London. Sitting in the rickety carriage, he thought whoever told him about this had to be lying. Why would any boxing coach train kids for free? But once a week, Dex opened the door of his club and children from the bad neighbourhoods could simply turn up. Alex used to save up his pocket money—a pound or two a week—to put in the tin, but it hardly compensated for everything that Dex did for youngsters like him.

Alex wouldn't look at Dex directly when he asked him his name and age. Despite his size, which easily intimidated people, he was shy and reserved. When he finally dared to glance at Coach, he thought he looked like Lewis, and the rest was history.

Coach said he'd taken a shine to him straight away. At twelve, Alex already towered over other kids of the same age. He didn't talk, wouldn't socialise, but he had the right attitude and killer instinct, and he was intelligent—all natural traits that made him a good athlete.

"You still run those classes?" Didn't the older man complain that he wasn't making enough money?

Dex knows what Alex is thinking. "Can't quit them kids. If there's another Alex Whale among them, it's worth it."

Alex would have become a delinquent or stayed in the dead-end town with a shit job and two point four children like all his schoolmates back home. That was another reason why he felt so ashamed after what happened; he had let Coach down. He was doing so well in the boxing world before making one gigantic, irreversible mistake, and he ended up in jail anyway like many of his childhood acquaintances.

Alex stares at the mid-distance for a moment.

"If I'm going to box at all, your club will be the first place I go to, I promise." The promise is the only positive thing he can give Coach right now.

Dex lets go of that line of questions. "What about your flat? How are you settling in?" He's thought of everything, making Alex wish his parents were as caring.

He nods. "It's okay. There are four of us. To be honest, I don't see the other guys much. There's a Russian and an Italian. And this young English kid. He must be a student or something like that. No one seems to recognise me."

Chris is the most gorgeous person Alex has met, but he's keeping that thought to himself.

At that moment, Paula opens the back door, letting out a whiff of delicious home cooking. "Hey, dinner's ready. Are you coming in?"

Dex turns to her. "We'll be right there, love." The golden couple makes the little sourness in Alex's stomach grow. As a kid, he marvelled at Dex and Paula's happy relationship. They must have been together for forty-plus years and remain strong.

Dinner is lovely, and the Johnsons are as loud and friendly as always. Alex sits among them, being treated like one of the children, except it reminds him of Sam and what could have been, and the imaginary knife sears through his heart once more. He closes his eyes and lets the weariness consume him.

~~~

Alex barely sees any of his flatmates. He ran into Dmitri doing a transaction in the lounge one day. *Great.* A drug deal in the middle of his fucking sitting room. Of course, he turned a blind eye as he would have done in similar situations in the nick.

The probation officer must have been desperate, putting him in shared accommodation like this. He wouldn't have allowed it if he'd known the easy access to drugs. No wonder lots of ex-cons recidivate. It's lucky Alex no longer takes drugs because even the prison was full of them. Alex was shocked to discover the availability of illicit goods there when he first arrived.

Another night, he heard Alberto shouting in Italian on his mobile for an hour, arguing with someone at the other end.

Chris.

Since Chris's room is next to his, Alex feels his presence all right. On his one night off a week from the late shift so far, Alex heard Chris and his companion. Alex shifted uncomfortably in his single bed. The narrow space and flimsy mattress are inadequate to accommodate a tall man like him, making sleep all the more difficult.

A woman with her middle-pitched *oohs* and *ahhs* and Chris's more muffled reassurance sounded like soft porn.

I'm going to make you feel so good, sweetheart. Jeez. It's the worst kind of torture to listen to sex through a thin wall when you're alone. The more Alex tried not to hear the noises, the more they became like surround sounds.

Alex's gaydar was pretty much dormant, but he did assume Chris's orientation after their first encounter on the stairs because of how Chris looked and behaved. Serves him right to be presumptuous.

A few days later, Alex returns home about six in the morning after the overnight shift. He should hate every day of his newfound freedom if it means sitting in an office and surveying empty spaces through the CCTV. At one point in the night, he began to imagine he was an insect trapped under a magnifying glass with nowhere to go. He laughed because it was better than crying; the lonely sounds he was making vibrated through the walls of the vacant building.

Chris and a guy are French kissing in the lounge. *Is this the same lover?* Alex tells himself off for analysing Chris's hookup habit.

Chris is clad in a small red thong and wriggling against his fully dressed boyfriend. *Thank fuck someone is wearing clothes.* He is the mirror image of Chris but less pretty: blonde hair tied up in a top knot, big blue eyes. Alex hovers, undecided whether to walk around them to his room and pretend he hasn't seen them. Either way, he'd look ridiculous.

He waits, trying to minimise his presence as Chris and the kisser break off after some prolonged and elaborate tongue-twisting. Chris glances at Alex and pushes the other towards the door.

"Shush, shush. Can't ever get rid of you. I've got to grab some beauty sleep. Work to do, people to see, et cetera."

"Yeah, yeah. Text me later, babycakes. Okay?"

Babycakes? Who ever says that? Have I just seen him squeeze Chris's arse? Alex can't help but stare at the two white, shapely globes.

After his lover has left, Chris turns and gazes at Alex with a perfect arch of his right eyebrow. "Have you seen enough?"

Alex can't believe Chris's cheek, but it's refreshing at the same time. No one speaks to Alex like that because of his size.

"I didn't ask to see you tongue-fuck your boyfriend in the middle of our flat. Sorry, if I intruded." Alex adds a large dose of sarcasm to those words, but he can't tear his eyes away from Chris's elegant and completely hairless body. A montage of what he and the top-knot were doing minutes before he interrupted plays in Alex's mind. He swallows and shifts to regain his composure.

Chris crosses his arms as if hiding his modesty from Alex's sharp gaze and meandering thoughts.

"Well, I don't expect people wandering in at the crack of dawn." He sits down and picks up a pack of cigarettes from the coffee table and lights one then holds the pack out to Alex. "You smoke? Want one?"

Now it's impossible to ignore Chris and go straight to his room. Alex sits down at the other end of the sofa, keeping a safe distance.

"No, I don't smoke." He is overdressed in his security guard uniform since Chris is as good as naked and is considering him with wide-open eyes. Alex forces himself to look away from Chris's very small underwear, which hardly conceals his size.

Chris holds the cigarette away with his long fingers, while he's not sucking it like a lifeline. He looks at Alex intently again as if he can bore into Alex's mind, as if he can access his soul with the intense indigo gaze. Under the bare light from the ceiling lamp, Alex can see Chris's irises—a mix of dark blue, violet and emerald. Is that anatomical detail possible? The combined hues make them turquoise. Chris wears red nail varnish and a hint of rose colours his cheeks.

Sensing Alex's paradox of fascination and restraint, Chris challenges him. "Like what you see?"

Alex swallows. "No…I mean, yes. You…" Damn the stutter. "You're nice-looking."

Chris laughs, sardonicism clear on his face. "Nice?"

Nice. Why couldn't he think of something else to say? Alex opens and shuts his mouth a couple of times but fails to defend himself for using such an innocuous word. He should have known that Chris would find that inoffensive word offensive.

After several seconds, Chris schools his face to neutrality. "So, what the fuck do you do? Why are you always creeping around in the middle of the night?"

Alex wants to point out that six o'clock is early morning for most respectable folks but thinks better of it. It's not the right thing to say to someone who has been staying up all night banging the next pop idol. "I've been working."

"As?" Chris raises an eyebrow like a question mark.

"Security."

Chris's eyes roam Alex's face once more, making him uncomfortable. Once Chris is satisfied with his effect on Alex, he yawns with raised arms and slowly stands. "Well, it's been a long night. I'll let you go to bed."

He sashays back to his room with the cigarette dangling from his mouth, reminding Alex of the dangerous dame from 1950s

Hollywood movies. *A femme fatale. Or Glenn Close who boils bunnies.* Dead bunnies.

Alex is out of his mind these days to be so intrigued by his flatmate. He has never met anyone like Chris in his life. He wants to find out more, and he is, without doubt, attracted to his neighbour. Blood rushes to his head, leaving Alex shaken with the realisation.

~~~

"Wow, we meet in broad daylight at last."

Chris's sultry voice startles Alex, whose head jerks up from his lunch of ham sandwiches and water, knocking a spoon off the table. He manages to catch the falling cutlery with his quick reflex.

Chris strolls into the kitchen area: an open-plan diner-lounge-kitchenette arrangement. The worktop and cooker are in an alcove to the side of the sitting room.

A sunbeam streams through the open window this late morning, gracing Chris's dirty-blonde hair.

Alex almost does a double take because this Chris has no make-up and is dressed in a plain tee and cutoff ripped jeans as though he's shed his androgyny. The fragrance from his shampoo or body wash wafts through the room like jasmine in the summer. Whenever his flatmate is near, Alex's keen heart races and his palms sweat. Alex blinks, trying to control his reaction.

Seemingly ignorant of the effect he's having, Chris makes a pot of coffee and a piece of toast and plonks himself down across from Alex. The tiny dining table sits only two, creating an intimacy that no one in the flat cares about until now. Chris's proximity causes Alex's heart to beat fast once again.

"Coffee?"

Chris has brought two cups to the table. Alex nods.

Chris pours two coffees and takes a bite from his toast. Speaking with his mouth half-full, he tells Alex, "Staring is rude."

"I wasn't." Heat rises in Alex's face.

They eat in companionable silence for a few minutes.

"How's your job going? Caught anyone breaching your security yet?" Chris asks but he doesn't seem interested in the answer at all.

"Funny."

Chris shrugs. "Yeah, comedian me."

Alex is not going to talk about his numbingly boring job at the office block down in Islington. "You're not really a comedian, are you? Whatever you do seems to be less time-consuming and more interesting than my job, though. Let me guess. A student?" Chris doesn't keep to regular hours and he's always sleeping in late. Alex imagines the college kids' lifestyle to be like that.

Chris huffs. "Nope. Been told all my life I don't have two brain cells to rub together. How am I a student? Unless you're talking about the School of Hard Knocks."

Alex has seen the way Chris speaks and how he subtly riles him up and observes him to work him out, all evidence of Chris's intelligence and curiosity. The hard-knocks part might be true. Alex wouldn't expect anyone well off to be living in this dump.

Chris finishes his brunch and lights a cigarette. A swirl of pungent smoke envelops them both.

"You seem clever enough to me. Bar job?" *All the young kids in London work in the restaurants and bars until they get better offers, don't they?* Alex sounds old to his own ears. Chris looks about ten years younger than Alex. He adds, "You're waiting to be a star or something?"

Chris scowls. "Why does everyone see my face and assume things about me? I am not only a pretty face. I think it's fucking stupid trying to be famous."

"I'm sorry. I didn't mean to offend you." Alex's mouth turns down. "Put me out of my misery. What do you do?"

Chris says, "I work as an escort."

Alex coughs, choking on his coffee, and covers his mouth with his hand as a hot flush reaches his cheeks.

Chris grabs some kitchen towel and helps Alex clean up. He watches with detachment; he must be used to that reaction.

"Say what you've got to say. Spit it out. Oh, right, you've already done that." Chris makes to stand up.

"Hey." Alex puts his hand over Chris's, around the handle of the mug. "Sorry. I didn't mean to act shocked. You don't need to leave."

Chris sits down again.

"That guy and the woman before. Are they...what's the word?"

"My clients?" Chris shakes his head. "No, I do out-calls to people's houses and hotels. I never bring them back here. Don't you worry."

"I'm not worried."

"I see other people, y'know?" Chris sucks in a chestful of cigarette smoke.

Alex is finding all the new information difficult to digest. If his brain is a computer, there's already a folder for Chris-related info. Alex has never given prostitution much thought, but he wants to understand how someone who seems so perfect to him would sell himself.

"You mean they were your lovers?" Inquisitiveness isn't in Alex's nature, but the info-bank is calling.

"Yes." Chris cocks his head.

Chris is bisexual. That must be who I am too.

For the first time in Alex's life, there's no need to hide from that simple fact. His admiration for Chris's openness nudges up another notch.

"Okay. And your clients? Do you sleep with men and women as well?"

"I don't like servicing women, so I don't. I earn enough. Guys are easier to find and more straightforward. Path of least resistance works for me."

Alex nods. "Wow. An escort. That's not a...usual job," he whispers.

Chris throws his teaspoon at Alex. "Seriously! What's your problem, man? What's a usual job? Security?"

After picking up the spoon, Alex is thoughtful for a second. "Is this an in-between thing?"

Chris blinks three times. "No."

Alex inclines his head to show he understands.

Chris sulks, seemingly annoyed with Alex's questions. He takes his cup and plate back to the kitchen to wash.

Alex can't stand the grumpy face on Chris. He picks up the rest of the dishes and follows Chris into the kitchen area. He leans against the worktop next to the sink and waits for Chris to finish washing up.

Alex's eyes travel Chris's body.

"Stop undressing me, Alex. I'm used to people looking at me funny when they find out what I do for a living. Unless you have a problem with sharing a flat with me? Or want my services? I can do you a neighbour discount."

"I have no problems, Chris. It's a job." Alex continues watching him. "I can see why you do it."

Chris's nostrils flare, though Alex thinks it's a good look on him too.

"What? Like I'm born a slut or something?"

Now Alex is a little unsure. Whatever he says always sounds wrong and irritates Chris. Alex doesn't want that. He wants to be on Chris's good side.

Alex picks his words carefully this time. "Sorry. I mean…you are sexy."

Chris's mouth opens, but the speech bubble is empty of comments for long moments.

"You're pulling my leg, aren't you?"

Alex wants to tell him how fascinated he is, but he doesn't mean to come across as a twat or a potential stalker. Chris has no shortage of friends or sex partners, so he'll think Alex is a weirdo if he tells Chris of his interest. Alex is a disgraced boxer and an ex-con. He can't get it up most days. What can he offer someone like Chris?

"I can hardly talk about my job. It's like watching paint dry. It doesn't make for a riveting conversation. At least yours is interesting."

Chris glances at Alex sidelong and tries to suppress a grin. "I suppose escorting has the same appeal as an exotic wildlife programme. The animals grunt and rut, and you can't take your eyes off them."

Alex chuckles. "A drug dealer. An escort. What does Alberto do?"

"He's a trainee chef. He works in a small family pizzeria in central London. Why?" Chris focuses his gaze on Alex again.

"Do you think he's a serial killer? He has access to knives," Alex says with deadpan irony.

Chris's answering laughter sounds like bells to Alex's ears. "No, I believe he only throws pizza bases and chops leaves for the salads."

"That's reassuring." Alex joins Chris, forgetting all his personal issues for a minute.

The way Chris giggles has distracted Alex, and Alex loves how Chris's cheeks show a flash of pink and his dimples deepen. He could watch Chris all day.

Alex is pleased he's made Chris laugh, too. Apart from Sam, he never used to make much effort of chatting people up. He has been told so many times that he's too intense.

Still laughing, Chris says, "Sometimes these flatmates are far too colourful. Feel free to tell me more about your dull security job."

Alex grins. Chris's invitation to a budding friendship is helping to heal Alex, to deal with the troubles that have plagued him for the past five years.

~~~

Chris flows down the aisles in the supermarket on autopilot. It's his night off, and he's officially off the meat market until next time. The last creep he hooked up with proceeded to stalk him on social media, telling everyone what a slut he was. *Fuck that shit.* Chris plans to stay home and make some proper food instead of thinking with his dick.

Shit. That big man currently examining the bread selection… Alex is unmissable, even with oversized Ray-Bans and his baseball cap. He stands out more because of the obvious disguise as if he was in a bad comedy movie. Chris shakes his head, turns down another aisle and plans to come back later for the bagels.

Displacement.

Now, which coffee grind? With the corner of his eye, Chris sees Alex approaching. *Why is he everywhere I turn?* Without thinking, Chris puts the nearest pack of coffee in his basket and starts to walk away.

"Why are you avoiding me?"

Busted.

Chris turns slowly, maintaining an act of innocence despite the blushing. Alex's forehead furrows.

"I'm not avoiding you. I thought you might want some privacy while shopping. You know, what with the glasses and headwear." He twirls his forefinger around his head.

An amused smile appears on Alex's face. "What? Because I'm afraid you know what I eat for my tea?"

"Oh, fuck off." Chris can't help but grin too.

Alex grabs a jar of instant coffee. "Do you want to walk home together, or am I violating your privacy knowing where you live?"

"Fuck right off." Chris is still smirking, though. "All right. I may let you walk alongside me."

Chris can sense the man's raised eyebrows and amused expression, hidden behind his large sunglasses.

"Why, thank you." *Snarky.*

"I'm nearly done."

Still with a smile, Chris surveys the contents of Alex's basket: loaves of white bread; tins of tuna; packs of ham, cheese and coffee. Diet Coke.

Chris tilts his head back towards the bread products aisle. "I'll grab some bagels. Won't be a sec."

When they walk out of the shop, Chris is loaded down with three bags of shopping while Alex has a single bulging sack.

"Shall I take one for you?" Alex offers, pointing to Chris's shopping.

Chris rolls his eyes and wonders if they'll stay on the top of his head if he spends any more time with Alex.

"I may not have as much muscle as you but I can definitely manage my own shopping, thank you very much."

Chris's sinewy biceps are mildly impressive. The hours spent in the gym are not only for cruising and his job.

"Oh, you're sensitive, too," Alex muses, seemingly enjoying Chris's tough act.

"Fuck you," Chris retorts.

"And very eloquent."

Chris stops and glares at Alex. "Are you sure about this walking back to the flat business? Do you think we'll make it to the front door without throttling each other to death?"

Alex considers Chris and smiles at his exasperation. "There's only one way to find out."

Surrender.

Chris dons a pair of Jackie O glasses, shielding his eyes from the slanting sun, and takes off, not waiting for Alex. Alex has to jog along to keep up with Chris, who marches on, his long slender legs carrying him along quickly.

Five minutes later, Chris stops outside a coffee shop. "Wait, I'm going to grab a coffee. All right?"

Eyeing the hipsters sitting on benches and working on their computers, Alex asks hopefully, "To go?"

"We can sit down for a few minutes if you want." Chris cocks his head to challenge Alex to spend more time out in public.

Alex considers it, hesitating outside the coffee shop. He looks from the patrons to Chris, his feet rooted to the spot.

Sensing Alex's fear of public places, Chris pushes open the shop doors without giving him a chance to flee.

"We're going in," he declares.

As they walk in, several of the customers gawk at Alex with curious gazes. *Is it because of his size and tattoos?* Chris glances over at his flatmate, who keeps his sunglasses on and faces straight ahead, as though he's trying hard not to be the centre of attention.

Alex walks quickly, his movements stiff, all the way to the back of the café, and sits at a small table.

Chris joins him and looks around the half-vacant shop.

"Can you tell me why we're sitting by the toilets?" Chris waves his hand to indicate the free tables around them.

Alex peers over his Ray-Bans. "I like it here."

Chris raises an eyebrow, but he can't argue with Alex's eccentricity.

Alex pulls out a ten-pound note. "Would you mind getting me a cold coffee?"

"What kind?"

"The dark-brown kind."

Chris points to Alex and shakes his head. "You! All right. A cold Americano it is."

He returns with two cups.

Alex sips his drink but keeps his head down, sitting uncomfortably.

"Blue. Is that you?"

Chris and Alex look up to meet the enquirer: a scrawny, middle-aged man with a moustache and greasy hair.

"I thought I recognised you as soon as you walked in."

Chris waits for Alex's response, but he's speechless for the moment, his hands tightening around the coffee cup. Beads of sweat grace his forehead.

Brake. Stop and hold.

Blue.

CHAPTER 3
BLACK

ALEX'S TENSION VIBRATES in the air like the humid oppressive atmosphere before a storm. Chris straightens and inhales, sharing Alex's discomfort.

The intruder carries on, oblivious to Alex's anxiety. "Are you going to box again? Man, I loved your matches. I thought you were the best heavyweight this country has ever produced."

Not eliciting any response from Alex, he quiets down. "I'm sorry...you know...for what happened."

After a pause, Alex mumbles, "I think you've mistaken me for someone else."

The man blinks. "Really? You're not Alex Whale? Are you his brother? I swear you're the spitting image of Blue."

Alex nods. "Yeah, I'm sure. Sorry to disappoint. It happens a lot."

The man scratches his head. "Okay. Uh. Sorry." He goes into the bathroom.

Chris watches Alex until after the interloper has re-emerged from the toilets and returned to his seat, with a few backward glances at Alex on his way. Chris asks, "Blue? I like it."

Alex draws a breath. "My surname's Whale, as you heard."

Chris processes that for a moment. A nickname for his size.

Chris should have known from the broken nose and scar on his cheek under the left eye socket. She has a hundred questions for Alex but promises herself she won't pry too much unless Alex wants to talk.

"You used to box. You had a nickname and people recognise you, so you were successful." Chris whispers as though she's uttering something illicit.

Alex shifts in the seat, away from Chris. "Yeah, I was doing all right."

Chris considers Alex, who takes off his sunglasses. His irises shimmer like tiger eyes in the cheap lighting of the coffee shop. Alex sits in a rigid way as though Chris's gaze is a spotlight shining on him.

"You were not only doing okay, though, were you? Your fights were on the telly. How famous were you?"

Alex shakes his head and sighs. "I'm sure you can find out all about me if you search the internet."

Chris frowns at the suggestion. "But I'm not going to unless you want me to know. Why don't you tell me about yourself when you're ready?"

Alex plays with his plastic cup of Americano. "I'm not sure if you'll want to speak to me ever again if I told you."

Chris absorbs what Alex has said. "Try me. My person specs definitely include discretion and being non-judgemental."

She also takes pride in being able to read people. She's mighty pleased with how she uses that transferable skill on her new flatmate.

She looks around the café, and a few people are still glancing Alex's way, but most of them have returned to their drinks and conversations. "You're so successful that a lot of people on the street will recognise you, right?"

Alex sighs again as a 'yes'.

"Something happened, and now you work as a security guard. Why can't you box again or train other people? Isn't that what athletes do when they stop competing?" Chris cocks her head.

Alex squeezes the bridge of his nose. "I can't face the boxing ring, but I'll think about training others. My old coach has asked me to work with him. For now, I only want a normal life."

"What's a *normal* life?" Chris pronounces the word with disdain while she stretches her long legs across the floor in front of her.

Alex shrugs. "You know, the kind where you don't have strangers approach you in a coffee shop."

Chris quiets while she drinks her coffee. Despite her usual annoyance with Alex, she wants to comfort him because he sounds so pained. She's not sure if he might welcome a hug or a distraction.

"Welcome to my world. I've no idea what I can do when I 'retire' and I'm not getting any younger." She's been looking for laugh lines in the mirror lately. Despite the fact that she has no career plans, she's tired of her life, her job, and some days she seems to be losing her sanity when she keeps dwelling on things that should remain buried.

Alex takes his sunglasses off. "How old are you anyway? If you don't mind me asking."

"Twenty-six. My birthday's soon. So, nearly twenty-seven."

"Fuck me. Look at your fresh face and bright eyes. Do you eat babies or something?"

Must the man's compliments be so backhanded? Chris gives him an eye-roll. "I won't fuck you, but thanks, I guess."

"I thought you were in your early twenties. And how long have you been a wh—I mean...escort."

Chris wags her eyebrows. "Since I was eighteen, on and off."

Alex whistles. Chris glares at him.

"Sorry. You surprised me with your age and how long you've been in the job. Eight years."

"Yes, I can count." Although she's lost count of how many times she's sold sex in that time. A thousand? Two? She's lucky and grateful for the fact that she earns good money. She knows there are other types of sex work and different conditions and prices.

Chris doesn't want pity from anyone, though. Why should she worry about what Alex thinks of her, anyway? It's not like she's not used to people's negative reaction to meeting a sex worker. It's refreshing for Chris to meet someone who isn't freaked out much by it. Chris always feels as though she repulses respectable folk. They are contemptuous and assume she's dirty and diseased. She's learned to refuse the hurt; a stony heart is the only way to stay immune.

Yet Chris wants to disclose more about herself when she's with Alex, while worrying about what he'll think of her. *Peculiar.* "Y'know, people don't aspire to be prostitutes when they grow up, but it's a job. I tried to make it as a model when I left school. It didn't work out."

Alex gaze meets Chris's. "What kind of modelling?"

"Pretty much anything. You know how it is." She shrugs.

"No, I don't know. Have I seen anything? I'd remember your face."

"I doubt it. I've done stuff like fashion catalogues, advertising. Some were…more adult."

"Oh, *that* kind of modelling." Alex's eyes widen. "You were a porn star?"

"No, it's not porn. Just glamour stuff and underwear." Chris frowns. "Well, it's still modelling. I've accepted lots of different gigs. That's all."

"You sure like taking your clothes off, don't you?"

"Work." Plenty of people enjoy looking at a body like hers, but they despise her for what she does. Chris sucks up the last of her coffee, then she purses her lips and licks them slowly to provoke the other.

Alex gazes at the soft lines of Chris's mouth, transfixed.

Chris returns the look. There's something very beautiful and expressive about Alex's beaten-up face, the scar and the sharp, strong planes.

"Don't you parade in front of people, show them your muscles and tattoos, and beat the shit out of other men? Do you call it entertainment?" she retorts.

"Sport," Alex replies with conviction and takes a sip of his drink.

"Same fucking difference. You were selling your body, man."
Deep down, Chris knows it is not the same. Alex must have
trained hard to be a top boxer.

Chris doesn't harm old folks and minors, and the men who
buy her do so willingly. She sells personal services at a price.
Why does Alex have this effect on her? For brief moments, Chris
has doubts. If she'd never started working in the sex industry,
might she be the one Alex wanted? She might be the one *someone*
wanted. Damn. What even is the meaning of their budding
friendship? Times like this, Chris has to agree with people who
tell her she's dumb.

Alex comments, "You must be good at what you do."

Huh? "How do you know that?"

Alex shrugs. "You've been at it for eight years, so you can't be
that bad. And look at that face. I bet men melt at your feet."

Another backhanded compliment.

Why have you not crawled at my feet yet? That's not a
question she can ask Alex. "Why do I find you really annoying,
Alex Whale?"

Alex grins. "I know that feeling. I find myself quite infuriating."

Chris smiles back at him.

"Listen. What are you having for dinner? Tuna sandwiches?
I'm making a pasta dish. Do you want some?"

"What's wrong with tuna sandwiches? That's what I've always
eaten. I need protein for training." Alex sulks.

"But you don't box anymore, remember? It'll be good for you.
Pasta, tomato sauce, vegetables and cheese. Get some vitamins in
you, my sweet. I can even put some tuna in it if you like?"

"Yeah, I'd love a home-cooked dinner. Thanks," Alex says.

"Well, drink up or take it with you, Alex Whale."

Alex smiles as though amused by Chris's use of his full name.
To Chris, a laughing Alex is gorgeous. His stern and broken face
lights up, revealing perfect white teeth.

Alex leaves the rest of his coffee and follows her out of the
shop, leaving his sunglasses off, as though he is unconscious
of the oglers. Chris turns to beam at him, pleased to know her

effect on him. All sunlight and starburst. Rainbows and glitter. For the moment.

At a crossroad, Chris moves forward while Alex hangs back. When Chris glances over her shoulder at him, he's watching her arse. He nearly trips up when he realises he has been caught.

Chris can't help but smirk.

~~~

They put their food away in the fridge and cupboards.

Chris turns to Alex. "So, you're going to help me cook?"

"What? You're trusting me in the kitchen?" Alex smiles. "I haven't cooked a full meal in my entire life."

Hands on his hips, Chris smiles. "What are you? A hunter-gatherer?"

"My mum used to make barely edible food while she rushed about. I ate school dinners and later trainer-approved protein-rich meals. There's takeouts and restaurants. I misspent my youth in the boxing ring. I can make sandwiches and that's about the extent of my cooking skills." Alex sulks, though not seriously.

Chris eyes his flatmate. Alex hadn't reached the peak of the boxing world without some hard graft. No one is born with muscles that ripped. How Chris would love to touch that strength, but he swallows and changes the subject.

"Well, it's about time you learned, then. Come on. Wash your hands! Onwards."

Alex smiles and follows Chris's instructions.

They spend the next thirty minutes cutting up the vegetables and bantering, conversing occasionally. Chris directs Alex to slice the peppers, onions and mushrooms. When he's finished, Chris looks at them and frowns.

"What have I done now?" Alex asks. Their faces are close together while Chris inspects the vegetables.

"They're all different shapes. I told you to cut them into strips. They need to be similar sizes so they are ready about the same time." Chris speaks with the authority of a head chef, his thumb and forefinger making the shape of a strip. He picks up a few particularly big bits and cuts them again. Chris misses the proximity when they straighten up, though.

"Not everyone's as perfect as you are," Alex says as he watches Chris's slender hands and fingers working the knives.

Chris glances at the other man and wrinkles his nose. "You being sarky again?"

"No. I'm deadly serious. You're good at your job. You take care of yourself. You can cook. Pretty sorted, aren't you?"

Chris considers Alex sidelong; he doesn't trust Alex to compliment him. Ever. "Thanks, I guess."

He puts the vegetables in the pan to fry, then turns back to Alex. "You're weird, aren't you? I mean, you must be the first person who thinks I'm sorted."

Alex fills a glass with water and leans against the worktop, watching Chris, who puts on a bit of a performance, moving about as if he's dancing to an inaudible rhythm.

"Most respectable people think your chosen occupation is less than reputable. From my perspective, you are fine as you are."

You are fine as you are.

It's the most beautiful thing anyone has said to Chris in a long time. He blinks twice, unsure if happy tears are prickling him.

He's still less than reputable, though. Chris stops and waves the spatula at Alex. "Man, I swear I will fucking kill you one day."

Alex pretends to avoid the wooden spoon and laughs. "Just saying!"

When the food's ready, Chris and Alex put the dish on the sorry excuse of a dining table and sit down. They crouch over the scratched, well-used surface as they spoon the pasta bake into their respective bowls. Seeing Alex tuck into his food with glee, warmth grows inside Chris. His past lovers never stayed for his food because Chris is not known for his culinary skills, is he? *No one wants me other than what my body can offer.*

Alex takes a bite and his eyes widen. "Wow, nice."

Chris speaks with his mouth full of his first spoon of food. "Nice. That's your choice word for me, huh? Anyway, I'm not only a pretty face, y'know?" He winks and adds more parmesan to his and Alex's bowls.

"Never thought you were." Alex stuffs more pasta into his mouth and issues some orgasmic hmms and ahhs.

Chris gazes at him with suspicion.

"And I'm glad I helped to make it. I told you I've never cooked." Alex looks as though he might finish his portion in three mouthfuls. "I'm going to grab some bread and butter."

Chris rolls his eyes at the other man as he gets the extra fodder. Alex must need a lot of energy to keep all that flesh going.

"How did you learn to cook anyway?" Alex asks after he has sat back down and helped himself to a second serving.

Chris is used to masking his shit with bravado and indifference, but he finds himself talking about the subject that he *does not* discuss. "My mum couldn't cook to save her life, so at some point, I taught myself. Otherwise, I'd have starved."

Stop talking. Please, shut your mouth.

Chris used to imagine a different life, sitting by the window of their flat and gazing at the London skyline. Beautiful orange and purple hues emanated from the windows of the high-rise blocks as if nature were mocking him by being so perfect and vibrant. The vantage point offered a view better than loft living.

Two burly police come to their door and announce there has been a mistake. Chris was swapped at birth with another baby. From a decent family. They will take him to his real family now. He waves goodbye to Annette while she dabs at her crocodile tears.

The scene never happened, and Chris grew up looking more and more like his mum. He learned that reality is nothing like his vivid imagination and his shitty life is all he has. *Laugh out loud.*

Alex considers Chris as if waiting for the next part of the never-ending story. Chris avoids his gaze and chews the pasta slowly and deliberately.

Alex has already eaten three-quarters of the dish. His hearty appetite amuses Chris. He makes a mental note that if he were to cook for Alex again, he'd need to make much more.

"Thanks for dinner. It's smashing. I don't know what I can do in return."

Chris could get used to being appreciated for something other than sex.

Alex leans back on the wooden chair and pats his full belly with a satisfactory sigh. The chair squeaks under the weight of the man. Chris worries for a second that it'll break. Disappointment is bound to follow, like the weak chair under stress.

Don't get used to Alex's presence. Don't show your hand. His usual confidence deserts him.

Out of habit, Chris masks his insecurity with flippancy. "No, have you forgotten I like your company? Don't worry about it."

"Here we go. How did I know sarcasm was coming?" Alex smiles. "At least we ate out of the same meal, so you definitely haven't poisoned me."

Chris grins, showing off his dimples. "Yeah, keep those comments coming. I'll give you poison next time."

Alex ignores the idle threat and smiles. He stands and grabs the cutlery, while Chris clears the plates. Alex's fingers touch Chris's as their hands land on the baking dish. Electricity courses through their digits, connecting them momentarily, like a scene in a soppy movie. Chris drops his hand and darts his eyes away.

"You cooked. Let me wash up," Alex offers.

~~~

The combined scents of leather, sweat, wood and adrenaline welcome Alex to Coach's boxing club. It takes him right back to the Essex boy who knew better, to the teenager who had to leave Coach because he was going to make it big. He didn't want to go, didn't want a fancy American trainer or to live in London away from Sam. She complained and sulked all afternoon, telling him he *couldn't* shag other girls because those women up in London were all *evil*. And, of course, Alex had promised her. He would have promised her the moon and meant it. At the time.

But Alex changed, and she would have changed too. He had the manager to feed and fans to please. The media frenzy and PR people after his stories. His parents' house got bigger and more opulent all the time. Gary's so-called business ventures always failed or were on the edge of needing bailouts. So who was the muggins who footed all the bills?

Before the accident, Alex had felt suffocated. For days, he didn't want to do anything while his life spiralled out of control. Clinical depression was the diagnosis according to the court medical report.

Sam had loved him, even when she found out about all the other women. That didn't stop them from arguing and fighting, always followed by desperate make-up sex. Sam had begged and cried, and she'd been distraught. They'd known each other for eighteen years, so there wasn't much left to say. Alex had thought he loved Sam, but he didn't behave like a man who was in love, and now he hates himself for having been that man once upon a time.

The images that come into his head these days are nightmares that morph into a living hell. Alex squeeze-shuts his eyes to screen out the memory but fails. Of Sam. Of how the guy might have pounded her on their new fucking bed, the one that he had ordered for the house. The Essex wild boy. It's not like Alex wasn't guilty of affairs, and he's not excusing himself. Two wrongs don't make a right. He accepted full responsibility for everything.

Alex shakes his head to chase away the big D. Swinging moods. They drown but never suffocate. Back to earth, and the pitch-black hole he finds himself in. Whenever he goes out, his palms are sweaty and his mouth feels dry, as though he's about to go back in the ring after a losing round without any way to save the match.

Dex sits down next to Alex on the bench, drawing him back from his musings. "Hey, how's it going?"

Alex forces himself to refocus, back to the present. "Good. The kids are working hard." He's come to watch the pay-what-you-can class on Tuesday. The half a dozen kids are mostly black and Asian, including one or two having a serious go at it.

"Still not interested in picking up the gloves? Not even to play around with these kids?" Dex urges while they survey the junior boxers.

Especially not with these kids. What do they say about power and responsibility? Some children need a role model, like Dex was to Alex when he was growing up. To these kids who are all from poor and deprived backgrounds like himself, Alex isn't sure if he should. Coach thinks differently, but Alex is content to sit and watch today.

Coach returns to the practice area, pairing the kids off to train. Alex hardly realises half an hour has gone until the class stops for a short break.

"I'm Devan." One of the teenagers sits down next to Alex. He has been watching this lad and noticing the good footwork and intelligence. Devan's not the biggest but he'll make a decent middleweight when he grows up. Ninety-nine per cent of Dex's kids don't go anywhere with boxing. Why would they? Some of the students are only looking for another out-of-school activity so they can stay off the street. Like Alex, these kids have never had any push to achieve anything. Alex was a tough, determined athlete who wanted success badly until he had all the spirit beaten out of him in the last few years.

"Alex." He holds out his large palm to shake the teenager's.

"I know. Coach never stops talking about you. 'You can be Alex Whale if you train hard.' That's what he says all the fucking time."

Alex knows his impact on Coach's club, even though Dex doesn't use his name to market himself enough. Alex has made a difference, a lasting legacy, for sure. On the walls are very old photos of him, of Alex posing with his teammates or Coach, and newspaper cuttings of his early wins. Anyone can see how proud Coach is of Alex Whale, his most famous graduate.

Alex chuckles. "Hey, you're not allowed to use that word. How old are you?"

"Thirteen." Devan tilts his chin, showing an innocent arrogance. "I've watched your matches on YouTube. My favourite is your win over Dill Thompson. I like the cross that won you that match, and I want a tattoo like the one you have over your heart."

Alex considers the kid and the fervent glint burning in his dark eyes. The ink over his heart is a skull with roses that he got in Mexico City when he won a match there. Alex was twenty-six, twice Devan's age, and he had the world under his feet. Sitting next to the teenager, Alex is at a loss what to say and how to help the kid. He has some suggestions for his training, but he thinks he should leave that to Dex.

The older man calls the end of the recess.

All Alex ends up saying is, "Nice to meet you, Devan. Keep up the good work."

~~~

Chris hauls his weary arse up the stairs to the flat. How the hell does he feel so tired? Oh yes, two clients one after another even though he tries not to work hard. He's not lazy, but this is not a career in which you get promoted for your performance. Chris does as little as possible; he knows his role inside out—could do it in his sleep. He hasn't actually done it since sleeping on the job would seriously lose him cred. His regulars love him, and he keeps them happy and turns down jobs that seem too much fucking hard work. Literally.

But the last john tonight always ends up hurting him a little. He doesn't mean to, but no matter how Chris prepares himself and lubes the gent up, he manages to angle in a way to cause discomfort. And the client is a man of habit. No amount of persuasion is going to change his preferred position and the order of play.

Chris sighs. He wants to have a joint and go to sleep for days.

The sight of Alex on the sofa, sleeping in a white vest and pair of boxers, makes him gasp. The TV is on but muted, the reflection of its images flickering on Alex's skin like a kaleidoscope of changing light while his broad chest rises and falls. Chris clicks the TV off. Once his eyes have adjusted to the dark, he watches Alex.

Chris should go to his room and leave Alex to rest, but he gives in to his compulsion to stay, transfixed by the sight of the other. He sits by the coffee table and rolls a joint. As he smokes it, he continues to observe his flatmate, illuminated only by the moonlight. His lips part slightly as he rests, betraying secrets of his dreams. After a few minutes, he twists a little.

"Sa. Sa."

Chris pays attention. Alex seems to be calling out for someone, but it doesn't make sense.

Alex thrashes about a couple of times. His arms and legs twitch, and sweat pours from his forehead. He bolts up and looks around, as though he's forgotten where he is. His face paints a picture of confusion and horror.

When Alex discovers his observer, he exhales. "Chris?"

"Here. Did you have a bad dream, honey?"

"Yeah. Shit." Alex runs his palm down his face to dry the sweat. "How long have I been sleeping?" He looks around some more, as though to check if they're alone.

Chris shakes his head. "I have no clue. I came back from work and you were already asleep."

Alex puts his feet on the floor, his elbows on his knees. Covering his head with his hands, he pants, trying to calm down.

Chris fills a glass with water from the kitchen and holds it out to Alex, who takes it and smiles wearily.

"Thank you."

Chris sits on the floor, at Alex's feet, like a curious cat. "You okay?"

Alex gazes at him. "Ah, I'm better."

Chris knows he's not and strips off his usual sarcasm, hiding his concern with a veil of calm.

Alex downs the whole glass of water in one go. "I had a nightmare." The haunted voice and the tremble of the words tell a different story.

"Was that why you quit boxing?"

Alex nods.

"And you went to prison for it?" Chris asks, almost in a whisper, allowing his lilt to help Alex focus, to give him a sense of security with a practised gentleness.

"How do you know? Did you check me out online?"

Chris stands and moves over to the empty end of the sofa. He leans against the back of the couch and faces Alex. "No, I didn't. I don't know much about you, sweetheart, but...do you want a hug?"

"A hug." Alex nods under Chris's hypnotism.

Chris shifts closer to Alex and winds his arm around his neck and upper arm because the man's is bigger. He presses his lips to Alex's stubbly cheek and inhales the scent of clean sweat, not infused by the smell of sex—what he often associates with being so close to someone.

"You called me honey."

Chris grins in the dark. "Yeah, and sweetheart."

Chris hasn't asked Alex about his past, about what he did to ruin his career, to deserve the intense gaze of strangers everywhere he goes. Alex has been in jail, so it's not a minor crime, and yet Chris gives him a hug, awarding him with a warm friendly kiss on his face and using endearments to comfort him. Chris doesn't always retort and argue and drown in sarcasm. He knows how to provide the soft warm safety that Alex clearly craves.

Alex melts into Chris's slender arms as if he wants to stay there forever.

CHAPTER 4
DANCE

C HRIS IS HAVING soup for dinner when Alex comes out of the shower. She wishes her flatmate wouldn't walk around half naked. It's distracting. But it has nothing to do with attraction. *Really.*

A few minutes later, Alex emerges from his room in a pair of shorts and a white vest that is too small. He makes ham and cheese sandwiches and a cup of coffee and joins Chris at the table. Looking at the pieces of limp white bread, Chris wants to tut. *Come on, the guy must be in his early thirties and yet he can't cook for himself?* Fuck if she didn't want to care about Alex like an idiot.

"Are you on early tomorrow?" Chris asks him when she finishes eating.

"Yeah, I'm covering the day shift for another guard this week. Why?"

"I'm heading to a club tomorrow night. You wanna come?" She can call one of her mates to go with, but if Alex is interested, she'd be happy to hang out with him. It has nothing to do with her little dancing heart because she's sitting close to Alex. Hell, no.

Alex wolves down three sandwiches in the space of as many minutes. He shakes his head. "I don't think so."

"Why not?" Chris dares him to come out of his self-imposed prison.

"I..." Alex hesitates. He swallows as colour rises in his rugged cheeks.

49

Seeing Alex's reluctance, Chris adds, "It'll be dark."

"Just you?"

"Yup. You and me, and a bunch of queers, I hope. Well, are you thinking it's not your scene?" She arches her right eyebrow as a provocation.

"No, no. It's not that. I'm a little nervous in a crowd."

Chris puts down her empty glass and regards Alex seriously. "When was it you last got laid?"

"That's…none of your business."

He picks up a pint glass of water and drinks from it to hide the colour rising in his face, but he gulps too fast and nearly chokes.

"It isn't my business but I'm asking." Chris stares at him, taunting.

Alex blinks a couple of times before uttering, "Getting laid…"

As he indulges in his jumbled thoughts, Chris continues, "Well, that confirmed my suspicion. Your dry spell has gone on for far too long, my friend. We're going out, and I'm getting you a woman to take to bed."

Alex opens his mouth twice but doesn't protest.

Chris takes his hesitation as a yes. "So, tomorrow night. Ten thirty. We'll order a taxi. Dress *smartly*." She cocks her head, studying his white vest that barely contain his big muscles, and points at his chest. "You do have smart clothes, don't you? You know, a shirt with buttons?"

Alex's eyes twinkle, then he tuts. "Yes. Don't you worry about me showing you up."

"I'm not worried about being shown up as long as you show up!" Chris tries hard to suppress her cheeky grin.

~~~

The next evening, as Alex takes his dress shirt and a good pair of trousers out of his wardrobe, he wonders why he's let himself be talked into going out. What is it about Chris that always persuades him to do things he wouldn't have done otherwise? *Recklessness.* He's never been one for it except that one time.

Alex realises that Chris gives him a sense of security. He does not feel uneasy around his new flatmate because of his nonchalance and lack of knowledge about boxing or Alex's past.

Public spaces make Alex break out in hives, but he's also desperate to spend more time with Chris. None of Alex's past acquaintances survived the test of hard times, and Chris is as different from them as he could be. Right now, he is the only person Alex is comfortable enough to go out with.

For the first time in five years, this new Alex wants to go out because he can imagine having fun with Chris.

Chris has brought out all Alex's hidden desires. At training, the boxers were fit, and he'd avoided watching them in the dressing room, but he loved it most when they were in the ring: the muscles, their feet moving, dancing across the square. The beads of sweat and stretched skin. Powerful drives that seared through his defences, and a secret that he needed to hide. He'd thought about how their bodies might feel. He'd convinced himself he could suppress his attraction to the same sex as long as he found distractions. It was too dangerous to reveal himself in Essex, in the boxing world, especially for a Heavyweight Champ. Passing for straight and suppressing his impulses was one of the many sacrifices he had to make.

Even though he's agreed to go out, Alex doubts having sex with a stranger will solve his problems, especially since he probably can't get it up. *Erotically challenged.* His right hand has been the only and infrequent sexual partner he's had in the past few years. He wants Chris's company, not an anonymous hookup. Even Alex knows about the apps for that.

Has he got smart clothes?

He used to have plenty: a huge house by the sea, several cars, fine clothes, jewellery. The house paid for the compensation ordered by the court, the barristers and court costs. Before he went to jail, he sold everything else and gave the money to his parents. They no doubt misused it on drinks and other vices. Money evaporates, and it doesn't buy a whole lot of things, least of all happiness. It's not a cliché at all.

Alex is not searching for happiness, though. No one offers counselling on being a famous ex-con so he definitely has no clue how to deal with his anxieties. Numbness is good enough for a man like him. He's still taking his pills five years later.

Alex pulls out his remaining couple of decent outfits. He hasn't let himself go. He has been working out in the park. When it's quiet at work, he carries on the training that has become second nature to him.

Even so, he lost weight in jail and has not regained it. The black shirt still fits well, but the tailored trousers are a little loose, so Alex tightens his belt. Chris is right about adjustments he has to make, now that he is no longer boxing. He doesn't own any aftershaves, so a spray of Old Spice will have to suffice. Alex sighs as he gets ready. He also questions why a beautiful soul like Chris would want to date an ugly, sick bastard like him. No, it's not even a date, not for the mesmerising Chris.

Alex can't back out now. He breathes in deeply to brace himself.

Chris is smoking in the lounge when Alex emerges from his bedroom. Chris stares at Alex.

Chris is his usual stunning self, even though he's only wearing a plain shirt and skinny jeans. He's applied light make-up and a single dangling earring adorns his left earlobe. There's a wide ring on his index finger and a silver chain around his wrist.

Alex asks, indicating his dress shirt, "Well, do I have your approval?"

"Yeah, great." Chris ogles with open mouth, revealing the tip of his tongue. He swallows and licks his lips.

Alex scowls at Chris's unconscious but seductive gesture and shifts his feet. "What?"

"You're tense." Chris waves his cigarette around.

"No, I'm not."

Chris purses his lips.

Alex groans. "I'm a bit nervous. I'll be fine, but it's been years since I went to a club. The media pressure. You don't understand it unless you have firsthand experience."

Chris cocks his head. "No, I don't. But I'll be there, okay? I've got you."

I've got you. Chris being so kind and supportive is suspicious.

"All right. Let's do it." Despite his reservations, Alex wants to make an effort and brave the consequences because Chris is worth it.

~~~

Chris says as they emerge from their taxi, "This place is perfect for you straights."

Alex is not ready to have that conversation with Chris, but he trusts Chris's choice and follows him into the club. The clientele appears to be a decent mix, and they are not too young and rowdy. Down in the basement dance floor, beautiful half-naked bodies are already wriggling to electronic music. Chris finds a quiet corner and two stools hidden in shadows.

"Sit and relax. I'll go to the bar. What's your poison?"

"Diet Coke, please."

Chris expertly weaves his way through the crowd. Alex watches his strong back and narrow waist and wishes he could touch Chris's body, especially his arse. Chris will freak out and bite his head off for sure if he confesses his growing attraction and gropes him.

Alex has to restrain himself and redirect his thoughts. *Just a friend. Repeat.*

Two men come forth, trapping Alex. They start talking to him before he can do anything. Chris seems to sense the situation from the bar and hurries back with their drinks, but the dancing crowd are in the way. Still, Chris threads through the pack of revellers with more skills than a figure skater on ice.

One of the two men asks Alex, "So good to see you out, Blue. Are you going to box again?"

Without responding, Alex glances past the intruders to meet Chris's eyes, as though he is sending an SOS signal for help.

"Can we take a selfie with you?" the other man asks, already holding up his mobile. Alex automatically shields his face with his right hand as the two men position themselves at his sides.

Chris plonks the two drinks down and puts on the most authoritative voice possible. "I'm sorry, but Mr. Whale is not answering questions or allowing photography right now."

The eyes of the one who asked for the selfie widen. "Oh. Are you his manager?"

Chris glares at him with enough venom to kill. "I'm a member of Mr. Whale's security team. I'd appreciate your cooperation, *sir*."

"Oh. Okay." The bloke sounds disappointed.

The two look at each other and step back, still glancing at Alex. Staring at them coolly, Chris waits till they have gone and hands the glass of Coke to Alex, who takes a large gulp. Chris sits on the other stool and drinks his whiskey.

Alex bursts out laughing, making Chris frown.

"I'm glad you find it funny. I don't normally expect to act when I'm out dancing."

"You? My bodyguard?" Alex's shoulders bob up and down while he tries to stop himself.

Chris points to Alex's broad chest. "Have you got a better fucking idea? Let's hear it."

Alex stops eventually. "No. It's just amusing. I think I can take on four of those men." He sips from his glass again. "Anyway, how'd you know what to say?"

Chris slices his fingers through his short, ash-blonde hair. "Pretending to be a bodyguard? I, um...have some experience of this kind of thing."

"What kind of experience?"

Chris bites his lip. "I've come across different situations with stars and celebrities. I was an actor."

"I thought you were only an escort and sometimes a nude model?" Alex considers Chris again and nods. "I suppose you might have been a failed actor. Been in anything good?"

Chris narrows his eyes. "I modelled for catalogues of children's clothes and some TV commercials. I acted in films and TV dramas as well. You know, the nameless-school-kid, teenage-friend kind of roles. It's been a while. And I didn't fail, all right? I grew up!"

Alex gazes at Chris as he considers the last part of his comment. "You were a child actor?"

Chris nods.

It makes sense, since what career options are open to a child actor and model when they retire? What does a former boxing champion do to make a living?

"Boy band?"

Chris's stare could fell a lesser man. "Do I look like I dance and sing to order?"

"I guess not."

As Alex digests the new piece of information about his flatmate, Chris jumps down from his stool, ready to tackle a couple coming towards Alex.

"Alex Whale?" the man asks.

When Alex doesn't reply, the imposter pulls out his phone and tries to snap. Alex hides his face again but Chris is ready to defend him. Without hesitation, he positions himself between the couple and Alex and blocks the man's phone camera.

"I'll have to call for my back-up if you don't step away right now."

"Uh. I'm sorry. We want to take a photo with him. That's all." The man addresses Chris instead of Alex, with much confusion in his face.

Chris answers with the utmost professionalism. "I'm not authorised to allow photography."

"Really?" The man regards Chris, then he turns to Alex. "No wonder they say you're a cocky bastard."

His partner pulls his arm, wanting to get away from the confrontation.

Alex continues to stare ahead, ignoring the couple. He has to mask his panic as blood rushes to his head and his throat goes dry. *Keep your head down and breathe normally.* As if Chris is guarding Alex, he steps forward to challenge the man.

"I'd leave now, if I were you," Chris tells the intruder. He is quite a few inches taller than the guy, but his physique doesn't give off the threatening bodyguard vibe.

The chap's companion starts to drag him away again. He retreats but not without the last word.

"Hope you're proud of what you've done." He turns to his partner. "Let's go. He's not worth it."

Chris glowers at them as they walk away, then puts his hand on Alex's shoulder. "All right, mate?"

Alex relaxes under Chris's soothing touch, but his heart thumps fast.

"Yeah. It doesn't get easier even though I've heard it a thousand times." He covers Chris's hand with his; the connection feels good. He needs to know what it's like to entwine their hands. As if Chris can hear Alex's inner voice, he slides his fingers between Alex's.

"I don't think this is going to work, mate. I'm sorry I've spoilt your fun. Shall we go home?" Alex reluctantly removes his hand. He's too chicken to rely on the entwinement for his sanity.

"Don't let them get to you. Come on. Let's stay for a bit." Chris knocks back the rest of his whiskey. "How about...we try something?"

Chris surveys the area around them, something mischievous lurking in his eyes. "Okay, Alex. Don't make it obvious, but you see that young woman over there? Your three o'clock?"

Alex moves the minuscule few centimetres to look at the target. "The one with dark hair?"

"Yeah, her. She's gorgeous."

Alex can see her black silky hair, neat fringe and bright eyes because she happens to be standing under a light, leaning against a small ledge and watching people. "Okay. What about her?"

Chris smirks. "Her mates have left her behind to go dancing. Let's go over and talk to her. See which of us she fancies.

Alexander, I've got a good feeling about this. It may be your lucky day, my friend."

Chris's use of his full name amuses Alex, but he's not comfortable with the suggestion.

"She's barely legal."

"Nah, old man. She's definitely legal. Early twenties, I'd say." Pinpointing an age must come naturally to Chris since he's such a champ of hooking up. "And she's unlikely to know who you are. Bonus."

"I warn you. I've never done this before." Alex puts his glass down, succumbing to Chris's persuasion again.

"What? You're asexual or something? Do you mean you've never fucked around? Was there a Mrs. Whale? Someone special?" Chris's eyes twinkle with amusement.

Alex rubs his nose bridge, avoiding talking about his past and about Sam.

"Yeah, there was a Mrs. Whale, but it didn't stop me fucking around. I never had to chat women up. They used to throw themselves at me after the fights." Realising how misogynistic it sounds, Alex swallows. "I'm sorry."

"Hmm. I hope you've learned a lesson now that Mrs. Whale has left you," Chris says.

You have no fucking idea.

"Anyhoo, the next stage of your love life starts right now. Here's what we do. We'll saunter over there, buy her a drink and have a chat. It'll be fun to see who she goes for. Next round of drinks on the loser." Chris grins.

Alex shakes his head. "Come on. A washed-up boxer and a young sex god. What do you expect?"

Chris stares at Alex, his eyelashes flickering. "You think of me...as a sex god?"

Alex coughs. "I mean...for a young lass like her. She must think you're sexy." Alex stops before he digs himself a bigger hole.

Chris swallows. He shifts his feet and downs his whiskey. "Well, if you say so. There's only one way to find out what she thinks. Come on, let's go, sexy."

The young woman is Lily, twenty-three, and she is gorgeous. Smooth, porcelain skin, big doll eyes; she's taken in straight away by Chris's charm. Her eyes haven't left Chris's face, mesmerised by every word he utters.

Amused, Alex knows when he's not wanted. Sure, there's a little sourness in him, though not from the fact that Chris is going to get laid with a beautiful woman. He wishes he was the one Chris was talking to and trying to woo. He makes the excuse of needing the bathroom, and after he has used the facilities, he buys a Coke and sits on the stool he vacated earlier. Across the throng of dancing bodies, the two younger people are deep in conversation. He'll leave Chris to his conquest and go back to the flat alone. He'll be fine with that since being alone is his new normal now.

Alex takes a sip of his Diet Coke and watches the dance floor while continuing his observation of Chris—his pretty, sinewy neck and body, how his face radiates from a distance amidst the dusk of the club.

~~~

An attractive woman with smoky eyes and golden-blonde hair approaches Alex. She's more mature than Lily, who is currently conversing with Chris across the room. This one, though, is definitely more the type Alex would've taken to bed five years ago. He doesn't feel threatened despite his wariness of the public these days.

Still. After the earlier encounters with the people who wanted photographs, Alex has little enthusiasm for chatting to another stranger. He's not looking for a casual hookup either. His recent sexual fantasies mostly consist of a naked Chris in bed. He was only humouring Chris when he agreed to come out.

The woman sits on the stool next to Alex and lifts her face to smile at him. "Is it okay if I sit here and we have a little chat?"

Alex nods and smiles back. "Sure. Let me get you a drink."

"I'm good." She raises her full glass of white wine, her slender fingers wrapped around the stem. "My name's Susan."

"Hi, I'm Alex," he replies. "But I think you know that."

Susan smiles. The woman has flawless skin and brilliant white teeth. She reminds Alex of the models and minor celebrities who used to chat him up all the time.

"So, are you taken?" she teases.

Alex glances over to Chris, who happens to look his way and winks at him. *The cheeky bastard.* Susan follows Alex's gaze.

"Taken? No."

Susan focuses on Alex's face once more.

"Really? I saw what happened earlier with the snap-happy people. Who's your companion?" She inclines her head ever so slightly in Chris's direction.

"My…he's my bodyguard." Alex winks.

"You're lying to me!" She grins. "He seems a bit too delicate and handsome for the task."

A perfect paradox.

Alex cannot tear his eyes away from Chris. He and Lily are talking, their heads close together, their faces animated.

"Appearance is deceptive. Chris is, eh, ex-military. He's the best I've had. You wouldn't know to look at him, would you?"

Wait till I tell Chris about this.

Chris may not have been a real guard, but he's been good for Alex. For keeping him in check, grounding him, rendering him safe. For the first time in a long while, the weight on Alex's shoulders lightens.

Susan laughs. "If you say so." She takes a large gulp of her white wine. "They say you're a nasty piece of work, but I've enjoyed your company very much."

"Likewise."

"I'd embarrass myself by asking to go home with you, right?" She scans in the direction of Chris and his latest conquest.

Alex turns his attention back to the woman sitting next to him. He does need to get laid and he should accept her interest, but he's rusty and less than horny while on medications. Casual sex is unlikely to help him get his groove back. Chris may only think of him as a friend and he likes to take the piss, but

Alex would much rather be in Chris's company than have sex with a stranger.

"You're absolutely gorgeous. But I'm not the same Alex Whale that everyone used to know." The new Alex suits him fine, too.

She smiles, her pretty eyes shimmering in the dark club. "I'd say you've become a better person. It's my luck to get to speak to you, if only for a few minutes."

He pecks her cheek. "It's nice that someone speaks to me like a regular man."

She giggles. "My pleasure. Have a lovely evening with that 'bodyguard' of yours!" She draws the quotation marks with her fingers in the air and stands to leave.

Alex smiles and watches her back as she walks away, and he wonders for the thousandth time recently what the fuck is wrong with him for not taking the woman home, having sex with her and living up to the expectation of an alpha-male.

~~~

Chris converses with Lily but his attention remains on Alex. The lovely young woman is touching his arm and talking, her mouth opening and shutting. Her longing eyes gleam brightly under the spotlights emanating from the bar.

"Sorry?" Chris realises he's missed what she's been saying for the past five minutes.

"Where do you live? Do you want to take a walk? It's a bit too loud for conversation here."

Chris is quite well aware what the euphemism means. She'll make a good distraction, even if she seems inexperienced and innocent. There were times when he wanted to leave someone like that heartbroken, but not tonight. He's getting too soft and caring for sure.

Chris was probably six when he found out he could either hurt others' feelings or risk getting hurt himself.

Chris's dick has been twitching, but it's for the unmissable Alex across the room. A little spark of envy settles in Chris's chest when a very elegant lady sits on the stool he vacated, and she proceeds to chat Alex up. Chris thought Alex might be too tense to talk with yet another stranger but he seems to get on with her. With the noise and music, she's been leaning close to speak to him, and he pays attention, nodding and smiling. When Alex smiles, his face lights up for a second, and he's stunning in Chris's eyes. But Alex shuts himself down after the briefest showing of happiness, as though the boxer has been trained to reveal no emotions. Different coping mechanisms to Chris's, but Chris recognises the result.

The woman is beautiful, but Chris is not going to be jealous of a couple of straight people chatting each other up.

I have only myself to blame. Duh. Will you want me if I tell you how I feel sometimes? Oh, I've forgotten Lily again.

"Ah, I'll stay and have another drink. I'm not sure what we're doing later. You see, I've come out with my mate." Chris points to Alex.

"Yeah, he's pretty impressive." She eyes Chris, then smiles. "Not my type, though."

When the blonde has left Alex alone, Chris's heart does a happy dance. He makes his excuses and beelines back to his flatmate.

"Hey, handsome. Do you come here often?"

Alex grins and shakes his head. "I've never been called that before."

"In the eye of the beholder and all that." Chris lifts her head and beams at him. "Come on. What's wrong with the woman?"

"Ah, she's just a fan."

Chris arches an eyebrow. "So? Does your dick feel different when you're inside a fan?"

Alex frowns. "Your face may be pretty but you've got a crude mouth."

"I was raised by my mother, not polite society."

Alex repeats the question back at Chris: "What's wrong with Lily?"

Chris grimaces. "I felt like the wolf enticing Red Riding Hood."

That makes Alex laugh.

Chris's clever comeback hangs in the air as 'Girls/Girls/Boys' blasts out of the monitors. "Oh, my gosh. I love this song!" Chris screams. "We've got to dance."

Alex glares at her. "You're fucking kidding me."

"No, I'm not. Come on!" Chris pulls Alex's arm.

"I don't dance."

"Yeah? You do now." Chris tugs the big man along. "You performed in front of millions, Alex. Are you scared of these people? In the dark?"

Alex slips down from his stool. "One fucking song," he says.

They dance along to the tune. The singer is pleading to another to change their mind and find him. Surprising himself, the boy abandons the girl for another boy.

Lost in the heady scent of body heat and sweat, they move with the rhythm. Being so close to Alex makes Chris all tingly and hot. Alex's body under the tight dress shirt does wonderful things—unfamiliar and tender things—to Chris's insides.

Chris dances like a pro, gyrating to the song, lost in the intoxicating scent of Alex. The other revellers ogle her and by default they take in Alex. Chris closes her eyes and grins. When she opens her eyes again, she is gazing at something close to magic. She throws her arms around Alex's neck and makes him swing along with her.

Alex is not a practised dancer, but heat radiates from his body as they rub against each other on the dance floor.

Chris closes in and puts her warm cheek against Alex's. Inches apart, Alex's hot breath tingles Chris.

"You're doing great."

"One song," Alex insists.

~~~

Chris stumbles out of the taxi and stands next to Alex outside their front door.

Alex wants to laugh, watching his flatmate struggle with his key. Chris has been drinking whiskey all night and at one point went to the toilet to smoke dope. His hand trembles slightly as he tries to aim at the keyhole but fails, and he looks up and giggles, his aquamarine eyes sparkling under the streetlamp. *Cute.*

Alex senses Chris's flirtation and the arousal. His cheeks are flushed and pupils dilated. Alex sniffs and indulges in that faint floral scent from Chris's shampoo, closing his eyes fleetingly.

"Oh, holy hole," Chris whispers, high and giddy.

"Give me it," Alex demands. "You're drunk, Christoph."

"I'm not, and my name's Chris. I don't use…that other name." He pouts. Surprising Alex, he reaches up the couple of inches and kisses him on the neck, his lips soft and wet.

Alex loves the impetuous gesture, but he's intrigued by the meaning of Chris's name. "It's on your letters."

"Well, I'm not my official self."

Alex is confused, but he puts it down to Chris being rather intoxicated.

Since Chris refuses to hand over the key, Alex takes his out instead and opens the door in one smooth movement. Alex helps Chris in, and for once, he doesn't protest. He sways, leaning close as they climb the three flights of stairs and negotiate the temperamental lighting arrangement like a pirouette, but the heat that passed between them in the club and outside the door cools, to Alex's dismay.

Once in the flat, Alex wrings his hands. "Thanks for the evening. I had a good time."

Lame, lame, lame. He kicks himself for not knowing what else he could have said to Chris, to tell him he's special.

"You're welcome." Chris stretches again and gives him another peck. Alex inhales the floral perfume that Chris's skin is laced with. He closes his eyes and imagines Chris's smooth pale body. When Alex opens his eyes again, Chris is gazing at him, almost coyly, before abruptly breaking eye contact.

"I've got to pee, sorry!" He runs to the bathroom.

Alex stares after Chris, watching his perfect small arse, tight against the material of the skinny jeans, sway slightly. Alex sighs. Chris is drunk and horny, but it doesn't mean he's into him. Otherwise, he would have said something.

Alex returns to his small box room, lies down on the single bed, his palms behind his head, and wonders what sex with Chris is like. Chris's soft skin glows and stretches. They'd kiss until the air between them vanishes. Maybe Chris hates sex, given what he does for a living, although Chris has plenty of sexual partners. Alex hears them through the wall, and every time he does, a spark of envy grows in his stomach. His insides have too many feelings these days because of Chris. He's going to be awake for a while, like all the other nights, listening to the hum of the distant city and watching the lights tango on the walls.

CHAPTER 5
WALLS

A LEX WANTS NOTHING more than a peaceful Sunday afternoon back in the Sussex he knew as a kid. If nothing had happened in these parts, it *would have been* like that, but too many memories linger in his brain these days when he visits.

His parents want to see him.

Ominous.

On the train down, he feels nervous enough to chew his nails and rub his hands on his thighs. The ugly apartment blocks of London soon turn to greener, flatter fields as he gazes out through the water beads on the window.

With trepidation, Alex ascends the steps to the once-beautiful home he bought his parents. The disrepair of the house is indicative of the way life has taken its turn. Unease sits deep in his stomach as he waits for someone to open the door.

"Alex!" His dad pulls Alex in with a firm hug. All the Whale family are tall and broad, perfectly suited to their surname. His dad has gone bald. The heavy drinking and a general unhealthy lifestyle accompany his pallid complexion. Alex might have smiled, thinking about how everyone needs some sunshine or a brightly lit person like Chris.

He walks into the chaotic front room to find Gary sprawled on the big leather sofa, watching football on the telly. Not bothering to get up, Gary points to a case of beers.

"Hey, man! Grab yourself one."

How can he get into that thick skull of his brother that he doesn't drink anymore? How *can* he drink when it has caused so much pain? He feels like an alien among his family.

Alex's mum is cooking in the kitchen; he can smell the Sunday roast. She's a poor chef, but roast potatoes and the scent of overcooked vegetables are familiar. He gives Gary a high-five as a sort of greeting and goes in search of his mother.

"Mum."

She turns around. "Here you are."

Alex gives her a quick hug. She doesn't stink of alcohol like his dad does, though she's still bloated and red, as if the alcohol has seeped permanently under her skin.

"Smells good."

"Gotta feed my boys, hey?" She smiles, showing tobacco-yellowed teeth—twenty a day for fuck knows how long. All three of them are heavy smokers.

"What's up with you? How's London?"

Alex leans against the worktop and watches her. Her big hands cut the carrots roughly.

"The job's fine. I'm too knackered to do much else, even though I'm in London." They are an hour away from the capital, but people who live *down* in Essex consider themselves in another world. Travelling *up* to the capital is a big deal.

She puts a pan of water on to boil. "You should start boxing again, though. Security, you say? That's wastin' your talent."

That's the extent of encouragement from his family he will ever get. Is there an ulterior motive behind those words? Most definitely.

"I'm not sure. After all—"

"I'm starving, love." Alex's dad appears in the kitchen. He rummages in a cupboard and retrieves a couple of bags of potato crisps.

"Hey, Alex. 'Aving a chat with your mum? It's 'bout time. We 'aven't seen much of ye since ye got oot. Come an' sit doon."

His regional accent comes out stronger when he's had a few drinks.

Alex is enjoying being in the kitchen, but he reluctantly follows his dad back to the front room and sits in an armchair while Gary and his dad share the big sofa, each with a can of beer in their hands. They tear into the packets of potato crisps as they watch the football highlights on the huge, flat-screen TV.

"Alex, are ye goin' to box again?" his dad asks without even a modicum of subtlety, but Alex has been expecting it.

"I don't know. After everything that happened..." Even these insensitive men must be able to see it's not easy for him.

"I say, it's all in the past. You can train again. Look at ye! You're fitter than before all that nonsense. There's no reason you can't manage a comeback."

Right. As if it's that easy.

Gary's eyes have been glued to the TV, but now he joins in his dad's plotting. "Tony was round the other week. He said he'd get you the best trainer, an apartment, the lot. Comeback tour and all that. He's talking serious money, bro."

Alex squeezes his eyes shut. Thinking about those things—the photographers, the journalists and Tony the smarmy businessman—hurts his brain. His chest tightens and he's light-headed. Don't they feel anything? Don't they know their son, their brother? Despite his tough appearance, he's always been highly sensitive and emotional. What he achieved when he was at his height was a pretence. He loved boxing, but everything else was a necessary evil. He got swept away in that life until he couldn't breathe—until that day when everything was taken away by one fatal mistake.

A crash landing.

He felt partly relieved when he was thrown in jail because there would be no more public appearances, no more interviews and photo shoots for commercials and magazines. He could be himself again; the scum of the earth.

"Tony's only interested in what's in it for him. Sam's family would kill me if I paraded around on the telly."

"Then get some security guards. It was an accident."

Yeah, try living with twenty-four-hour bodyguards!

Gary always sees the world in simple black-and-white terms, but his remark brings a smile to Alex's face. Chris and his security-detail act were funny, and his new flatmate understands him better than this lot combined. Chris appreciates why he's living the way he does. Chris knows the present him, while his parents and brother see the Alex he was five years ago—someone who metaphorically died and should never be resurrected.

Alex's brother and dad return their attention to the sports programme on TV while drinking, but he knows the conversation is not over. There will be more demands for money. He needs to decide whether he can part with his last fifty thousand in the bank, his last bit of security for an emergency if anything happens to him. *Damn it!* Besides, it's not going to last forever.

Nothing lasts forever.

Alex is thankful when his mum eventually serves up the Sunday roast so he can focus on the food.

His dad, as usual, complains about one thing or another. The gravy is too watery. The roast is a bit too small. How many people is he feeding, exactly? Colin Whale is sexist and obnoxious, but everyone knows better than to contradict him.

"Thanks, Mum," Alex offers while Gary and his dad don't even have the decency to express gratitude.

"We have to do this more often. I missed you, Alex."

Yeah? Then why didn't you visit me more often inside?

Alex nods and tucks into his food. Bland, overcooked and lacklustre, like the house and his family, who are waiting for the day when they can't carry on.

"Say, when the weather's better, we need ta do some remedial work on the 'ouse."

"Can you and Uncle Kieran sort it out?" Even Gary questions why their dad can't repair the house, since he was a builder before Alex started to earn money.

"Kieran retired two years ago." He's also not their 'real' uncle, just one of Dad's builder mates, so there's no familial obligation. "And with me leg and back, it'll kill me." He takes a swig of his beer.

It'll kill me to be forced to box. Alex shuts his eyes again to tune out the ongoing conversation. He can't do this. Can't be part of this anymore.

"Alex?" his mum calls.

"Hmm." Alex refocuses.

"Dad asked you about going back in the ring. Your manager has been round."

Alex takes a deep breath. "Mum, there is no free lunch with Tony. And Sam's family won't be happy. You must see that. I can't take the pressure of a comeback right now."

His mum's mouth shuts dramatically and the crocodile tears come out. "I know it's hard for you, Alex. You heard—your dad's getting on a bit now. We both are."

What about the waste of space that is your other son? A couple of years older than Alex, Gary has never earned an honest wage and leeched off Alex until he exhausted everything. Alex can't remember how many of Gary's 'business ideas' he's funded, and he's never seen any return from those investments.

"Mum, I've got nothing left after the court costs. The house was sold. They seized my assets and Tony took a chunk. I'd have helped if I could."

"Then, man up and go and do what you do best." His father raises his voice.

Man up. Why me? What about the other men in this fucking household?

Alex remains silent for the rest of the torture meal.

Eventually, when it's clear that no one is sober enough to take him back to the train station, he calls a taxi.

The taxi driver steals glances in his rear-view mirror. "Are you Alex Whale? I thought so when they called me out to their house."

"Hmm. Yes." That's why his PO won't allow him to live here anymore since people in the local area know the family.

"Didn't know you were out, man." The taxi driver's eyes light up.

Alex can't wait for the fifteen-minute journey to be over.

"What are you doing these days, Blue?"

Stop asking me the same fucking question.

~~~

London comes as a welcome relief after the Sunday lunch ordeal, and Alex feels even better when he sees Chris in the lounge smoking a joint. The hazy afternoon sun has created a beam in the air as dust dances along. Chris looks up and smiles, lighting up the room, reaching out to Alex with that simple gesture. He's shinier than the sunlight. The bedsit has rapidly become more of a home than the mansion Alex bought his family. Money can't buy happiness. It's not a cliché when it's true.

"Hey."

"Hey, yourself." Chris blows out smoke, and all Alex can think about is licking Chris's pursed lips.

He sits at the other end of the couch while the tension from the trip to see his family eases. Here's someone he doesn't need to pretend with and who doesn't want money from him. Chris sure doesn't care if he's going to do a comeback tour or help with the repairs to the house.

Chris regards Alex's leather jacket—the one piece of clothing Alex believes makes him half presentable. He bought it when he first went professional, so it is now nice and weathered. He feels self-conscious under Chris's gaze, though, so he takes it off, exposing the black tee underneath. Something changes in Chris's face, but then he coughs as if to hide the blush on his cheeks. Butterflies flood Alex's stomach. *Butterflies. What the fuck?*

"Where've you been? Anywhere nice?"

"Lunch with my family."

"Oh, and where's that?"

"Southend-on-Sea."

Chris nods, but no comments come forth.

Alex wants to hug him and touch his pretty, delicate face, and that scares the hell out of him. Alex should go back to his room or go for a walk to calm himself down, but he is glued to the spot so he can be in the other's company.

He asks Chris, just so he can listen to his honeyed timbre, "What about you? Are you working today?" Heat rises in Alex's face. "Sorry, I didn't mean to—"

Chris chuckles. "It's all right. No, I don't work on Sundays."

"Really? Is it a common thing?" Alex shuts his mouth after the question.

Chris only laughs louder. "Yeah, I'm a pretty common kind of prostitute. No, I don't know how other people work, but *I* don't work on Sundays."

"Oh. Sorry. I meant..." *Alex, shut the fuck up.* "Is it a religious thing?"

Chris is belting it out now. His face colours from the laughter. "No, Alexander. It's a principle thing. *I deserve a day off a week* kind of thing."

Alex squeezes his hands between his thighs. "I'm glad you find me funny."

"That, I do. Sometimes. Other times, you're kind of a miserable fella. Far too serious." Chris giggles.

"Oh, I know," Alex concedes. "By the way, I didn't think you'd call yourself a prostitute."

"What? Cuz escort sounds better? It is what it is. I am who I am." Chris stubs out his joint. "I have sex with people and get paid for it. That is the definition of prostitution, and I'm okay with it. My job makes people feel better, if only for a little while."

Alex gets the logic, but it also hurts as if Chris has thumped his heart with the truth.

Chris reaches out and pats Alex's thigh. "What are you doing now? Wanna go for a walk?"

Alex gazes out of the dust-smeared window and sees the sun, reluctant to set yet, even though it's nearly three o'clock in the afternoon. "Okay. Where are we going?"

Chris stands. "We'll see. This is the kind of escorting I don't mind doing on a Sunday. Coming, then?"

They get ready quickly and walk out of the building into the slanting sunshine.

"Hmm. I love the smell of smog." Chris stretches his arms out and inhales, winking at Alex.

Alex laughs. His worries and the depressing lunch with his folks fade in importance. "Lead the way."

Chris squints at the sun and smiles, causing Alex's stomach to flip-flop again.

They start north, walking side by side and mostly in silence. When they get to the main stretch off Finsbury Park, Chris turns and grins. "I've got to get some bagels. Come."

He takes Alex's hand and drags him along to the bakery. Alex stares at their joined digits, captivated by the sensation of Chris's skin against his own.

The sweet, warm fragrance of yeast hits them as soon as they enter the bakery. It's busy, and Alex and Chris squeeze between the counter and the racks of baked produce, towering over the other customers.

"Hey, what would you like? They have ten different sorts of bagels. Look!" Chris sounds like he's thirteen and just discovered a treasure cave.

Alex has to smile at Chris's enthusiasm, but he doesn't want bagels. He surveys the sweet treats. When he was training, he had to be extremely careful with his diet. The occasional buns were fine since they all burnt up in the hard work. Now that he's not boxing, he wants to indulge instead of counting his calories and worrying about his body shape.

"Hmm, I'll have an iced finger."

Chris gives him an eye-roll and hollers to the young staff behind the counter, his voice carrying above the bustle of the bakery. "Can I have two onion bagels and two sesame seeds, and may I have cream cheese in one of the onion ones? And an iced bun, please. Thank you."

When Chris detaches his hand from Alex's so he can pay, Alex misses the warmth and the connection straight away.

They wind their way outside again. Chris gives Alex his iced finger and takes out his cream-cheese bagel and bites into it. He chews and swallows with glee.

As they resume their walk, Chris glances at Alex and his bun. "Yuck!"

"What's wrong with it?" Alex speaks with his mouth full of sweet dough.

"Mum used to feed me them. She said it was good for my figure. I swore never to have them again."

"How's this good for your figure, though?" Alex devours the bun in three mouthfuls.

Chris rolls his eyes again. "If you don't eat anything else, that is."

Chris shares Alex's experience of always thinking about food and what's allowed or not. Their appearance suggests a certain polarity, but they have a lot in common and Alex is happy about the discovery.

"Well, I'll never eat another iced bun in front of you. I promise." Alex holds up two fingers like a pledge.

Chris giggles. "You don't have to do that. As long as you don't make me eat it, I don't care!"

As they walk along, Alex wishes Chris would hold his hand again, but he doesn't. Chris marches through the edge of the large public park and onto the footpath that was a railway track.

"This used to be the train line to Crouch End," he tells Alex as if giving information to a tourist.

Alex stayed in London when he trained here, in between going to his Essex home and Sam, but they'd put him in soulless serviced apartments and hotels, usually in Central London. The only things to do were watching TV and porn in the room, which Alex didn't care for. He couldn't go out and get pissed if he was training, and he was too famous to wander around by himself too much. Alex's training days were nothing but hard work and otherwise full of unfeeling, faceless encounters that left him cold. Remembering those days fuels his guilt like a burning fire inside of him.

"Alex?" The way Chris says it sounds like he's been calling out to him for a while.

"Oh, sorry."

"It's okay. You look like you zoned out for a moment." Chris hooks his arm around Alex's and walks along as if they are a couple, making Alex feel content and relaxed. The sun is low now, leaving the late-afternoon air cool. They meet fewer and fewer people on the way. All Alex can hear is the crunching of fallen leaves underfoot and the distant hum of traffic. Along the disused railroad, a scent of musky decay fills the air, which he finds oddly soothing.

A couple of graffiti artists are already out tagging under one of the railway bridges, and Alex and Chris stop to watch one of them. After a few minutes, she turns and smiles at Chris. "Hey."

"Hi. How's it going?" Chris replies.

Her eyes run past Alex and focus on Chris again. "Wanna have a go?"

"Yeah, sure." He approaches.

The artist has drawn letters with black lines. She holds out a can of silver paint to Chris. "You can fill that letter out with this if you want."

Chris takes the paint, and the two of them work together for ten minutes or so. The heady chemical smell surrounds them. Chris fills out a letter under the artist's instruction and converses with her along the way as Alex watches from the sidelines.

When they're done, Chris says, "Thanks so much for letting me do that."

The young woman smiles. "You're welcome. Thank you for doing a good job. You'd better go back to your man."

In the approaching dusk, Alex may have imagined Chris blushing.

"Oh, my friend...yes." Chris glances at Alex, then runs back to him. His genuine joy reminds Alex of a time of innocence. Chris's broad grin is so bright it helps Alex to focus on the here-and-now, though.

"That was such fun!" He winds his arm around Alex again and they walk on.

"Do you know her?" Alex asks.

Chris shrugs. "Sort of. I've seen her around a few times, and we've chatted. We don't know much about each other—not even names."

Chris relates to people easily, perhaps as a result of his job, and Alex wonders if he's reading too much into their budding friendship. Chris's friendliness towards a new flatmate doesn't mean he's interested in him. *Why would the drop-dead gorgeous Chris want me, with my broken nose and complete lack of tact?*

They have walked half a mile or so along the disused railway line when Chris stops.

"There you go. My favourite thing in the whole of North London." He presents a lichen-covered wall to Alex with a flourish and a playful tilt of his lips.

"Huh?" Alex looks around and can't see anything other than the disused track and overgrown banks.

Chris tightens his grip and tugs his arm a couple of times. "Look up!"

Alex does. Under the rail arch, peering out from above, is a gargoyle, observing them with a mischievous grin. Its arms are outstretched as if to support itself on the wall, its only leg perched high. It's covered in moss that issues a mysterious green hue. In an instant, the magical atmosphere envelops them in a timeless and eerie fashion.

All sounds stop in a dramatic moment.

"Wow!" Alex marvels.

"I call him the green man. Very original." Chris laughs.

Alex wants to capture Chris's laughter and put it in a can. When he feels blue, he can open it a little, like a music box.

They stand there, admiring the strange sculpture and sharing a fairy-tale moment. Chris nudges Alex, who reluctantly tears his eyes away from the statue and refocuses on Chris's dreamy face. Chris glances away as if he's too shy because of Alex's interests.

When they start walking again, Alex asks, "So, you come here often, Chris?"

"Cheesy chat-up line." Chris pushes him. "You can walk all the way to Highgate Woods, then Ally Pally, but it's too late today. It'll be dark soon. Let me take you to the cemetery in Highgate another time."

The joy in Chris's voice is infectious, so Alex giggles. "Okay, if you say so."

"Lots of famous people are buried there. It's one of my favourite London places." Chris takes out his phone. "Type in Highgate Cemetery and famous boxer." He hands the mobile over.

Alex does and gives Chris the search results.

He squints to read the text slowly, the faint backlight illuminating his face. "See? Tom Sayers, famous boxer. Did you know him?"

"Who?" Alex raises his eyebrow and grabs Chris's hand to read the screen. "He died in 1865! Did I know him..." Alex can't help but chuckle at Chris while their faces are close, hovering above the small text.

Chris loads the Wiki page on Sayers and strains to read. "Look. He was only a small guy...bare..."

Alex helps out. "Bare-knuckle prize fighter. He was a national hero...who won the first world championship. Okay. I'll be sure to check the little guy out when you take me to the cemetery." Alex's shoulders go up and down as he tries to suppress his laughter. Chris joins him.

After another few minutes, they come to the platforms of the old Crouch End station.

Chris stops. "Well, we'd better head back."

Dusk has fully descended, so they turn around. Alex almost deflates with the end of their stroll.

Chris brings out a small torch.

"You're prepared," Alex observes.

Chris shrugs. "I've done this a lot."

Alex gazes at Chris's profile. "Thank you."

He doesn't only mean the walk. He's grateful to Chris for making him laugh, for allowing him to forget what a sorry state he lives in and the pressure from his family.

"You're welcome." Chris squeezes Alex's arm as though he understands.

~~~

Alex arrives at work—a drab and soulless modern building in Islington. He has been covering the late shift from eleven to six. Mike, his boss, is packing up to leave, so he must have swapped shifts with someone since the manager rarely works late.

"Whale. Evenin'." He looks behind Alex as if he's expecting someone else. "Where're the paps?"

Alex wishes he could deck the guy like an opponent in the ring. Mike's been doing the same joke every time he sees Alex, but there's no point rising to the bait. Alex takes a deep breath. "Just me, Mike."

Mike puts a pile of papers away and locks them in the metal cabinet. As he passes Alex, he instructs him, "The control room's a bit messy. Would you mind cleaning it up, ready for the daytime crew? And the toilets are a bit, you know, unsanitary."

"Yes?" *I am not a fucking janitor.* Alex hopes Mike isn't serious about the staff bathroom and scowls as a kind of threat.

Ignoring Alex's displeasure, Mike crosses his arms. He's not a tall man, but he's muscular and tattooed, and he's likely been in security for a long time—one of those bouncer-turned-manager types who enjoys his ego-games far too much. "Well, the cleaner is off on holiday for a week. We have to muck in."

Then why didn't you fucking do it?

"Fine." Alex's reluctance drips off him.

His line manager shoots another look his way and bids goodbye. Mike's enjoying his power trip, and Alex has to give it to him. He can only escape this drudgery by getting a better job, and he promises himself he will do it soon.

CHAPTER 6
BOXED

C HRIS STEPS INTO the flat to face a hell of a shock. Their mother and Alex share the sofa. She clings onto Alex, pretty much sitting on his lap and smiling like an infatuated teenage fan, gazing at the boxer with her big blue eyes.

Chris prises her away from Alex's arm and face as though they are unsticking chewing gum from the furniture. "What the fuck are you doing here, Annette?"

She looks up, but her eyes are glazed. *Shit.* Annette is in her early fifties. Chris looks like her, a fact that hits them every time they lay eyes on their own mother because Chris doesn't want to end up like her in twenty years' time. Her hair appears artificially ironed to a peak at the top and reminds Chris of a pile of dry straw. She has been crying, so her dark eye make-up has smeared. With the rather thick blusher and bright orangey-pink lipstick, she looks like a Barbie wannabe, trying to reach some kind of impossible beauty standard. Annette was once a beautiful young woman, and Chris has seen plenty of evidence in photographs and videos, but today their chest tightens watching her.

Chris grabs hold of her arms and tries to drag her up. "It's two in the fucking morning. Move."

Chris is embarrassed to let Alex see their family like this—their sorry excuse of a mother. They've stuck with her all these years, even though they were the one earning money a lot of the time when they were growing up and should have been studying and being a kid. Chris never complained, though, not about the work, cooking and, later on, paying the damn bills in case Annette had forgotten. All Annette wanted was to find boyfriends or husbands who would take care of her and her child. Three times she'd married, and they'd all failed her and left. *The bastards. Why would anyone want to be their meal ticket?* At six years old, Chris learned they needed to rely on themself, and that is what they have done for twenty years. The young Chris never believed in fairy tales when the reality had always been grim.

Chris doesn't know any alternative ways to make a living, and when it comes down to it, they are used to having sex with strangers. Most of the time.

Clearly, Annette's latest conquest hasn't worked out. *Now, that's a surprise.*

Alex shifts uncomfortably on the sofa, making a crinkly noise. Chris can see the pink lipstick marks on his cheek and neck like a child has been let loose with a crayon on his person.

Annette struggles against Chris's grip and falls into the space between the coffee table and the sofa in a heap. "Oh, give us a hug and a kiss, Chris. I haven't seen you in ages."

The longer the better. Chris puts money in her bank account every month. Not much—five hundred. Two fucks. They sometimes wonder why they're still doing it and when this life as they know it will ever stop. Do other people's parents grow up?

"I didn't know you lived with Alex Whale!" Trust her to recognise Alex and know the celebrity gossip. She tries to stand up and reaches for the arm of the sofa for support.

"Mrs..." Alex stretches his arms to support Annette.

Alex helps Annette up, and as soon as he's done that, she clings on to his strong arms again. Chris takes a good look at her now. She's still in one stiletto, and the dress is so short and small it almost reveals her arse. Most of her breasts are visible under the flimsy red straps that are barely holding them up. Around her chest and neck, the skin has sagged so grooves gather, and her tan clearly comes from under the lamp rather than the natural sun.

Even from a couple of feet away, Chris can smell the alcohol. They want to scream at her, but their anger bubbles and fizzles, as always. Twenty-odd years of rage turns into resignation. They had tears, wondering if it'd been their fault, if they'd deserved a childhood like theirs. After a while, the exploited and ignored child was all out of tears.

Chris scowls at Annette, clenches their jaw and prises her away from Alex again. "Time to go home. Now!"

Annette's pupils dilate like a cat entering a dark room. "Oh, you see. I'm scared. Jimmy thinks I've got a job on, and he's jealous. He chucked me out this afternoon. I can't go back there until he's calmed down."

Chris fails to keep up with Annette's boyfriends, and they don't want to. One thing they're sure about: Annette has no job on. She probably hasn't had one for fifteen years, even though she fails to recognise that the career of a porn actress and adult model is extremely short. Their mother is delusional when she's drunk or high…or both.

"No. No." Chris starts to drag her away from Alex again. Their eyes meet above Annette's head, and an acknowledgement flickers between them. Annette is not a small woman, as Chris's height testifies, but against Alex, she seems to have shrunk since her last rare visit.

"See? One room. And I ain't sleeping with my mother." Chris points to the direction of their room. "So, knock it off now."

Annette starts to cry; her tears ruin her make-up further. Her long red nails dig into Alex's side.

"Ah, I…she can have my bed, Chris," Alex offers.

Chris has already sussed that Alex is a big softie. They knew from the first time they had a proper conversation that underneath the scary appearance, Alex Whale is a compassionate man. But they can't let Alex do that for a woman—an intoxicated mistress of misery—he hardly knows.

"Don't be daft. She's so going home." Chris urges her mother. "Come on, Annette. Where's your other shoe?"

"It's no problem, honestly. I'll stay here on the sofa." Alex gazes at Chris.

You've got to be kidding. The couch is not long or wide enough for him.

"Oh, Alex darling. That's so kinda you," Annette slurs and flashes a big smile while letting the eyeliner run down with the tears. If she was not their mother, Chris might think this was a poorly scripted TV sitcom that had gone on for far too long.

"Fucking hell." Frustrated, Chris throws their arms up. "Annette. Alex doesn't know you. You *can't* have his room. Now, come with me. I'll get a taxi for you."

Chris rips out their phone to call a cab.

Alex puts his hand on Chris's. "Hey. It's okay. She's pissed. We should let her rest."

Chris is surprised at how soothing Alex's big hand and words are. "But…"

Alex is already pushing Annette along gently to his room, her one stiletto dangling from his forefinger. They'll have to locate the other one later.

Annette slurs. "Darling. You're not like my Chris, are you? I can't believe how nice you are! You were fierce when you boxed."

Chris follows them. "Oh, shut up, Mother."

They have always called her Annette because, growing up, she didn't want people to know she had a kid. So the name had stuck. When Chris gets mad at her, though, they call her 'Mother' just to piss her off.

Together, Alex and Chris manoeuvre Annette into Alex's room. Chris wants to take the make-up off to save her complexion, but the woman's too far gone. She stumbles and falls over the short distance, even with Chris's support. Alex's pillow's going to look like a Picasso painting tomorrow. Chris silently laughs about that.

Annette falls onto the bed. Chris picks up their mum's heavy legs and deposits them on the mattress, then they pull up the duvet. Annette mumbles something about Chris being a good kid.

Chris rolls their eyes. As if they had a fucking choice.

Annette thrashes about to get comfortable, while Alex and Chris stare down at her like two white-coat scientists examining an experiment gone wrong.

Annette slurs. "You're so sweet…wouldn't know you killed your wife looking at you…"

Chris's eyes snap wide open as they stare at Alex.

Alex turns his head to avoid their gaze, and wrings his hands.

Annette tries to get up. *For what? Fuck if I know.* "Come on, now. Get under the cover and shut up already."

Chris has always spoken to Annette like that because they have that kind of relationship with their mum in their fucked-up family. All their life, they've been Annette's nurturer, partner-in-crime, cash cow, but never their child.

Maybe it all started that one time. When she stood in front of Annette to protect her. *Whack.* She had to stay at home so the school wouldn't question her mum over the bruise. They would have sent Chris away, Annette had told her. *Yes, it was a bout of very bad flu.* Chris lied, just as Annette had told her, and she's been lying about a lot of things ever since until she never knows what's real and what's not, and her heart has gone cold.

Chris sighs in relief after Annette finally lapses into oblivion. She and Alex head back to the sitting room.

Alex scratches his head. "Well, I'll rest here. I don't sleep much anyway."

Alex approaches the couch, but Chris places her hand on Alex's arm. "Hey, come here."

She holds Alex's right hand and leads him to her room.

Once inside Chris's room, she puts her hand on Alex's chest and touches the fabric of his T-shirt against the solidity it sheaths.

"Thanks. She's…she's always this over-the-top."

"Don't apologise. Should I have turned her away?" Alex asks, scratching his five o'clock shadow at the same time.

"Well, that's almost impossible. You've seen how she is." Chris smiles apologetically, angling her head and squinting in the low light.

Alex sighs. "About what she said—"

"You don't have to tell me anything," Chris insists. "Or, you can tell me in your own time. I'm good with secrets. Anyway, I won't judge. Okay?"

Alex rubs his temple. "Okay."

She looks up and sees a moment of naked vulnerability in Alex's dark eyes. "Come with me, Alex."

Chris climbs up the bed and sits cross-legged, then pats the empty space on the mattress.

Her eyes meet Alex's. It's that simple. *It.* Something they don't quite know, and yet it is drawing them together more and more.

Alex joins Chris, sits on the edge of the bed and twists around to face her. He takes a deep breath, and speaks with a husky voice. "I crashed our car one night, killing Sam, my wife. I was drunk and high on crack."

Alex squeezes his eyes shut.

More quietly, he confesses, "And I killed the driver of the other car."

"Fuck," Chris mutters.

"I went to jail for causing death by dangerous driving. Two counts. Five years. I served four years and three months, and I just got my parole, as you might have guessed."

Chris has already gathered that Alex is an ex-con, like so many other people who have passed through the flat.

Alex sighs. "Now you know. I'll go for a walk and you go to sleep." He turns to leave, but Chris holds him back once more.

"Alex."

He still won't face Chris. "Don't. It's okay. You'd have found out sooner or later. The whole world knew except you. Now you do. Why do you think I can't face the public?"

Chris pulls Alex back and reaches over to lay her hand on his warm back, resting her face against his shoulder as she whispers, her voice gentle and calming, "It's okay. You made a bad mistake. You've served time. You torture yourself, don't you, Alexander?"

Chris can see it all in Alex's face, can feel what's unspoken and the pain in Alex's disturbed sleep.

"I should go." Alex moves away a few inches, but Chris pulls him back again.

"Alex, sweetheart, stay with me. Let me hold you tonight. Please. Come and lie down with me." Chris takes off her top.

Alex steals glances at her. "Are you sure?"

"Lie the fuck down with me. I'm not going to bite." Chris strips down to her underwear and gets under the cover. Alex gawps at the tiny piece of garment on Chris. He peels off his shirt and jeans, revealing a pair of boxers, and gets in. They face each other.

"So, now you've met my mother and see what a hot mess she is…my middle name is embarrassment." Chris grimaces.

"Come on. You haven't met my family." Alex shudders.

"It's hard to be worse than Annette."

"She mentioned a job earlier?"

Chris tuts. "What job? She was a porn actress. Who wants to see her looking like this now? She's a fucking joke." The bitterness cuts through her words.

"So, she encouraged you to be a child actor?"

"Encouraged is not the right word. How about pushed? Forced? Cajoled?" Chris stalls for a moment. "You're giving me that 'screwed-up freak' look."

"Sorry."

Chris shrugs. "It's fine. When you have a mum like her, the only way is up!" Setting the bar low has been Chris's *modus operandi*. "Mum was a pretty woman when she was young, y'know. The industry fucked her up. Aren't we stereotypes?" She exhales and squeezes her eyelids to soothe the onset of a headache.

Turning to her side, she pulls Alex's arm across her chest. "I'm cold. Hold me."

Alex wraps himself around Chris and plants feather-like kisses on her hairline, earlobe and neck. "Is this okay?" he asks.

"Yeah." Chris has forgotten all about her troubles and focuses on the sensation of Alex's soft lips on her skin.

They lie spooning each other.

"You're the one who looks after her now, right?"

"A little. She always has a husband or boyfriend, but they have all been spineless cunts."

"My parents are alcoholics. My brother too. I can feel your pain." Alex treks down Chris's soft, hairless arm, his finger pads rough. Chris shivers inside with the gentle touch and Alex's light breaths on her neck, dragging her fingers along Alex's arm in return, trying to make out the colours of the tattoos in the dusk and caressing the skin and muscles underneath, wondering what Alex's strength is capable of.

"Were you fierce when you boxed?"

"I had to be. I was pretty aggressive when I was in the ring. I couldn't show my emotions."

"You're the gentlest person I've met." Chris chuckles. "Granted, I have come across a lot of scumbags."

"Are you tired? It's half past three. I can leave you to it."

"Don't go. Let's get some sleep." Chris can feel Alex's erection, and she would have offered herself to Alex out of habit. It's expected of her, so like a robot she usually has sex as a means of connecting with people who ultimately all reject her. But she doesn't want to fuck Alex right now, as though to do so will break a special bond between them. A connection, a friendship.

"Okay." She drifts off to a restful sleep as she feels Alex's breaths on her cheek.

~~~

Chris kisses and gently massages Jeff's back after a hand job. He treats the older man like a pliant dough and cleans him up with care.

"How has your week been, dear? Anything more about the man you've been dating?" Jeff asks about Chris's love life every week but never keeps up.

Chris chuckles. "Well, the guy I've hooked up with a couple of times has gone a bit creepy. So I don't think I'll see him again."

Chris rubs in divine-smelling geranium massage oil. He has bought a whole set of these super-expensive aromatherapy oils for Jeff because he knows the older man loves these moments.

"How's he a creep? I worry about you with the weirdos out there"

Chris has had a fair share of bad dates and has known Jeff long enough to have told him some of *the stuff he doesn't talk about.*

Chris shrugs. "He texted me way too often, as if he's my boyfriend or something."

"Uh-huh. It was a long time ago when someone stalked me! Are these stories real or do you make them up to amuse me?"

Chris only laughs.

"I hope you know what you're doing."

"I'm fine." Chris sobers for a second. "Mum turned up at my flat and embarrassed me," he adds. He has already told Jeff an abridged and sanitised version of Annette and his childhood, which is more than he's revealed to anyone else.

"I'm sorry to hear that."

"The strange thing is..." Chris stalls for a few seconds. "I slept with my new flatmate. You know, the one who's moved into Liam's room?"

"Huh?" Jeff half turns his face but his voice is muffled. "The big guy? What's so strange about that?"

Finishing off the massage, Chris wraps a big fluffy towel around Jeff, helps him up and gives him a full glass of water to drink. That's the extent of 'erotic massage' Chris can manage.

"I mean we slept, not fucked. We talked and cuddled. He kissed me everywhere but my lips. Alex is all muscles, but that night he was so gentle, so tender."

Jeff's eyes widen, before he breaks into laughter. "That is unusual, dearie. I didn't think you'd ever refrain from fucking the person you slept with."

Chris giggles. "You're implying I'm some kind of nymphomaniac, aren't you? I know I have a bad rep for a high turnover of sexual partners, on and off the clock. Just as well I don't give a fuck."

"You are who you are, Chris. Anyway, tell me about this guy. He must be pretty special."

"Oh, yes, Alex. This huge beast of a man. I drool every time I see him. He was a famous boxer, but something happened and he went to prison. He's just been released." Chris shivers with the arousal, remembering the strong arms and the tattoos and how safe he'd felt in Alex's embrace all night.

Jeff drinks some water and frowns. "Alex? Do you know his second name?"

"Whale. His nickname was Blue."

"Oh my God! It was a huge story. I feel sorry for him, killing his wife like that—"

"Stop!" Chris puts his hand up to interrupt the older man.

Jeff gazes at him with a scowl. "You didn't know?"

"I know the bare facts, but I told Alex I wouldn't try to find out about him, like from the internet or something. I want to hear it from him."

"Ah." Jeff shifts a little in the seat. "I only remember the media stories anyway. What do you know?"

Chris tells him.

Jeff sighs. "Yeah, if my memory serves me right, the other driver's wife and two kids were injured. The only person who came away with only a few scratches was—"

"Alex."

Jeff nods. Everything about Alex makes sense to Chris now. Chris spaces out.

"You all right, dear?" Jeff lightly pats his hand.

"I...yeah, I'm fine."

Jeff gazes intently at him. "You shared a bed with him, you say. I assumed he was straight. I mean, he had a wife. He was a boxing champion, after all. If he wasn't, everyone would know about it. What's he like?"

Chris shakes his head, trying to shake out the confusing thoughts. "He is... I felt comfortable with him. He's so sweet. Annette said he was a tough boxer, but I couldn't see him like that. I don't know. Maybe he's bi. I have no clue what we are exactly, and I haven't talked to him about it."

Jeff winds his arm around Chris. "Well, something is going on in that pretty head of yours. That's for sure. Are you falling for this guy, hmm? Just a little bit?"

Chris stares at Jeff wide-eyed. "I hardly know him. He only moved in a few weeks ago."

"Sometimes it takes no time for us to find ourselves falling for someone. It's called love at first sight, dear." Jeff squeezes Chris. "Someone who's lived through something like that is likely to be very complicated, no? You need to take care of yourself."

The older man considers Chris again.

A little spark of rare and precious emotion grows inside Chris, something he has never experienced in his life.

Alex is definitely complicated, and Chris is emotionally closed off. Perhaps they'll be a good match after all. A match not quite made in heaven.

~~~

Alex is hitting the speed bag when Dex comes up beside him. "Hey, how's it going, son?"

Alex stops. The scent of sweat fills his nostrils, interspersed with the grunts of the other boxers. "Good." He picks up again. He has tried to keep his stamina up, first in prison, and then at home. Coming to the club to use the equipment feels natural to him, even though he still has no wish to box professionally. The small club is exactly what he needs right now. He was hoping to tire himself out enough to sleep for a while tonight.

"Your punches are almost as good as when you were competing, Alex," Dex observes.

"Thanks. I try to keep it up." Alex stills the bag and tilts his head a little to Coach's side. "I see Devan's working on the footwork."

The teenager is practising on the workout ladder, and he's quick. Coach has always taught Alex to work on his feet diligently because that's often the downfall of a heavyweight—being slow in their movements.

"Yeah, he's doing well. Why don't you spar with him for a bit? I'm sure he'd appreciate it."

Alex considers Coach's advice. He said he wouldn't train others, but watching the youngster so absorbed in his drill, how can he refuse? After a few moments, he exhales. "Okay."

He picks up his headguard and approaches Devan. "You finished with that? Wanna spar with me?"

Devan stops dead and stares at Alex with wide eyes. "Yeah. Defo!"

He quickly picks up a headguard and they move over to one of the rings. They start slow, then build up speed. Alex focuses Devan on various techniques—punches, movements, footwork, body positions—and Devan learns fast. The concentration on his face gives Alex a much-needed boost of energy, too. Devan reminds him of his younger self with all the passion and love for boxing. Focusing on something physical helps kids like him to temporarily forget about whatever shit's going down at home.

Alex feels the old flame reigniting in his heart. He was only here to train, but the sparring exercise has pitched him against someone for the first time in five years and he loves it. Devan reacts like a sponge, soaking it all up. The teenager reminds Alex of himself, of being free in the ring. If only that freedom could stay with him when he stops sparring.

CHAPTER 7
COLOURS

ALEX IS DOING press-ups and sit-ups in his room. It's almost impossible for him in the confined space, but some days the gym feels too oppressive.

After twenty minutes, he can't ignore the angry noises emanating from Chris's room.

He has heard it all before since the walls in the flat are paper thin. Listening to Chris and his partners fuck is torture because it sounds like porn without the visual. Arguments with his lovers are frequent occurrences, too, and they are the worst kind of intrusion for Alex when his mind is already scrambled.

Shall I put some music on to drown it out? It sounds like something else today, prompting Alex to stop the workout. He concentrates and listens, his breathing slowing. The flat is quiet apart from the altercations currently taking place in his neighbour's room.

Thump. Something heavy drops on the floor.

"Fuck right off! Get off me, you fucking cunt!" Chris raises his voice.

Alex strains to hear the other person. "You freak...stupid whore." More bangs against the wall.

"Fuck's sake," Alex mutters under his breath. He hates himself for wanting to intervene and protect, but he can't ignore this. The arguments so far haven't escalated to violence, but this signals that something vicious is about to erupt. It reminds him of fights he had with Sam when they were both drunk or drugged up. Even then, he would never lay a finger on her except that one day.

But there's no doubt that Chris and his latest partner are getting into a physical fight.

Alex stands and moves over to outside Chris's door. *Bump. Bang.*

"I said, get your filthy hands off me!" Chris shouts.

The other voice sneers. "Yeah, you were begging for my dick not so long ago."

Against his better judgement, Alex presses his ear against the door to listen.

There are more movements in the room, and the man dry laughs. "You're gagging for me, aren't you? Don't get all virginal on me, Chris. If you want kink, you only have to say."

"Get off me! I'm sick and tired of your bullshit. I don't need to beg for anything." Slapping. *Clap. Clap.*

"Yeah? Is that why you're a fucking prostitute?"

Wham. Against the wall.

"Fuck right off. Twat!"

Adrenaline rushes to Alex's head. Before he can talk himself out of it, he bangs on the door. "Chris. Chris. Open the door. Don't make me break it down."

The noises stop momentarily.

"Who the fuck is that?" the unfamiliar voice asks.

"My flatmate. Now piss off." Chris calls out, "It's okay, Alex."

No, it's not fucking okay. I'm not going to be fobbed off.

"You do let everyone use your arse, don't you? Dirty slut."

"If I'm a slut, you're a filthy bastard!"

A knock. *Thwack.* The man curses. *Good.* It sounds as though Chris is giving the other guy hell.

But enough is enough. Alex pushes the door, hard, assuming it's locked. It isn't and it hits the wall with a thud. The heap on the floor is Chris, wearing only a pair of small briefs and black lace tights that are ripped in a few places. His soon-to-be-ex kneels in front of him, pressing him against the wall. Both of them look up at Alex with wide eyes. Alex quickly scans Chris and can only see a few small bruises. *Good, but not.* His dark eye make-up has smeared, though. Chris rubs at it, and Alex's chest tightens. He turns to survey the other man.

Now, who's this clown?

The man stares at Alex in shock. A black eye and bruise on his left cheek confirm who was winning the fight. He's shorter than Chris but bulky and full of bulging muscles—a gym rat with tattoos—and dressed in a vest and tracksuit bottoms. Alex sees red, imagining the twat touching Chris.

Chris's assailant stands, challenging Alex, who towers over him. "Who the hell are you?"

"Alex Whale."

The other man steps back; recognition flashes in his face. He's about to make a comment.

Thump. It all happens quickly. Chris's knuckle reddens straight away when it connects with the guy's right cheek. The boyfriend falls on the floor, landing on his arse.

"What the fuck?" He stares at Chris, then back to Alex.

Chris frowns at his ex with a cold detachment that Alex has never seen, arms crossed at his front. He picks up the guy's jacket and throws it to him without a word.

Alex pulls the guy up and pushes him out of Chris's room, almost lifting him clean off the floor. The man smells of alcohol and other chemicals. Before he can protest, Alex has deposited him outside the flat and shuts the door in his face.

He bangs on the closed door. "Stupid whore. Chris, you'll fucking regret this. I promise!" Alex waits until the messy footsteps down the stairs have faded and the loud crack of the front door stops reverberating before returning to Chris's room.

Alex's heart aches when he sees Chris sitting on the edge of the bed, his elbows on his knees, hands covering his head. Alex steps close and sits next to him.

Chris looks up, rubs his eyes again and smears the black kohl even more; it matches the nail varnish. Alex notices the red lipstick, too. He's looking less thrashed than his latest ex, all things considered.

"Thanks, but I want to be alone now." His voice quivers ever so slightly.

Alex knows better than to tell him not to get involved with the scumbag in the first place, but Chris is so upset and vulnerable Alex wants to stay with him, so he stubbornly sits there. He wants to hold Chris, chasing away his sadness.

Chris doesn't ask him to leave again. He retrieves a bottle of make-up remover and cotton wool and cleans up his face, reverting to his porcelain skin. He finds a discarded T-shirt and pulls it over his naked torso. Then he opens his tobacco tin and starts making a joint, his hands shaking.

Alex gazes at him and resists the urge to hold him and kiss his blues away. He stares at Chris's shaved chest. Shaved everywhere.

Chris regroups, skilfully rolls the joint and takes a toke. He scants sidelong at Alex. "Say whatever the fuck you want to. Or fuck off."

Alex knows whatever he does will rile Chris, but Chris needs him. He lets himself be distracted by the couple of holes in his tights.

"Did you dress up like that for him?" As soon as those words come out, Alex regrets that he might have sounded jealous. Stupid mouth of his.

Chris rolls his eyes. "No, I don't do that for anyone. That's what I am today."

Alex frowns. "What do you mean? Do you like wearing women's clothes? I mean…I can dig that."

Chris tuts.

"I'm not a cross-dresser, Alex. I'm gender-fluid. Queer." Chris blows smoke and it obscures Alex's vision. "Have you heard of that?"

Alex shakes his head. "No, not really. I mean, I know you're queer. Enlighten me."

Chris gives Alex another eye-roll for emphasis. "I am a woman or a man. Some days I'm both. It depends."

Alex racks his brain to digest this latest Chris-related information, seemingly fundamental to who Chris is, but he admits defeat. "Is it an escort thing?"

Chris stubs out the joint. "What escort thing?"

"Is that because of what the guys want?"

Chris shifts away from Alex. "I give my clients what they want. What I perform sex-wise has little to do with my gender."

Alex is afraid to think about what Chris *does* perform.

"Ah. Do you want to cut off your willy?" Alex scratches his chin.

Chris stands up and pulls at Alex. "Get out. Get the fuck out of my room."

Chris's voice is steady, but it betrays resignation and weariness. Alex lets Chris drag him up but instead of leaving the room, he pulls Chris into a hug, forceful and firm, wrapping Chris's lithe body in his arms. He cups Chris's head and lets it rest on his firm shoulder.

"I only want to know more about you," he whispers for Chris's ears only. "Whoever you are, the scum has no right to abuse you. What would've happened if I wasn't home?"

Chris pushes Alex but doesn't try too hard to get out of the hug. "Fuck you. I'd have kicked him out, too, without your stupid arse. Who do you think you are? Waltzing in here and pretending to rescue me!"

Yeah, yeah. Chris would have won the fight without Alex's interference, but that's not the point. Alex already knows Chris is a fighter. He pulls Chris back and squeezes tighter. The scumbag has no right to hurt Chris, and that's that.

"For your information," Chris's voice is muffled against Alex's neck, "I finished with him and he freaked out."

"Damn right. You're not dating the creep. Why did you even go out with someone like that in the first place?" Alex is aware he sounds possessive. Well, maybe not. He's truly baffled. That's all. In his eyes, Chris is perfection and no lover is good enough.

"He wasn't so bad. They all eventually flip, though. It's because of my personality, my gender or my profession. Usually all three."

"I'm still here," Alex says. "I like your personality. You're rather unique and special."

"You're a masochist and stupid."

"You're keeping your dick, too. It's good, cuz you look good with it."

Chris laughs. "Yeah, but my gender has nothing to do with what's between my legs and how I use it. Do you know how many times I've been asked if I want to cut off my dick? 'You're either a boy or a girl.'…'You can't be whoever you want to be.'…'You must be sick to dress in women's clothes.'…'Do you want surgery?'… 'You are mentally ill.' Or the worst one—'*What* are you?'"

Alex blinks as he digests this. "Okay." He hasn't let go of Chris. He wants…*them*, he supposes…to stay in his arms forever, to keep them safe.

"Talking of which, I gotta pee."

Alex smiles and lets Chris go. Chris takes off their tights and walk out of the room. Alex stares at the shapely and pert bottom, clad in the smallest black briefs.

When Chris comes back, Alex stands. "I guess I'll leave you in peace." He heads towards the door.

"You can stay if you want, if you've got nowhere to be." Chris wrings their hands. Alex turns back, raking his fingers through his hair. "I'll go and brush my teeth."

Chris turns away from him. "Yeah, that's a good idea."

~~~

Alex joins Chris in bed later. The whole thing sags under their combined weight. Alex awkwardly moves his arms about, unsure where Chris wants them. Like last time, Chris grabs him and winds Alex's arm around their chest. Alex inhales, allowing himself to be intoxicated by Chris's unique scents—jasmine and spice and all things nice.

He wants to hold Chris all night and more, and that desire scares him. It's best not to start anything right now, what with his emotional and psychological state, but he can't suppress his attraction to Chris at all.

"So, you are basically a tranny?" Alex feels the smooth skin of Chris's back.

"You shouldn't use that word."

Alex plays with the soft, short strands of Chris's hair. "Oh, I didn't know. I'm sorry. Is it not politically correct?"

"No, it's not."

Alex kisses Chris's neck. "Okay. I won't use it again."

"I'm not transgender. I also don't want to transition. I like my dick enough too!" Chris tightens Alex's arm around themself some more. "And I am okay with the rest of me. I like shaving, and some days I want to put on my make-up. I feel pretty and natural that way."

You are pretty, Alex wants to tell them, but he remains silent so he can hear Chris talk because their whispers in the night are the best sounds in the world.

"My appearance doesn't define me. Some days, I love my make-up. I feel like that today. Sometimes I want to be bold and careless. I can behave the way most *boys* have been brought up to behave. Do you understand?"

Alex has seen Chris's different gender presentations. "Uh-huh."

"Does it…me…does it bother you I'm like this?" Chris sounds cautious and hesitant, without the brashness they usually present to the world.

Alex smiles, even though Chris can't see it. "I like the way you dress, and I like it when you boss me around. You're sassy when you do that. I sort of…like everything about you."

Chris chuckles and half turns. "Hey, I'm exhausted. It's been a long night dealing with that idiot. I'm going to sleep. Don't try anything, okay? Don't think because of my job I'll put out for anyone."

Alex laughs. "Have I dared to try anything with you? I don't think you're easy. Jeez. What kind of man do you think I am?"

"You're as much of a twat as the next man. That's what I think."

"Yeah, yeah. Sure you do. Now go to sleep. Good night, Chris." He kisses their cheek.

Chris falls asleep a lot faster than Alex can. Alex caresses Chris's soft skin with his fingers as he listens to their faint snores. Their chests move in unison to a peaceful silence. He can see Chris's face in the dusk, their lips apart, an innocence betraying them in the dead of night. Much later, Chris's presence lulls Alex into a dreamless sleep, the first night after days of insomnia.

Chris wakes when Alex tries to move, to hide his unfamiliar arousal.

"Where's your arm?" they mumble.

"I've got work," Alex tells them apologetically.

"Go and take a shower. I'll make some breakfast for you."

"You don't have to do that. Why don't you sleep in?" Alex pulls on his T-shirt while watching Chris rub sleep from the corners of their eyes like an overgrown child waking up to go to school.

"I want to." They're already sitting up.

Alex loves the sweet Chris with messy hair and sleep marks. He grins with affection.

When he comes out of the shower, Chris has brewed coffee and made some toast. Together, they bring their breakfast to the table, sit and look at each other. Smiles dance between them. Alex feels as though he's fourteen again and discovering that he loved Sam. Now, he's looking at Chris, and they're an enigma. They let the fragile bond between them deepen. Chris breaks the spell by coughing.

"You better eat your breakfast or you'll be late for work." They tilt their head to indicate the food in front of them.

Alex nods and bites into his toast, washing it down with some coffee. "Yeah, my idiot boss will try to get me fired."

"He sounds like a piece of work." Chris tears a dainty corner off the bread and dips it in their mug. "What time are you getting off tonight?"

"Not until after six. Eight-to-six shift. It sucks."

Chris makes a face, their dimples appearing for a second. "I'm not working tonight. I'll make some dinner for us. If you have no plan, that is."

Alex shakes his head quickly, in case Chris changes their mind. "No plan. No. It'd be lovely."

~~~

It comes as a surprise to them both, but whenever they are not working nights, they end up in the same bed. They share breakfast and dinner sometimes, too, and Alex finds Chris cuter by the day but is afraid to tell them because Chris will definitely bite his head off.

Alex has come home from work to find Chris still awake, so he crawls under Chris's cover and snuggles up.

Chris giggles. "Stop this, Alex Whale."

"What's that?" Alex asks with a smile.

Chris turns on the table lamp, the yellow light shining on them, creating a halo. For a fleeting moment, Alex thinks about angels and celestial beings, like Chris.

"I don't know. Being needy? Cuddling up every night? I'm not a cuddler." Chris pretends to sulk.

Alex laughs. "Who's the one who holds on to my arms when they have bad dreams? You like me being here."

"Ha! And vice versa." The expression on Chris's face changes, like a wave calming. "Alex. Have you been with someone with a dick before?"

Alex shifts a little so he can see Chris more clearly. "No. I…I've ogled plenty of them, though."

Chris frowns. "Explain yourself."

Alex rubs the back of his thick neck. "I've found other men attractive, yeah? I've never acted on it."

"Why not?" The turquoise in Chris's eyes shimmers in the light. They shift to hover above Alex. Under that intense gaze, Alex flinches from the guilt of not having admitted this to anyone.

"I was a famous, successful boxer. What do you think? They'd have given me hell for it."

Chris cocks their head to consider Alex. "Hmm."

"Have you had a boxer punch your face before?" Alex muses.

"No...been battered, though."

"Oh." Alex waits for Chris to elaborate, but they only look away.

Alex shakes his head. "Imagine making a pass at the wrong man. I know who I fuck should have nothing to do with my sport, but the media and the whole boxing world would have had a field day. Not everyone's like you. You don't ever compromise. You have your gender thing and you fuck whoever you like. You can call me a coward."

"I'm not going to call you names. I dig it's hard to be in the closet. But if you'd come out, it would've been so cool for people to know this famous, bisexual boxing champion exists. Isn't that the assumption? A macho man like you can't be interested in cocks? That queers are effeminate or some shit like that." Chris's indigo eyes glimmer in the dusk.

"I guess so. You think that's who I am? Bi?" Alex kisses Chris's shoulder.

"Seems that way to me, but you don't have to use a label if you don't want to. I don't go around telling people that I'm gender-fluid."

Alex nods, thinking about sexual desires as natural needs, like air and water. "Okay."

Chris leans forward, creating an intimacy that engulfs them both. They touch Alex's arms, the soft tips of their long fingers tingling Alex. Chris's hand stalls at the dragon tattoo.

"Tell me about them. Tell me your stories."

"Stories about my tats?"

Chris nods.

Alex points to the intricate dragon on his left bicep. "That one's from Hong Kong. Together with the tiger and panther on my back. I had them done over a few years. It was one of the things I did enjoy, apart from boxing. I got to travel to some cool places."

"They are pretty distinctive. The tattoo artist must have been talented," Chris muses.

"Yeah, I think the three animals are related to the Triad or some shit. That's what the tattooist said."

Chris smiles. "So, you'd signed yourself up for the Chinese Triad, huh?"

Alex laughs. "I might have. My fans out in the Far East loved the ink. That's good enough for me."

"I've never travelled. I don't even venture out of London," Chris admits with a giggle.

"Would you like to see the world one day?"

"The world… Are you one of those frivolous people who plan for the future? I can't spend my hard-earned cash on reveries." Chris pouts. "Anyway, I'm not sure if the world's ready for me." They dip their head.

"No, it'll never be ready for you!" Alex kisses Chris's forehead. "There're places I'd love to return to. I can show you."

Chris licks their lips. "I'll check my schedule and get back to you."

"You do that." Alex reads between Chris's lines as he tunes in to Chris's idiosyncrasies. They both have their insecurities from their past, but Alex used to think about the *future*. For a fleeting moment, Chris's face is a map of dreams, their emotions expansive and searching, and Alex understands why it's a scary concept to grasp since travelling together sounds like science fiction right now.

Most of Alex's right shoulder and bicep are covered by tribal designs. Chris kisses them, tracing the lines down with their tongue.

"I had that done in San Diego but the artist has Polynesian blood. I loved his work."

Chris touches Alex's lower stomach. "Alex Blue."

The name is carved in a joined-up, flowing script as if Alex has signed the name himself. The one on his lower back is an ornate sundial with a full wheel of rays.

Alex traces the contour of Chris's face. "You've never thought about getting some?"

Chris grins. "I don't want anything permanent. I only have my lip and ears pierced."

"They're beautiful on you," Alex says.

Chris plays with their left nipple. "Maybe here, a small bar."

Alex considers the pink tip between Chris's fingers and imagines licking the cool metal.

They touch Alex's left shin—his entire lower leg is covered by a kaleidoscope of gothic motifs: skulls, thorns and blackbirds—and then draws along Alex's thigh. "Are you going to get any more here?"

"I haven't thought about more ink in the last few years. When I was in the ring, they were part of Blue's persona, you know? Now I have no one to stare at them and they're not plastered on every tabloid newspaper and sports website. I don't see the point."

"I want to see them." Chris continues to scroll along Alex's skin with their fingertips as if drafting an atlas of their interest. They lower their eyelids, the long lashes forming two small crescents over their eyes, as though they're shielding themself from Alex's gaze. "I love looking at them. At you."

Chris's light touch makes Alex's heart thump fast. Alex smiles. "Me too. I mean, I like looking at you."

"Hmm. I suppose you can say you've had enough ink." Chris's eyes are drawn to Alex right forearm. "I know what this is now."

"Yeah. It was my first."

He had Sam's name done when he turned eighteen. The capital 'A' with a Roman font represents a big Alex in her heart.

How the strongest love for someone can turn to shit.

Is this infatuation with Chris just a phase? Can attraction change without warning? What if I'm simply not relationship material?

And you think you're having a relationship with Chris right now? Alex has no answer to the questions at all. *Who am I kidding? Who'd want a partner like me?* Long-term doesn't seem to exist in Chris's vocabulary, and Alex is a depressed, disgraced ex-boxer with no future.

Yet Chris burrows underneath Alex's defences, deeper and deeper, day by day. Their impression is already as permanent as the art on his skin.

~~~

The waxing this afternoon was painful as usual. In the bathroom, Chris gazes at the mirror and her smooth torso, her fingers traversing the milky skin. She closes her eyes and remembers Alex's tattoos and his low drawl telling intimate stories about himself. She draws a sketch around her nipples. *Am I someone Alex would fall for? What does he look like as he comes? Those biceps will stretch, but he'll be gentle. He will unravel only at the last minute, pushing them forward, burying all his reservations. They will move in unison.* She trembles with the imaginary scene.

Chris's breath has misted up the mirror, like a shroud of white dust. She can't always tell who she is, whether she's ever happy. She steadies herself against the basin. Her hand meanders down to her lower body and she starts to stroke herself, remembering the power of Alex's arms and legs. She imagines those thighs rubbing against hers. She rests her forehead on the cool mirror surface while her hand speeds up, pushing herself against the porcelain until the sensation explodes like colourful fireworks.

Chris opens her eyes and stares at her reflection as her breathing slows.

Afterwards, she returns to her room and picks out a dress shirt even though she'd prefer something else today. She has an appointment with a regular who likes a sharply dressed model in his bed. Two hours' work and it's back to her real life.

Real life. *I've been doing this for far too long.* There isn't another life. Her hands stall at the task of buttoning the shirt. She shakes her head and summons her butch self, her hidden identity. It's not quite happening today.

Dark suit, expensive cologne and no make-up. She feels naked. Some days Chris is only pretending, passing between the gender boundaries, desperate for a comfortable position.

~~~

Chris can do this with his eyes closed. Leon is a little guy who calls on his services every few weeks. He's a gay man in his forties who seems very shy. He mustn't have been able to find a partner. Chris performs as always and makes Leon come. As Chris gets dressed, Leon watches him, wringing his hands.

Chris stands and rights himself the best he can. "Thanks. I'll see myself out." He pecks Leon on the cheek.

"Wait." Leon brings out a small, gift-wrapped box from the drawer of his bedside table. "It's...for you."

Chris's eyes fall on his client's present.

Fuckety fuck. "That's very kind of you, Leon. Thank you."

He leans down and pecks Leon again on the forehead. It's not the first time a john has expressed interest in him. He's had offers of moving in, becoming exclusive, and declarations of love. Chris summons up a smile. "You know, it's awfully kind of you, but you don't need to give me anything, sweetheart."

Leon fidgets. "Uh. Are you not going to open it?" He sounds so mild and scared, but this crosses the line—a thin line barely protecting Chris's dignity.

"Would you like me to?"

Leon nods.

Chris maintains his smile as he takes off the small bow and opens the wrapping paper to reveal a bottle of expensive perfume. Leon asked him a few weeks ago what he used because it smelled nice.

"That's very sweet of you." He wishes he could reject the present and tell him he would never be interested in a client. But it'd hurt, and Chris doesn't want to break a client's heart due to a vague notion of professional courtesy.

Leon glances down. "I was wondering if...if we could go out." He looks up, hope rising in his face. "You know, as friends."

Chris looks away. He doesn't know anything about the john other than that he seems fine. The sex is vanilla and he's cordial enough. He lacks the allure of a certain fallen boxer. Chris does a good job as always, but he has absolutely no attraction to Leon.

"I'm sorry. I'm flattered but I don't date." He smiles apologetically while telling the decent white lie.

"What do you mean? You won't date anyone or just not your clients? Is it me?" A frown develops between Leon's brows.

"Leon, come on. We have fun, don't we?" Chris puts on a charming face and a big grin to hide how he feels inside. This conversation is so pointless, like his life.

It dawns on Leon. "Oh, I get it. You don't do anything without getting paid, do you? So, if I pay you, you'll go out with me?"

Chris suppresses a sigh. Why does Leon have to force him into this position?

"Leon, you're a lovely man. Why would you... No, I don't do boyfriend experience. I make a really lousy partner. Sorry." Chris is reluctant to use that line, but Leon gets the hump anyway.

"There! I thought you were different. That you're...into me. I was so naïve. So stupid. I guess you lie to everyone, don't you? You really are a money-grabbing prostitute and nothing more. Here, have a fucking tip!"

Leon throws some notes at Chris that land on his lap. The soon-to-be-lost client might as well have shot a spear at his pride.

"I've got to go. I'm sorry." Chris stands, letting Leon's tip fall onto the floor. Leaving the upset client, he steps outside to face the chilly, dirty streets of London. He turns up his collar against the wind.

"Well, that's that, then," he mutters to himself and pulls out his phone to arrange a taxi.

I don't love you. I don't want you.

Evenings that ended with Chris being made to feel cheap and unworthy. Names that the men like to call him in bed. They play out their fantasies of power while Chris goes along with the role of the subservient, his insides hollower every time something like this happens. His job is to bring them happiness and fulfilment for a short time, and Chris believes he's good at his role. He's not the future or the long-term solution. That's all.

The job of an escort isn't glamorous or at all exciting despite the number of literary pages and feature films devoted to it. Most of the time Chris feels adrift, and lately, he's been thinking a lot about quitting. If only he had actual job-worthy skills and career options.

Chris prays Alex is at home.

He finds Alex in bed and collapses into his arms.

Alex stirs and mumbles, "Hey."

"Hmm. I feel like shit. Give me a hug, will you?"

Alex does, wrapping his massive limbs around to comfort Chris. "What's the matter? Did something happen?"

Chris sighs. "The client asked me out. I'm okay."

"What? Why? Does he know you well?"

Alex sits up, and Chris follows suit, covering his knees with his arms. In that gesture, he hides his vulnerability.

"No one knows me well." Chris is not including Alex in this, but even Alex. Even Alex. Chris shakes his head to get rid of the thought. "He got angry when I said no."

Chris doesn't like that nasty taste in his mouth. There are times when deeply hidden emotions bubble up and make him go back to being a little kid before he was forced to grow up and face the contempt of the whole world. This kid would sit in his classroom among other shiny happy children and feel a jealous rage. His mother stole years from him, and he couldn't bear to see the innocence and naivety of the other children. Leon's hurt little face reminded Chris of his classmates: entitled kids thinking about their future.

What are his classmates doing now? In their regular jobs, having romantic nights in with their partners? Fuck knows. If he hadn't been trading his body, he might be one of those regular people worthy of someone. Not Leon, though. Not a client who has only ever seen the façade.

"Wanker. Did he hurt you?" A deep V forms in Alex's forehead as he considers Chris's face.

"Nothing like that. He shouted abuse. The usual—that I'm a greedy whore. Don't worry. Let's get back to sleep."

"How dare he!" Alex's indignation on Chris's behalf cheers him up.

"I've heard it all before. You win some, you lose some."

Alex pulls him into a hug. "There are some wackos out there. I'm worried about you getting hurt."

Chris gazes at him. "It's part of my job. I can take care of myself. Public workers get shouted at, verbally abused, don't they?"

Alex shakes his head. "But you're not a public worker. You're in people's private homes and hotel rooms. He could have murdered you then. How do I know you're safe?"

Chris knows the bad times, too, and wicked violent people. He's vulnerable to their slurs and attacks. His head never clears of the memories of their kicks and fists. He remembers the sounds of footprints raining down, moments before everything fell silent and dark.

But he smiles. "Don't be dramatic. I'm safe, okay? I've done this for long enough to know. I share my schedule with another escort and we look out for each other. I have a pepper spray. I don't ever drink on the job, et cetera. Plus, this guy was a regular. I should have seen it coming, but I hadn't paid enough attention."

Chris blames himself for growing too complacent. He sighs, betraying weariness.

Alex opens his mouth to say something but then shuts it.

"Now, I am knackered. Can I sleep, pretty please?" Chris grins, flashing his teeth, and lies back down. He feels much better after seeing Alex's reaction. Someone cares. Isn't life tolerable?

As Chris falls into a slumber, he finds brief happiness in his colourful, scattered dreams.

CHAPTER 8
DRAG

A LOUD THUMP AND the sound of breaking glass cut through the quiet afternoon.

"Fuck!" Alex has been in the bathroom for a while.

Chris knocks on the door. "Alex, what are you doing in there? Everything all right?"

"Uh, okay. I'm...fine," comes the muffled reply.

Chris hears him moving about. More expletives seep through the gap at the bottom of the door, like an involuntary SOS.

"Chris, is there a first-aid kit in the flat?"

"Shit. Have you hurt yourself?" Chris tries the door handle but it's locked. His chest tightens. "Open the damn door, Alex."

He's not dumb, not really, despite what everyone thinks. He is quite aware of Alex's mental health, and he could be in there slitting his wrists.

After a few beats, there's a click and Alex opens from the inside. Chris quickly assesses the damage. Blood has splashed all over the sink. Pieces of the mirror from the bathroom cabinet are scattered around like shards from a broken heart, and there are white tablets amidst the carnage, as though Alex has sprinkled snow on the red and silver.

Alex holds his bleeding left hand up and looks away in embarrassment.

Chris urges him out of the bathroom to the kitchen area. "I think there's a first-aid box under the sink. Someone left it. Now, run your hand under the tap. The cold water will sting a little."

Alex does while Chris holds Alex's forearm steady.

"It's starting to feel numb."

"Go and sit down on the sofa," Chris directs when he's satisfied the bleeding has slowed enough.

He finds the kit under the sink. Fuck knows how long it's been there. He rummages further in the low cupboard but can't find any clean cloths. Armed with the first-aid kit and a roll of paper towels, Chris sits next to Alex and dries his hand, dabbing it with care. It's not as bad as the amount of blood suggests. It's only a gash on his palm that will heal.

Chris pats the cut dry with a towel soaked in saline solution. Then he finds the gauze and wraps up Alex's hand. As he tends to him, he can feel the man's breaths on his neck, their faces close together. He loves the callus on Alex's hand and imagines how good it'd feel on his own skin. A lover's touch, not strangers' need, on his body. Heat rising inside of him, Chris shakes his head to clear his wandering mind.

"Take the gauze. You'll need to change this if the blood soaks through later," he tells Alex after taping on the bandage.

Alex takes the pack. Chris gazes at him and comes face-to-face with his own features reflected in Alex's dark eyes, flinching from Alex's intense look.

"What were you doing to cause such chaos? Do you need to be bathroom-trained?" Chris smiles to show he's joking, anything to distract Alex from peering into his soul.

"I...lost it." Alex blinks and sulks.

"So, you fought with a bathroom cabinet?" Chris chuckles.

"I'm glad you find it funny. I always forget my own strength." Alex shifts in the sofa. "The cabinet door wouldn't shut. I dropped my bottle of pills and got frustrated. I tried pushing it shut, then the stupid mirror fell out."

Chris stares at Alex, returning a look so penetrating that Alex can't hide from it and moves to stand. Chris stills him with a hand on Alex's thigh.

"Where are you going?"

"To sort out the mess in the bathroom."

Chris stands up, too. "I'll do it. How are you going to manage with one hand?"

"But…" Alex looks up, but he has no argument for refusing Chris's offer of help.

In the bathroom, Chris crouches to pick up the broken mirror. Luckily, they are rather large pieces.

"Be careful with that. You'll cut yourself," Alex tells him.

He turns to see Alex leaning against the door frame, watching him while he picks up the glass fragments with a towel and then gathers the white diamond pills; some are in the sink, more on the floor. The small, white bottle lying empty shows a brand: Prozac. He puts the tablets back in the bottle.

"You can't take these now. They've been on the filthy floor. You'll have to get another prescription."

"They'll be okay. I don't think the doc would give me more of them in case I overdose." Alex takes the bottle from Chris. Their fingers touch.

"They're for depression," Alex explains.

Of course, Chris knows they are antidepressants, given his mum's history of taking prescribed and over-the-counter drugs. Annette used to take them all the time as though they were bloody love hearts. Chris is not around to see her on drugs anymore, but he suspects little has changed. To show his defiance, he hasn't followed his mother and descended into drug and alcohol abuse—part of his inverse control mechanism.

"I know. Still." Chris finds a bottle of cleaning stuff and an old sponge and starts to mop up the blood.

"Why are you cleaning my shit?" With his good hand, Alex takes the sponge from Chris and wipes the sink himself.

Chris's face is so close to Alex's, again. He shrugs. "I don't know. Because there's blood and glass in the bathroom?"

He watches the pink water disappear down the drain hole, the little eddy like the stirring in his heart. "It's okay. I know you're depressed. It doesn't make you a lesser man," Chris whispers. "Look, it's done already."

Alex steals a glance at him. "Thank you."

Alex might mean Chris's comment on his depression, for wrapping up his hand or the cleaning. Chris gives him an eye-roll anyway.

"I won't say 'anytime', cuz I'm not that fond of gore fests." He flashes his bright white smile at Alex.

Alex coughs. "Well, I'll get a new cabinet to replace this one."

Chris stands, distancing himself from Alex. "Just as well. We'll have years to wait if we ask the landlord. And I want to see myself when I shave."

In the naked light of the bathroom, Chris imagines a world more perfect than theirs. "Magic mirror in my hand, who is the fairest in the land?"

Just like that, Chris drops Alex's hand and sashays back to his room, hoping Alex knows the answer to that question.

Chris, of course.

~~~

Since the day Chris had a fight with his last boyfriend, Alex and Chris have cuddled up and slept together most nights. A couple of times, Chris worked till two or three in the morning and woke Alex up to go to his room. They still haven't done anything sexual, but Alex doesn't mind. He worries about his libido, which has been affected by his depression and the medication, and he wonders what their relationship means, whether they're officially together. Chris is everything to him right now, but they may also be nothing. He's supposed to be a man of the world, and yet he is confused as hell. Whatever they are, Alex can't help but smile when he thinks about Chris.

Alex hasn't slept at all, and it's about two thirty in the morning when Chris comes home. He stares at the door in the dark, waiting patiently for Chris to wake him up like he's done often lately.

Hey, Big Blue.

Alex listens to the faint noises of Chris using the bathroom, but he is not coming for Alex tonight.

Chris has not refused him so far, so why shouldn't Alex go to him instead?

Alex puts on a T-shirt and a pair of boxers and opens the door to Chris's room. In the darkness, he can work out Chris's shape in bed.

"Don't come in. I want to be alone tonight."

Alex doesn't know what he's done wrong, but if there's one thing he's guaranteed to do when Chris tells him not to it's to behave in the exact opposite way. Alex approaches Chris, sits on the edge of the bed and puts his hand over the lump.

"What's the matter? Did I do something? Are you ill?"

"I'm not ill. Fuck off."

Alex remains.

Chris switches on the desk lamp and sits up in bed, pulling the cover over his body. Alex glimpses the marks on his neck.

"What's that? You're hurt." Alex tries to pull the duvet away.

Chris holds on to it and scowls. "Alex Whale, if I tell you to move, can you do it? I want to sleep. I'm knackered."

"No, I won't leave. What are the bruises on your neck?" Alex demands again.

Chris lets the duvet drop a few inches. "It was the collar. I was in a scene."

Alex is confused, as though Chris is talking in another language. "Your client put a collar on you? What the fuck is that?"

Chris sighs. "That's what he asked for, among other things. That was the job tonight. Can you leave me alone now?"

Alex squeezes his nose bridge. "No, I'm not leaving until you tell me what's going on. Where else did he hurt you?"

He yanks the duvet away and takes a look at Chris, who struggles to pull the bedding back. Chris always sleeps only in a pair of knickers so Alex can see there are other faint finger marks. He turns Chris around roughly. Chris fights back but Alex is stronger.

"Shit!" Alex can't believe the angry lines on Chris's back and the patches of dark bruises on his arse, his perfect skin marked by someone who paid for this kind of shit.

"I thought you only have sex with them. Why did you do that? Did he force you?"

Chris turns back, quite nonchalant. "No, and it's not as bad as it looks, okay? I know what I'm doing. He's a regular. Can you please forget about this already? I'll speak to you tomorrow." He starts to push Alex out of his room, but Alex wouldn't budge.

"No, I don't understand. How often do you see this wacko?"

Chris deflates. Alex won't leave him alone until they've had a conversation about it.

"I see him every few months. He pays well and he wants kinks. I don't need to work for a week or two because he pays good money for a session. We do a scene, and we fuck. Do you want more details? It's only an occasional special request. I'm not going to explain myself to you." Chris's voice cracks as though his anger is bubbling.

"I can't believe you'd voluntarily get cuffed and flogged for money. It just seems dangerous to me." Alex shakes his head. "I'm not judging you or anything, but what do you get up to in your job?"

"I do what I gotta do." Chris pouts. "I'm not answerable to you. In fact, you're not my keeper, or…or special friend or anything!"

"I thought… I don't care I'm not 'special'." Alex draws the quotation marks in the air. More quietly, he says, "I don't want you to see this guy again or anyone else who pays to hurt you. How am I going to know you're safe when you're out there if you let men do this kind of thing to you?"

Chris's face turns cold and stony.

"Before you came along, I was fine about selling myself. Not even to the highest bidder, just the right amount of money would buy me. And I was fine with that. You fucking changed me. I don't even know how or when. Now I wish I'd never met you. You're nothing to me, Alex Whale."

After the rant, Chris exhales. He stares at Alex with an impassive face. "Fuck off. Don't come to me again," Chris adds for emphasis. He switches the light off and burrows under the duvet once more, with his back to Alex.

Alex wants to say 'what the fuck?' but thinks better of it. Is it so bad to be concerned when your friend comes home from work covered in black and blue?

Alex returns to his room and sulks like a lovesick teenager, staring at his bare walls. He wishes he had a punch bag. He is hurt, wound up. Fifty press-ups and sit-ups in the narrow space between the wall and his bed should occupy his body, if not his mind.

Alex is nothing to Chris.

~~~

For days, Chris ignores Alex whenever she sees him in the flat. Whenever Alex says hello, she looks the other way, and every time he feels like she has punched him and his heart is hollower.

About a week later, Alex can't stand it anymore. When he's sure Chris is in her room one night, he enters without permission, pushing his chest out and prepared to face her fury. Chris is sitting on her bed, a cigarette dangling from her lips as she taps something on her phone. Her stare is harsh and cold, but Alex stands tall and returns his own glare.

Instead of telling Alex to leave, Chris stubs out her cigarette, turns the light off, and lies down. *No, no.* Alex kneels down next to the bed.

"Chris, listen. I'm not trying to control you or criticise you, all right? Not like all your previous boyfriends. I worry about you when you're working. It's not right to be all bruised up because it's not like you're into that stuff. I know that."

When Chris fails to respond, Alex continues, "Talk to me. Tell me I'm *something* to you!"

"No, leave me alone."

"Chris. You lied about me." Alex's voice trembles, betraying his desperation, because he wants Chris to know he cares. When he went to prison, he lost everything and he existed only to go through the motions. Their relationship *has* to mean something because Chris has given him reasons to hurt. The epiphany makes Alex's heart thump so hard and fast he fears she can hear it.

Let her know. Let her see how much.

"I said, 'Fuck off.'" There is little force behind Chris's words. She turns the table lamp back on and sits up.

"I've been doing this for years. And before that, I looked after myself and my mum. I don't need you to tell me how to do my job, to protect me."

She blinks as if to stop her tears from falling. She whispers, "I wish you were nothing to me. I wish I could walk away and forget about you."

Alex blinks. He grabs hold of Chris's hand. She stares at their joined hands.

"I do want you to be safe, but I won't be the big man trying to tell you what to do. I hate being the big man. Just…don't lie about us." All Alex can see are the big blue eyes hiding fear. He wants a fighting chance with the owner of that horror.

Chris's tears form two rivulets down her cheeks. She wipes them and stares at the tears as if surprised. "No one's safe. Nothing's guaranteed. Promises are words that offer false hope. They all treat me like a freak and leave eventually."

"I'm not good with words. Let me prove myself to you. I'm here and I want to be here, with you," Alex pleads.

"How can you promise me anything? You don't even know me."

"Then let me get to know you and you'll find out about me, so I will be something to you. I'm worried you *will* leave when you do." Alex says the last part with childish petulance, earning a reluctant smile from Chris. He knows she likes a challenge.

"How can I leave unless we're together? If you tell me what the fuck we're doing, then I can make a decision." She arches her eyebrows in a perfect inverted V.

Alex grins. Now they are getting somewhere. "That makes two of us. We don't know what we're doing, but will you? Let me stay?"

"I wish I knew how to quit you, Alexander." Chris adds, "That's a line from *Brokeback Mountain*."

Alex frowns. "What mountain now?"

Chris sighs heavily. "Never mind. Two het-boys playing gays in the hills. It's quite romantic, though, if you're into that kind of thing. I'm not."

Alex nods. Then he remembers what Chris said about the film. "Would you like it if we do something romantic, like having sex?"

Chris is silent for so long, Alex thinks there won't be an answer. She rolls a joint and smokes as if to stall the conversation. Alex sits and waits with his customary patience.

"Sex is not romantic for me. It's a…commodity," she states.

Alex gazes at her, trying to empathise, to consider something that he assumes to be part of a romantic relationship.

"No, it's not for me. I know how this may sound, but you probably haven't met the right person yet."

Chris laughs and gives Alex an eye-roll. "You've gone from nothing to telling me you're my Prince Charming. You've woken me up from a hundred years of stupor? I don't believe in *the one and only*, and we're not going to have angry make-up sex, Alex Whale."

Alex chuckles. "I didn't think so. I don't care about angry sex, as long as I've got angry Chris rather than sulking Chris because you know what?" Alex waits for a moment before saying quietly, "I mean something to you. Admit it."

Chris chuckles. "If you say so. Are you coming to bed or what?"

"Can I? Have I survived our first argument? I've not been sleeping cuz you're not next to me. I reached out and you weren't there. I missed my Chris-shaped lump."

Chris touches Alex's five o'clock shadow. "How are you feeling?"

Alex feels like a kicked puppy. A rather huge kicked puppy. His depression is a larger-than-life shadow that trails both of them. His dreams are reruns of a horrific slice of reality. He can't forget the scene that has been so vividly etched in his psyche, his nightmares and every waking moment ever since the accident. His horrors can only be dulled by the pills.

He shrugs. "It's okay. I'm not better or worse." The meds make him feel flat and hollowed out, but Chris is the spot of red in a sea of blue.

Chris draws Alex's head close and whispers in his ear, "I'm here. Yeah, you're something, Alex."

Alex grins.

~~~

Chris has coaxed Alex into going out to Soho.

When she comes out of her bedroom, Alex gawks and swallows. She's wearing a little black dress, flesh-coloured tights and her usual jewelled pumps, her make-up understated as always. Her short, cropped hair reveals two small earrings dangling from her delicate ears, her long neck punctuated by a small leather necklace.

As Chris puts her black coat on, she smiles. "Stop staring."

Alex opens his mouth a couple of times before replying, "Can't help it. You're beautiful. When did you start dressing like this?" He plays with the lapel of her coat.

Chris checks her phone, wallet and keys. "A long time ago. I enjoyed the dressing-up part of modelling and acting, even though the rest was bullshit. I hated the uniforms at school. I started wearing things I liked when I was about fifteen or sixteen."

"At school as well?" Alex asks. She can almost see him sorting and storing the Chris-related information in his head.

"Yeah, I wore earrings, painted my nails, put on eyeliner and things like that. The school wouldn't allow jewellery, so I got into trouble for it a bit. I sometimes wore dresses and skirts. By that time, I wasn't going to school much anyway."

Alex kisses her cheek. "Did anyone bully you over this?"

"Oh, yeah, you bet. Some of the kids tried, but I wasn't exactly a pushover. I was the tallest in class for quite a while, even though I was a bit too lanky to be a good fighter."

"Wish I was there."

"I didn't need no protector. I had a reputation for being a bit of a headcase. I was a freak and I acted up. That was my weapon against those assholes at school. The teachers didn't care to force me to learn and the other kids kept their distance. A few taunted me relentlessly but I survived anyway."

Her school days are simply not something she dwells on.

Alex says, "I love your independence. You're a free spirit, Chris."

"I certainly don't need help."

Alex smiles. "I will always offer it though."

She winds her arm around him. "Come on. Are we going or what? You look like you want to stay here and gape at me all night."

Serious flirtation hangs in Chris's voice.

"Okay. Let's go. I'd like us to do something when you're out of that dress, though. Properly. Soon."

She hits him. "I told you I'm not that easy."

That earns a dry laugh from Alex.

~~~

It's ten thirty by the time they arrive at the club. There's no way Chris won't get into the place with her familiar face and genial disposition, but the bouncers give Alex a once-over. They recognise him but are discreet enough to let them through without any fuss. Chris directs him down to the basement where he surveys the clientele, taking note of the setup in the underground room before she leads him by the hand through the packed floor to the bar. She addresses the barmen by their names and gets a beer for herself and a Diet Coke for him. They perch by a shelf near the end of the bar.

Chris leans close to speak to him above the loud music. "Is this okay? Not too crowded?"

The fact that it's busy works fine for Alex. Most of the punters don't seem to take notice of him. He kisses Chris's soft cheek. "Yeah. I'm good."

The cavernous room isn't set up for dancing, though. There's no dance floor, but a low stage stands to one end of the central space.

A pair of lean arms circle Chris from behind, and the guy they belong to kisses her cheek. "Hey. How's it going?" He comes around to face Chris and Alex.

Chris returns the kiss. "Mwah. We're good. You're not working tonight?"

"No. I should be fucking studying, but I'd had enough. I'll take advantage of my staff discount and get you two some cheap drinks in a second."

He holds his hand out to shake Alex's. "I'm Liam."

"Oh." Alex wipes his hand on his thigh and takes Liam's. "Alex. I replaced you in the flat."

"Aye, aye." Liam's twang betrays his Irish heritage. "Everything all right there?"

Alex glances over at Chris, who flashes her signature enigmatic smile.

"Yeah. More than all right," she admits.

Liam looks between the two and nods. He asks what they'd like to drink and wanders off to order.

When he returns, Chris asks Liam, "Who's performing tonight?"

Liam laughs. "Victoria Leather."

Chris coos. "Holy moly. I love Victor!" She turns to Alex and explains, "Drag act on the last Thursday of every month. *Victoria* is exquisite."

Alex can only imagine RuPaul, even though he hardly ever pays attention to the programme. Soon, Chris spots a couple of people she knows and strays over to say hello.

Liam holds his pint up to salute Alex, his eyes peering over to Chris at the other end of the room. "Chris is quite a handful, yeah?"

Alex grins. "You can say that again."

"They're a bit of a *character*, like." Liam utters the word like a veiled warning.

Alex's temperature cools with that threat.

"How long have you two been…you know?" Liam twirls his forefinger once and takes a big gulp of his beer.

Alex's smile returns. "It's hard to say. I'm…interested in Chris. I can't remember when we started." Everything—the beginning and middle—was fuzzy, but his beam stays because, somehow, they have ended up dating.

Liam raises a single eyebrow. "Intriguing." He thinks about it for moments. "I've not seen Chris like this. Ever. The way they smile around you, acting kinda coy. If I didn't know any better, I'd say they're happy. Chris pretends they don't care about anyone, but they took me in when I was a fucking mess."

Chris has told Alex a little about Liam, who used to be an escort too until he met his boyfriend and moved out. The recovering drug addict has cleaned up his act and gone back to university to study for a music degree. As a kindred spirit, Alex can imagine the troubles behind Liam's eyes.

"It's good, isn't it? I mean, Chris being happy?" Alex asks tentatively.

Liam swallows his beer. "Sure. Yes. Cuz Chris pretends to be jovial but they push people away, force them to treat them badly. Nasty break-up. Repeat. So, I guess you guys are doing great."

Alex smiles. His eyes drift over to where Chris is talking to her friends. She is laughing about something and seems relaxed. The warm fuzzy sensation, now almost familiar, surges inside him.

"We're taking things easy. Chris is sweet underneath all that bullshit, you know."

Liam almost chokes on his drink. "Slow and sweet? It doesn't sound too much like Chris. They're a champ of three-minute relationships. You must be special. I can see why you might be a perfect match for them because they need a great big fucking beast to tame them, that's for sure."

Alex smiles and shakes his head. "Yeah. When I first moved in, all I could hear was, hmm, her sexual activities or her arguments with people. But, we've only held hands and cuddled in bed. It's as if we're dating back in the 1950s. We're waiting till we get hitched or something like that."

Liam's eyes widen. "Wow. You mean…you haven't had sex yet? Holy shit!"

Alex shrugs. "I don't miss a thing."

Chris comes back and she folds herself around Alex, interrupting their conversation. Alex looks at Chris and the blue-green of her eyes, mesmerised by the mild pink gracing her cheeks and the big smile on her face.

"Hey, what are you two talking about?" Chris asks.

Liam gives her an eye-roll. "You, of course, and how you seem to be totally smitten! I've never seen you like this."

She laughs, rubbing her nose against Alex's thick neck. "Personality transplant. They perform those on queers-in-need. Where's Ali?" She explains to Alex, "Liam's boyfriend. They're too sickly sweet for my liking."

"You're just jealous. His friend's on holiday, so he's pet-sitting. They have two dogs and a cat. I can't say I'm much of an animal person, so I was going to do my assignment—"

Liam is cut short when the lights dim and canned drum rolls announce the appearance of tonight's drag act.

"Woohoo!" Chris moves off from clinging onto Alex to clap her hands, her laughter lighting up her face once more.

The drag artist who comes on stage is beautiful and way more femme than Chris. She has a long blonde wig and colourful stage make-up. True to her stage name, her padded-out body curves inside the white leather corset. A black miniskirt, garter and tights, and a pair of glittery six-inch silver platform boots complete her outfit.

Glitter. Glitter. Glitter.

She puts her thumb and forefinger in her mouth and whistles loudly, so the room hushes immediately.

"Good evening, ladies and ladies!" She has a voice that betrays a hint of harshness, but Alex thinks she'd definitely pass for a woman if the make-up wasn't quite as stage-dramatic. Liam smiles at Victoria.

The crowd cheers her on and a few of them whistle back. Chris glances at Alex sidelong and winks. Alex watches the performer with much curiosity.

"Are you ready for your compère?"

The audience screams 'yes', while Victoria further eggs them on by shouting back.

After more banter, she introduces herself, "I am your one and only Victoria L-E-A-T-H-E-R."

She breaks into a perfect rendition of an eighties hit, her voice strong and sultry. The next twenty minutes pass in much the same way and, drag or not, Victoria is a talented performer. She does not lip-sync like RuPaul's contestants, and she can hold a tune better than most pop idols. Her jokes are funny, too, without being too cheesy or vulgar.

"Now, before I sing my last number, I *must* say hello to my dear friend." Victoria pouts and points her long finger with the expertly painted nail at Chris.

Chris mutters under her breath, "Oh, fuck! This is the last time I'm coming to see the bastard."

Alex looks between the drag queen and Chris, all eyes in the crowded room on the latter. Instead of feeling uncomfortable, Alex has forgotten about the pressure and enjoys the moment.

"Come on stage, my little Chrissie. I'm not coming down in my platform shoes to *drag* you up here."

She laughs and claps her hands together. The audience follows her lead and begins to chant, "Chrissie! Chrissie! Chrissie!" Liam joins in.

"And that's not my fucking name." Chris shakes her head, but she can't ignore the calling. She kisses Alex and threads through the throng of people to reach the stage. She and Victoria hug and kiss. On the lips. The crowd cheer even louder. Alex can't help but smile at the playfulness. Chris is blushing, bringing crimson to her pale cheeks.

"Now, boys and girls. Is Chrissie hot or not?" Victoria announces, her arm around Chris's shoulders. The answer is, again, a unanimous 'yes'.

Victoria nods. "Let me tell you. This is her natural self." She presents Chris to the crowd with a flourish. "It takes me two fucking hours to transform my ugly mug to look like this, people." She points to her face and down her body.

The revellers respond with a collective sigh and then laugh. Chris's face is now scarlet.

"My darling, you've *dragged* along a fine gentleman to see my act tonight. I am absolutely honoured, so I'm going to dedicate this final song to you." She kisses Chris again and then directs her eyes to Alex and winks; Alex grins even wider.

Before Chris leaves the stage, Victoria leans in and whispers, though the microphone picks it up, "Thanks for coming, my old pal. I'll see you in a mo."

Chris smiles, showing her dimples, as Victoria launches into a rendition of The Kinks' 'Lola'. Chris makes her way back to a smiling Alex as Victoria starts to sing about the fluidity between boys and girls. All eyes are on Chris as she negotiates the packed room of people to come back to him.

Alex clips Chris's shoulder, dips his head and shouts over the music, "Take it you know her?"

Chris laughs. "Obviously! Him. Victor. He's one of the very few friends I made when I was an underage actor."

Liam sidles up to them. "You're a star, Chris. And you're a lucky man, Alex." Heat rises on Chris's cheeks again while Liam smirks at her unguarded embarrassment.

Once the set has ended, Victoria/Victor comes over to have a drink with them after he reverts to his cis male self.

~~~

Chris and Alex continue their intimate whispers in bed that night. "Was it okay at the club? There were a lot of people." She caresses Alex's broad chest.

"Yeah. It was fun. Victoria's kinda cool." Alex chuckles. He hadn't known he had a thing for drag performance before meeting Chris and her band of queer friends.

"Victor's only a part-time drag act. His parents aren't like my mum. They put him through proper schooling. He's a computer programmer."

"Wow! No, I wouldn't have guessed it."

"I know, right? He's like a geeky drag!" Chris laughs. "The two friends I was speaking to are trans."

Alex comments. "I'm glad you don't want to cut off your dick." Chris huffs.

"Sorry to be selfish. I've...I think about how you might feel inside me." Alex wrings his hands, remembering the few erotic dreams he's had about Chris lately.

"What? Really? You've not done it with someone with a penis, right?" Her chuckles sound like bells.

"No. And I don't mean I won't want to hammer into you." Alex laughs. "I'm kind of curious."

"Okay. Alex Whale is bottoming-curious. Very interesting." Chris continues to giggle, while Alex encircles her in his embrace.

He pulls her close, their bodies pressed together so he can feel her erection, and plants kisses on her smooth skin that smells sweet and spicy.

"Jerk off for me," he requests gently.

Chris's heart races so hard Alex can feel it. She reaches out to switch on the small lamp and retrieves a bottle of lubricant. Alex pulls down her knickers to reveal her erection. Like the rest of her, it's perfectly proportioned and proud. She opens the top and drizzles the clear gel on her long fingers, massaging and letting the liquid cool her palms. Alex absorbs the scene as though it's a classical tableau of sexual pleasure painted in muted hues.

Her eyes lift to meet his. Blue and ochre. Alex ruts against her, his big hand covering her smaller fist as it rubs and pulls. Chris's head rests against Alex's wide shoulder. She bites her lip and she groans, sounding incoherent with the sensations. Her moans become more desperate. Their entwined hands quicken, and Chris whimpers as she comes. Her seed spills on Alex's hand and sprinkles down his thigh.

Later, Alex gazes at Chris's soft face, the light pink in her cheeks as she sleeps, and the long lashes under her closed eyes. She seems so young then.

CHAPTER 9
KISS

THE FIRST TIME it happens, Alex's arm jerks away, knocking Chris sideways. All dazed and confused and half-awake from his sleep, Chris lifts himself back up the best he can.

"Alex?"

He's turned into a nocturnal keening animal. "Eeeh…qui…"

"Alex?" Chris pushes Alex's arm. "Sweetheart, wake up."

"Ahh…" His arm flies and hits Chris in the face.

Shit! That'll cause a bruise or a black eye.

"Alex, wake up!" Chris uses more force and shakes him.

Alex struggles against an unknown threat, a source of terror. His eyes open wide, but he's not seeing. Then, he bolts up, staring into space. When he comes to, he's sweating and breathing hard in a fit of hyperventilation.

"Alex, it's a nightmare. It's okay." Chris wipes the sweat from Alex's forehead.

Alex whispers, "It's not okay. Not okay." He hisses as though he's been running, and he's trembling. Chris hugs him.

"Do you want to talk about it, sweetie?" he asks softly.

Alex swallows and takes a sip of water from the glass Chris keeps by the bed. "Not much to tell. I have these nightmares. They're vivid, as if I'm reliving the accident again and again." He wipes his hand over his face, drying the rest of the sweat. "I'm hit by the full force of the crash. Sam's bloody and dying in my arms. I scream and scream until there's no more. It's always the same—an extreme impact pushing me back to square one. I can't breathe, as though my lungs are airless."

"It must be frightening."

Alex stares at Chris; the magnitude of horror that has been haunting him for five years is imprinted on Alex's face.

"The thought of a life in terror…reliving the scene. Tonight… It was your face instead of Sam's."

"It's only a nightmare. I'm here. Safe."

A single tear tumbles down Alex's cheek.

~~~

Six in the morning. Alex finds a taped note on the countertop in the kitchenette—*Eat me!*—complete with a smiley face. Chris's writing looks childlike; the lines of the letters zigzag across the small piece of paper. Some days, Alex imagines he has stumbled into a dream spun by Chris, and he can't help but grin at the invitation. The dish contains the pasta bake Chris knows he likes. He glances at the door to Chris's room and pictures him in bed, asleep. With the beam still on his face, Alex puts the food in the microwave to warm up, tapping his forefinger on the worktop to pass the time as he waits. When the machine pings, he takes the hot plate and a fork to the table.

In the corner of the lounge sits an old stereo. In purple plastic casing, it must have belonged to a kid once, but one of the ex-inmates has left it. That's how Alex has come to think of his accommodation—a step away from prison, with more colourful inhabitants.

Since none of them own CDs anymore, they rarely use the stereo, but Alex turns the radio on low as background noise to keep him company while he eats. It's tuned to an unknown station, playing a song that sounds vaguely familiar. Alex recognises the singer's voice—a hoarse, low growl, as if he smokes forty cigarettes a day. Haunting but beautiful.

He sings the story of a late-night encounter in a café, telling himself not to fall in love with the lonely woman.

Does falling in love make him blue?

Alex's hands still. He tries to focus on his very late supper, but he can't. The realisation he's falling for Chris is elating and absolutely terrifying at the same time.

Since the accident, the pills and the frequent dark episodes, his heart had been still until he met Chris. Alex closes his eyes, swayed by the song, and imagines the soft curves of Chris's body. Chris has made him less blue. Alex takes the food back to the kitchen and puts it away. He has a quick shower and brushes his teeth, remembering how Chris warns him about his stinky breath if he doesn't.

Alex tries Chris's door and finds it unlocked like always, as though it is Chris's open invitation, with the generous promise of intimacy brought by his smiles and touches.

Alex can make out the dark shape of Chris in bed, and the tenderness he feels makes him shudder. He watches Chris for a few moments. He is breathing evenly, his mouth slightly open. Alex's fingers itch to caress the silky warmth of Chris's face. Alex climbs over the other side of the bed and slips in under the cover as quietly as he can.

Chris shifts a little. "Hmm."

"Thank you," Alex whispers, not wanting to wake Chris, assuming he has gone to bed late. The two of them are often up all night because of their work or insomnia. That's why Alex finds his security job dull but acceptable. He is usually awake in the middle of the night anyway; he might as well work through the small hours.

Chris seems to be able to work or sleep at any time of the day. He often whispers 'good night' to Alex and falls asleep within seconds like an overtired child. Alex smiles into the dusk about that.

Alex shifts close to Chris's body heat, and he can make out the smooth skin on his back and shoulders. Alex's cock has gone hard again. All he can think about is how he wants to pin Chris down and fuck him fast.

How do you fuck someone with a penis?

As if Chris can hear Alex's thoughts, he turns to face him. His eyes are still closed, but he raises his hand to touch Alex's stubble.

"Hey, you're back."

Alex takes hold of Chris's smaller hand and kisses it. Chris smiles and opens his eyes.

Alex's kisses turn to Chris's hairline and face. "I want you."

Chris chuckles. "Where's that come from?"

"My dick. I wish you wouldn't laugh at me." But there's amusement in Alex's voice, too, as his lips trail down to Chris's knuckle.

"Hmm. Unless you make your intention clear, I'm not going to fuck you."

Alex laughs. "You want me to promise I'll marry you first? Or take care of you when I knock you up?"

"No, but I don't want to give myself away too easily." Chris pouts. "I've already told you."

Alex can't stop his giggles. "If you say so." He drags his fingertip over Chris's smooth lips. With lightness still in his words, he asks, "Do you not kiss either?"

It's Chris's turn to chuckle, but the chuckle soon morphs into a grimace. "Oh, fuck off. I hate that stupid film. Of course I kiss—"

Alex's mouth claims Chris's, reluctant at first as if the permission isn't enough. Their mouths are tender and light on each other, but soon that tentative exploration melts away. Alex pushes his tongue into Chris's mouth so he can lick Chris's full lips—the first thing Alex noticed about him all those weeks ago when they danced on the stairs. He's lost count of the times he's wondered what they'd taste like.

Chris smells like nectar and sweet vanilla, and Alex can't get enough of him. Chris bites Alex's lips while teasing him with his tongue. Alex reciprocates, their tongues swirling, arousing. Alex's hand cups the back of Chris's head, steadying him as though they're in another tango. There's no music, but the air between them is thick with their heavy, rhythmic breaths.

Time stands still when the imaginary dance ends, but Alex is not ready to let go. He pulls Chris closer, and his lips are on

Chris's once again, kissing him with passion and impatience. Alex's vision turns white; his breath catches. All he is aware of is Chris's heat, the scent that he's come to associate with him.

The *ying* to his *yang*. The two become the way.

"I want you so much," Alex murmurs, betraying everything he's been thinking and feeling about Chris.

Freno. A brake.

Chris sucks in a hasty breath and moves away, his palm on Alex's chest, pushing, creating distance between them.

"Don't kiss me like that."

"Like what?" Alex is breathless and confused by Chris's alarm.

"Just don't, all right?" Moisture glistens in Chris's turquoise eyes.

Alex's brows draw up. "But you kissed me back. What's the matter?"

"It always starts this way and inevitably ends another. This whole thing was a mistake. I don't wanna lose you."

"Why would you lose me?" Alex is as confused as ever. "What are you talking about?"

"Don't you understand? Because sooner or later people leave. I let them kiss me and touch me, and I have sex with them, and soon they tire of me. Too much too fast. They'll find some mysterious flaw in me by the third date or the sixth fuck. Sometimes I don't even progress to that stage." Chris frowns at Alex, his face turning pink from fear.

"I'm not like them. I mean, I want to kiss you and touch you, and maybe we'll fuck. I've never slept with a man before. Or queer, not male or female. You get my gist."

Alex scratches his head and gazes at Chris. He adds steadily, "But we don't have to do anything if that's what you're scared of."

"I'm not scared. I'm being sensible. You and I. We've been doing it all arse-wise. We go out and have fun even though you're frightened of the crowd, and we cook. We go for a walk and talk about shit. You don't expect me to have sex unless I want to. You ask silly questions about me, but I like that. When something is too good to be true, it usually is."

"We're back to that, are we? If I care too much about you, I'm being controlling. If I worry about you getting hurt, I'm undermining you. We're never going to get anywhere if you don't ever tell me the truth. What the fuck are you frightened of?" Alex seldom talks so much in one breath.

Chris laughs bitterly. "The truth? There's no such thing. I haven't lied to you if that's what you're insinuating."

Alex is stunned silent while he reminds himself what he has come in to tell Chris. How have they managed to have an argument instead?

Chris schools his face back to nonchalance—the default that Alex recognises. "I don't know what I was thinking. It's better we stay friends. Only." Chris shakes his head, wags his forefinger and moves further away. "Sorry. I think you should leave."

"Chris."

"Leave me alone." Chris pushes Alex's chest. "Go! Go back to your room."

When Alex refuses to move, Chris shoves him again. "Leave, Alexander Whale. I mean it."

Alex reluctantly stands up, but he stares at Chris's slight frame as he departs. Chris has turned to face the wall, refusing Alex. *Fucking stubborn idiot.* Chris made him stop breathing with the kiss, and yet his reaction was to push him away. Alex sighs and walks out.

~~~

Chris shuts the door behind Alex and stares at the discoloured paint on the panel as if it can protect him from the world, from Alex. He'll stay in his room, where he *should* feel safe. He sits on the bed, opens his tobacco tin and, with the meagre remnant of hash, rolls a joint.

A stupid kiss.

Why are you acting like this?

Chris is so angry with himself he wants to lash out. The only thing stopping him would be Alex barging in to check on him because the man would do that. And he cannot see Alex now without turning into a helpless heap in his arms again.

The beginning.

Chris was twelve. Annette had taken him to the set. He never knew what the shoots were about until they got there. Half a dozen people: the photographer, the director and his personal assistant busied themselves with preparation; two other kids, a boy and a girl about Chris's age, sat on the plush sofa, absorbed in some kind of handheld device, playing games.

One of the young women with a clipboard approached him, "Christoph?"

He frowned. "It's Chris."

She bit her bottom lip, which sported a piercing. Chris stared at the small silver stud. "Ah, okay. Chris. Would you come with me, please?"

Wow, someone who could actually speak properly. Said *please* as though he mattered. He was already impressed with this job, whatever it turned out to be. He looked around to see what his mum was up to, but she was nowhere to be found. Chris could only guess that she'd gone outside for a smoke or a sneaky happy pill.

He shrugged and followed the woman. She gestured for him to sit in the chair in front of the short bank of mirrors. She left him with, "Okay, make-up will be with you shortly."

Chris knew the drill. He had already found out he liked cosmetics. Even so, those long sessions were boring.

The make-up artist was another cookie-cutter creative hopeful.

"Okay." She immediately sponged foundation on him before Chris could close his eyes. The sweet smell of face powder travelled up his nose. "You're pretty, kid."

Kid? She was only young herself.

"Not too much of this, though." She put some blush and the faintest eye colour on him. "They want you boys to look natural."

Boy or girl. Not between or both. Naturally. They wanted the illusion of happy, healthy pre-teens.

Chris had already gathered it was a catalogue shoot. He knew how fucked up his life was, while his 'jobs' all seemed to be about selling unrealities.

When the truth is too ugly, believe in the lies.

Next, the wardrobe guy came in with his call sheet. "Hey, Christoph, isn't it? I'm Jude." He offered his hand, and Chris shook it.

"Just Chris." He looked up and was dazzled by Jude, who had a top knot in his hair, red cheeks and twinkly brown eyes. Chris felt warm suddenly. He'd known for a few years that he liked more than one gender.

Chris thought about attraction, but he was confused.

At that age, he'd already seen sex—too much of it—starting with his mother in videos that no one thought to hide from him. It wasn't a secret that sex brought them money to live on. So, what do you call the sensation in your groin when you see someone? Is it only sex? Does it have anything to do with that thing called love? Chris had heard the fairy tales, the princes and princesses and Father Christmas. He understood the falsehood of those stories. That consciousness had come long before he realised he was different from most other kids—those with doting parents and brains that weren't contaminated by matters they had no business knowing.

Jude smiled, showing neat, white teeth. He was the same age as the make-up artist, maybe only ten years older than Chris, but they were adults. *Right.* Chris had always worked with adults. He'd been working for about ten years already. His earliest memories were of shooting commercials for toddler products—some healthy yoghurt or shit.

Jude handed him his first outfit. "Can I help you, or, do you want to put it on yourself, hmm?"

He was speaking to Chris as if he was six, and he didn't like it, so he grabbed the clothes without a word and headed towards the changing cubicles. No adult ran him around their fingers, not since Chris was three or four.

He changed into the bog-standard boy's T-shirt, turtleneck and jeans. His dick twitched when he thought about Jude and his elegant face. Chris would be thirteen next month, and he'd been jerking off for a few years, but the want to touch another was new.

Later, Chris stood in the changing room again, with the nth set of clothes. Seriously, the outfits all looked the same to him, and he was so tired and hungry. He was given a Danish pastry for lunch because Annette told him he shouldn't eat much when he was working. *For his figure.* Chris had repeated many times that he hardly gained weight; Annette never listened. Besides, boys' clothes were usually baggy, but his mother still imposed her body insecurity on him.

"Chris. They're chasing. What are you doing in there?" Jude must have been calling his name for ages.

He stared at the fabric of the curtain as though it concealed a premonition.

Jude pulled it back and ogled him.

Chris realised he was in his underwear and his dick was at half-mast, which would be quite obvious to the assistant.

Jude looked over his shoulder, then drew the curtain closed again and scrutinised Chris's face. "You're pretty. Eleven, you say?"

Chris huffed. "I'm twelve, nearly thirteen."

"I see." Jude elongated his two words.

What happened next seemed so quick, Chris was completely caught off guard. Jude pulled down Chris's briefs, wrapped his hand around Chris's penis, stroking it and massaging the base and the head. It was unexpected and so different from masturbation. Chris gazed into Jude's dark eyes; he'd never been this close to another. Jude whispered *pretty boy* into his ear while Chris was paralysed by the scent of Jude's cologne and the heat that coursed through him. Over the years he had wondered if he was addicted to those senses, allowing him to fall for the illusion that there was more to sex.

Chris came in about two minutes. His heart was pounding hard and he froze in fear once his arousal had died down.

Jude passed some tissues to him to clean up. Chris managed to pull his underwear back up when Jude moved away.

Jude dried his hand and picked up the clothes Chris was supposed to put on. As if they hadn't done a thing, Jude ordered, "Come on. Let me put these on for you."

Chris let him then and held out his arms like a toddler being waited on by an adult. He turned his face away, though, so he wouldn't have to see Jude's face and those dark eyes.

Chris had seen in some men's eyes what they wanted to do to him. Annette told him again and again, "Don't let them touch you." It was the only useful thing she had taught him, but he had let Jude jerk him off. *I'm an idiot.* It felt good even though it was wrong.

For the rest of the shoot, Chris avoided Jude, frightened by the strong attraction he had felt and the guilt of letting the man play with him and enjoying it. He feared everyone on set could tell what had happened.

Finally, the producer declared the shoot wrapped. Chris was eager to get home. He had homework to do and his studies were getting harder and harder. He was in his first year in secondary school. The teachers seemed to do nothing but frown at him and, in turn, he scowled at the books. The words always looked jumbled up to him. Chris had learned later on that it was likely dyslexia but he was never diagnosed. His formal education ended at sixteen with two GCSE passes to his name. Annette had never managed to help him with his education. After all, he was just a pretty face and, in a few years' time, a hot body.

But hang on.

Jude ran up and whispered something to the man in charge, who shouted, "Chris. Daniel. Wait!" The girl had already left with her mother.

"We've missed a couple of the planned photos. Can you stay for a few more minutes? We'll make it as quick as possible."

Jude shifted on his feet. "Eh, but they are for a boy and a girl."

The camera operator looked at them and pointed at Chris. "Can't you make him up? I'll fudge it with the angle and lighting. He's got girl's features."

He's got girl's features.

Chris liked being a girl sometimes. He remembered how he felt so beautiful in the pink and purple dresses, with a hint of rouge painted on his face and a hat to hide his short hair. The photographer told them he'd take one from the side and another one with more shadow on his face. Chris wanted to ask him not to because he wished to see himself as a girl in full, not shadowy and fuzzy.

The two photos were his favourite for a long time. He soon pushed aside the excitement and shame of the hand job in the changing room. He was ridiculed for being like a girl. Some girls at school wanted to be like him; some became his girlfriends. He had crushes on some boys and fought the bullies. He wanted so desperately to not care about what everyone said because it felt nice to be a girl as much as a boy. He should refuse to feel ashamed of his beauty.

As Chris remembers the tangled beginning of his being, he stares at the door—the portal beyond which is Alex's strong body. He recalls others who have departed from his life and deserted him. Tears begin to fall and Chris can't stop them. He hates crying and dislikes himself for being out of control of his feelings. He crawls to lean against the headboard and holds his knees tight to his chest. He lets himself bawl while rocking back and forth until there are no more tears. Chris can blame his mum and all these other people who make him feel worthless. He has used the one thing that his mum has taught him to use, to make a living, to support both of them. All the men and women who recoil when they think of Chris as ugly inside, so incongruent with his beautiful anatomy.

Alex. The one who has accepted him, despite his own darkness. Only his useless soul holds Chris back from wanting this nameless yet profound thing the two of them have shared. The lack of control of his feelings drives him insane. He needs to go back to that place of emotional security. He doesn't know any alternatives but to hurt Alex with his words.

~~~

Alex retreats to his room and takes a headache tablet before he lies down and stares at the ceiling. Chris is too good for him, but the kiss was…sweet and right. It seemed to him the most instinctive thing to kiss Chris, and Chris responded with sensuality and surging intensity. What did he do wrong?

He definitely can't sleep now, even though he is utterly exhausted with a grief that shouldn't have been there. He can't miss something that hasn't happened yet. He should have told Chris how he felt. He should have done a lot of things, but he's broken inside and out. He's going to spend the rest of his days on antidepressants. Alex has no career to speak of, no money. He has little to give, and it's unbearably discouraging.

Alex wants to think of Chris as his, someone he will protect and provide for. Despite everything, he smiles to himself.

Yeah, right. If he utters those thoughts to Chris, he'll get a mouthful.

Who the hell needs you? I can take care of myself.

Alex can imagine Chris's scowl as he dismisses the idea. All he can think of is how cute Chris looks when he gets annoyed and calls him an idiot.

But then Alex remembers Chris's face when he told him to leave, his eyes full of fear and confusion. Alex can't process the barrage of thoughts flooding his brain, so he has to shut down. He wants to scream, and yet no sound comes out as a silent darkness fills him.

No one will ever be able to understand the nightmares Alex lives through again and again, and how they eat him up, turn him inside out. The explosive impact of the two vehicles and the screams of those badly hurt vibrate long into the night. Blood, so much blood, cradling Sam's lifeless body while waiting for the ambulance.

It's for the better that he doesn't get involved with Chris. Alex is hardly a prize. Anyone who has a relationship with him will have to deal with his depression and guilt for years to come.

He finds his phone and texts his boss, feigning illness. *I've got the flu. Sorry.* He sinks down under the cover. He may have slept, but more often than not, he gazes at the stains on the walls.

~~~

Chris has come back from an appointment. He has a quick shower and puts a frozen pizza in the oven. He glances at Alex's closed door and wonders if he'll want to have dinner with him.

Stop. Surely he can't give in and allow himself to get close to Alex again. Alex will find out what a despicable person Chris is. They won't even stay friends and that will be a real tragedy. He remembers the look on Alex's face as he left: the downturn of his mouth and the deep groove between his brows.

A justification for his concerns.

How long has it been since that early morning kiss and his rejection of Alex? Two days? Three? Chris turns around and sees white as if someone has hit the side of his head, and he suffers a whiplash. His resolve not to care about Alex disappears.

He intercepts Alberto as he walks past on his way out. "Hey, have you seen Alex?"

The Italian raises an eyebrow. "No. What's up? You should know. He's your boyfriend."

Chris narrows his eyes. "No, he's not...oh, never mind. Thanks."

Alberto shrugs and continues on. Chris considers Alex's door and knocks on it. If Alex has the same shift this week, he should be at work. No answer. He texts Alex to see if he'll reply, and then takes the disgusting readymade pizza out of the oven. *Guess Alex is not missing much.*

As he tucks into a slice, Alex's door opens and the man himself emerges. Chris's hand freezes in mid-air, his mouth open.

"Why are you texting me when I'm right here?" Alex asks.

He's wearing a faded T-shirt and boxers, his hair a great big mess. Alex's unshaven face tells Chris he has holed up in his room for three solid days since Chris refused him. Alex folds his arms in front of his chest and frowns.

Chris stares at Alex's bloodshot eyes, at the grief and sadness. His dinner completely forgotten, he reaches up to him and hugs the big man, but Alex stands there in stony silence.

"Why didn't you answer your door, then?"

Chris sees the state of Alex's room now. It has been turned upside down: a chair has been broken, the slats scattered on the floor, and clothes and bedding strewn around. Alex smells of stale sweat and musk.

Is this his fault? All his fears and confusion dissipating, Chris only wants to help Alex, to embrace him and take all his sadness away. It won't matter if Alex hurts him in the long run.

This time Alex pushes him away. "No. Don't."

Chris steps back a foot and gazes at Alex.

"Don't touch me and be nice to me." Alex's voice is low as a forbidden whisper. "Don't make me fall in love with you and then tell me to fuck off."

Chris takes a deep breath. He sinks down into the chair, his body heavy as if he's weighted down by the effect he has on Alex.

They are a fucking disaster waiting to happen.

"You scare me because you're saying you love me. I'm doomed to fail and then I'll be hurt, and you'll be pissed off too. And fuck knows you're a big mess already."

"I know I'm a mess…but why will we fail? I mean, I won't hurt you, not if I can help it." Alex's eyes shift to far away.

"How can you promise me that? How can anyone say that?"

Chris runs back to his room and buries his head in his hands. Despite his best efforts to hold back, he starts sobbing, thinking about all these people who have promised him the moon and then deserted him when it suited them. He remembers one of his ex-lovers called him emotionally stunted. *Well, fuck off, then.* And that's what all of them have done.

Alex pushes the door open and stands so Chris can see his legs, thick and solid. When he gazes up, Alex's face is distorted, masked by a kind of anguish familiar to him. Alex kneels down and hugs Chris, but Chris fights him, trying to get away from the contact. Alex grips Chris's wrists to stop him from struggling.

Chris stills, letting Alex hold him. "I missed you, you stupid fuck," Chris admits. His tears keep falling. Big fat ugly tears of frustration and anger.

Yeah, a pair of idiots. A giant, tattooed ex-boxer and a hardened escort who shouldn't be like this. Chris is not crying for Alex or himself, though. He's mourning in acknowledgement of the things he was deprived of, a lost childhood, unconditional love. Whatever he lacks is unknown and frightening. The man in front of him makes him want things that are the most terrifying of all.

"Missed you too. Couldn't sleep cuz you weren't next to me," Alex replies.

Chris looks up and smiles through his tears. "You keep saying that. Get a hot-water bottle already. You know this will come to no good, right?"

"Maybe we're worth the risk, Chris. You are definitely worth all the heartaches in the world." Alex hugs Chris tightly and lets him cry himself dry.

Cradle.

CHAPTER 10
RAINBOW

THE RINGING WAKES them up in the middle of the night. Chris retrieves her mobile from the bedside table. She rubs her eyes and presses speak. "Hello?" … "Yes, I am." … "What's wrong with her?" Chris's brows draw close with irritation. "Which hospital is it?" She promises to be there as soon as she can and clicks off.

"All right? Who's in the hospital?" Alex moves closer.

Chris gets up to locate clean clothes. "Who could it be? Her Majesty Annette, of course. They wouldn't tell me much over the phone, just that she's not in danger now."

Alex follows Chris and gets dressed. "I'm coming with you."

Chris nods. "Okay. Thanks."

~~~

Without the make-up and the latest revealing clothes, Annette's more herself. Chris hasn't seen her like this for years. Her natural beauty shines through despite the circumstances, and she seems younger, so much so she could claim to be Chris's older sister.

Chris goes around the bed to help Annette as she tries to sit up. A small, reluctant smile appears on her face. Her eyes land on Alex, who's standing a foot behind Chris.

"Hey, Chris. Alex." Her voice is rough. "My throat hurts from the tube."

"What tube—"

A white-coat comes in, surveys the room and guesses the relationships between those present correctly.

"I'm Dr. Philips. Are you Ms. Neeser's son? Mr. Neeser?" He holds out his hand to shake Chris's.

Chris nods. "Please, call me Chris. This is my friend, Alex." The doctor acknowledges the other visitor.

"Ms. Neeser, do you want me to speak to Chris about what happened?"

Her eyes glisten. She answers with a voice so small and vulnerable it may break Chris's heart if it hasn't already been broken too many times. "Yes, please. Chris, I'm sorry."

Dr. Philips delivers his spiel about alcohol poisoning and whatnot. Chris already guessed most of it. Annette binged and became violently ill, vomiting blood, among other things. In her delirium, she also took painkillers and other drugs, and couldn't quite remember what and how much. Her latest boyfriend is nowhere to be seen.

"We gave her a gastric lavage, otherwise known as a stomach pump. It's not as bad as it sounds. The procedure's not as intrusive as it used to be. Have you any questions?" He addresses Chris.

"When will she be discharged?"

"She should be all right to leave in the morning, in a few hours after another check-up." The doctor turns to Annette. "I'll ask the nurse to talk to you about alcohol and drug use before you go."

Annette nods again, her shoulders hunched. Her effort to smile is strained by embarrassment.

Dr. Philips departs, leaving Chris and Alex to stand awkwardly for a couple of minutes.

Annette watches them. "Are you two seeing each other?"

Chris and Alex's eyes meet. Chris would like to shout about their budding relationship, but she doesn't owe Annette an explanation. "It's none of your business. You've done enough to fuck up my life as it is."

Annette shifts in her bed and offers another timid smile. "I'm sorry. I hope you find happiness, Chris, and Alex seems like a good man."

It's the first sensible thing she's said to Chris in years, and yet, Chris can't let go of the angry fire in her heart. "I don't rely on you for my happiness, so that's something. And you wouldn't know a good man if he hit you in the face. Hell, that's contradictory in terms."

Annette's face dims. "Yeah, you're right. Sorry."

"I'm not going to be hurt by you anymore. Don't worry about it." She schools her face to hide the emotions threatening to surface.

Annette looks pale and grief-stricken. For once, she is not acting.

"Jimmy left. For good." She swallows. "I'm going to sort myself out. You may not believe it, but I will stop drinking and go to AA."

"You say that every time some dude dumps you." Chris can't help but disapprove.

"I know. I know. Let me prove it to you this time." Annette gazes at Chris and Alex again. "You'll do better than me, Chris. I know you will… I'm very tired. Thank you for coming, you two. I'll be all right. I'll let you know when I get home tomorrow."

"Shall I come back to help you? You can text me," Chris grudgingly offers.

Annette shakes her head. "I can manage a taxi. You head back and get some sleep. I told them not to call you in the middle of the night. It's not like I'm dying or anything."

Annette is dismissing them, so Chris and Alex bid farewell. Once they're outside of the hospital, they seek out the taxi queue and climb into one. Alex takes Chris's hand in his large palm and holds onto her tightly all the way home. Through the window, Chris watches the hazy orange sun appearing on the horizon. Is it what hope looks like? Does it always struggle to shine through the clouds? She closes her eyes to concentrate on the safe sensation of Alex's skin.

Once back in their flat, Alex pulls Chris into an embrace. "Let's go back to bed."

They seem to be spending more and more nights like this, lying in Chris's bed, chatting and getting to know each other. Alex plays with Chris's soft hair. "What are we doing, Chris?"

"I honestly don't know. I like being with you, but I don't know how to be happy, how to make someone else happy. You heard my mum. You know what's wrong with me, don't you? So, are you interested?"

"Am I interested? Chris, I'm totally into you. There's nothing wrong with you. We must be two wrongs, and they seem to make this feel right." He leans forward and kisses Chris. She doesn't want it to end this time.

When they eventually pull apart, tears prick at the back of Chris's eyes. "Annette's first sensible thing to say to me was about you being a good man."

Alex laughs, but it's a bitter kind. "I tried to be a decent man. To be a good boxer, a responsible son. An honourable husband to Sam…but see what happened." He sighs. "You don't seem to realise I've killed, and in the eyes of most people, that's definitely pretty evil."

Chris kisses Alex's forehead. "You did a terrible thing, but it doesn't make you a bad person. What am I even talking about? I don't believe in good and evil."

Alex's smile returns. "Good or bad, I think you're great."

Chris *actually* feels shy when she's the centre of Alex's attention. Alex is the first in so many ways. When was the last time she felt nervous in the company of another? "Still, don't think I'm going to put out just because you said that."

"What?" Alex chuckles. "You honestly think I'm only nice to you so we can have sex?"

Chris smiles through a paradox of sadness and happiness. "Don't forget I've been programmed to distrust everybody."

Alex is still grinning. "I'll wait for you to beg me."

"Oh, fuck you! I will never do that!" Chris pushes him in jest. "Don't you think it'll be strange? Have you slept with someone like me before?"

"I've never met anyone like you, Chris."

Chris giggles. "I have a penis."

"What's your point?" Alex frowns.

"Have you thought about your sexuality?"

Alex nods. "I was attracted to some men but I didn't dare do anything about it. It wouldn't be acceptable to my family or in the boxing world, y'know? Then, I married Sam who was my first girlfriend, and I thought any gay feelings would go away." He dry laughs. "So, yes, I have been thinking about it since I first met you. I'm nervous but I want you sexually, yes."

Chris takes Alex's hand and puts it over her own heart. "Well, you never stop being who you are. I'm bi and queer. When I sleep with a woman, I'm not straight, like when I fuck a man, I'm not gay."

"I think you're one of a kind." Alex grins.

"I doubt it." Chris places their joined hands over Alex's heart. "Unlike you, Alex Whale."

"If you say so. We should sleep. Why do we always do this? Talking till the crack of dawn."

"We've got stuff to talk about. That's why."

Alex rubs his stubble on Chris's cheek, prickling him. "I think it's a good thing."

"Hmm." Chris is almost too sleepy to talk.

"And Chris?"

"Hmm." She's dropping off.

"I'm falling in love with you."

Her heart is thumping so fast she's afraid Alex can hear it. She almost gives in and tells Alex she loves him too, before a lifetime of habit stops her from showing the one true emotion she has lately. She hates herself for being scared by the uncertainty of wanting a relationship.

"Good," she mumbles instead.

Alex's smile illuminates the little dusky bubble around them.

~~~

Coupling.

Alex asked Chris out, to go on a proper date. He wanted Chris to decide what to do—Alex says he hasn't dated since he and Sam were twenty—so Chris has come to Liam and Ali's house for tea and a bit of advice.

Chris's old flatmate Liam moved in with Ali, which was marvellous for Liam, and because he showed Chris there might be light at the end of a dark tunnel—a place she's been her entire life, wading against the tide and never reaching the end.

"I have no clue, either," she says. "I know places for hookups, flirt on Grindr or whatever. But Alex means a proper date." She lights up her blunt at their dining table, waiting for Ali's vegetarian shepherd's pie. She has already told them all about Alex.

Ali whistles. "Wow, I remember Alex Whale on the sports channel…" He hesitates as if pondering whether he should mention the sensational news but instead goes with, "What's he like?"

Chris smiles, appreciating her friend's consideration. "He's sweet. I know what happened and his reputation, but he's been nothing but gentle and respectful. He treats me like a lady."

Liam laughs. "I'd hope so and all."

Ali serves up three portions of the pie and they all tuck in.

"How about you head down to Dalston? You say he's trying to avoid crowds, right?" Liam spoons food into his mouth.

"Sounds like a good plan. We can grab some dinner and have a quiet drink."

"I never thought I'd see you like this, Chris," Liam comments.

"Huh? Like what?" She stirs the peas on her plate, making patterns with the food.

"Fucking in love, is what it is. Look at you, worrying about going on a date. You never used to bother. I thought you'd mistaken fuck buddies for lovers." He chuckles.

"Laugh at me, why don't you? Monogamy is a bad look on me. Seriously, who'd want me? Really?"

Liam shakes his head. "Who just said the M-word?"

Chris winks at Liam and raises her eyebrow at Ali, who grins back.

"But this is you, Chris. You never take shit from anyone. I didn't know you could be serious like this. You're getting soft in your old age!"

Chris tuts. "Are you suggesting I've turned into some kind of tart with a heart after all?"

Liam smiles. "Don't fucking deny it. You help your friends in need. I call that the definition of someone with a good heart."

"It makes me feel superior. Cuz my acquaintances are all losers—drug addicts, whores, homeless beggars, society rejects. Gah." Chris shakes her head fast until her cheeks tremble.

Liam and Ali laugh. Liam fulfilled all those identifiers in his bad old days. When Chris first met him, he'd been a fucked-up junkie, but she'd helped him with a place to live and more.

After they've settled down again, Liam tells Ali, "I checked Alex out at the club." Liam chews his food and takes a sip of his beer. "He's impressive. A big beast of a man."

Ali nods. "Yeah, I don't watch much boxing but I can remember."

Liam says, "Maybe we can get together sometime, the four of us. Ali will love that. Won't you?" He directs the last part at Ali, who smiles.

"Your friends are always welcome here. Of course."

"How fucking domesticated—a dinner party like proper grown-ups." Chris huffs. "I'll ask him, but he's wary, you know. People come up to talk to him all the time. They want photos and stuff. You never know if they're friendly or not."

Ali nods. "I'm not surprised, given what happened."

There seems to be something that passes between Liam and Ali as if Liam's asking for permission.

"Have you, uh, done it yet?"

Chris shifts in her seat, uncomfortable with the line of questioning. "We still haven't had penetrative sex yet. No."

"Whoa, what the fuck!" Liam chokes on his mashed potato. "Are you kidding me?"

Chris blinks several times, signalling to her friends she's deadly serious.

"Are you all right, Chris?" Liam frowns in mock concern.

Chris pouts. "Well, it seems that everyone expects me to behave like a nymphomaniac. I'd take it as a compliment."

"Sorry. I was next to your room for two years. The amount of sex I heard broke some record for sure."

Chris hits the side of Liam's head.

"Ouch!"

"Alex plays to different rules, or I've changed. I have no fucking clue what I'm doing. I really don't think I should be allowed out. Bring back the Victorian asylum and lock me in! Throw away the keys!" She forks some more pie into her mouth as a distraction, but she's been mostly stirring the vegetables. Her plate looks like a tan face made out of a harvest of carrots and peas.

Ali takes a sip from his beer, ignoring Chris's self-doubt. "I say go with how you feel. If it's right, it's going to happen." His eyes twinkle when he gazes at Liam. "Who cares what's expected of you, or what *ought* to happen." He reaches out to hold Liam's hand.

The couple are so in love that in the past Chris would have felt a twinge of envy or faked throwing up, but she has Alex now, and she can hold Alex's hand too, so all is well in her world.

~~~

Chris comes out of her bedroom in a long-sleeved black dress with gathers at the waist. Smudgy eye colour and lipstick. Strappy black pumps. Alex swallows because he loves seeing her like this. He loves Chris in anything or nothing. Full stop.

"Is this okay?" Chris smiles. The light shining on her makes the small stud under her lip glitter.

"You're gorgeous. Hot. You're pretty stunning."

Alex has put on his good shirt again and a decent pair of black trousers. Chris reaches out and touches the kink of his nose.

"Glad you know a few words, but they all mean the same thing." Her eyes twinkle when she's amused. "Anyway, stop staring. Let's step out before we end up peeling all our clothes off and screwing."

Alex barks out a laugh. "Good luck with that."

They head out.

"I'm sure you're punishing me for some reason," Alex murmurs, keeping up his jokey tone. "Withholding sex…like some women do."

Chris orders a taxi on her phone while she replies. "I'm not some woman, and it's sexist to assume only women do that."

"Sorry! I like it when you tell me off for things like that."

"Everyone uses sex. Sex is power. You negotiate with sex. Sex in exchange for something else. I only go about that in more obvious ways than others. Call it honesty."

Alex considers her face. "It doesn't have to be that way." He squeezes her hand to reassure her.

They descend the three flights of stairs to the street and wait by the front door to the building.

Chris hooks her arms around Alex's as they stand waiting by the door. "So, sex is one thing. My genders. Some days I'm passing for a man, especially if that's what the johns expect. Other times people look at me and think I'm a freak. It's exhausting."

Alex leans down and kisses her cheek. "I'm sorry. I hope you can be whoever you are with me and never have to pretend."

"You're not very politically correct, but you're a quick learner when it comes to my queerness. I could forgive you." Chris smiles and elbows Alex, whose grin spreads across his face.

The rumbling of a taxi approaching tells them they've got transportation.

They decide on the cosy little pizza restaurant after walking up and down the high street in Dalston a couple of times. Instead of wearing his usual baseball cap, which looks a little ridiculous at the best of times, Alex has put on the beanie with a visor that Chris bought him a few weeks ago. Chris has insisted that he ditch his Ray-Bans.

"They stare at you *because* of the stupid sunglasses!"

Alex sniggers. That's another thing he likes about her: she tells the truth and nothing but the truth.

As if proving Chris's point, every pair of eyes in the restaurant fall on the two people who have strolled in. Whether people recognise Alex or not, the two of them turn heads. Chris asks to sit in the corner of the dining room, which should afford them some privacy. After all, this is an up-and-coming area of London where the punters must be quite used to spotting minor celebrities.

They peruse the menu.

"One or two…" Chris glances up to Alex and shrugs. "Silly question. I don't think I can manage a whole pizza, but still."

Alex nods. "Definitely two. I can finish off yours. I didn't have a snack earlier. I was too nervous waiting for you."

"You were nervous because we were going out on a date?" Chris tries to hide her laughter behind the oversize menu.

"Yes."

"Okay." She squints at the menu and then pushes it over to Alex, pointing at the name of a pizza. "Is this the one with pesto?"

He reads it. "Yeah."

"And a salad to share?"

"Perfect."

Chris surveys the wine list on the back with the same concentration. "May I have a glass of white wine?"

"Of course. I'll have a Diet Coke."

She asks for a glass of house white instead of negotiating the names of the different bottles.

Once they've ordered, they sit back and try to relax. Alex avoids the gaze of the imaginary public; Chris surveys the other patrons. Most of the diners have turned their attention back to their meals.

"Some days I don't want to go out, to go to work and face the world. It's hard not to picture the whole restaurant ogling at me," Alex admits.

"It's okay. Don't forget your bodyguard's here." Chris grins and takes his hand across the table.

Alex smiles too. "You look even less like a bodyguard tonight."

"Hey, have you seen *Charlie's Angels*?"

That cracks Alex up. "I'd love to see your stiletto moves, darling."

Chris rolls her perfectly made-up eyes, and her long eyelashes flick. "I don't do stilettos."

Converse and women's pumps and flats like tonight's, but no heels or platforms in Chris's shoe collection. Perhaps she's too tall for them.

Their food arrives, and the stringy mozzarella threatens to splash tomato sauce on Chris's pretty face, making Alex smile. Whenever they catch each other's eyes, fuzzy feelings are all around. After a couple of slices, Chris stops, wipes her mouth and clears her throat. Alex stares at her, knowing she's preparing for a serious talk.

"I don't know why. Since we started with the talking and getting to know each other, it feels weird—thinking about 'proper' sex with you." She draws the quotations in the air with two fingers. "We'll do it soon, though. What do you think?"

Alex exhales with relief and chuckles. "Yes. It'd be marvellous if you let us, Chris."

"So, I get to decide if we have sex or not. I can't tell you how much I'm enjoying this power over you right now." Chris looks deadly serious.

Alex scratches his head, conscious of his wild hair. "You've completely overpowered me, Chris, with or without the sex. I can't understand what happened! It's like losing round after round at boxing. I'm not used to that!"

Chris can't keep a straight face anymore and laughs.

"Mr. Whale?" Alex and Chris look up at the young man waiting with the restaurant's menu in his hand. "Sorry to intrude, but… Could you sign this for me, please?"

Alex has switched to fight mode and is vaguely aware of Chris tensing too, but then he sees the young man's earnest face. He relaxes a little.

"Okay. I'm not the chef, though." He takes the menu and the offered pen. "What's your name?"

"Ben. Ben Chapman."

Alex writes out the guy's full name carefully, then adds, 'All best, Alex Blue.' He shows it to Chris and then offers it to his fan.

The younger man is so chuffed. "I watched your fights all the time…" He glances at Chris. "Are you…going to box again?" He would have been a teenager when Alex was still in the game.

Alex closes his eyes for a split second. "Sorry, but I've retired now."

"Oh, okay." Ben takes the menu back and reads the autograph. "Thank you so much!" Clutching it close and smiling, he returns to his seat.

"Alex Blue. I like that." Chris's dimples deepen. "So, is that who you are now? Retired at thirty-three?"

~~~

A small V forms between Alex's brows as he tells her how hard it is for him to even sit in a public place like this, let alone cope with the televised fights. She notices the little crow's feet that have appeared around Alex's eyes. She loves them on him.

"My old manager wants me to do some comeback fights." Alex wrings his hands. "But going back professionally means trainers, a manager and media circuits."

"Oh. Will you? Do you want to?"

Alex sighs. "Not if I can help it. I don't need the money, though my folks could use some help. Sam's family. They're still pissed off with me, as you can imagine."

"Oh!"

"I won't bore you with the legend of Sam Taylor senior. Some may call him a gangster, but I've always thought Taylor is a shrewd businessman who's happy to do the dodgy deals. He could use his connections to track me down. He probably hasn't done it because he's not an unreasonable man. The Essex lot don't know that."

"He sounds like a tough Essex gang boss, all right."

"Well, he liked me from the start and he always treated me like a son. But then, I haven't seen him since the court hearings and at the sentencing. He looked impassive across the sea of black suits, like we were at a funeral for the living." Alex looks away, and Chris reaches across the table to hold his hand.

Alex continues. "I'm sure part of me died during those weeks, but it was what I deserved. I wished I were dead instead of Sam. I deserve all the punishment I get."

"But you're here, doing the best you can. She'd be proud of you, don't you think?"

Alex sighs. "Maybe. I've been helping out at the boxing club."

"You gonna train the kids there?" Chris inclines her head, curious to hear more.

Alex's face lights up as he tells her about Devan's small outfit, waxing lyrical about the pay-what-you-can sessions 'Coach' offers so poorer kids can go.

"Sounds cool. You should so totally do it!"

Alex grins. He picks up Chris's hand and kisses her knuckles.

Later, as they walk the few hundred yards to the bar that Chris promises will be pretty stress-free, Alex winds his arm around her shoulders. He can do that with the few inches' advantage.

They choose a small table in the corner of the cavernous bar. They say cheers, clinking their glasses together.

Chris looks down at her OJ. "It's my birthday."

Alex nearly chokes on his Coke. "Oh, why didn't you say? Twenty-seven, is it?"

Chris gives him an eye-roll. "Old enough. I didn't want you to fuss."

Alex kisses her, and it goes on for several minutes, sucking the air out of both of them. When he breaks off, he shrugs. "Who's going to fuss? I don't care for you at all."

That earns him a thump on the shoulder. "Ouch!" Alex feigns pain.

"Apparently, my life isn't much to celebrate. It's damn luck I'm alive." Chris stares at the mid-distance, her mind far away.

Alex frowns. "What do you mean?"

She purses her lips, hesitant to dwell on her past. "Annette was drunk and high one day, and she told me she went to the abortion clinic. This boyfriend—not my biological father, I might add—turned up and vowed to take care of her. They got married. He was her first husband. The cunt left after three months. By that time she couldn't get rid of me."

Alex's mouth drops open.

Chris forces a smile. "It's nice to know you're wanted, isn't it?"

Alex kisses her gently. "Hey, you *are* wanted."

Chris snorts. "Apparently, I was a *really* cute baby. I suspect she had an idea about how I might help pay the bills. Otherwise, she'd have given me up for adoption." Her jaw clenches.

"Chris...thank you for telling me. I can't begin to imagine how that made you feel."

She flashes a false smile and changes the subject. "Twenty-seven. What am I going to do when I'm too old and wrinkled?"

Alex opens and shuts his mouth, and opens again. "You and Annette could sell cosmetics together?"

"Bastard! I'm sick of selling my appearance. I have thought about quitting sex work."

"What would you do instead?" Alex's dark gaze focuses on Chris.

She takes a deep breath. "I've been thinking... Don't you fucking laugh, all right? I want to look after kids, like working in a nursery or something like that."

Alex tries hard not to laugh, making his face scrunch up till it turns a rosy colour.

"Don't laugh! Don't fucking do that." Chris punches him, forgetting her strength and leaving a small dent in his arm. It doesn't stop Alex letting out the giggles, though.

"I'm trying hard not to." Still grinning, Alex teases, "Are you ready for nappy changing and shit? Literally."

"You think I'm scared of a bunch of crying babies? I've made grown men and women cry many times. I can handle a few helpless kids."

Alex stops laughing and looks at her intently. "Hey. You'll be good at that."

"Really?" Chris's eyes widen in disbelief.

"Really. I hate to say it, but you're more caring than you like other people to know. Your hard-as-nails routine is a front, isn't it?"

"This is the second time in as many days someone's told me I'm kind. I'm becoming one of those *kind-hearted losers*." Chris snorts, but it's bullshit, and Alex knows it too. He hugs her firmly and kisses the side of her head.

"Now that you have a pipe dream, what are you going to do about it?"

"No idea. I've been thinking about this for a while. I did badly at school, but I'll give it a go if the college will have me."

They are on their second drinks. Alex insists on buying Chris a glass of champagne for her birthday since he didn't know he needed to buy a present.

"Oy, I can't believe you're out and about. Aren't you the boxer who killed innocent people? You're disgusting." The words are like an entire quiver of arrows flying across the bar from a tweed-jacketed woman in her fifties.

Alex quiets and puts his head down, his body tensing. He's breathing so hard he looks as though he's going to hyperventilate.

Chris faces the intruder with her usual unflappable calm. "We're having a quiet drink. You should mind your own business."

But instead of leaving, the woman points at Chris and addresses Alex. "Have you forgotten all about your wife? Moving on now, are you?"

Chris glances around the bar to see where the woman came from as a young, well-dressed guy and an older man approach them. The anxious pair appear to be the woman's son and partner.

"Viv, what are you doing?" the older man asks.

Her eyes are red with anger. "You know that boxer who was done for drink-driving and killed his wife and the other driver?"

"Viv, please! You can't do this." He puts his hands on her shoulders to try to move her away from Chris and Alex's table.

Alex is keeping his head down, so Chris can't see his expression. Under the table, she places her hand on Alex's thigh.

The woman's son also pleads, "Mum. Come back to our table. We're leaving in a minute."

The older man manages to drag her away while she mumbles, "It's not fair. Lord have mercy…"

The son watches his parents' backs as they return to their seats. "Ah, I'm sorry. She lost…her dad…my granddad. He was killed in a car accident."

Chris offers, "I'm very sorry."

"No. I apologise if we disturbed your evening."

Chris nods. "We'll be fine. I'm sorry for your loss."

After the man leaves, Chris puts her hand on Alex's shoulder. "You okay?"

Alex is pale and sweating. Chris hugs him and whispers, "Close your eyes and take normal breaths. I'll break out that massive tub of ice cream for my birthday treat when we get home. Do you want to join me?"

Alex does as he's told and breathes, shallowly at first. He clenches and relaxes his fists. "Dance with my legs. Here. Now. The ring is like a battle of life. Face the opponent," he mutters.

"Like preparing for a boxing match?"

"Hmm."

Chris plants small kisses on his cheeks, hairline and neck. Alex keeps still, inhales and exhales. After a while, he leans into Chris's arm as he comes back to planet Earth.

When Alex is finally calm, Chris takes out her phone for a taxi. "Let's go home, shall we?"

Alex lifts his head, his eyes full of unshed tears. "Sorry I ruined your birthday."

"Hey, you've done nothing. I'm good. I had a great time." Chris wipes the wet from Alex's cheeks and kisses him again. She takes his hand. "Since it's my birthday, I say we definitely break out the ice cream, then I want to stay in your arms all night."

CHAPTER 11
PROMISES

T HE KID CAN'T be more than twenty years old, but with his hard, cold stare, short, cropped hair and a stud in his ear, Chris wonders if he's Dmitri's latest drug deal. He runs his wary eyes up and down Chris, who's wearing a T-shirt long enough to be a nightdress and nothing else.

Thanks for the eye fuck, kid! Chris's instinct is one of distrust, and his first impression is rarely wrong. He ignores the younger man and continues to make his morning coffee.

"Hey, can I bum a cigarette off you?"

Chris turns around in a theatrical arc. "Oh, excuse me. And who are you?" His raised eyebrow challenges the other.

"Paul. I've just moved in." He indicates the last room in the flat that has been vacant for a while. "What's your story?"

Chris has been in the flat longer than anyone else, so the tone in the kid's question piques him.

"I don't have none. And get your own fucking cigarette if you're going to speak to me like that." He turns back to his coffee making. The hairs on the back of his neck prickle, but he's not going to be intimidated by a teenager!

Behind Chris, Paul must have huffed and returned to his room because within minutes, he re-emerges dressed in a dark tracksuit and is out of the door without acknowledging Chris.

What the fuck! Chris makes yet another mental note about moving. It's becoming impossible to stay in the shared apartment and remain civil when the landlord keeps letting every little shit in London move in. Ex-delinquents galore. Admittedly, Alex was another ex-con acquisition, and Chris is glad his desperate parole officer had to put him in this particular accommodation. Chris wants to ask Alex if he would be willing to move in with him. A one-bedroom would be more than enough for the two of them, and it's all they can afford in this area of the city.

Thinking about Alex is enough to make Chris forget about the rude new flatmate. Alex has gone to see his parents this morning, and Chris takes his cup of coffee back to bed with a smile, though he misses Alex's larger-than-life shape next to him. In lieu of the real man, Chris sniffs the pillow that smells of his faint scents: musk, sweat, Old Spice. He might have even blushed thinking about how they'd kissed last night. He hadn't known what he was missing until he'd found out he could talk to Alex and let the man touch him all night long, drowning in Alex's manna-like kisses. Last night, Alex let Chris rut against his muscular thigh until he came.

Chris closes his eyes and sighs with complete contentment, remembering the sensations, then shimmies out of his briefs and covers his erection with his hand. Closing his eyes and imagining the feel of solid flesh, he smears the pre-cum around until he can quicken his strokes without hurting himself. *Think of Alex. Wanting him, desiring him. Touching, kissing, caressing. Flying high like a jaybird.* Chris shudders and shakes, letting the waves sweep him along.

~~~

How Alex wishes he were at home, with Chris, breakfast in bed or a simple brunch and cuddles under the duvet. He must be smiling because when he looks up, his mum is scowling at him. Sometimes he wonders if his darkness has a deeper root than the car accident because there had always been little joy in this family.

Alex plants himself at the breakfast bar in his parents' kitchen and watches his mum prepare Sunday lunch, surprised to see her movements slowing down. Her joints are all a little red and swollen, as if the alcohol she's consumed over the years is finally taking over her body bit by bit. She seems to be doing something, then forgetting what she's doing, and starts another task. It's painful to see. After all, she's only in her mid-fifties. His dad's a bit older, sixty-one if Alex remembers correctly. Gary is eighteen months older than Alex, who was the result of a contraceptive failure. He supposes his folks were happy to have him when he proved to be the more sensible and successful of the two sons until his dramatic fall. If there was love in this family, Alex could never tell from the way they treated each other. 'Family' exists like a habit in the Whale household.

"They told your dad it's the rain and the wind. We've got excessive erosion or something like that. We can't understand it. The house is pretty new."

Alex tunes in again to what his mum's saying.

She goes on, "We had to evacuate last spring when we had that freak storm."

Well, you wanted to live by the sea.

"What are you saying, Ma?" It's obvious this chat is leading somewhere that will consume money. A lot of money, usually.

She sighs, tossing her head back, as if to emphasise the point. "We had the first lot of repairs covered, but it's so expensive. The social don't pay for things like that, y'know, even with your dad's disability. Gary's using our money instead of helping us out. The roof needs doing, and Dad's talking about renewing the damp course…"

Alex tunes out again after that. The house has been a money pit from day one, but his parents wanted it because it sat on the water's edge. Alex had known there would be problems: structural issues, weathering, flooding. It might have been an architectural wonder but it was always going to be expensive to maintain. He hoped that as a retired builder, his dad would be better at keeping things going, but he was wrong.

"…so Dad's wondering if you'd help with the rendering. His mate could do it quite cheap but, still… We've no savings left."

Alex knew this was coming. He doesn't want to dig into his account. Now he's more settled, he needs to think about his future, to move to his own place, so the savings will be useful. He doesn't have the means to support his mum and dad and Gary anymore. It's high time he took care of himself first, but Alex has always been a good son, which means he can't ignore his mum's ageing face and her needs.

"Ma, I don't have much either. Let me think about what I can do, okay?" And just like that, his parents' problem sits in his stomach like lead.

The whole Sunday lunch remains as painful as it always is. Gary arrives as his mum is about to dish up. Gary is almost as tall as Alex, but he abuses his body with an unhealthy lifestyle—downing twelve pints every Friday and Saturday night, consuming copious amounts of fatty foods and no exercise.

The brothers hug. "What'ya up to, bro?" Gary's jovialness is not helping. He's such a typical untrustworthy geezer.

"Nothing much. You?" Alex sits in one of the armchairs in the lounge.

Gary plants himself on the couch, next to their dad, and lights a cigarette. "Yeah, the business is good, man. The garage is raking it in."

Alex is sceptical of any of Gary's claims to success, but he doesn't call him out. His brother's latest venture is the garage he runs with a mate. Gary's a pretty good mechanic if he puts his mind to it, but he exercises little effort in any of his ventures. Alex has lost count of the number of businesses Gary has run. Of course, they have all failed. Gary has managed to scrape through his entire adult life achieving as little as possible but he always has his next idea for a new project. Alex used to subsidise him, but for obvious reasons, he has not been able to. Instead, his brother has been draining his parents' savings. The whole family is financially fucked, and there is not a damn thing anyone can do about it.

"You should come down and look at the bikes. Some of them are absolute beauties." Gary flashes a toothy smile. Alex can't drive or ride a motorbike. He would not, even if they could give him his driving licence back.

Football, rugby or whatever programmes Gary and their dad are watching play on the massive wall-mounted television. Alex used to be on the sports channel. The thought of it makes him shudder now. Excusing himself, he goes to his old room, where his mum has kept his belongings as if preserving a shrine to the living legend—the boxer known as Blue. He is long gone. Alex gazes at the sea-misted window. Essex used to feel like home when he was training in London because of Sam. Between training and fights, he looked forward to coming back to something familiar. Now, his family is nothing but a chain around his neck. How he longs to be back in the city with Chris.

He turns away from the view to consider the room. On the shelves are his trophies and medals. He kept everything from the first one he won when he was only thirteen and touches his teenage prize now: a small gold-coloured medal. He remembers it well. Coach wanted to encourage him to take up boxing professionally, and the way to do that was to give him a taste of winning. It sure opened his mind to all the possibilities that boxing might bring. The competition was only a local youth contest with some other London boxing clubs. The fact that he beat a bigger boy, older by two years, was a real confidence booster. He could see where boxing might take him, how doing something he loved would bring respect and an escape from his family of origin.

To be free until one fatal error.

Alex shakes his head to clear his mind since he has come into his bedroom for a reason. He opens the drawer in the bedside table and finds the small pendant. After he went out with Chris for a drink and they told him it was their birthday, he has been thinking about a small gift: a small silver disc with a pair of encased boxing gloves made with solid black stone. Dex gave it to him on his eighteenth birthday. It must have been from Coach's youth since the back is marred and the metal could do with some buffing, but it will make a perfect present for Chris. Alex will buy a thin chain to thread through the small hole—he imagines it around their long, pale neck.

Thinking about Chris makes him forget the guilt in his gut, forget where he is; he has been swimming in a deep, dark hole filled with a sticky mass as thick as oil. Thoughts of Chris calm him, slowly bringing him to light. He does not need to get out of his depressed state if he can see the radiance beyond.

The knock on his door startles Alex, and his dad pushes the door open before he can answer. He and Gary have been at it since before lunch and now he is halfway to drunk, his face red and puffy. When Alex was a kid, he used to think he would turn out like his father. He nearly did, and it cost him his entire boxing career.

"Why you hidin'?"

"I'm not." Alex puts the pendant in his pocket in case his dad asks about it. He's not ready to tell his family about Chris yet. "What's up?"

The older man sits down on a chair. "Your ma spoke to you about the 'ouse?"

Alex nods.

The lead, the guilt, the darkness.

"Some guy roughed Gary up a couple of weeks ago." He lights up a cigarette. Alex doesn't like smoking in his room, but then this house no longer feels like his home. Even his box room in the flat has given him a stronger sense of belonging. He can't envisage coming back here to live, so it doesn't matter.

"Why? He tried to chat a married woman up or something?" It's the kind of idiotic things that Gary would do.

His dad shakes his head. "Hard to tell. He was a bit vague. I suspect he owes someone money."

That would be it. Damn it.

"Tony spoke to me, y'know. He can fix things up. He said a few matches, and you'll be back on your feet." His dad's eyes are on Alex, waiting for his response.

Back on my fucking feet. Alex frowns. "Wish he hadn't contacted you. Going over my head like that."

"I know Tony's a bit of a shark, but he's always delivered. It's not only about us. If you don't want to help, that's fine. Your ma and I will figure something out. It's about fucking time Gary grew the fuck up anyway. But you're too young to retire, Alex. Too much of a waste, if you ask me."

That's why I don't ask you. But Alex isn't going to argue with his dad. "I'll think about it. I will call Tony, hear what he's got in mind."

His dad stands. "Good." They are similar that way. Men of few words. At least Alex's dad has never been a loud drunk. Instead, he's usually sullen and morose. Alex was drinking way too much by the time of the car crash, but it was the easiest thing to give up. It's the blame and shame that Alex will never be able to shake. Sobriety has become his fodder in the permanently locked prison of his mind.

~~~

The restaurant Tony chooses to meet him at boasts a couple of stars awarded by a gourmet list. It is light and airy, autumn sun streaming through tall panes of glass, but it doesn't entice Alex at all. He would prefer to turn back and forget about the whole thing. Despite the fact he is now dirt poor and working in a job he dislikes, he values the freedom away from all the bullshit associated with fame. The thought of returning to the ring only fills him with dread. *So what the fuck are you doing here?* Because he's a good son, and he promised his parents he would speak to Tony.

Alex only wears his beanie today without the sunglasses. Over the past few months, he has come to realise that with his size and stature, disguises serve no purpose, and being with Chris has given him the courage not to hide behind dark glasses anymore. He walks through the expensive restaurant, following the maître d', with half of the diners and all the waiters watching him. He tries to ignore the discomfort inside of him.

Tony waves him over. No matter how sharp his suit is, Tony is still a lowlife underneath. But then, Alex is an ex-criminal on parole. Who is he to judge? He sits and is immediately presented with the heavy leather-bound menu. He glances at the fancy words and opts for the safe-sounding fish and chips of the beer-battered exotic fish variety with potato curls and lemon tartare mayo. That's a whole eleven words for the same thing. Tony asks for a steak, medium rare. Sharks are always after bloody red meat.

Tony chitchats, bringing him gossip about the boxing world that's as alien as the restaurant. At the third forkful of their food, Tony gets to the real topic of conversation. "So, Blue. You've thought about a comeback?"

Alex wishes he could choke on a fishbone, but there's none in the perfectly cooked fillet.

"Yeah, thought about it. What's your proposal?"

Tony is used to him. Alex's reticence means he won't say more than the absolute minimum, except when he talks to Chris, who can coax anything out of him.

Tony puts down his fork, the remnant of a piece of steak glistening ruby blood on the shiny silver.

"You know Lewis Keane?"

Keane's a big, strapping beast, an Irish heavyweight who was a few ranks below Alex and whom Alex has beaten twice before. As far as Alex knows, Keane retired two years ago.

"He wants to fight a few matches, add to his retirement fund, you understand?" Tony cocks his head to gaze at Alex.

Alex understands, all right. If his circumstances were not so different, he might be doing the same. Now, he's wary of the limelight. Lewis Keane would be a good match, though. The audiences will love it—two veteran heavyweights of similar skill level.

"How much?" Alex is going to do the necessary to keep his family afloat. But what happens next time they need a bail-out is anyone's guess.

Tony's shrewd eyes roam Alex's face and body.

"After my expenses, trainers, insurance..." He taps some numbers on the calculator of his mobile and shows it to Alex. As Alex thought, it's enough to buy a small family house in Essex.

"And I can negotiate sponsorship, a percentage with the venue and a TV deal with a sports channel," his ex-manager adds. More than one house, then. The start of a little savings for himself too.

Alex doesn't trust Tony, but he's a good businessman. For his own benefit, Tony would get a good deal for Alex. That's why Alex stuck with the twat over the years and why Tony managed to screw him over. Can he do this? Can he face the world again?

"As little media as possible. No junkets, no commercials and let me see the contract when you're ready." Alex knows Tony won't be able to stop the media interests, not if he wants the TV deal. "I'll need some intensive training nearer the time."

He will train with Coach, but for at least a few weeks before the match, a pro would be good. After all, it'll be a demonstration fight, not a proper tournament or championship.

Tony assesses Alex for a moment. "You won't come back for real?"

"No." Alex answers without hesitation. His hands are already clammy. Anticipating a match never felt like this, as if he were being forced to stand naked and humiliated in front of millions. He sighs soundlessly and pops a few more chips into his mouth.

Good but hardly worth the thirty quid they charge.

~~~

Alex kisses the soft skin of Chris's neck, drinking in the delicious scent: spicy yet floral. He can always tell who Chris is as if they are viscerally in tune. There's something natural about Chris's scent when they aren't working. The rich fragrance they wear to appointments doesn't suit Chris in any form—expensive, bland cologne as if they've just come from the perfumery of a department store.

Alex traces a line down to her shoulder and tastes the sweet flesh. His fingers make a parallel line along her smooth chest, stopping at the nipples. A wisp of sensation flows through Alex while he licks her belly with a feather-light touch before he sits up and considers her. For the thousandth time since they met, he can't quite believe he's here, holding and savouring her.

Chris pulls herself up and gazes at Alex, too. A hint of a smile rivals Mona Lisa's.

Alex reaches out to his discarded trousers and retrieves her gift from the pocket. He places the small medal in Chris's hand. He went to the Jewish-run jewellery shops near Farringdon and found a thin silver chain to accompany the pendant.

"Happy birthday."

"For me?" Chris's face lights up, radiating a beauty and grace incongruent with their grotty surroundings.

Alex nods.

Chris examines the silver disc, fingering the encased boxing gloves. When she looks up, tears glitter in her eyes. "It's so beautiful. Thank you. Put it on for me." She turns to let Alex reach the back of her neck.

Alex struggles to clip the small hooks together because of his thick fingers, but when he succeeds, he beams.

"I didn't win this one. Coach gave it to me when I was eighteen."

Chris turns to face him again, touches the surface of the small disc and leans forward to kiss him.

"It's the best gift anyone has given to me." Her big eyes shine with so much warmth and happiness.

Alex grins. "I wanted to give you something personal, a gift that means a lot to me."

"And you have. You do." Chris asks, her voice low, "Seriously, why aren't we having sex?"

Alex sighs. "I don't know. I've been wanting you ever since I laid my eyes on you on the stairs."

His words are not enough because he's aroused and Chris must be able to feel his woody.

Chris's eyes shimmer in the dusk. "Then, why are we still dancing around? Is there something wrong with me?"

Alex cups her head in his big hands and kisses her. "No. There's absolutely nothing wrong with you. Maybe I want you to think of us as special."

"We are… You are special."

"And you are too, Chris, and I want you to know that. It's not a threat or anything like that. I want to wait for our first time when I'm confident. Until I am not scared that I won't be good enough for you."

Chris leans in to kiss him again. "But you are good for me."

Alex touches his head of wild, thick hair. "Chris, I'm afraid... Sometimes I've not been able to get it up."

Chris blinks. "Since when? I've felt your erections."

Alex looks away, embarrassed. "With you, yes. When I was in prison and with the meds... I sometimes want to, y'know, jerk off, and then... I can't."

Alex's eyes turn down, afraid of Chris's reaction.

"I love being with you, Alex. I don't need a working dick. I like your penis when it's sleeping."

Alex grins. "It's often sleepy these days."

"Then I like it a lot."

Alex pulls Chris closer to him, his heart dancing with her easy acceptance. "Why do you want me, though? Why are you interested in battered old me? And I'm not fishing for compliments."

"And you won't get any, Big Blue." Chris kisses him. "I wouldn't call thirty-something old."

"You know why I feel that way."

Chris lies flat on the bed. "Well, you're depressed. It doesn't make you...flawed. I should be the one no one wants."

"Plenty of people seem to want you."

Chris opens her mouth to protest, and Alex raises his hand to stop her, but she goes on. "They want me for what I sell them, give them the illusion that they get what they want."

"I want you, no pretence, no illusion. You're not kidding when you said you're my security guard. I feel safe with you. I trust you."

Chris smiles.

"Well, do you trust me?" Alex asks as if he's posing a challenge.

Chris covers her face with both hands. "Gah. I'm so off this conversation. I don't do this. I can't do this."

Alex laughs, forgetting his moroseness for a second. "Do what? I told you I love you and trust you." He tickles Chris under her smooth armpit. "Tell me you love me too?"

Chris wriggles and starts chuckling. "I'm not telling you anything! I don't like…talking about feelings."

Alex tickles Chris some more because he knows he can.

"Get off me! Get off, now!" Chris tries to move away, but Alex grips her by her wrists. In one fluid motion, Alex overpowers Chris onto the bed and hovers on top of her, still gripping her arms over her head.

"This is so unfair—"

Alex's mouth claims Chris's over her protest and kisses her and tastes her sweet and fresh lips and tongue until she stops struggling against his rawness. He releases Chris's arms. Heavy breaths fill the air between them. When he moves away a few inches to catch his breath again, Chris kneads Alex's hips with her smooth palms and pulls him down against her, whispering, "Stop acting like a big romantic, just… Rut against me, Alexander."

Alex does. Chris arches and they move in unison, building their need together. Move. Press. Kiss. All rational thoughts leave Alex's head. He closes his eyes and forgets about his fears, drowns in the sensation of Chris's body against his.

His dream moves along her body.

Alex opens his eyes and sees the indigo of her dilated pupils. Heat bubbles and consumes them until Alex tenses and shouts as if his fist has been raised by a referee.

It's been five years since he was intimate with someone like this, and he feels the threatening tears as he gazes down at Chris. He moves off the beautiful body underneath him and flops down on his back.

They stare at the ceiling.

"Fuck. You made me come in my underpants."

Chris smiles. "You got it up no problems, mate."

Alex laughs. After stilling himself, he touches Chris's briefs. They're damp, too, and he grins. "We're going to have dried cum in our pants. Go and clean yourself up."

Chris turns and now looks down at Alex, their legs entangled and hanging outside the bed. "That's it, isn't it? You're a prude. You think spunk is dirty."

"No, I don't!" Alex protests.

Chris giggles. "You better not. I work with the stuff." She puts her hand in Alex's boxers and scoops up a mouthful of his seed. She licks her hand and fingers clean, saliva and white streaks everywhere. Chris eating his cum like that has aroused Alex again.

She beams. Before Alex can say any more, Chris hops off the bed like a Jack-in-the-box. She goes off to the bathroom to have a pee and comes back to bed in another clean, tiny thong.

Alex follows and uses the bathroom. When he's under the warm cover again, he kisses Chris. "Thank you."

"Pleasure's all mine."

~~~

Alex approaches his parents' house with dread. His mum's panicky voice on the phone was not unexpected.

Gary's been roughed up.

She ushers him into Gary's room as soon as he arrives. Gary's face is covered in bruises, one around his left eye socket, and the eye almost swollen shut. He also has a busted lip, though it's not that bad, all things considered.

Gary lights a cigarette and refuses to look at Alex, who about has enough of his brother's antics.

"What's going down, Gary?" The least he can do is be honest.

"My mate and I borrowed some money for the garage. When we have the cash flow sorted, we can pay them back, y'know?" He sucks hard at the cigarette. They would act like idiots and go to the loan sharks, wouldn't they?

Alex sighs. "How much?"

"Twenty grand." It's not that much—if Alex were still at the top of his game. But he's not, and his family is leaning on him to do something.

He clenches his jaw as he considers this.

"I've seen Tony about a comeback, but there won't be a next time. All right?"

Their mum has been hovering near the door. She pipes up, "Your dad and I are going to do this place up and sell." Directing her comment to her older son, she says, "Gary, what you got to do, huh? You can't live in dreamland your entire life. You've long sucked us dry of the last of our savings."

Gary looks up. He seems so tired and weary; his hunched shoulders make him appear a good ten years older. "I swear I won't get into trouble again. I promise ya."

For some people, promises are cheap, but he's family to Alex. *I feel like I'm prostituting myself.* Alex thinks about Chris and what they said about boxers parading in front of people and showing their muscles. The comeback gig has become increasingly like selling his body to millions of unseen TV viewers.

Gary exhales, and for once, he's not flippant or cracking a cheap joke. "I'll work for my mate's garage. Good, honest work. Okay?"

"You understand the concept of good, honest work, then?" their mum remarks with an arched eyebrow.

Alex will have to do the fight, but it will be the absolute last time. Then he's going to retire for real and persuade Chris to move in with him. A new beginning for them.

CHAPTER 12
FLIGHT

ALEX HAS BEEN withdrawn with the prospect of the upcoming boxing match. Tony sent him the contract, but he has avoided reading it. Now Tony's left yet another message on his mobile to chase him up.

Chris and Alex haven't touched each other since the night they held and rutted against each other so tight that they both came. Alex is on the night shift and he's plunging lower and lower into the deep, debilitating him, afraid he'll let down the people closest to him, especially Chris.

~~~

Chris is making dinner when the revelation comes to him. He stares at the spatula he's holding, sadness filling his heart as he becomes infected by Alex's darkness. Most days, Alex goes to work, comes home and stays in his room, avoiding his flatmates. Chris tries to coax him out, cooks for him and makes jokes, and Alex politely goes along with it as though he wants the distance between them to grow.

"Knock, knock. Hey, you fancy some pasta? It's your favourite!"

Alex opens the door, but he seems half asleep, his hair spiking in all different directions. He's wearing an old T-shirt and tracksuit bottoms.

"Hey." The lack of energy in that one word hits Chris in the gut.

"Come on. I put extra tuna in it for you and your protein!" Chris puts on a big smile, trying to be as cheerful as possible. He grabs onto Alex's elbow to drag him out of his room.

Alex sits at the dining table, and Chris serves up a huge bowl of pasta, as always.

"You working later?" Chris asks.

"No, not today. I've got the day off. I was going to Dex's club, but…" It's Tuesday; Alex normally goes to train the kids and work on himself, *but…*

"You okay?" Chris stops eating because Alex has been stirring his food around. The giant usually has an appetite to match.

"Yeah, fine." Alex puts some pasta in his mouth. "You?"

"I've got an appointment later." Should he worry that Alex will flee like all his previous sexual partners? After these past two weeks, Chris is starting to doubt Alex wants him even though he's said he loves him. Chris distrusts any declarations of dedication. Alex has lost interest already, even before they've properly started. Just another page in the tragedy of Chris's life.

"Why don't you come in the taxi with me? I'll drop you off at the club. The guy said he'd pay me the cab fare to the hotel."

Alex stabs the table with his fork, causing the plates to jump an inch. Chris leans back in his chair, willing himself to be absorbed by the scratched and faded patterns of the table.

"Fuck's sake. I don't want to know you're spending the night in a hotel with some guy, Chris."

Here we go. Seeing Alex react is better than nothing at all. It means he does care after all.

Chris has looked into the nursery nurse qualifications. He needs a few good GCSEs and then two years full-time or three or four years of part-time study. He has saved some money, but how is he going to stop working for four years to support himself through college? How much does waiting tables pay again? He knows daydreaming doesn't do any good. He learned that from an early age.

Alex rakes through his hair. "I'm sorry. I'm exhausted."

He looks it. Bags have appeared under Alex's soulful eyes, revealing a darkness almost as bad as his mood. He doesn't return Chris's gaze but picks up the half-finished bowl of pasta to take it to the kitchen, leaning against the counter as though he's trying to regain his composure, to gather up some courage to go on.

Chris follows him into the kitchen.

Alex wraps his bowl with cling film. "I'll eat the rest later. I need to go and lie down. Thanks for dinner." He kisses Chris's forehead.

Damn it. Chris watches Alex retreat to his room. It's as if Alex is fading away right in front of his eyes, and Chris hasn't a clue what to do to make things better or at least back to how they were. Chris has lost his appetite too, so he puts the dish in the fridge and gets ready for his appointment. The client is not a regular, and they are meeting in a business hotel in the rejuvenated dockland area in East London. The john is paying more than his usual rate, making it worthwhile. Chris has given up the client whose sessions left him with the bruises Alex saw and was outraged about.

During his appointment, Chris can't help but become preoccupied with Alex's depression. Sex with the john is pretty vanilla, so he can do it with his eyes closed and his mind someplace else. He calls Chris 'babe' as he comes. *Right.* Chris often wonders about his clients and what they say in the heat of the moment. It doesn't take a genius to know the endearment is often involuntary.

Chris gazes out of the taxi on the way back, suffocated by the loneliness inside him. He knows about Alex's moods, but it's still hard to accept that it's not him; it's not rejection. It is depression. Deep down, Chris knows that, but it still hurts. Whether he hurts for Alex or himself isn't clear. Chris has always believed physical and emotional pain are indistinguishable, and now Alex's have become his. A big cosmic joke on Chris that is not remotely funny.

The neon lights and the blurred rainbow colours of the shop signs fly by, making him want to reach out and grab hold of something vibrant and unreachable. Like happiness. Or euphoria. He has never known it. He doodles on the moisture covering the cool window of the taxi.

Chris alights the car still engrossed in his thoughts when the stale night air hits his face. About ten men and women crowd the door to the building. It takes him several seconds to realise who they are. One of the women surges forward.

"Hey, do you live in this building? Have you seen Alex Whale, the boxer?" She has a notepad and a pen, and another reporter with a camera paces by her side.

Fuckety fuck. Chris wants to punch the living daylights out of the pair of them. He hesitates. The other paparazzi are coming forward like zombies in a terrible B-movie.

Chris retreats, trying to reach the door, away from their threats.

"No." He turns on his heel, unlocks the door and runs upstairs. He's panting and sweating by the time he arrives home.

"Have you talked to the paparazzi downstairs?" Chris snaps at his Italian flatmate once safe in the apartment.

Freshly rolled joint in hand, Alberto looks up. "Nice to see you, too. Haven't seen you in days, bud. What's up?"

"Sorry! Did you speak to those people about Alex? There're a dozen of them downstairs with cameras and everything."

"No! I didn't speak to anyone." Alberto lights his blunt. "What's going on?"

Instead of explaining everything to Alberto, Chris glances over to Alex's room. "Is he in?"

Alberto shrugs. "I guess so."

Chris knocks on Dmitri's door as well. The zany Russian appears in his boxers, showing his tattooed torso. In the past, Chris might have jumped the man. That Chris—the one who never cared about anyone or himself—has gone; the realisation causes his heart to miss a beat.

"C. What do you want? Drugs. Those I have." The Russian speaks with his familiar accent.

"Fuck, no! Did you have anything to do with the paparazzi downstairs?" Chris demands.

"The what?" Dmitri's eyes widen with shock.

"Someone alerted them that Alex lives here." Chris folds his arms across his chest.

Dmitri frowns, grooves deepening between his brows. "Hey, would I involve the media given what I do? And...you know I don't dare to cross you, Christine."

Chris has to smirk at that. Chris has ripped him one quite a few times in the past for doing what he does—like selling crack to Liam, who's a reformed drug addict.

Dmitri shakes his head. "What has your boyfriend done now?"

"Alex used to be a famous boxer, all right?" Chris flips him off with his hand. "Anyway, he's not my boyfriend."

Not yet. They'll deal with that after this emergency. Chris is determined not to let the pack downstairs win.

Dmitri rolls his eyes. "You'd have fooled me, the way you two carried on with each other. What about that new kid? Paul?"

Chris forgot about the latest addition to the flat, the fucking rat-arse kid who looks about eighteen and is fresh out of prison. If anyone might want to make a quick buck by tipping off the media, that creep is the prime suspect.

"Is he around?"

Alberto pipes up, "Don't think so, no."

"I bet it's that twat. Don't you speak to the newspaper people, okay?" Chris directs that to Alberto and Dmitri. He knocks on Alex's door.

Alex's muffled voice drifts through. "Hmm?"

Chris twists the doorknob and finds it unlocked. He enters. Alex's room always strikes Chris as like a prison cell, and it's particularly oppressive tonight. Alex is lying sideways but he's not sleeping. Chris sits on the edge of the single bed that's barely big enough for Alex.

Alex sits up. "Hey, you back from work?" He reaches out and cups Chris's head and kisses him with some urgency.

"Yeah."

Another gentler kiss. "I'm sorry I snapped at you." Alex rubs his day-old stubble on Chris's neck; the friction feels like heaven. Chris inhales, loving Alex's unique scent.

"It's okay. We'll talk later. Have you been sleeping?" Chris ruffles Alex's messy hair.

"No, I can't…" He lifts Chris's shirt and touches his chest and back, still rubbing his prickly beard on Chris's skin. The hard-as-nails boxer and the cynic—as Chris used to think of himself—turn to putty in each other's company, and Chris doesn't have the heart to tell Alex what's waiting for him downstairs.

"I can't sleep if you're not next to me. I feel so dark inside when I reach out and you're not there."

His callused fingers touch Chris's face as though asking for help.

Chris decides he won't mention the paparazzi until the morning. He will protect Alex. "Are you going to work, darling?"

"Hmm. I've got a seven o'clock start."

Chris stretches over to have a look at the time on Alex's mobile. It's nearly one o'clock so Alex will need to be up in a few hours if he is going to work, and the man needs his rest.

"Alex, try to sleep. I'll talk to you in the morning, okay?" He takes off his clothes and burrows under the cover, his body warm and fresh after the quick shower in the hotel.

Holding on to Chris's body, Alex finally gets to sleep, though he moves in the night as peace eludes him.

~~~

The alarm announces the start of a difficult day. If Chris had a say, her day would start at twelve, and everyone would only need four hours' sleep without getting scratchy like old cats.

Alex shifts. The two of them have slept uncomfortably because they have been pressed together in the confined space. They should have gone to Chris's double bed, but Alex was far too confused and cute a few hours ago for Chris to ask him to move. At least they managed to shut their eyes.

Alex's rough palms caress Chris's arse, sending a smile to her face. "I've got to get up."

He stretches.

Chris places her hand over Alex's. "Ah. It may be a good idea for you to take the day off."

Alex frowns with concern. "Why? Are you okay?"

"I'm fine." Chris gazes at him, and sighing, she tells him the bad news.

Alex runs his hands through his sleep-tussled hair. "Fuck."

Chris hugs him. "I have an idea. It's not a very good one… Basically, we run."

Alex pulls away and scowls, while she tells him her plan.

"Is that all you've got?" He looks so miserable. "I can't go to my family. Coach's house is too crowded. Anyway, I can't bring troubles to my family and friend like that. I'm sorry for burying my head in the sand."

Seeing Alex like this makes Chris more determined.

"Come on. I'm your bodyguard, remember? Trust me." She grins despite the impending threat.

Alex nods. "There is no one else in the world I trust more."

Chris instructs him to gather some clothes, essentials and his medication in a holdall. He has few other possessions anyway. While Alex gets ready, Chris makes the call.

She knocks on Alberto's door first. The Italian opens, his hair messy and his big brown eyes half closed. "What the fuck? Do you ever sleep?"

"Get dressed. You're helping out," Chris orders. "No time for chitchat."

Dmitri is next. "No way, Jose! I'm not speaking to no paparazzi."

But he puts his clothes on eventually, still sulking and stealing frightened glances at Chris. It's inexplicable that the part-time drug pusher should be scared of her, but he is.

Chris brings out her Jackie O. sunglasses to give to Dmitri.

"Put them on. Once they find out you've got nothing to say, they won't print anything. Trust me." Chris has been saying that to everyone; she's beginning to believe it herself.

Finally, she gets dressed quickly in another understated black outfit and canvas trainers.

Alex wears his beanie and Ray-Bans. For once, Chris approves. "Are we getting a taxi?"

"No. These people like chasing cars. Don't you remember Princess Diana?" Chris touches Alex's arm to reassure him.

"I'm no Princess fucking Di," Alex grumbles. If the circumstances were different, they might find this vaguely amusing.

Chris laughs anyway. "No. That's in your favour. They'll leave you alone soon enough."

When Alberto and Dmitri both emerge from their rooms, still bleary-eyed and half-asleep, Dmitri sporting the ridiculous, large sunglasses, Chris declares the early morning strike ready. Alberto looks out of the window and tells them only four of the paps are still around.

Stunt.

The gang descend the stairs. Alberto is the first one who will distract them. He leaves, and five minutes later, Chris receives a blank text.

"Okay. Dmitri. We're leaning on you." Chris points at her flatmate, the red nail varnish a kind of warning.

Dmitri grimaces. "*Pizda*." Cunt. But he puts on his game face and opens the door.

Chris counts ninety seconds, then turns to Alex. "Ready? Three. Two. One."

They emerge. A photographer is poised with his camera but one of his other colleagues is deep in conversation with the Russian. Another young woman moves forward.

As the door is shutting behind Chris and Alex, they take off running, hand in hand. The camera guy shouts to the other paparazzi. Abandoning the decoy—Dmitri—they all give chase. Alex is naturally fast, but Chris with her long legs keeps up without much difficulty. They can hear footsteps behind them, especially the clacking of the women's heels against the concrete pavement. When they get to the main road, they jump on the first bus that comes along.

"Shut the door. Please, shut the door," Chris shouts at the bus driver, who frowns at her. "Bad, bad people are chasing us. Please." Chris urges her to help.

The driver stares at her and Alex, then glances in her side mirror. "Okay." She presses the button to close the door, moving away from the kerb as the cameraman and reporters reach the side of the bus.

Regarding Alex, while keeping her eyes on the road, the driver smiles. "This one here could take on a few of them. What are you worrying about?"

Chris grins, her bright eyes sparkling. "We don't believe in violence."

The driver laughs. "Go and sit down, you two."

Chris leads Alex up to the top deck. They must be in luck since the front seat is free. Sinking into the soft bench, Alex hides his head in his hands again. Chris chuckles as she looks back through the smeared and dirty windows to find the three paparazzi staring after the departing bus.

Alex glances at her sidelong. "I'm glad you find this funny."

"Did you hear Dmitri? He was talking about the Cossacks. What the fuck has that got to do with the price of eggs? Cossacks!"

Alex has to laugh along. "And Alberto?"

"He's taken one of them to a coffee shop and is getting his first caffeine intake of the day for free." She instructed the Italian to say nothing.

Alex shakes his head. "So, what now?"

Chris calls up her map on the mobile. "I'll text Liam."

Liam and Ali are waiting in their small black car by the time Alex and Chris reach the appointed bus stop. They get in and greet each other.

Liam turns around. "Hey, have we missed the excitement?"

Chris laughs. "You're part of it. It's like that programme on the telly. *Pet Rescue.*"

Alex rolls his eyes. "I'm not your pet, Chris, though as we're talking about animals, when you run you look like a pretty lynx."

Chris is grinning wide, enjoying the adrenaline rush and the triumph over the paparazzi.

"Oh, my friend, Liam, you've met. This is Ali, Liam's boyfriend—I told you about them. Ali, this is Alex."

Alex pats Liam's shoulder. "Thank you so much, mate."

Ali replies, "Of course. We heard it's an emergency, friends in need."

They've come out to pick Alex and Chris up without a moment of hesitation.

Once they arrive at Ali and Liam's house in Islington, Ali offers his hand to Alex. "Welcome. Make yourself at home. The guest room is yours for as long as you want."

Alex shakes the offered hand, and grateful tears threaten. "Thank you, again."

"No problem. I've got to go to work. I can't believe I've already done a run-along the A1 and it's not even nine a.m." He reaches out and grabs Liam for a kiss. "You get them settled, okay? See you all later."

Liam gives him the grooviest smile before turning to Chris and Alex. "Actually, I've got a class too. Do you need anything else? As Ali said, treat this like home. All right? Here's the spare key." He passes it to Chris.

"I...thanks," Alex mumbles. "Hopefully, we'll figure something out soon."

"Don't worry! Mi casa es tu casa." Liam winks. "Alberto taught me that."

"It's Spanish," Chris counters.

"Really? Same difference." Liam looks at his mobile. "Sorry. I've got to run. Classes to get to, courses to fail."

Chris shakes her head.

Liam goes into his room and picks up his flute and backpack full of college stuff. He departs with, "Let us know if you need anything, okay? Don't be a stranger."

The new Liam is breezy, bouncy and full of love, a changed man. Gah, Chris used to despise people who change for the better because they are happy! Before she met Alex, she'd already accepted that the gooey love of coupledom was never going to happen to her.

L.O.V.E. Forever and ever. Unspeakable and unknowable.

Am I happy? Chris doesn't know. She and Alex have too much to deal with right now to think beyond the immediate crisis, but Alex squeezes her hand as if he understands.

After Ali and Liam have left, they sit in the quiet house. Alex draws Chris close, laying his head on her shoulder. "My depression has got worse, Chris. This is not helping."

"I know. Is there anyone who can help? Your parole officer?"

Alex pulls away a little, resting his forehead against hers. "No, my PO is not a head doctor. He's business-like but not particularly helpful. And he's already told me this would happen one day. I went to some drug and alcohol courses in prison. Now all I have is the medication."

"Alex, whatever you want to do, what's best for you...I'll be right here. You're my charge, remember?"

Alex's lips lift at that.

Chris makes them both some toast and coffee, and they sit together. Chris tilts her face to be in the warmth of the sunlight streaming through the windows.

"Do you think they've heard about your contract?"

"Probably, and they haven't even started the promotion yet. It's supposed to be hush-hush, rumours only." Alex sighs.

Chris curls her wearied fingers around the cup handle. "That new kid Paul might have called the media to earn a quick buck."

Alex considers the situation for a moment. "You think so? I guess he recognised me right away. I doubt my story's worth that much."

Chris takes a sip of coffee. "He's a twat who'd sell his parents if money's involved."

Alex takes the day off, and he and Chris relax in Ali and Liam's house. Both of them are tired from having little sleep last night. In the afternoon, they relax on the settee and watch some mindless daytime TV. Her head rests on his broad chest as they lie back.

"I'm Alex Whale. I don't run from the paps," he declares all of a sudden, in the middle of a reality show rerun.

Chris grins. That's the man she admires. She asks, "Do you know why I don't own any heels?"

"Hmm, cuz you'll look like a giraffe in a crowd?"

Chris hits Alex on the arm. "Says the man who looks like his nickname. Anyway, I'm only six two."

Alex chuckles. "Tall enough. You look gorgeous in anything, though. Why do you always wear flats, then?"

Chris takes a sharp breath. "About five years ago, I was beaten up so badly I was in a coma for two days. I tripped and one of my heels broke, or it might have been the other way around. Anyway, the three blokes called me a tranny and kicked the shit out of me while I was on the ground. They stamped on my head. I had my hands and arms up to protect it, otherwise... They broke one of my arms, a rib, an ankle.

"You should've seen me when I first regained consciousness. I looked like the Elephant Man. The hospital told me I was very lucky not to have permanent brain damage."

Chris takes Alex's hand and places it on her scalp just above her hairline on the left. "Can you feel it?"

A hard lump—a sign of transphobic hatred.

"That's a reminder of the attack. Those men wouldn't have cared if they'd killed me. How could human beings do this to another human being? I escaped death, Alex. Someone walking past screamed for help and called the police. They never caught them. Maybe they didn't try very hard.

"I used to have long hair down to the middle of my back. I wore dangly jewellery and stilettos when I wanted. After that, I stopped wearing heels and I cut my hair. I don't want anyone to grab my hair or for my shoes to break again when I try to run."

She'd lost her accommodation and couldn't work for months, instead couch-hopping with acquaintances, living from hand-to-mouth. When she finally went back out there to face the world, she had to force herself one step at a time.

Alex touches Chris's cheek with his fingertips. "I'm sorry that happened to you. I can imagine how beautiful you were with your long hair." He cards his fingers through Chris's short blonde strands. "I like this, too. You're flawless and pure gold inside and out. You know that?"

"Now you're encouraging me to be conceited. It was lucky my face survived. Imagine!" She hums the chorus from 'You're So Vain'.

Alex laughs. "You remind me of these tough old boxers who always get the fuck up no matter how many times they are knocked down. Or a roly-poly toy."

Alex gently massages her head. She smiles and leans into his palm and feels inspired by him.

"I've grown to like my short hair, but I love heels sometimes. I'm queer and I will wear whatever I want. I won't be afraid of falling down and not being able to run. I won't let them win."

"Then let's go home in a couple of days. What's the worst that can happen?" Alex asks.

Chris touches her chin and thinks about the question. "Not much. They'll snap a few photos and try to speak to you, I guess. You may be lucky and there'll be some other bigger news that day and they'll have forgotten all about you. Yeah?"

Now Chris has put it like that, Alex relaxes a little and sits back.

"I know I'm a miserable bastard and you deserve someone better, but… Do you want to live with me? I mean, not like sharing a flat because we do that already. I mean, do you think we can move in together?" Alex bumbles along with the words. "To share a flat with me, but not like the way we are now."

He grimaces at the garbled delivery of his veiled declaration of love.

Chris considers Alex as he waits in hope. She swallows hard.

Alex sighs. "I know. I'm no good to anyone. This depression." He rubs his temple as if that will make it go away. "I want to hold you every night. I want you to be mine."

Chris screws up her nose, mirroring Alex's little insecurities.

"It's the most beautiful thing anyone has said to me. Yes, I'd love to live with you, Alex. You know...I can't give up work. Not yet, but I'm looking into it."

She tells him about the childcare course, about studying part-time, trying to change her life. They both pay pretty high rent now, so they should be able to afford a small flat together. Pooling their resources, Chris may even be able to work less.

Alex caresses her face. "I know." He kisses her. "I'm not easy to live with. The psychiatrist said there's nothing she can do to cure me. I can only control it through the pills. I'll ask her about therapy again. I've been dreading having to talk about it, but I want to be able to live with the illness. I want us to be able to live with it, y'know?"

Chris kisses him, brushing her hands over his strong body.

When they break away for air, Alex breathes out to steady his tremors. "When I'm down, I want you to know it has nothing to do with you because you make me happy. As happy as someone in my condition can ever be."

Chris smiles, tears threatening to fall from her eyes.

"I've never made anyone happy. Not like that." She puts her hand up to stop Alex from arguing otherwise. "Not truly. A good fuck is just that. I didn't think I knew how because I'd never had anything. Love, trust, someone who wanted me for me. They always wanted me for something else—for what I could do for them, for sex or money."

Alex smiles. "If I didn't feel so down in the dumps and I wasn't so scared of rejection because you are way above my league, I'd have fucked you the first time we met. It's good that we didn't jump straight to sex. For you, I mean."

Chris considers it. "I like the stuff we do in bed."

"Yeah, I like doing the stuff we do as well. In bed, out of it..."

Chris rubs her head in Alex's neck. She can't have enough of him like that. She whispers, "You know most people think of me as a slut. It's work, nothing more. With my other lovers, I tried to prove I wasn't a sex machine, but it never helped. They made me feel cheap because...because I was offering them free sex and it should feel good, but I couldn't get away from worrying about whether I was performing right. Whether I deserved their attention. So…I'm fucked up, Alex. I want you to know that. Do you still think I'm worthy?"

Alex pulls Chris close. "Worthy of my love? Of course you are. I want you to feel good, to have what you need. When you are with me, you never have to perform, all right?"

Chris bites her lip. "Yeah, all right."

CHAPTER 13
FIGHT

Tony accidentally leaked the news about the upcoming fight, of course, to coincide with the media interest. He offers to pay for a hotel room for Alex and wants him to receive extra training from a professional coach—a US-based heavyweight trainer—instead of Dex. Alex refuses to move to a hotel. Even though the flat is a dump, he wants to be there with Chris, but he has a good virtual chat with the American trainer, knowing he will never be psychologically ready for the upcoming fight.

After a few days at Liam and Ali's, they move back to the flat. The paparazzi manage to snap a few photos, and they're featured on page four of the newspapers and the sports section for a couple of days.

Chris laughs at his blurred profile. One paper has posted a question mark over him: 'Who's Alex Whale's companion?'

"Who, indeed? Does my face look gaunt in this?" Chris's comment makes Alex laugh.

~~~

"So, how much for a fuck?" Paul surprises Chris when he is making lunch one afternoon.

Even though Chris is not usually that easily intimidated, Paul creeps him out. Paul is standing about a foot behind him, his hand on the edge of the kitchen unit, trapping Chris in. Too close for comfort.

Chris considers how close he is to the sharp knives in the kitchen. *I will use them in an emergency.* He moves Paul's arm away and peers down at him, making his disgust absolutely clear. "For you, no amount of money can buy me."

He takes his coffee and sandwich to the couch, ignoring the stupid kid. Alarm makes the hairs on the back of his neck stand up, though he makes sure he appears unfazed. Chris always acts as though he's unflappable; hiding his fears has become second nature.

Paul gazes at him from the kitchenette, a nasty glint in his eyes. He forces out a chilling laugh. "No whores I know refuse money."

"I refuse dicks who want a piece of my arse." Chris reserves *that* glare for the assholes of this world.

Paul is startled, then he snickers. "Oh, so you give Blue freebies, or what?"

His knowledge proves Paul was likely the culprit for alerting the paps to Alex's location.

"What's it to you? You want to sell that story as well?" Chris puts his food down, then summons his seductive face to mock his slimy flatmate. "Or, you're jealous cuz you can't sample the merchandise?"

Paul laughs but there's no joy in it. He approaches Chris now but stops a few feet away, attempting to stare him down. He reminds Chris of all the smarmy bastards he has ever met.

"Don't worry, bitch. I only like pussies. Real cunts. It ain't something you 'ave, is it? I ain't spending money on getting some from a poof. I should be the one getting paid for risking it with a dirty AIDS slut. Anyway, I asked cuz I'm trying to work out what the fuck's going on in the flat—"

Chris stands so quickly that the coffee table nearly tips over. He grabs Paul's shirt collar and shoves him against the nearest wall. He tightens his grip and knocks the back of Paul's head against the wall behind. Paul's face turns ash-white from the pain.

"Don't you call me dirty. I may sell myself, but I never sell out, unlike you, you fucking rat."

Chris pushes Paul hard again before releasing his shirt. This brutish Chris only appears when provoked.

Paul's eyes are full of cold hatred. He takes a packet of cigarettes out of his pocket and lights one up slowly. "You'll pay for this, you piece of shit."

With that, he storms back to his room.

Chris scowls at Paul as he walks away, swears silently and makes a note to tell Alex to be careful with the little cunt. Paul is probably all mouth and Alex has about eighty pounds on him, but still. There's something in those intense stares. Chris picks up his food again and finds he has lost his appetite.

~~~

The phone calls from unknown numbers have been coming in daily, an incessant alarm that fails to frighten Alex. He dismisses them as sale pitchers or 'journalists' wanting to interview him, trying for an exclusive.

Ignoring the latest call, Alex arrives at the pub to meet Chris for a drink after the adult boxing class that he helps Dex to teach. The bar smells of stale beer and sweat, in contrast with the aroma from Chris as he kisses him on the cheek and the lips.

Chris makes his heart flutter every time. Alex marvels at how the turquoise of his irises shines like glitter, and the hint of lipstick makes his lips too kissable.

"Hey, you look like a gorgeous dyke tonight."

Chris beams. "You mean like a butch lesbian?"

Alex laughs. "Oh!"

"Absolutely. I think of myself a butch woman sometimes. I would be careful calling a lesbian gorgeous, though, Alex."

Alex chuckles. "I know. For you, it's a compliment. I wouldn't go around talking about the appearance of just any woman—cis, bi, lesbian or trans!"

"Damn right. You're learning fast, aren't you? You sound like you're familiar with all the right lingo."

"Yeah. I've been reading up on the internet. If I'm going to come out as a bisexual man, I can't be ignorant, right?"

Chris becomes serious. "There's plenty of biphobia and transphobia among the so-called LGBT community. Everyone can be uninformed. Besides, there isn't one way to be queer."

"I tried for so long to pass as straight. The macho culture of the boxing scene made me uncomfortable, but I couldn't challenge the status quo then. Now, I want to try, to understand you, to be truthful about who I am."

Chris kisses Alex. "So, are you? Coming out?"

"I am not hiding my interest in you too well, am I?" He smiles and Chris joins him.

Alex asks, "May I take you home sometime? I mean, to see my family in Essex?"

Chris's eyes twinkle in surprise. He hesitates. "Like I'm official or something?"

Alex nods. "Yeah, you are official."

Chris squeals. "Wow. Okay. Yes, you may. No one has ever asked me that before."

"Your exes were idiots."

That makes Chris laugh.

Alex gazes intently at Chris, then blinks several times, his thoughts drifting, but he notices Chris incline his head and the concern in his eyes.

"You okay?" Chris asks.

"Yes." Alex sits up. "I'm thinking how I'd like to ravage you. All of you. Properly, with penetration. If it's okay with you, that is."

Chris bursts out laughing. "That's kind of romantic. Yes, I'd like that."

Alex laughs, too. "No one has ever told me I'm romantic. I've got to work tonight and tomorrow day shift, though. Do you think I'll get lucky tomorrow night?"

Chris's smile deepens his dimples. "You might."

"Damn, that twinkle in your eyes. And I really don't need a hard-on in the bar." Alex shifts his legs. His phone buzzes again. He pulls it out and stares at the screen.

"Are you not going to answer that?"

"Hmm. No caller ID. I've been getting a lot of calls like this. They're sales or sports news people." He casually tosses the phone on the table. Chris frowns. Something doesn't feel right, but Alex can't quite put his finger on it.

"Oh, I almost forgot!" Chris says. "I've arranged to see a flat near Holloway Road tomorrow at six. What time will you come home?"

"I get off work at six thirty. It's too late, isn't it? It's okay. I trust your judgement. You go ahead and view it."

Chris has cut his hair again, so the short blonde strands cling to his well-shaped skull. Alex touches the lump, the remnant of the attack on his lover. "Just be careful, okay?" Alex adds, and kisses Chris's temple, near the bump.

Chris finishes the last of his beer in one gulp. "I'll be fine."

Alex follows Chris's lead and downs his Diet Coke. "I'm off to my double shift. See you tomorrow night—see if my luck's still valid?"

Chris giggles, and it sounds like ringing bells. "We'll see if you're extra nice to me, yeah?"

"I'll think of you when I stare at the surveillance screening of empty corners tonight. My new favourite hobby." Alex checks the time. "Sorry, I've got to run."

They kiss goodbye.

~~~

The flat is nice if a little small for the money, making Chris wonder if it's worth paying so much to stay in zone two. If they move further out, Alex will need to get a bike to go to work. In the back of Chris's mind, she wants to work less. Despite being distracted by the worries of moving and money issues, she walks up the flight of stairs, grinning to herself and looking forward to talking to Alex about the flat and finally having 'proper sex' with him, as Alex puts it. She will make some dinner and wait for him to come home.

The smile stays on her face until she opens the door.

A fall.

Terror seizes her.

Paul sits on the sofa with a guy dressed in a leather jacket, who has small, beady eyes that home in on Chris straight away. She flinches, noticing two other men standing at opposite corners of the lounge. They're big and burly, but they mustn't be as strong as Alex. No one can match Alex's physical strength. These two have their arms across their chests as if they're bouncers standing in front of a club, ready to pounce on anyone who crosses their path without permission. Bomber jackets, dark trousers and hard faces.

Waiting, staring at Chris.

They are not Paul's friends and they are dangerous. Chris knows that by instinct. She frowns at Paul, but he avoids her eyes and stands up to leave the flat instead. Chris should have turned around, walked right back out of the door and run, but she freezes. Paul gets there first; Chris hears the click of the door and the turning of the lock from the outside. She reaches into her pocket for the pepper spray, but more importantly she needs to run. Without a word, she goes to her room. *If I can lock myself in and call Alex.*

Or the police.

Laugh out loud. How long is it going to take them to respond to a call like this? She'll be long dead if these men want to kill her.

Chris's hand is on the knob. Just half a second more and she'll be semi-safe in her bedroom. The men move behind her, so fast that Chris has little chance of out-manoeuvring them. The boss's dress shoe wedges the door open as Chris slams it, and she hears him hiss with the pain. But now she can't get inside the room. Her attacker grabs her arms to push her into the bedroom, already bruising her up. She stumbles backwards, almost falling down onto the floor. She reaches for the edge of the bed to steady herself.

"Who the fuck *are* you?" Springing back up, she pushes out her chest to appear as tall as possible. Her height isn't much of an advantage, as her slight physique suggests weakness in a situation like this.

All three men stare back, their contempt clear on their faces.

The boss scowls at her; his henchmen stand coolly by his sides. He smirks. "Alex Whale always prefers the pretty ones, doesn't he? My sister was smitten with that dickhead."

Chris pushes Sam's brother. "Get the fuck out of my room. I don't know you."

Chris draws her pepper spray and squeezes, aiming it fully at the man's eyes. He partly blocks the spray with his right hand as it hits his face. "Fuck!" He coughs, squeezing his eyes shut, while tears and snot run.

One of the thugs pulls Chris away from his boss, grabbing her can of pepper spray and throwing it away. It lands in the far corner of the room. Without her weapon, Chris raises her hands to force her attacker back, but he catches her wrists and shoves her roughly into the side of the bed.

"Alex!"

They all know he's not there. Screaming his name is no more than a distraction.

The main man laughs through obvious discomfort. "No, your scumbag of a boyfriend can't save you now, bitch."

Chris knows how to fight, but one against three is bad odds. An insurmountable situation only makes her see red. She stands up and throws a punch against the gang boss.

"I'm not a bitch, you fucking twat." Having nothing to lose makes her brave or reckless, depending on one's perspective.

Still disorientated with the effects of the pepper spray, the man touches the heat on the left side of his face where Chris has hit his jaw so hard it swells and reddens right away. The two beefy henchmen surge forward and grab her, dragging her back while Chris struggles against their firm grip.

"Get off me!" She tilts her head back to butt one of them, but her opponent's face is a couple of inches out of reach. Chris kicks out at the boss and catches his thigh, but she's too far away for any real impact. She elbows the men, hard enough for them to strain to maintain their grasp.

The main man jumps back a little and stares at Chris, running his reddened eyes up and down her body. A flicker of recognition flashes across his face.

"The tranny's not just a pretty face." He laughs, amusement in his mockery.

The man on his right must have been distracted, so Chris takes advantage of the momentary lapse, pushes and headbutts him hard. Blood spurts from the thug's nose on impact.

"Fucking hell!" He squeezes his the bridge of his nose to stop the flow. "Ryan, I don't care what junk he's got. Stop the stupid fag, will ya!"

Ryan's right hook sends Chris back onto the floor. She sees stars, and her cheek and nose throb. She's so dizzy that the other thug doesn't need to hold on to her anymore. Ryan's hand is on her neck as well, trapping her. Disorientated, Chris's vision blurs, but she can make out Ryan's distorted face, his tears and red nose as a result of the spray.

Chris uses the opportunity and pushes her attacker back. The men return, one on each side, and hold on to her legs, trying to stop her from kicking.

Ryan scowls. "The little shit said you're a whore. Let's see the package you're selling."

He unzips Chris's jeans and pulls them and her knickers down in one sweep, exposing her penis.

Not again. For fuck's sake.

"No!" Chris frees her left hand and she tries to throw another punch at Ryan. One of his men reacts first, locking Chris's neck with a meaty arm and deflecting her punch.

Chris kicks at Ryan instead.

Ryan shifts back. "Fucking bitch. Hold him back."

"He's stronger than he looks, boss," one of the men says, perplexed.

The more Chris struggles against the headlock, though, the more her neck is wedged, and she's going to choke if she continues to struggle. Another hand now grabs her right leg to still her kicks.

Chris roars. Using her free hand, she reaches back to jab her fingers at the man's face, but he must have moved and avoids her attack.

Ryan stares down at her again as he unfastens his belt, unzips his trousers and pulls them down along with his boxers so they're slack around his thighs.

Chris strikes with her one free leg but Ryan catches it and pulls it back, exposing Chris's inner thigh and arse.

"No!" Chris's fingers desperately pull at the arm across her throat.

The tattooed arm. Something to forget, but it's imprinted in her psyche.

Ryan tells his men, "Turn him around. I don't want to see his dick." The strong hands on Chris tighten further as the other two pull and push at her legs. She's exposed, vulnerable. She lashes out against the constraint. She crawls, attempting to kneel, but the men pull her thighs and calves out again.

She can feel the head of Ryan's hard cock.

"Getting fucked is better than murder, you fucking poof. Alex Whale will love my gesture."

He pushes forward and his cock invades Chris's arse crack. Chris clenches, resisting and wriggling and hurting herself in the meantime. Her vision turns white, mentally blocking what's happening, but images of other attacks and violent sexual encounters flood her brain. Chris panics and seizes up, frozen with fear. She's almost grateful she can't see her assailant.

She imagines floating in mid-air and observing the pathetic display of inhumanity: another invasion of her person, exposed and on show for the haters.

The searing pain slashed across their thigh.

Stop.

The pressure is gone. Chris glances back. Strong hands lift Ryan up and throw him to one side. Out of the corner of her eye, Chris sees a mass of legs and arms. She hears grunts and shouts from the men. She turns around.

"Alex!"

Ryan is standing next to the big man who dwarfs him. The gangbangers try to hold Alex back, but that only exacerbates his anger. Like a cornered animal, Alex's eyes are on fire. He pushes the two men aside and throws a punch so impactful it sends Ryan to the wall with a loud thud. Ryan collapses in a heap on the floor, blood pouring from his nostrils.

Alex howls, the veins in his neck and arms visible. He hasn't finished with the man who moments ago was trying to violate Chris. He kneels down and pummels Ryan's face like a sandbag until it's a bloody pulp. It might have been only thirty seconds, but the damage is done. Ryan's two men drag Alex away, back from their unconscious boss on the floor, but Alex is not going to be stopped. He morphs into a large wild tiger, growling and throwing blows at the two thugs, who almost match him in size but not power.

Chris pulls her trousers back up and whimpers, "Alex, stop!"

The two men can barely restrain him. Chris turns to see Ryan struggling to open his eyes and writhing in pain. She stares at Alex fighting with the two men, his arm muscles bulging, but it's nothing like a boxing match with rules. They hit each other messily, two against one, but Alex is holding his own.

Chris tries again. "Alex, don't!" She needs to stop him, but it's not for Ryan and his men. Alex is on course to kill someone by accident.

When Chris catches the flash of a hand and an object with the corner of her eyes, she freezes.

No!

But no sound comes out of her mouth, and she has no time to find her voice. Chris scrambles over to Ryan to grasp his hand. Ryan is semi-conscious at best, yet he holds up the small handgun to aim at Alex's back.

Alex is engrossed in his fight with the two larger men. When Ryan glimpses Chris approaching him, he moves the gun out of her reach.

Seeing she's too late to stop Ryan, instead of reaching for the revolver she staggers closer to Alex, who has his back to the barrel of the gun.

"Alex! Alex!"

The split second plays out like a slowed-down sequence. Still suffering from Chris's earlier pepper spray attack, Ryan aims the gun at Alex the best he can. Chris nears Alex as he frees himself from another man's iron grip and finally turns around to see why Chris is shouting.

Too late.

Chris stands up fully and puts herself between Ryan's extended arm and Alex.

Pop.

Chris always thought the firing of a gun should sound louder than the click she has just heard. Was the shot muffled by the screaming? There are other noises. The men calling out to Ryan to drop the fucking gun.

Chris can only see one person while everything else has receded into nothing. She remembers falling to the floor in front of Alex. Her lower back feels strange and wet. The movements and light flash in and out. Alex sinks down in front of her, talking to her…

~~~

The shot.

The scene appears like Alex's recurring nightmare, except this time, he can move. All blood has left Alex's head and flows out of Chris's wound.

Chris's hand covers her waist on the left, where a stream of blood is seeping through her fingers. Her eyes are closed; the pain has distorted her features. On autopilot, Alex finds his phone to dial for the ambulance, telling them there are two injured parties.

Alex is vaguely aware of the other men. One takes the small revolver from Ryan and speeds off. Another stays with his boss, who stares at Chris and Alex, rendered speechless by the consequences of his own actions.

Alex wraps Chris in his arms as though he's holding onto his biggest fear. His recurring nightmare is no longer about Sam but a doomed future for him and another person he loves. Chris is already slender, but right now she feels fragile and featherlike in his embrace. Her eyes remain shut and she's breathing erratically—the greyness of her skin betrays the massive blood loss. He strokes her cold face, soothing the pain with tenderness, paralysed by helplessness.

"The ambulance will be here very soon. How are you feeling?" She grips his arm. "It hurts a lot."

Alex starts to talk. He's never seen anyone get shot before. *Are you supposed to speak to them? To keep them awake?* Chris's breaths on his neck are laboured and intermittent.

"Of course it does. What did you think you were doing? Trying to block a fucking bullet?" His voice sounds surprisingly calm, even though his heart hurts so much. *Why would anyone do this for me?*

Chris's chuckle is weak. "I'm...bodyguard...I...so love your black widow tattoo." Is she hallucinating? She hisses with the sharp pain.

"I didn't know you'd take the role so literally." Alex wishes he could laugh.

"Who...they? Sam..." Chris whispers.

"Yes, Ryan is Sam's brother."

Alex moves a little away so he can see Chris's face; all colour has drained out of it. She has passed out because her weight in Alex's arms has suddenly increased. They're both covered in blood now.

Ryan and his crony are talking. Alex avoids their gaze and focuses only on Chris.

The wait seems like a millennium. In the back of the ambulance, as the paramedics hook Chris up to who knows what, Alex stares at her face. She looks as though she's gone to sleep; her ashen cheeks scare him. At least they've pumped her up with meds so she won't feel the pain for now.

Another time, on the way to emergency, he'd screamed so loud he lost his voice for days. They gave him an injection at one point. *Why didn't you let me die instead?*

Blue and green scrubs whizz Chris away as soon as they arrive at the emergency room. Alex is left in the corridor. He can focus on nothing but the hurrying legs of the nurses and doctors wheeling the trolley down the white-tiled floor. He stares after them when they refuse to let him go with Chris.

"Sir. Sir." The receptionist has been calling Alex for a while.

He turns and approaches the desk.

She hands over a clipboard with a form and a pen attached. "Could you fill this out, please?"

Alex takes it and tries to focus on the words, but the world has blanked as if he's gone blind.

"I…" He glances around. Ryan's underling is on the phone. No doubt word will have gone back to Sam Taylor senior.

He looks at the form again and the various boxes. They had a drink on her birthday, but Alex can't remember the exact date. He writes down Chris's name and address and hands the board back to the woman behind the counter.

"Is he your friend? You don't know much about him, do you?" She glances at the registration and frowns.

I don't even know her date of birth or anything about her medical history. He hesitates. Who's Chris to him? "I'm her boyfriend. I just can't remember her birthday."

"Her?" She reads the form again where Alex has ticked the 'M' box for gender since it's designed for the binary world.

As if explaining to himself, rather than to the staff, Alex states, "Chris prefers her some days."

The receptionist's eyes widen, but before she can respond, another crisis unfolding next to Alex catches her attention. Someone with a serious head wound has been brought in. She hurriedly asks, pointing to the bottom of the form, "This is your name? Alexander Whale?"

Alex nods.

Her focus is already elsewhere. "Waiting room's over there."

Alex moves to a bank of plastic chairs and sits down. It might be minutes or hours later when Dex occupies the seat next to him. Alex can't remember calling him. Dex puts his big hand on Alex's shoulder.

"You all right, son?"

Alex stares at his hands and the spot in front of his seat. "No. Chris took a bullet for me."

"You said it was your ex-brother-in-law. How bad was it?"

Alex shakes his head. "I don't know. It went through her waist. I don't think it's the kidney or any vitals. I hope not. She's lost a lot of blood, though, so I couldn't tell."

Dex leans forward to look Alex over, prompting him to notice the blood drying and darkening on his clothes. Dex lifts Alex's hand, twisting it from side to side. Alex's knuckles are raw and caked in blood. "You should get that seen to."

Tears swim in Alex's eyes. "Chris tried to protect me. She could die because of me."

Dex clears his throat, opens his mouth a couple of times. "The receptionist said the patient's a young guy. You're dating a man?"

Alex cocks his head. "Chris sometimes thinks they're a woman." That has come out wrong, but Alex doesn't have the words for it at that moment to explain the fluidity of Chris's gender.

"He has a penis, doesn't he?" Dex nods, as though he's convincing himself. "Then you're having a relationship with a man unless he's one of those…transsexuals?"

Alex looks over to Dex. "I wouldn't say that to Chris's face if I were you."

Coach's mouth forms an 'O', but there's respect there for what Chris did.

A dark shadow looms over Alex. He looks up to see Sam Taylor senior and some of his men standing like a brick wall in front of him. His ex-father-in-law is dressed in his usual sharp business suit. He stares hard at Alex, a massive frown between his brows. The dark, wild hair is now peppered with white strands.

Taylor is not tall, but there's something fierce about the man that demands attention.

Alex is Taylor's daughter's killer and now he's beat up his son pretty bad. The latter, though, was provoked by what he saw when he came home from work. If Alex had a bit less self-control, Ryan would be dead by now.

When Sam Taylor speaks, the harsh tobacco behind the voice hits Alex in the guts.

"I should have known the first time you came into my house that you're fucking trouble."

Alex met Samantha when they were nine years old—in the same class in primary school. He opens his mouth to speak, but Sam puts his hand up. "I know what went down. Who's that in emergency surgery?"

Alex swallows. "My boyfriend."

He is not going to have a third conversation about Chris's gender tonight, and certainly not with a gang boss from Essex whose son he's beaten to a pulp.

"So, what my men told me was true. You're now a fag. You surprise me, Alexander." He turns to Dex. "You know about this, Coach?"

The older man shakes his head. "It's all news to me as well."

Sam's sharp eyes flicker with contemplation. He leans down to keep his voice low. "No one's going to find the weapon. If they do, I have men who can identify the shooter. You got that?"

Alex stares at him and slowly nods.

"We're even on this one, but Ryan's mother's upset."

Alex knows Sam's mum well. She is as tough as her husband, but these few years have been hard on her. Alex feels bad for what he's done to her daughter and now her son.

"Please tell Jean I'm sorry." He can't apologise for thrashing Ryan. In fact, he and Ryan got on fine before the car accident. They weren't exactly like brothers, but they respected each other enough as in-laws went.

"Ryan will live. From what I heard, he deserved it."

Alex nods.

Sam's facial expression is unreadable for a few seconds before his frown deepens. "Cancel your match with Lewis Keane. We don't want any more media attention on the family."

Alex swallows. He thinks about it briefly, but he has no option but to accept Sam's truce. "Consider it done."

He gazes intently at the gang boss, neither resentful nor grateful for the man's discretion because Ryan and his henchmen had started it. Before Alex needs to say more, Taylor leaves as abruptly as he appeared.

Dex, having witnessed the whole exchange, pats Alex on his back as if to console him. Alex wonders how long he's going to be waiting before they tell him how Chris is. He has already bothered the reception desk of the surgical unit enough. He wants to pace like a caged animal, though he's considerate enough about the other people in the waiting room not to do it. Dex keeps them both in coffee supply.

Alex has lost track of time when more pairs of legs appear in front of him.

He lifts his head. Four police officers line up in front of him, officious in their black uniforms and white shirts and felt hats, their hands on the batons. *What the fuck?*

"Alexander Whale. Metropolitan Police. You're under arrest for assault. You do not have to say anything, but it may harm your defence if you do not mention when questioned something which you later rely on in court. Anything you do say may be given in evidence. Do you understand?"

Alex takes a deep breath and nods once. He can remember being read the rights five years ago like it was yesterday. An officer holds out a pair of handcuffs. Without protest, Alex lets him put the cuffs around his bloodied fists.

CHAPTER 14
RED

ALEX INSTRUCTS DEX as he's being led from the hospital. "Chris's phone should still be in the flat. Call Chris's mum. Her name's Annette. And call Liam."

Coach stares at the sea of officers' black escorting Alex away. They must have thought he would resist arrest and become violent. Alex would never fight the police when he knew he'd done wrong.

Dex approaches the nurses' station again and asks about the progress of Chris's surgery. When they learn that Dex is neither a relative nor close friend, they refuse to give him further information and suggest he contact Chris's relatives. Without any option, Dex goes to Alex's flat.

Their flatmates are appalled by the incident.

Alberto refers to Paul. "That twat. We'll chuck all his stuff out. I don't think he will dare to come back."

Dmitri frowns. "Do you need anything else for Chris?"

Dex shakes his head. "I don't know. The police took Alex from the hospital to the station. He didn't tell me to contact his family. He asked me to come here and find Annette and Liam. I'm not sure what Chris might need." Coach is a practical man and he wants to help, but at this moment in time, he feels out of his depth.

Alberto says, "To be honest, we don't know much about Alex. He keeps himself to himself. Chris is the one who's closest to him, y'know? They're like...really good friends."

Dmitri tuts. "Man. You can say it. They fucking sleep together."

Coach forces a smile. "Yeah, it's okay. I know. Don't think because I'm an old man I won't understand these things. I didn't know Alex liked men since he was married and all, but I'm not prejudiced."

Alberto shakes his head. "No, no. I wasn't trying to hide their relationship or anything like that, but I didn't know for sure."

"None of this 'special friend' bullshit. Alex is Chris's boyfriend," Dmitri informs the older man.

The Italian nods. He rubs his neck and comments with fascination on his face. "Anyhoo, I can't believe this kind of thing could happen in our flat. It's like an episode of TV drama! First the paparazzi, then a shootout. Under our roof!"

Dmitri gives him an eye-roll. "I don't think Dex has the time for that shit, Al."

Dex looks at his watch. "Sorry, but he's right. I'm meeting Liam and Annette at the hospital. I'd better head back in case Chris woke up from the operation. I'll let you know if there's any development. Thank you, my friends."

Alberto says, "I didn't do anything. I may go to see Chris when he's a bit better. Text us the details, please?"

"Okay." Alberto and Dex exchange numbers before Dex shakes their hands and rushes back to the hospital.

~~~

"The surgery was successful. He's very lucky. The shot went through here."

The doctor points to a poster of the body on the wall. The cartridge grazed the left side of their waist, as Alex told Coach. "The bullet missed vital organs, which is good, but he's lost a fair amount of blood. The wound is clean. We'll monitor him over the next three to five days to see how he is healing, to make sure there's no infection."

Dex nods numbly. Annette starts crying with relief. He puts his arm around her shoulder to comfort her.

Liam asks the surgeon, "When is Chris likely to wake up?"

The doctor glances at the clock on the wall. "I'd say in the next hour or so. He'll be very tired, though, so you can't stay long. I hope none of you are currently ill."

They shake their heads.

The surgeon dismisses them. "Okay, the nurses at the recovery room will issue you with scrubs and hats. You can have a few minutes with him."

Annette dabs her face with a tissue. She's as dolled up coming to the hospital as usual, but her concern for Chris seems genuine enough.

It feels as though they wait for hours until a nurse comes out of the ward. "Christoph's visitors? You can go in now. Keep it down and please don't touch him for now." She distributes the protective clothes and makes them all sterilise their hands.

Liam can't believe how pale Chris looks. Tubes and IV lines snake from their arms and under the blanket covering their body to the humming monitors and drips. Their eyes are closed.

Annette approaches first. "Chris darling," she whispers.

Chris opens their eyes, but they're glazed, as though they don't know where they are yet.

Liam approaches his friend. "Chris. How are you feeling, mate?"

Chris moves but then flinches. "Alex?"

Liam and Dex exchange looks. "Alex is not here at the moment. It's me, Liam. Dex and your mum are here too. Do you want your mum?"

Chris closes their eyes again, suffering from the lingering effects of the anaesthetic and exhaustion. Their voice is low and weak. "Alex. I want Alex." A single tear falls from the corner of their eye.

Annette gazes at Dex, who nods in support. "Alex had to report to the police station. How are you feeling, sweetie?"

"Why are you here?" Chris responds, their eyes hooded. "I want Alex. Why is he with the police?"

Dex comes forward. "He'll come to see you as soon as he can." He looks around to make sure the nurses are out of earshot before whispering, "Chris, the police will want to speak to you as soon as you're better. Remember you didn't know who fired the shot. It wasn't Ryan. Will you do that? It's important."

Chris watches Coach and forces the words out. "I didn't see who."

"No, you didn't."

Understanding flickers in Chris's eyes.

A nurse knocks and comes in at that moment. "He'll need to rest now. You can come back later, but I don't think the patient is going to be very responsive today. He'll be better tomorrow. Why don't you come back then? Visiting hours for the ward are two to nine."

Dex goes home to change. Liam and Annette stay on, but Chris sleeps until visiting hours are over.

~~~

"Where's Alex?" Chris asks Liam as soon as he arrives the next day. Chris's eyes are more open and alert, though their face remains pale as the hospital bedsheet.

Liam spoke to Annette the night before. It's Liam's call how much he's going to tell Chris, not that they know much about what's going on with Alex since his arrest. Liam leans forward to talk in a low voice.

"Alex was arrested for assault. That's why you have to keep his ex-in-laws' family happy, okay?" He turns around to check if anyone can hear them, just in case.

Chris shifts in bed and winces with the pain. "The police have kept him?"

Liam sighs. "He hasn't come back. I'll ask Coach to contact his family, to see if they know anything. I'm sorry, mate."

Chris grabs hold of Liam's hand, their palms cold and clammy. "Are they going to send him back to prison?"

Liam hurts for Chris. "I don't know." He squeezes Chris's hand. He has never seen them like this, caring about one of their lovers with all their heart. The hospitalised Chris has been stripped bare of their bullshit. With their pale face and fragile limbs, Chris looks like a frightened child lost in a busy place.

Desperate tears fall down their face. "Please, can you find out what has happened to him? Promise?"

Liam nods. Chris has always been there for him when he was homeless and struggling with his addiction. He must do everything he can for his friend now.

~~~

Alex contacted Dex from police custody.

"They want to charge him with grievous bodily harm," Dex tells Liam. "Ryan wouldn't cooperate with the police, so they've got nothing on Alex. Both Alex and Chris would have told them they didn't know who fired the shot."

Liam's brows furrow. "So, why are they keeping Alex?"

Dex sighs. "Parole violation. He was suspected of a serious crime and it was enough. Come on. They know Alex beat Ryan up, and they also know Ryan or one of his men shot Chris."

"So, why are they harassing Alex? Don't they have a criminal to catch?" Liam purses his lips.

"Because they can't bother Samuel Taylor, his son or his men."

Liam's mind is musical, not legal or criminal, and none of this makes sense to him. "What's going to happen to Alex?"

"The parole board will make a decision. They might have already. Alex only called me once after his arrest."

"What does that mean?"

Dex sighs. "They might send Alex back to prison."

"What a clusterfuck!" Liam wants advice from Coach. "What do you think I should say to Chris?"

"You know him. How is he going to react if you tell him the truth?"

"Coach, Chris loves Alex. They always put on a brave face, pretending they didn't give a shit about anyone.

This is… Chris is finally showing their true emotions. You tell me how they're gonna be."

~~~

Alex has been through this before, but it doesn't make it easier. Unlike last time, there's no crown court hearing, no barristers, no media circuit or the scrutinising eyes of the families he hurt. He met with the parole board and his probation officer in a small office. That was all.

They explained that a fixed-term recall of twenty-eight days was the minimum. Four long weeks.

He doesn't care that they have revoked his licence, but he desperately wants to stay with Chris, to see them wake up and know they're all right. The sense of complete powerlessness within the legal system only adds to his despair.

The police have been observing him.

Suicide watch.

A bench sits to one side of the holding cell, and it's covered by a plastic blue sheet. A washbasin occupies the other wall. Hard concrete floor and discoloured tiles surround him. Alex needs his medication, but he won't get it until they transfer him to prison. He has to see the doctor there, who will no doubt treat him like the scum he is. Alex stays on the narrow bed, his mind occupied with thoughts of how he has endangered Chris. In his brief call to Dex, Coach assured him that Chris would be fine, but it doesn't stop the all-consuming guilt.

The frantic fight for vengeance and Chris's bloodied body play in his mind all day long.

If there were something, anything, in the cell, he might have done it. The world is clearly better off without him. The thought of never seeing Chris's brilliant smile, though, is also killing him. Alex drowns in a whirlwind of mixed emotions. In between, he loses track of time and where he is.

The heavy door whooshes open; harsh light from the corridor hurts him as if his brain has burst. Alex hides his head under his hands. Where's the fresh blood from? It covers his knuckles.

Three burly guards charge in and grab him. Alex struggles against them, so they hold him and press him down, pushing his face hard against the cold concrete floor that smells of detergent and bleach. Dazed, he sees white spots. His nose throbs with a dull pain from the way the guards are restraining him. They handcuff him with his arms behind his back, cutting into his wrists, but they would have done so 'for his own protection'.

Alex is exhausted from his jumbled thoughts, from the emptiness of the cell, from the constant darkness that hangs around him like a millstone.

One of the policemen must have been a rookie because another has been speaking to him as if Alex was not there. "This one is waiting for psychiatric assessment, but since he's being transferred tomorrow, he'll be seen by the prison psych. Our job is to keep him alive here."

To keep him alive. Alex wishes he could *feel* alive, too.

As the metal door slams and locks, Alex's heart sinks further. He wishes they'd been more violent, to punish him for what he has done to Chris.

Heavy footsteps move away, but Alex can hear the young policeman ask, "Was that Alex Whale? He looked rough."

"Yeah, he was recalled…"

Alex closes his eyes to shut out the mix of expressed pity and disgust in the officers' conversation. *At least Chris can't see me like this.*

By the time Alex is transferred back to prison, he is numbed and dazed, though nothing can take away the pain inside. He needs to carry on. He must get to the other end. His only worry isn't whether he'll survive prison, but how Chris is doing.

A week later, the prison psychologist assesses him as a low-suicide risk. Alex doesn't agree with the diagnosis, but she gives him his antidepressants. Three weeks more, he's a free man again.

~~~

The closing of the gate behind him sounds final. Alex remembers last time, when he was completely hollowed out and

Gary took him home and tried to ply him with drinks, making him more desperate for calm and sanity. Then he met Chris that first night when they had the incredible and elegant dance up the stairs. Even in the dark, she was so radiant to him that he couldn't take his eyes off her.

Alex's stomach knots as he steps out into fresh air, but his apprehension eases when he sees Chris. She's waiting by Coach's car, wearing a long-sleeved plain cream and blue dress. Sharp features on her pale face with only a hint of pink on her cheeks and lips, she looks like a movie star—classic Hollywood Hepburn or Kelly. Alex gazes hard at Chris because he can see beyond the surface, beyond the way Chris dresses. The person beneath is so pure that she's willing to trade her life for his. So pure that Alex cannot match. He gasps.

Chris smiles and the clouds dissipate.

She was discharged from hospital after four days but immobile for another ten. In the four weeks inside, Alex managed to call Chris twice, but by the time she was well enough to arrange a visit, he was about to be released. Twenty-eight days have been far too long, like a lifetime compacted into a feature film. The emotions trapped behind bars now flood Alex, making him shiver.

Alex grabs Chris and kisses her, closing his eyes to inhale her unique spice and sweet jasmine. When they part, their eyes lock and Chris smiles again.

"I missed you so much." Alex touches her face to make sure she's there, that this isn't all an illusion. Even though twenty-eight days was finite, Alex had worried that a mysterious force was going to keep them apart.

Interruptus.

Chris is there in the flesh, right in front of him.

"Missed you too. It feels like we're on a film set. I'm playing the gangster's moll collecting her man from jail." Chris angles her head.

"Don't say that. It's not fucking funny. I'm no gangster and I have no intention of committing another crime for the rest of my life," Alex whispers, tears swimming in his eyes.

Coach coughs behind them.

Chris stands aside. Alex blinks to control his feelings and gives Dex a bear hug.

"Good to see you, son." Moments like this, he wishes Dex was his father. "Let's get you lovebirds home."

Chris covers her mouth to hide her chuckles.

Alex and Chris sit in the back of the car because they can't keep their hands off each other, or their mouths and lips for that matter. Dex pulls out of the parking space with a shrug. He has to look in the mirror, and the couple in the back seat barely notice. They break off, resting their foreheads against each other.

"Does it hurt?" Alex places his hand on Chris's waist.

She shakes her head. "It's still a little tender, but I'm fine."

Alex rubs the back of Chris's head and slides his hand down to her neck. He attacks her mouth again with his teeth and lips. Alex wants to taste, to savour, to binge on every sense of Chris-goodness. Chris opens her mouth and lets Alex invade her with his tongue; they want more and more of each other, like two kids who have been deprived of sweets for far too long.

Alex catches Coach's smile in the rear-view mirror. To Coach, Alex must seem the most content man on earth right now, despite the circumstances. The recall, the comeback tour that got cancelled and Sam Taylor's lingering threat all pale into insignificance.

When Chris and Alex break apart for another brief moment, Dex laughs at them. "Come on. Let me concentrate so I can take you two home and you can carry on in the bedroom!"

Alex grins and Chris blushes.

Dex leaves them alone as soon as he delivers them back at their apartment. Alex and Chris walk up the stairs hand in hand, breathless for no good reason. Chris leads Alex to her room.

Alex cups Chris's face in his hands. "Wait a minute. I need to wash the prison off me." At the mention of Alex in jail, tears fill Chris's eyes.

When Alex returns to her room, she's sitting on the bed in a thong and is almost done taking off her make-up. He remembers not so long ago, before the nightmare of the last month, he had asked her permission to have sex.

Alex sits on the edge of the bed. "Chris, I'm so sorry."

She puts her face cream away and gazes at Alex in surprise. "What for?"

"Everything." He extends his hand. "Come here. Please."

Chris does and sits cross-legged, facing Alex.

Alex touches the wound on her waist—a dark shape that doesn't look sore anymore, but she's going to have it as a permanent reminder of that horrific night.

"It's all my fault. My past, my crimes. How can you ask me why?"

Chris cocks her head and blinks. "But without your past, I wouldn't have met you."

The simple logic doesn't make things right.

"I brought them to you, and you were violated. I'm not sad at all that I beat Ryan up, but I wasn't there when you woke up, and I couldn't look after you. For that, I'm very sorry." Alex brings her close to him, their chests pressed together, his warm skin covering Chris.

"Ryan didn't do it. He didn't…he didn't get inside me." Her eyes are glittery with tears waiting to fall.

"Still." Alex would have beaten Ryan up again if he saw him now. "Why did you do it? Why did you put yourself between the bullet and me?"

"It was a split-second decision." Chris frowns as she thinks back to that day. "I did it for me. I was stopping Ryan getting what he wanted. He tried to rape me. At least I could die a heroine or some shit like that."

Quieter, she adds, "Fucked up, I know."

Alex knows that wasn't completely true, but he smiles. "Thanks for accidentally saving me." He kisses her. "You wouldn't have done it if it was someone else, though. You *are* my heroine."

Chris looks down, almost coy. "If you say so. I was more worried about you in jail than my recovery. I mean, once I knew I'd survived."

"Chris." Alex is so overwhelmed by the events of the last month that he can't find the words to express himself.

Chris winds her slender arms around Alex's body. "I missed you so much when I woke up and you weren't there, but Annette looked after me some. Can you believe it? Liam, Ali and Dex came and helped, too. And Alberto and Dmitri. All these people around me—I don't know what I've done to deserve them, but I was fine."

"They are around because you're an amazing person, Chris. I'm still sorry for my role in this."

Chris rests her head on Alex's broad shoulder. "Is that all you're going to do? Apologise? Hmm?"

Alex kisses her hair. "No. I seem to remember I was going to get laid that night when the fuck-up started. What a horrible interruption! So, do you think…I'm going to get lucky now?"

Chris pushes Alex away, and she smiles, two deep dimples appearing. Instead of answering, she claims Alex's mouth. The kiss is full of hunger and lust, and it sucks the air out of Alex. Chris removes the towel from Alex's waist and marvels at his arousal.

"Alex, you're so special to me. I don't know how to do this. I thought I had the right to use my body any way I wanted. You've given me the real power. You'll stay around, won't you?"

Alex promises, "Of course."

In one clean move, Chris straddles Alex's thighs, pushes him down on the bed and kisses him along his neck and down his chest. She sucks on his erect nipples until he moans and then moves her mouth down the faint line of hair to his groin, burying her smooth face in Alex's pubic hair, still damp from the shower. She sucks the hell out of Alex's dark crown.

"Jeez, Chris. Not so quick. You're gonna hurt yourself, sweetheart. I want us to enjoy this. I can't come yet!" Alex focuses, determined to savour this magical moment.

Chris looks up, pre-cum smeared around her mouth. "You look out for my well-being first. That's so sweet."

"Chris, your waist—"

"I don't care."

She takes Alex's cock in her mouth again, all the way to the back of her throat. It's been years since someone deep-throated him, and his vision bursts with the sudden surge of arousal. "Fuck!" He shifts to see her face. "Chris, what about you? What do you need?"

She seems determined to see Alex unravel as quickly as she can. She reaches out to her bedside table and yanks the drawer out with such force the whole thing falls out, revealing numerous packs of condoms and other supplies.

Alex draws his knees up. Chris removes her mouth from Alex's cock only to lick her fingers. She returns to blowing Alex and inserts her wet finger into his arsehole. It feels strange and cold at first, but Chris has already found where he is the most sensitive. The strokes alongside the rhythm of Chris's teasing are giving Alex brand-new sensations.

She releases him for a moment. "Alex, I need you to fuck me. It's been a long time coming. I'm very horny." She looks at him with such intensity, her turquoise eyes seem ablaze in the chill of the room. She tears open the condom and sheathes Alex quickly, then she spreads lube everywhere. She lies down on her right side and draws up her knees.

Alex stares at Chris's perfect arse and then cups it in his hands and pulls her back. Aligning the tip of his dick, he pushes in. Alex has always enjoyed anal, but he can't believe how Chris feels as she yields, pushing back, engulfing him and tightening around his erection. Alex's right hand holds the back of Chris's head, while his left steadies himself on Chris's left shoulder.

"Is this okay?" he asks, knowing his own size and strength, and worrying about Chris's wound.

Chris squeezes around his cock as an answer. "'S more than okay."

Alex starts to thrust. He doesn't want to hurt Chris, but her incoherent moans are too sexy and he loses himself as he picks up speed. When he shifts, he hits Chris's sensitive spot, enough for her to shout out, "Faster, harder. Don't fucking stop."

Alex complies, pulling out and pushing back in at the same spot. Chris rocks back at the same time. Soon the two of them are moving the bed, its headboard knocking against the wall. Chris grabs Alex's hand to cover hers, and they milk Chris's cock in unison. Their hips dance, smooth and graceful at first. Alex can't shift easily, but it's okay; he needs to be gentle. Chris starts to clench around him, her movements soon becoming wilder and more sensual. Then she erupts and arches back like a last jump before collapsing in Alex's embrace in a boneless form.

"Do you want me to come, Chris? I don't have to."

Chris mumbles, "Yes."

Alex resumes. Within seconds, he feels the build-up of the tingling feeling in his balls. He yells and thrusts until he sees stars bursting. The waves come more intensely as he shouts like an animal, primal and frenzied, screaming for the plateau.

Sex felt different before when he was with Sam or other partners. Alex used to play the active role in bed, while Chris and Alex are equal, neither dominating the other.

Their breathing rhymes as if they are playing a finale before it eventually slows to a murmur.

Alex withdraws and takes off the condom. "I hope I didn't hurt you."

Chris turns around and hooks her leg over Alex's. "I feel a tug, but the wound shouldn't tear open now. You made such sweet love to me."

Alex sighs. "It was sweet. Different."

Chris looks at him intently. "I hope it's a good difference. I mean, I don't know how this goes…"

Alex frowns. "What do you mean? I'm not being…but you're the professional here?"

Chris's laughter betrays bitterness and uncertainty. "Yeah, I can do it on the job. I do it with my hookups, but sex is a series of physical actions and reactions. It's disappointing like my life. I liked that I didn't have to have high expectations of my sexual partners, and they didn't think much of me other than what I could deliver because I did it with everyone, right? I might be a confident performer, but sex meant little for me. So, yeah. My sense of sexual performance is absolutely screwed."

Alex considers Chris and nods with understanding. "Was it a performance?"

"Oh, hell, no!" Chris shakes her head. "No. I tried very hard not to perform. Was it rubbish?"

Alex smiles. "If that's rubbish, I'll happily have bad sex with you the rest of my life. But...I see where you're coming from. Perhaps you've been giving too much in bed. Clue me in so I know how to make you feel good, okay?"

"Okay." Chris beams.

Alex leans in to claim her mouth again, his palm holding her close, his lips chasing hers. Chris gives. Their tongues circle each other and twist as if they're resuming the dance. They snake around each other until they run out of air.

Chris breaks away and considers all of Alex, naked and true. "You have a boxer's body and a fighter's mind. You're so beautiful, Alex Whale."

Few people see Alex's harsh lines, brokenness and loyalty as beauty. Only Chris.

~~~

There is a time when lovers are discovering each other's bodies and they want to navigate every contour and fold, reading them as if drawn on a map.

The scar is a faded line, across Alex's cheekbone. Chris touches it, her finger feather-light on his rough skin. She moves the tip across to the small kink on the bridge of Alex's nose that mesmerises her; she touches the scar, and Alex shudders and closes his eyes.

"Where did the scar come from?" she asks.

Alex inhales deeply. "The accident."

Chris whispers, "Tell me about it if you want."

Alex opens his eyes.

"I haven't... The police took a statement from me when I was supposed to be sober and calm enough. I was prescribed medication for PTSD—tranquillisers first, then sleeping pills, antidepressants. The judge ordered an injunction against the media reportage of some of the details." Alex hesitates.

He picks up Chris's hand. "You risked your life for me, so I owe you the truth. If I tell you, you'll think I'm a worse person than you could ever imagine."

Chris kisses him. "I won't. You see, people think certain things about me, but no one gets me more than you do. I want to know everything about you, Alex. I don't believe you're capable of truly ugly things because I've found beauty in you. Anyway, I'm used to pretty people and nice things that are rotten inside. You're kinda the opposite."

Alex swallows. Silence stretches while he gathers the words.

Fortifying himself with a deep breath, he begins, "I didn't only kill Sam and the other driver that night, Chris."

Chris's turquoise eyes dilate. "What do you mean?"

Alex shakes his head again and squeezes the bridge of his nose. He sighs. Chris holds on to his hand, refusing to let go while Alex recites his nightmare.

CHAPTER 15
WHITE

I TOLD MYSELF I wouldn't fall into the same trap as other successful athletes and celebrities. The lifestyle of being away from home, training hard, then playing hard. But I did. I came from a family of drunks, and I hated myself for drinking and taking party drugs. I had to be careful because of the drug tests. I took cocaine and amphetamines because I knew how they worked and when they'd be out of my system. I'd had plenty of sex with starlets and models that I now regret.

Sam snorted coke too, with a habit much worse than mine since she didn't need to worry about being busted. I was out of touch with what she did while I stayed in London and trained.

I was home in Essex during a three-week break and we argued a lot about stupid little things like another car or something for the house or whatever she wanted to spend my hard-earned money on. Sam had a go at me for the phone calls I was receiving on my mobile.

Who the fuck was it? You'd better not be keeping a mistress up in London.

There were women but never a mistress. Despite everything, I loved her with all my heart. We grew up together, and there was no one who could ever replace Sam for me. I knew I shouldn't be unfaithful to her, but I justified it by the fact that I loved only her, so everyone else was there to scratch an itch. I felt like a real bastard while trying to stay on top of my game and providing for her and my family. We argued and argued, had fights when we were drunk and drugged up.

That day, she got high and she was mad at me for something. I had tuned out because the arguments were always the same. I went to my home gym and worked out. Sam came in and she was furious like a big black cloud had descended on her. She tore at my clothes and said I didn't touch her anymore. I did. We'd had sex a couple of times since I came home: angry, make-up sex rather than something between two people who love each other. She was bawling her eyes out, telling me I had stopped loving her. It wasn't true.

I tried to keep her still in my arms. It wasn't hard given she was a slender thing and about a foot shorter than me. I almost cried thinking somehow I'd hurt her. I didn't know how to make her happy anymore, how not to upset her whenever I came home to Essex. She stormed off.

I buried my head in my hands, sitting on the floor in the gym. My physical strength was an illusion because I was emotionally broken. I hadn't faced the fact that I'd been suffering from depression.

When she returned, she shoved a pregnancy test in my hand. Two red lines in the small window. I stared at it, but I was confused.

"What?" I asked.

She rubbed her eyes, her make-up already smudged. "Positive. I'm fucking pregnant, Alex."

I'd been on a bender. I ogled her, trying to understand what she was telling me. I assumed that she was pregnant with our child. Why wouldn't she be? Shouldn't she be happy? Shouldn't we look forward to being parents? My thoughts were going wild in ten different directions.

"That's great, isn't it?" I asked when I saw the frown on her face.

She hit my head with her fists. "It's probably not yours. D'you know what I'm saying to you, you stupid twat?"

Her tear-streaked face came into focus. "What do you mean? I'm glad we're having a baby. Don't you want it? Why?" We hadn't used contraceptives for a year or so even though we didn't discuss it. I thought she had wanted a kid, and it was fine by me.

She pushed me again. "Wake up, Alexander. I wasn't going to tell you. I was going to have an abortion as soon as you went back to London."

I became angry then. *Why is she getting rid of our baby? Why was she going to lie to me?* The alcohol was clouding my head, so I couldn't think straight.

"It might be Charlie Tait's." She added this last bombshell in a whisper.

Charlie was one of her dad's henchmen, for want of a better word. He was younger than us, and he always seemed like an arrogant prick to me. Sam's face was close to mine, and now I saw the challenge in her eyes. She was taunting me.

My vision went nuclear.

"What the fuck? You're fucking Charlie Tait! Bitch." I spat the last word out. I would regret everything I said and did that day.

"Yeah, when you've got a woman up in London," she shouted back. "Why shouldn't I fuck whoever the fuck I want?"

"Stop saying that. I don't have a woman in London."

It didn't matter. Sam was venomous.

"Do the fucking maths, Alex. It's been six weeks or so since we had sex. What if I don't know whose baby this is?" She put her hands on her belly.

"How many months are you, then?"

She shrugged. "The doctor said eight weeks. You weren't here eight weeks ago, Alex."

I was furious. It could have been mine if the doctor was wrong, but I knew in my heart Sam was pregnant with Tait's baby. I was desperate to go and find Charlie and kill him. The image of Sam having sex with him enraged me.

"Fucking bastard. How many times? How long have you been having an affair?" I shook her. She felt so vulnerable in my strong grip.

"No, I wouldn't call it an affair." Her eyes reddened, but she refused to look at me.

"How many times?" I demanded again. *Does it matter, Alex?*

"I don't know." Her voice was small and pathetic, and full of regret.

I slapped her but took care not to hurt her. Even in that state of mind, I wouldn't harm her. I couldn't beat her up. She bawled and said she was sorry.

Sam held on to me and wouldn't let go. We bickered some more and fought. Deep down, I knew it wasn't Charlie's fault. Even if it was not him, it would have been someone else. I drank some more alcohol—whiskey or brandy, I can't recall—and I did a few more lines. Anything to numb myself until I had to face all the problems in our relationship. I asked Sam to stop drinking. If I'd known she was pregnant, I wouldn't have let her drink and take drugs, but she was already high. All afternoon, I tried to persuade her to keep the baby. Even with a chance that the baby wasn't mine, I didn't want her to get rid of it. I would support her. She cried some more and said she was sorry.

I felt like my whole world was crumbling into dust, and I didn't know what to do other than to stop myself feeling through more alcohol.

At some point, we had sex, the kind of after-argument sex when we were raw and emotional. Sam agreed that she wouldn't have a termination. Instead of relief, I felt completely, utterly exhausted from everything: from the fights, from being there with her. I wanted to escape back to London and my training even though she needed me to comfort her. I planned to go back to the city the next day to give us some breathing space. We could talk about things later.

It was early evening when Sam told me she'd been having backaches and cramps. She had started bleeding, and soon it turned heavier with blood clots.

My Sam was wild. I loved her for that. She panicked and was hysterical. I felt helpless, so I carried her out to my car without thinking whether I was fit to drive. That's what being a destructive drunk does to you. I was coming down and was more sober than earlier, but I was still too intoxicated to drive. All I thought was that I needed to take her to the hospital.

She didn't put the seat belt on.

No one knew about the baby other than her family. The details all came out during the court case, hidden from the public because of the media reporting restrictions. Sam's dad would have killed me if not for the fact that they had all known about her affair with Charlie and they never told me. The pregnancy and the miscarriage had completely tipped me over the edge. My father-in-law had some sympathy for me. The judge took pity and gave me a lighter sentence.

The road was windy and narrow, and it was dark. The night was opaque, as though the moon had decided not to appear at all. The bright headlights approached out of nowhere, dazzling me, sending me into a tailspin. I was speeding along on an icy surface in deep winter.

Tipped over the edge. I remember feeling free for a moment, a split second when I was flying. The moment was cathartic but far too fleeting.

I woke up in the hospital with this scar and screaming. Sam had died instantly. She was having a miscarriage. The other man drove a small family car, and, against my fast sports car, there was no way he was going to survive.

~~~

An innocent man and the family he'd left behind. Sam shouldn't have died either. Alex should be the one being punished. That's why he accepts the hopelessness, the guilt, the depression and insomnia as his punishments.

"I wish every day, every waking hour that I could take back that momentary lapse in judgement," Alex concludes.

Chris has been holding Alex's hand, and now teardrops fall on her arm. She looks up.

"You didn't kill the baby."

"Didn't I?" Alex is overcome by grief, sadness and self-hatred. "If I hadn't crashed the car, Sam might have survived. It might have been mine. I wouldn't have cared either way. I'd have been happy to be a dad." Alex rakes his fingers through his messy hair.

Chris is speechless.

"This was…is my crime. I've had nightmares. They come almost daily. In them, I always hold Sam in my arms after the crash and she is bleeding to death right there. I try to scream, but no sound ever comes out. In reality, I couldn't move in the wreck and I couldn't reach her. I was trapped unconscious behind the damn airbag until they managed to pull me out. I couldn't comfort her in her last moments. What kind of husband was I?"

Alex trembles so Chris moves closer and hugs him tightly. "One fucking mistake, and my whole world just…"

Crumbled. Destroyed.

Chris holds on to Alex and lets him cry.

"I've never cried like this in front of anyone."

"You cry all you need, honey. You have a heart."

Finally, Alex lifts his head and asks, "Do you still want me, Chris?"

Chris kisses his scar so tenderly it breaks him all over again. "Yes. Why wouldn't I?"

Alex lowers his head, and points to his chest. "Because this here is dead. What would you do with that?"

Chris puts her hand over Alex's heart, then places it over hers. "I'll take your broken heart and you can have mine. It's not pretty, either, but it's yours if you want it. You know, like an organ transplant? It's a few years younger if nothing else."

Alex nods and forces a smile. "I'll cherish it…cherish you. I want you. If you ask me what my intentions are, I'll love and care for you if you let me."

"I do. We sound like we're exchanging bloody wedding vows."

Alex has given his promise and she hers.

"Do you want a wedding? You'll look great in a white dress." Alex seems serious.

Chris pushes him in jest. "No, I won't. Who's going to marry you anyway, Big Blue?"

"You love this big man." Alex kisses Chris with force, bruising her lips.

"Oh, fuck off! We should be taken out to be shot. People making promises to each other…are clearly wrong in their heads. Gah!"

Chris feigns annoyance when they break off for breath, but her flushed cheeks tell a different story. Alex forces a smile despite the wet tears clinging to his cheeks.

~~~

Alex faces Sam Taylor's mansion for the first time since his crime. As he approaches the tall black gates, two security guards step forward. They eye Alex up in the most unfriendly and threatening way possible.

"You're trespassing on private property." One of Taylor's men challenges Alex, flexing his muscular arms in preparation for confrontation. His padded jacket likely conceals some kind of weapon he might draw on Alex.

Unintimidated, Alex pushes his chest out. "I want to see your boss, Samuel Taylor. Can you tell him Alex Whale is here?"

Alex never likes to throw his weight about, but there is no other way for him to get close to his ex-father-in-law.

The two guards look at each other because Alex's name still commands attention. After several beats, the one who spoke tells Alex, "Wait here."

He walks back towards the house while talking into his mobile.

Alex turns away, squinting at the sun behind his dark glasses. He has impulsively come to talk to Sam Taylor, and now as he waits, nerves creep in. A good ten minutes pass before the guard returns and asks Alex to follow him. His colleague stares with the same coldness, reminding Alex of a hawk considering its prey.

Nothing much has changed in Taylor's sitting room. The TV got bigger in his absence. The leather sofa is new. The décor's bold and expensive, but Alex hasn't a clue how to judge the aesthetic taste of Taylor's home.

"What is it you want, Alexander?" Sam's voice has always been gruff as if he smokes forty a day. As far as Alex knows, the gang boss doesn't touch cigarettes. Whiskey and cigars, yes, but not ciggies. His sharp eyes penetrate Alex as though tempting him to spill all his secrets.

Alex watches the older man sit in the plush sofa. He swallows to prepare himself.

"I cancelled the tour, or rather, the main sponsor dropped me after I went back to jail."

Sam is quiet for a few seconds, then he nods with slow deliberation. It dawns on Alex. Tony, the promoter, the sponsor, and everyone else involved should have been madder than they were. Sam Taylor and Alex's gazes meet with the flicker of recognition.

"You paid them off, didn't you?"

Sam inhales. "I oiled the wheels, Alex. Your sponsor was a bit dicey about your comeback gig anyway after you were recalled." He views the younger man levelly.

"Thanks. It's worked out fine for everyone," Alex admits.

He didn't want to fight in the first place. It would have drawn too much media attention back to the original court case and Sam Taylor's family. Neither of them want that. Alex wonders how Ryan is. Chris gave a statement to the police while they were still in the hospital, claiming they didn't see who shot them. Taylor's men managed to persuade the law that the man had fled the scene with the gun, which was never recovered.

The older man taps his ringed fingers on his lap. "Anything else?"

The honest answer is anything and nothing. Alex can do little to ease the pain he has caused. Taylor is a hard and dangerous man, but he is also devoted to his family. Alex looks intently at Sam's lined face. His dead wife resembled her father, except the blonde hair. Something bitter bubbles in his throat, threatening to gag him.

Alex stands shakily and approaches Taylor. He drops to his knees, his fists hitting the ground beside him. Chris has taught him that men can cry, so he lets his tears run down his face freely. Five years of hurt and remorse erupt and Alex has no desire to stop them.

"I'm sorry. So sorry."

Alex's voice is breaking, the words barely coming forth, and they are suffocating him. He gasps, trying to breathe. He should have done this a long time ago. He loved Sam so fucking much. In one moment, he destroyed two families.

He would repent. Then, now, and forever.

Through the tears, Alex can see his ex-father-in-law's feet and the shiny dress shoes. Taylor lets him cry. The mansion is silent but for his sobs. Somewhere in the distance, a clock ticks and it sounds like his beating heart, the one he has exchanged with Chris. Chris didn't have much more than him, but they gave it anyway. Chris has been like a balm soothing Alex enough for him to carry on.

Eventually, Sam's rough hands are in front of Alex, taking his arms and pulling him up.

"I know, son."

When Alex faces Sam again, he can see tears on the older man's face. Two small rivulets that are drying, as if he, too, has been healing and coming to terms with his family tragedy.

~~~

Liam and Ali come along to help Alex and Chris move even though their meagre possessions hardly merit the extra people power. Still, Ali is the designated driver. With a borrowed van, Ali and Alex have already transported the larger items—Chris's double bed and wardrobe, Alex's training equipment and a small dining table that Ali has donated to them.

Liam peers out of the car window on the way to the new flat, licking his lips in contemplation.

"Wow, Green Lanes. You guys are going to move to suburbia soon," he teases.

They've chosen to move north, along a thoroughfare of Turkish businesses. Liam reminds Chris that when she came to see the flat, she couldn't hear a word of English on the bus. It was almost exclusively Spanish and Turkish.

Chris muses, "That's me. Two point nine children and a semi-detached house."

Ali interjects, "Two point four."

"Nearly three, aren't we contributing to the human race in a reproductive way!"

Liam says, "They say two point four, Chris."

Deadpan as always, Chris ignores them. "I was a champ at maths in school, me. Decimal, dismal."

Alex shakes his head and smiles, joined by Ali and Liam.

"The flat's nothing fancy, I'm afraid. You'll see," Alex tells their friends.

"We can't afford anything else. Alex wants to leave his security job soon, and I want to work as little as possible. My arse is getting old."

Liam rolls his eyes. "Jeez, Chris! We don't want to hear about your anatomical details."

Chris has kept some regulars, but she's thinking of other part-time jobs. Money will be tight if she gives up sex work altogether, but for once in her life, she has plans for her future and they involve Alex. She's going back to school and looking for some other work experience.

Alex and Chris are holding hands, grinning with contentment in the back seat.

Liam half turns around. "I was only teasing. I'm so proud of you, Chris. So happy for you two. You guys are too sickly sweet." He asks his boyfriend, "Hey, what do you think?"

Ali, the quieter one, beams but offers no comment. Alex rubs Chris's neck and they gaze into each other's eyes and smile.

Ali and Liam help with the unloading and stay for a coffee, but they make an excuse to leave so that Chris and Alex can cherish their first night alone in their new accommodation.

~~~

It has been an exhausting day. Excitement and euphoria from finally moving out of the shithole they've lived in are quickly followed by apprehension. Chris has never lived with someone. No one has gone past all his defences to reach the three-month stage, let alone this kind of commitment.

Caresses.

Alex traces his fingers down Chris's smooth chest. "It feels great to have our own place, but it's been a long time since I lived with a partner. You're not only starting a life with me. You'll have to live with my depression."

"Oh, honey. Believe me, my life with Annette has tooled me up to deal with personal crises."

"I'm not sure if I can always get it up. It's a side effect… You're probably looking for some steaming sex. The woody when I sleep next to you? It sometimes disappears when I touch myself. I can't always revive the little fucker."

Chris kisses the line of hair down Alex's front to shut him up. He lifts his face. "You were great the other night. I don't care about that, Alex. We'll take it as it comes. Remember, whatever happens, it won't change how I feel about you."

"I want you so much. Some days I feel as though my dick doesn't belong to me anymore." Alex sounds frustrated.

Chris chuckles. "Because it belongs to me now. Personally, I think sex is overrated. Look at the exorbitant prices people pay me." He winks at Alex.

Chris teases the head of Alex's semi-hard dick with his cool fingertips, and Alex's cock jumps. Chris sits up, observing Alex's body and grinning as if he hasn't a care in the world.

"Alex, this is what I call an erection, and I'm happy to see it."

He moves down again and uses his palm to massage Alex's balls while licking and sucking him at the same time. The divine smell of Alex down there engulfs him. He indulges in Alex's unique scent. Doing this in their own space means so much for Chris, this momentous, beautiful thing infused with yearning and a knowledge that Alex is all he wants. Being with

Alex feels like the first non-fucked-up thing Chris has done in his entire life.

He wraps his mouth around Alex's cock, and Alex follows Chris's lead, pushing himself deeper down Chris's throat.

"I've been wanting you...so much." Alex's quivering voice is low and tender.

Chris lifts his eyes and considers Alex, contemplating all his solid flesh and boldness, his past, his present laid out for Chris to explore. Chris cannot tear his eyes away from Alex. He loves Alex—a feeling that has been so alien—as if he has learned to see the world anew.

Alex gazes at Chris intently, as though he understands this fragile, yet strong, connection between them.

"I love you too, Chris."

Chris smiles, happiness reaching every part of his face. "Our first time wasn't a fluke. You haven't forgotten how to have sex after all."

He returns to Alex's cock. He has one purpose now—to make Alex feel good, to chase his demons away. Alex has awakened his latent superpowers.

They face each other with Chris hooking his legs around Alex's powerful body. Alex closes his eyes. Chris's senses heighten, shrouded in Alex's heat. They move in unison as Alex chases his orgasm. He wraps his big hands around Chris's erection and strokes until Chris lets out a deep and primal groan and comes.

"I'm getting addicted to your post-sex smile. I want to make you happy like that," Alex says.

Alex's rough fingertip skates across the scar; it's faint but still noticeable close up. On Chris's inner thigh, the three-inch line starts close to his arsehole.

Chris touches the mark as he tells Alex his secret.

~~~

I was living in another shared flat. This guy moved in, and he was a bodybuilder type. We didn't get on, but I wasn't too bothered.

I never had problems before in the flat, letting the other sharers know what I did for a living. But I could see something dangerous lurking behind the glint in his eyes when he found out I was an escort, as though he had me in his viewfinder. I avoided him like a plague, but he used to creep me out on purpose: being too close and making transphobic remarks because of how I look. One day, I'd slept late and he should have been at work.

I had woken up about two in the afternoon and got up to use the bathroom. I wore a long T-shirt. When I came out of the bathroom, he was standing there, smoking and watching me, his eyes travelling up and down my body, leaving me vulnerable to his hatred.

"What the fuck do you want?" I asked.

He licked his lips. "Why don't you suck my dick? I'm sure you're pretty good to get paid for it. A pair of firm lips you've got there."

He was wearing sweatpants that were faded and too small for him. His hand meandered to his groin where the pale grey fabric stretched.

"Are you fucking serious?" I spat and turned to go back into my room, but he grabbed me from behind and pulled me back.

I elbowed him and tried to wriggle out of his hold. He was a brawny gym rat, so he was way stronger. His iron grip was hurting me.

"Get your hands off me." I twisted and brought my knee up to kick him in his nuts.

He only tightened his hold and laughed at my attempt. The more I struggled, the more he managed to lock me with his arm. I can still remember the anchor tattoo on his skin, the fading blue seeming too vivid on the tan arm. The only advantage I had was my height, but he was trained and recognised he needed to drag me down. He used his arm to choke me and pull me onto the floor.

I was breathless, but I elbowed him again and kicked out my legs in the hope I'd loosen his hold. I upturned the coffee table and everything on it scattered on the floor. I thought about dying on that dirty carpet with the contents of the ashtray and the empty beer cans.

"Stop fucking moving, Chris."

The anchor was still right under my chin when I felt a cold, blunt object against my neck. It was a flick knife. I froze, sweat chilling my skin.

"How about this? You'll have a hard time selling yourself with a long scar on your pretty face, right?" Glee filled his words.

My body stiffened. I couldn't take any chances. I went still, paralysed by his threat.

"Thought so. Stop fucking moving."

"What do you want?" I asked, my voice barely audible.

"I wanna fuck you. I've never had a man-whore before. I bet your arse is tighter than most pussies."

I couldn't do anything but comply, while the tip of the knife pressed against my neck. He pushed me into his bedroom.

"Strip off. What are you waiting for?"

He raped me. He was harsh, brutal and laughing at me the whole time. He must have seen me in my dresses sometimes because he kept calling me a dirty slut and a freak. Hopelessness gripped me while I was face down on the bed, and I let him get away with it. I was thankful when I heard him open the condom packet.

The familiar crinkly sound brought a sense of worthlessness.

As soon as he finished, I got up to dress, but he grabbed my hair and pushed me back down on the mattress. I had longer hair that I usually tied up then. I stared at his ugly face.

I hissed as the sharp pain seared through my body.

Wanting to escape as soon as I could, I hurriedly dressed, while he laughed at me.

"A little reminder for you freaks out there." He used his thumb and forefinger to lift my face up. "And I wouldn't tell a soul if I were you. Anyway, no one's going to believe a pretty whore like you, are they?"

He released me finally. "Now get out of my room."

I rushed back to my room and saw how he had shanked me. I used only tissue to stop the blood, enough to pack my stuff and leave, and I never returned.

~~~

Chris's eyes are full of unshed tears, glimmering in the soft light in their bedroom. He uses his fingertips to dry off the moisture.

Alex's jaw clenches. "What the fuck! And you never reported him?" His fists tighten, as though he is ready to kill the man.

Chris shakes his head. "He was right. Who'd believe me? Or care?"

Alex pulls him close in a tight hug. "They should. I do. He might hurt other people like you." He kisses Chris tenderly.

"Like me, huh? After the attack, I hated myself so much. I knew it wasn't my fault, but it didn't make it easy to like myself. No one respects me."

"Oh, Chris. You have a pure heart. Did no one tell you that?" Alex kisses Chris's cheek. "Was that before or after the attack on the street?"

"It was after. Yeah, these things keep happening to me because why? I am queer. I sell my body, so that implies I'm cheap. I couldn't fight a group of men intent on hurting me or a psycho who thought it was all a bit of fun. I can only protect myself. Sorry if I don't try to help other people because it's fucking hard enough as it is to help me!"

Chris sniffles.

"Ryan and his men. That's my fault. I'm so sorry, Chris."

Chris was glad to accept help that day.

"Hey, we've been through this. It's their fault. No one else's. Men like them think I'm fair game because of the way I look, my profession. I hate them." Chris's voice breaks with the heartache.

"No, you don't hate, not really. You always survive because you're so strong and…together. You know that, right?"

Nonetheless, Chris has pushed the experiences to the netherland of his consciousness so he can ignore them. "You think I'm together because I refuse to let the bastards win?"

Instead of answering, Alex kisses him again. "Why don't you cry? Hmm?"

Chris huffs. "I've cried myself dry too many times, Alex. I have few tears left."

Alex plants more kisses on Chris. "I'm right here. If you find those tears, I'll lend you my shoulders or chest."

Chris smiles. "There's a lot of you for me to cry on."

"Exactly." Alex pats the back of Chris's head as though he's comforting a child. So Chris cries, remembering things he doesn't want to. Small details of the attack, the man's tattoo. Snippets of insults he'd hurled at him. The cheesy-sock smell of his attacker's bedsheet. After a long time, since there's a lot to remember, he stops. Alex's skin is soaked through because he has offered his body to catch Chris's sorrows.

Chris sits up and straddles Alex's massive thighs. "Y'know, my middle name is Jay. Christoph Jay Neeser. Annette's family moved to England from Germany."

Annette's lilt, hardly detectable, comes from her German origin.

Alex touches Chris's nipples. "Your name's beautiful."

Chris reaches for his phone and taps something in search. He hands the phone to Alex. "Could you read this for me, honey?"

"Blue jay breeds in both deciduous and coniferous forests... Sexes are similar in size and plumage." Alex looks up to meet Chris's gaze.

Chris points to an image of the North American species. "The blue and white together are pretty. Don't you think?"

That piques Alex's curiosity. "And your point?"

Chris gets like this. His mind operates a hundred miles per hour, travelling in several directions at once.

"Annette taught me very little, but this she told me when I was about four and I still remember. My dad's Canadian and from the Algonquin country park. He was a big fan of the Toronto Blue Jays, the famous baseball team. He gave me nothing but the sperm and my middle name. And now the jaybird has found Blue!"

~~~

Alex smiles.

It's Chris's lyrical mind, even though he knows nothing about literature or prose. Chris, like the blue jay, has become a beautiful creature, dazzling Alex every day and adding elegant stanzas to the poetry in their lives.

CHAPTER 16
PRIDE

I'LL WRITE YOU a reference. I can say you've been my carer for... How long have we known each other, Chris?" Jeff squeezes her hand.

Chris gazes at Jeff, thinking about their long friendship. "Six years? On and off. Fuck! You've seen me lose my baby fat... But what I've been doing with you is not exactly personal care—"

"Rubbish!" Jeff barks, but not with menace. "You're better than any of these community nurses I see. Sure, they cover the procedures and make sure I take my ART and stay healthy. I look forward to you coming every week. Don't tell me I'm too old and senile to notice. You bring expensive massage oils, nice food, takeaways, trashy magazines and art books for me to read. You're paying to come to work and I let you because I know you'll argue otherwise. You *care* about me."

Chris can't help but smile. "Busted. I don't know. It'd sound silly if I told you I see you as a friend, sometimes even a parental figure cuz I don't have one of those. I know I have this messed up sense of the world, but it's nice to pretend I'm not only an escort once in a while."

"You are not only an escort. Not to me. That's it. Life's too short to mind whatever you call me or however you think of yourself. I'll provide a reference when you need it." Jeff beams at Chris with warmth.

Chris kisses Jeff's cheek. "Thank you. I need better GCSE grades, too, so I'll have to start with those. Damn. Twenty-seven years old and going back to school. It's fucking embarrassing!"

Jeff chucks Chris's cheeks as if she's a child. "It's not. It's a disgrace that this country's education system couldn't put a clever girl like you through school. It's a damn shame. Now, you go and show them how it should be done."

Chris laughs, though she's still scared of the prospect of 'returning to school'. She remembers how it was: the bullying from the other kids about her gender, the teacher's indifference. If the school and teachers realised she had a learning difficulty and a troublesome home life, they did nothing to help.

~~~

Chris stands outside the youth centre, greedily smoking their second cigarette.

Come on. You've looked forward to starting, so why are you so scared?

Right. Before they allow themself to think twice and turn back, they push the door open to the drab building.

The weekly LGBTQ youth group meets on the ground floor of a nondescript multistorey block in Kentish Town, North London. It's as noisy and scary as Chris imagined. So at least no surprise awaits. On the walls of the room hang several boards packed with notices, posters and bits of paper, photos and artwork, some barely clinging on. What frightens Chris most are the dozen or so teenagers who scatter around. A group of three surround the pool table, waiting their turns. Another couple are shooting table-football. Four sit around a bench with their heads over workbooks. Two sit on a tattered sofa talking, their faces animated. Hip-hop pipes out of the stereo system, though it's not too loud that the participants can't converse.

Chris swallows. They move over to the homework table and clear their throat to catch the attention of one of them, a girl in her early teens. When she looks up, Chris realises that she's most likely assigned male like them. The teenager wears a long bob and dark nail varnish, reminding Chris of themself when they were her age. Chris smiles and relaxes a little. They may be able to relate to the kids if they're going through what Chris experienced when they were younger.

"Ah, I'm here to see Rosie. Do you know where I can find her?"

The teenager scowls and shouts, "Rosie! Someone here to see you!"

She sounds as though her voice has just broken. Chris hated it when theirs did. They liked their voice soft. They still speak in a particular way now, so they don't sound gruff. The teenager is so loud that all the other participants turn their heads towards Chris.

Oh my G. If they could only run away right fucking now without appearing like a twat.

Before they can escape, this small muscle-bound black woman appears to save Chris from further embarrassment. Shaved head, sharp eyes, a tattoo on her skull, Rosie casts her analytical eyes on Chris.

"Well, you're the newbie." She offers Chris a firm handshake. "Rosie."

"Chris. Well, you know." They scratch their head.

Rosie gives them the slightest nod. "Follow me."

Okay. She's not a woman of pleasantries. Chris is already debating with themself whether they can come back to work here. These are teenagers and not the kind of people they have ever worked with or serviced. But that's why they wanted the work experience in the first place. After the conversation they had with Alex and Jeff, they went to the local library, the first time in their adult life and looked up everything they could find about a career in childcare. Their eyes hurt, but they kept reading about work experience.

Work experience. They almost laughed out loud in the library. Acting, modelling and sex work.

Great on an escort's curriculum vitae. Professional skills: plenty. Transferable: not so much.

Rosie leads Chris into a small office to the side of the big room with a glass window so the staff can keep an eye on the activities of the young people. Rosie goes behind a desk covered with files and pieces of paper. She gestures to the chair opposite, so Chris sits down, their hands hidden between their thighs.

"I've seen your application form and the police checks came back okay."

Chris nods.

Rosie barks out a loud laugh. "I hope you're not as tongue-tied as this when you deal with the kids out there. They'll eat you alive."

Somehow her laughter breaks the ice. Chris tuts. "Fat chance. I can definitely hold my own. Thank you."

Rosie pats the desk, causing all the files to jump an inch. "That's the spirit. Hope you don't mind, but I asked Eric and Sasha about you. I don't need official reference if I have the word from those two."

Chris approached their friend Sasha who in turn contacted Eric, the vicar he worked for, to see if he knew of any social or care work for them. They don't need the money. Eric has recommended Chris to the youth centre on Sasha's recommendation. Chris is ever so grateful for their friends' trust since they're not exactly employable in polite society.

Chris has given Eric and Sasha permission to tell the youth group anything about them, but now they worry about their bad rep.

Chris is a pain in the arse and has a smart mouth. Their profession is a bit dodgy, but they're pretty reliable when they want to be. Give them a go if you're desperate.

Rosie asks, jolting Chris out of the comedy sketch in their head, "How were you at school? Do you think you can help Jess out there with her homework?"

Chris is confused. "Jess?"

"The kid you spoke to." She explains, "Jessica. She started secondary school in September."

Chris nods. "I only got two Es at GCSE, so I'm not sure if I can do much to help with school stuff. I flunked out, I'm afraid. I think I have dyslexia, but I was never diagnosed."

Under her dense lashes, Rosie considers Chris for a few seconds. "I doubt any of our participants are at a level they're supposed to be at. They're all vulnerable. Some are bullied at school, and many like to stay away, pretending to be sick or playing truant. Quite a few have issues at home. Their parents won't accept them for their sexualities or genders. Jess didn't go to school for one reason or another for six months. So if you want to, I'm sure you can supervise them with their homework."

Chris is not surprised by any of the issues the kids have because they all sound so familiar to them. "I've been there, done it and got the T-shirt," they tell Rosie.

Rosie nods. "It figures. Once a month, an education support worker comes in. I'm sure he can see you next time he's here and you can ask him about your dyslexia. It's never too late to do something about it."

Chris is amazed that somewhere like this exists, and they wish they had some support when they were growing up instead of a mother who was usually drunk or high. Annette did her best in a way, but she'd never encouraged them educationally. It wasn't entirely her fault since she was never expected to achieve much in life herself.

If there was even one role model, someone who had their back, they might not have been where they are now.

"Okay. I will."

"Well. How does that sound to start with that? See how you get on with helping the homework table?"

Rosie has made it difficult for Chris to run away. They make to stand up and go to help the teenagers as she has suggested when she comments again, "I wasn't going to let you volunteer."

Chris stops and lifts their right eyebrow. "Sorry?"

"Your, eh, other job isn't exactly illegal and your criminal record check was fine. I still wouldn't ordinarily have someone who does sex work here. I'm sorry."

Chris's stomach drops. "I thought...never mind."

Did they imagine that Rosie asked them to help the kids? *Fuck my stupid life.* Now how are they ever going to get out of their rut?

"Sasha and Eric talked so highly of you. They said you're fucked up but basically harmless. I'd give you a chance if I was desperate." Rosie sighs.

Chris bursts out laughing, only stopping when they can see Rosie's serious face. "Sorry. I reckoned they'd say some shit like that."

"I'm not too short-staffed, just so you know. But I want to give you a chance, and I don't know what else you do for a living if anyone asks."

She stops to let that sink in.

She continues. "You must be very sensitive if you're going to talk about sex with the teenagers. Some of them have already been through the mill because of their sexual orientations or gender identities. I can't tell you about their history because it's confidential, but some of them might have been sexually abused. You understand?"

A furrow develops between Chris's brows. "I may be an escort and messed up, but I'm not daft. I know a thing or two about young people and what's inappropriate."

Unlike the adults around them when they were growing up. They were practically raised in the sex industry.

Rosie nods. "Good. I try to warn all my volunteers. It's not just you. I wouldn't have agreed to you coming if I didn't think you were suitable. Your friends are right about giving people a second chance. You're here because you're queer and a great person, or so Sasha told me." Her smile returns. "Don't disappoint your friends or me."

Chris arches an eyebrow, but they are too stunned to respond.

"And as soon as you walked through that door, I got a sense that you had it bad when you were their age."

Not only at that age. It feels as though I've never fit in since the day I was born.

Chris agrees. "All right, I'll help the kids study now."

"Good. You know our Rainbow teens' drop-in is every Wednesday six to nine. Will you be able to come every week? It's hard for the kids to get used to someone only for them to move on quickly. Inconsistency, you know?"

"Yes. I'll keep every Wednesday evening free."

Chris is determined to make the best of this chance. They don't know where their boldness comes from. Before speaking to Rosie, they'd wanted to turn back and forget about gaining work experience. But the more they have talked to her, the more they want this. How difficult can it be to try to relate to these queer kids even though Chris is at least a decade older?

Chris offers to check Jess's homework. She looks everywhere but directly at Chris, but then she gives them the maths workbook she's done. Chris's numbers are not as bad as their reading, and they cheat a little by checking the results and guidance at the back. They help Jess correct a few of the mistakes.

In the end, she stares at Chris and stutters. "You...you're beautiful. Are you going to be here every week?"

Chris grins. "Thanks. You're pretty too. I'd like to come every week if it's okay."

Jess lowers her eyes again.

The participants are wary of them at first, but they offer to help and don't push. If the teenagers seem resistant, Chris sits quietly. Gradually they make small gestures to involve them. Even something as small as eye contact is a kind of triumph.

Chris can't believe a couple of hours have gone by when a delivery worker turns up with half a dozen pizzas. The teenagers all abandon what they are doing, descend on the central table and tear into the pizzas with gusto.

Rosie appears all of a sudden and stands beside Chris, observing the kids' fighting over the pizzas.

"A few of the local takeaways donate food to us. They do it in turn, so we'll have Chinese food one week, pizza the next, and sometimes curry. So far, pizzas are the most popular."

Chris can't help but smile at the participants, behaving like six-year-olds at a birthday party. All they need are jelly, party hats and balloons. Chris never had a birthday party.

"How's your first night been so far?"

"Good, I think." Chris winks at Rosie. "I managed not to corrupt the kids. Yet."

She laughs. Then she stops and sighs. "I doubt you'd make things much worse than what some of them have been struggling with."

Alex said something about helping others like him. It's the first time Chris has done work that doesn't rely on their looks and body, and that has made a warm and gooey mess of Chris's insides. They beam at the teenagers fighting for their slices of pizza.

~~~

One of the volunteers at the youth club, David, is a special needs school teacher who attends once a month. Chris meets him for a diagnosis of her educational needs. As Chris already knew, it was not her intelligence but years of neglect at her school and undiagnosed dyslexia that caused her to drop out. Unfortunately, there are no free services for people with dyslexia. David refers Chris to websites and other resources that might help her. He has written a letter for her to present to college when she starts. All these are so much hard work, but once Chris has made up her mind, she doesn't back down easily.

Chris and Alex sit at the dining table, their heads close together. Dark brown and dirty blonde hair hang over a college application form. Chris draws the letters carefully, but they are still of different sizes. She bites her lip and frowns as she struggles to write everything out as neatly as possible. Chris J. Neeser. Date of birth. Address. Alex reads through her writing and has to correct some when she has the wrong spellings and added extra letters at the end.

"So, what did the special needs guy say?" Alex asks.

Chris squints at the paperwork in front of her until her eyes hurt. "Oh, I've got a report to take to college and they'll do a healthcare plan to support my study. It sounds like I have a long-term illness or something."

"Well, it's not that bad. All this stuff is over my head as well. Anyway, have you got dyslexia or not?"

"Ah, yes. He thinks I have mild dyslexia. He said I should have had help at school." Chris purses her lips. "Like anyone there cared enough."

Chris was so bad at most school subjects that when she obtained a high mark for a maths test once, the teacher accused her of cheating. She refused to pay attention in her class after that.

"Okay. But you will have help learning now?"

Chris nods. "That's the idea. The college may have someone who specialises in assisting students with dyslexia. There are things that can help and I can have more time for my homework. That sort of thing."

"Hmm." Alex picks up the college prospectus and the application form. They told Chris she had to apply online, but she doesn't have a computer. The staff needed some persuading to print out a paper copy for her. No wonder education is one hurdle after another for someone like Chris.

Chris hits Alex's head with her pen. "Are you going to make sure I'm doing this right, Alex? No slacking now."

"You're so bossy! Yes, I'm watching you. I only managed to scrape through my schooling, too, you know." Alex was already training semi-professionally when he did his school exams and studying was not a priority for him either.

Chris looks over. "But I bet you can read and write better than me." She squints at the various boxes of the form and struggles to fill them out. She is so slow at this and she hates herself for it.

At one point, she kicks her long legs out with frustration brought on by the whole process. "I can't do this!" She throws her pen down.

Alex picks it up and shoves it back in her hand. "Come on. Don't be impatient now."

Chris has to force herself to carry on. Damn it. If she can't even pass this first test... She stares at the next question. "What's this? Highest quality...?"

Alex takes a look over the form. "Qualifications."

Chris pouts. "What does it mean? I don't have any qualifications. Isn't that the point of me going back to college?"

"No, it means the last thing you studied. Like what were your GCSE grades? Did you pass any exams?"

"Oh!" Chris is grateful that Alex is always so patient when it comes to helping her. She returns to the question and carefully writes them out.

Alex reads Chris's grades and grins. Chris scowls at him.

"Sorry. I'm not laughing at you. I'm thinking about my own results."

"What?" Chris is still staring at Alex with mistrust.

"I only got two passes as well. A 'D' in human biology and an 'E' in English. What a pair we are!" Alex shakes his head.

Chris rolls her eyes. "Why don't you apply to come to the classes with me? I can picture you sitting at the back of the classroom!"

In her imagination, the room has these kid's size desks and chairs; Alex would struggle not to break them.

Alex smiles as if he can see that image too. "Nah, I don't think so. I'll leave the studying to the brainy one. Besides, I've got to bring home the bacon."

Chris hits him with her pen again. "I don't need your money and I don't eat bacon."

Alex laughs. "All the more for me. So, what subjects are you taking?"

Chris looks pained, her eyes feeling funny from concentrating too much. She should take an eye test, too. "I need three good grades, so perhaps English and biology. And I'll retake maths to get a better result. I don't need to decide until the beginning of term."

~~~

Chris chews the top of the pen when she's not writing.

"You're so cute with your big eyes and pen-chewing."

She stares at Alex until he backtracks.

248

"I mean, your determination is kinda catching." He reaches out and kisses her.

When they break off, Chris pushes him away. "No time for this kind of thing for me now. Education and career come first!"

Alex laughs some more, prompting Chris to punch his arm again.

"Take me seriously. Damn it!"

"I do! I do!" Alex pretends to dodge the blows, which are hardly making a dent. Then he grabs Chris's wrists and stops her. "I take you seriously. I love you, Chris."

Chris's eyes widen as she stares at Alex and her vision turns white. So many have said those three words to her over the years because they were in lust and fucking her, or they wanted to. That's why she spent years believing love was overrated and it only gave people false hope.

"You…mean it?"

"Absolutely."

She could reconsider it. It. Love. Big fucking scary word.

Chris opens her mouth to say something, but Alex puts his forefinger on her lips. "Shh. It's okay. You don't have to love me back out of obligation, but I do love you."

Chris wants to love Alex. She'll have to learn how to, like the education that she'd missed out on. She'll sign up now and see what happens. She will learn to care for another person and get a good grade in it. For now, she thinks the world of Alex and that's enough. He's strong and gentle, calm and patient, serious and vulnerable. He deserves to be loved and Chris will get there. That decision makes her chest swell, so she smiles in acknowledgement and marvels at the sight of Alex that has made her dare to hope.

~~~

Later that night, Alex comes home from his shift and walks straight into their bedroom. Chris grins, pretending to be asleep. With her eyes closed, Chris imagines Alex is pleased to see her, how he strips in the dark, revealing his hard body covered by the tattoos. All his ripped muscles capable of protecting her and warming her every night.

She feels the mattress dip when Alex gets in. His strong chest close to her back and rough fingers on Chris's cool skin, the connection arouses her from her sleep.

"Hey. I love the smell of sweat on you."

"Sorry. Should I shower?" Alex offers.

"Hmm, no? I like to rub my face against your armpit, especially after sex."

Alex giggles. "Kinky. Go back to sleep. I didn't mean to wake you."

"It's okay. I was awake."

Alex circles his fingers on Chris's neck and shoulder. "How was the youth project?"

Chris smiles in the dark. "It's good. Really good." For the first time, she's contributing something and not getting paid. She understands now why Alex volunteers at the boxing club.

Alex kisses her shoulder with such a sweet, tender stroke of his lips. No one would believe that's what Alex Whale is capable of. "Great. I knew you'd be a wonderful carer."

"Oh, fuck off."

Alex chuckles. "I hope you don't talk to the kids that way."

"I'm sure they've heard worse."

Alex's kisses become more urgent, and Chris responds as heat grows inside of her. Alex turns her around and trails his tongue down Chris's neck and front, licking the hard nipples and down the pale flesh. He wraps his mouth around Chris's cock and sucks, using a little teeth as Chris has taught him.

"Fuck!" Chris moans and bucks up, pushing further into Alex's mouth. Chris can tell Alex is trying hard to please her, applying techniques that remain a little alien to him. His admiring brown eyes, not skills, are enough to turn her on.

When Alex finally releases Chris's cock, she's ready to combust.

"You've got a perfect dick, Chris, like the rest of you." Alex smears pre-cum around the head. "Do you wanna top?"

Chris cups Alex's head in her hands. "You want me to? Are you sure?"

"Yeah, want you." Alex takes off his boxers, revealing his own erection. Chris imagines he'd be intimidating for a smaller sexual partner. Chris doesn't mind because when Alex leaves her a bit sore after sex, it reminds her of him in her, within her.

"Turn around."

Alex does, and Chris lifts his arse up. Chris uses her tongue on Alex, pulling out all the stops to prep him. Alex responds by groaning and wriggling, desperate for his first bottoming experience.

Chris smirks at Alex. "Big Blue's tight arse. I'm so spoilt."

She finds a condom from their bedside table, tears the foil packet open with her teeth and rolls it on. She drizzles extra lube on the condom. She's determined to make Alex's first time special.

Alex steals a glance at his lover. "I've been wondering about your dick inside me for so long. It's one of my favourite sexual fantasies about you."

Chris leans down and kisses Alex's cheek. Her erection aligns with Alex's arsehole. "No pressure! Relax and it won't hurt."

"I trust you," Alex says.

That brings out a crooked grin on Chris's face. She admires the muscles of Alex's back and the tattoos. The beautiful lines of the wild animals, like Alex, who is soft and strong at the same time. Life is a paradox, too. Sometimes Alex finds it reassuring when Chris laughs at the bad stuff. If they can find humour together, they will survive.

"Can I see you when you fuck me?" Alex's voice is muffled on the mattress. Their favourite sex positions allow them to maintain eye contact. One of them lies down on the bed or they face each other on their sides. When they don't want to fuck, they touch and kiss, sometimes for hours in their own non-sex heaven.

"Sure. Turn over."

Alex does and Chris pushes his legs back at the knees. Chris considers Alex, now slick with her saliva and lube, and inches in, stretching Alex, who issues soft appreciation of the fullness. When Chris is buried, she angles to hit the sensitive spot inside of Alex and is rewarded with a pleasant sigh. Sweat beads on Alex's chest and face, his eyes dazed from the intensity of his first experience of getting fucked. Chris slows down as she nears climax and takes Alex's cock in her hand. That way, she controls their orgasms. Chris lets herself go only after she knows her lover is satisfied. She delves into Alex hard until her whole body shakes and stiffens.

Chris gazes at the deep tawny of Alex's eyes.

"Come here." Alex beckons.

Her breathing calming, Chris withdraws and disposes of the condom. She scoots up to reach Alex's broad chest and puts her ear against Alex's heart, marvelling at the wild thumps. Chris inhales the fresh sweat from Alex, her favourite scent.

"How was it? Your first time with a cock up your arse." Chris smiles against Alex's bare skin.

"It was…great. I didn't feel weird. It felt right to have a dick inside of me. Your dick." Alex laughs and Chris follows him, her shoulders shaking.

"What about you? Tell me about your first time," Alex whispers, as though he's asking about something elicit.

"My first time?" Chris winces. "You don't want to know."

"Yes, I do."

Chris inhales. "I was fourteen, and he was this other kid in the school. Big and hot. We did it in his bed when his parents were away one night. That's it."

Alex frowns. "Was he your boyfriend?"

Chris shakes her head. "No. He didn't use a condom, saying he'd never done it without one and since I was a virgin, it'd be okay. It was painful as hell, but he wouldn't stop when I told him to. He was a lot stronger than me. And as soon as we'd fucked, he stopped talking to me. He said I'd been gagging to take him up my arse since I was a slut anyway. They used to laugh at me and my mum at school. That's it. It hurt. A lot."

It was a combination of physical and emotional hurt, a mix that would soon become familiar to her.

Alex kisses Chris's cheek. "What a stupid fuck."

"Well, I used to specialise in dating assholes and bitches. What can I say? I'm an idiot."

"They didn't deserve you, and you didn't love them. Not really."

Chris's eyes dim. "That's a cliché but true."

"You really do deserve better. I want to chase off the memory of every fucking terrible thing that has happened to you."

Chris blinks. Over the years she has built herself a fortress, brick by brick, commemorating every hurt she has suffered. Its walls are thick. To let Alex in, she will have to let him open this fortress, dismantle the walls.

Chris can hear the door opening. It squeaks due to lack of use, but still. Alex has the key.

"I guess your first time was with your childhood sweetheart?"

"Sam. Yeah."

Alex steals another kiss from Chris, who can't keep her eyes open.

"Now, go to sleep," Alex whispers.

Exhaustion washes over her. It's been a long day.

"Night, Alex."

"Night, Chris."

CHAPTER 17
FAITH

J ESS WANTS CHRIS to paint her nails dark blue.
"Are you sure it's all right with school? I still remember the shit I got for violating the uniform code," Chris says. She has noticed Jess's make-up today.

Jess lifts her face and squints. "It's half-term holiday. I'm not back to school till Monday so I'll take it off on Sunday night, okay?" She gives the small bottle of varnish to Chris.

"All right. As long as you don't wear it to school, I guess it'll be fine." Chris smiles. "Listen to me, talking like a responsible grown-up telling the kid off!"

They giggle and enjoy the closeness between them as Chris concentrates on Jess's nails. The teenager blinks at Chris. "When... when did you start to think you are a girl?"

Chris can't look up so she answers without eye contact. "Hmm. I was twelve. Actually, I don't want to be a girl. I don't want to be only a boy or a girl if that makes sense?"

"Oh." There's a hint of disappointment in Jess's voice but then she nods. "I understand. Gender-fluid, right?"

"Yeah. Generally queer, I guess." Chris finishes one hand and looks up at Jess. "So, what about you? Tell me about yourself, if you want."

Jess bites her lip. "I was about eight or nine. I hated everything that boys were supposed to do, and I felt wrong. I'd like to transition someday." Jess is thirteen. The public health service provides some help for trans kids under eighteen, but accessing advice can be a problem without her parents' support.

"Have you seen a doctor or spoken to your parents about it?" Chris asks gently.

Tears swim in Jess's brown eyes. "My mum may be okay with it, I guess. I've always told her I'm not a boy. She's nice. She listens to me. My stepdad would rather see me dead than believe I'm a girl. I've only been reading about it online."

Chris hopes Rosie and the youth group can help Jess face the obstacles ahead. Hope. She didn't have much of that either when she was Jess's age.

Chris grins in encouragement and finishes Jess's nails, blowing on the lacquer to help them dry. "You should speak to your mum, then, and maybe see a doctor and take it from there."

Jess glances at Chris. "I don't know. My stepdad won't have any of it."

"Perhaps Rosie will have some idea what you can do." Chris arranges Jess's hands and spreads her fingers for the nails to dry. That, at least, Chris can do for Jess. As an untrained volunteer, she can't and is not allowed to counsel the kids.

"I want to be like you when I grow up." Jess gazes at Chris again. She smiles shyly. "You are...you're so beautiful."

Chris laughs and Jess joins in. "That's flattering. Thank you, but being me is not that special. Trust me. You can be whoever you want to be, Jess. Don't be me."

Jess frowns, seemingly not convinced that Chris isn't special. "Did you want to be anyone else when you were young?"

"I'm still young!" Chris starts to giggle again. Working with teens has given her brand-new perspectives on her own life. She thinks about her childhood and what she's been doing to support herself. "I was always pretending to be someone else, so I dreamt about being me. To be left alone."

She tells Jess about being a child actor but skips the bad bits. Jess seems to have forgotten all about her worries and listens with fascination, prompting some kind of special bond between them. Jess's large, innocent eyes are full of admiration for Chris.

Chris still can't believe the kids take to her so well. A few months ago, she wouldn't have imagined she could work with young people like this and be a role model to them. She's perhaps not as much a fuck-up as she thought.

~~~

A step.

"So, how's the new love nest?" Jeff beams. "I enjoy Christening your accommodation with that term."

"I wouldn't have it any other way. I mean, it's…nice." Chris can't help but smile, his head already full of images of the marvellous intimate times he and Alex have been having since they moved. They play like a montage of his favourite movie sequences.

Jeff rolls his eyes. "Now, that face is worth all the heartaches in the world." He stands to search for a wrapped package from his storage cupboard and presents it to Chris. "Congratulations on your new home, darling."

Chris stares at the gift, shaped like a painting or mirror and wrapped in plain metallic paper. "Jeff. You shouldn't have."

"Yes, I should. You've had a crazy year. I'm so glad you've found someone. It's a big step moving in with your boyfriend, dear." Jeff tilts his head to indicate the present. "Come on. Open it."

Chris's eyes are misting up. He tries not to tear the wrapping paper open too quickly so he can savour the reveal. It's as if he's getting approval from a parent, twenty years too late. When he can see the artwork mounted in a simple wooden frame, he is stunned silent. It's a line drawing of two naked people kissing, and they are genderless. They are two people deeply in love, in a pure and simple embrace. The strong brush marks, muted colours and lines elegantly spread across the surface.

"I…" Chris stares at Jeff. "It's wonderful. I can't thank you enough." He kisses the older man.

Jeff smiles. "You can thank me by enjoying your life. Chris, I want you to come and see me sometime. You let me know when you're free. I love your massages, but I don't want you to provide any sexual services anymore. I'll pay you the same. Is that okay?"

Chris only gives Jeff hand jobs these days, but still. He frowns. "I'm not a therapist or a masseur."

Jeff covers Chris's hand with his. "As I said, I enjoy your company and you can help me relax with a good rub. I don't need anything else. Okay? You save yourself for your man."

You save yourself for your man. Chris is sad that his relationship with Jeff is changing, but he also understands Jeff's request. He thinks of Jeff as an older friend, a mentor, too.

Reluctantly, Chris agrees. "Okay, but if you change your mind, let me know."

"Good." Jeff smiles and pats Chris's face fondly. They raise their glasses, even though Jeff's is only filled with water.

"To your new life."

"To good health." Chris beams.

~~~

Chris enters the small boxing club. The mixed scent of body odour, rubber and old, distressed wood fills her nostrils. Grunts and sounds of punchbags being hit intersperse with Alex's firm instructions.

Alex coaches a tall black teenager who is throwing some strong punches. Alex holds on to the bag while the youngster punches fast with his left. Chris salivates, gazing at Alex's bulging biceps and calf muscles that remain steadfast as the young boxer strikes repeatedly. The developing scene only reminds her of how she has loved Alex from the beginning. Someone who is invincible and yet sweet. Someone who complements Chris in every way possible.

Her soul mate. She shivers at the thought.

Chris approaches the pair gingerly. The teen glances at Chris, alerting Alex to her arrival with a tilt of his head. Alex turns and a wide grin appears on his face. Both Alex and the boy move away from the equipment. Chris steps forward.

"You made it," Alex says.

"Yeah." Chris hides her arms behind her back, feeling self-conscious in the middle of a rather macho place. Alex told her they wanted more female boxers but they were the minority among the learners.

Alex leans forward to peck Chris on the cheek. Someone makes a cat-call, and Chris blushes, almost coy. Alex has the most groovy, gooey grin on his face.

"This is Devan." Alex introduces them. "Chris—my partner."

Devan takes his right glove off and shakes Chris's hand. "Nice to meet you."

"Likewise." Chris smiles. Devan blinks before looking from her to his coach.

Dex emerges from the small office, taking a large gulp from his water bottle. When he sees Chris, he joins the group.

"Whoa. To what do we owe the pleasure of your visit?" His eyes are twinkling, set against his dark skin.

"Ha. Pleasure's all mine." Chris smiles and hugs Dex.

When they come apart, she twirls her forefinger around. "This is an awesome place. I'm sorry I've not visited before. Alex talks about the club all the time. It's like his other lover!"

Coach laughs.

Alex joins in, too. "I've practically grown up here."

Devan quietly observes the adults converse. The history behind Alex and Dex's relationship is well known in the club and the teenager clearly idolises Alex.

Alex glances at the clock. "We'll be done in fifteen minutes or so. Why don't you wait in the office?"

"Sure."

Dex leads Chris to the small room at the corner of the club, while Alex and Devan resume their practice.

Once in the office, Dex offers to make Chris a hot drink.

"Water's fine. Thanks!"

Dex gives her a bottle.

As soon as they've sat down on the two uncomfortable chairs, Dex clears his throat. "I want to leave Alex this club when I retire, which should be soon if my wife and children have their way. What do you say?" He gazes at Chris, waiting for her answer.

"You're asking me?" Chris swallows.

"Who else? You're the most important person in Alex's life. That's quite clear to everyone. And he's the love of your life. Don't deny it."

Chris giggles. "I've never been someone's love of their life. They usually run for their lives! You asked for my opinion on an important matter. I don't know what to say right now."

She doesn't think beyond the rent, one month at a time. Planning the future has always been a frivolous pursuit.

Dex declares his admiration for Chris. "Alex will need you because you're a tough cookie, Chris. Knowing what you did for Alex... You're stronger than me, and I am not comparing muscle mass."

"Thanks, I guess. I know nothing about boxing, though."

"Well, talk it through. See if this is what you both want," Dex suggests.

"Okay. We will. Thank you." Chris knows Alex would love to do it, though their finances will suffer. They'll sort something out if this is what Alex wants. Everything Alex wants, he should have.

~~~

Chris walks along the main street leading up to the youth club among a few high-rise apartment blocks. This is the quieter side of Camden towards Kentish Town. The other end boasts the canal and the busy markets, hordes of tourists and eighties punk wannabes.

The night air flows in a damp fog through the remnants of an earlier drizzle.

"Chris." A croaky and uncertain voice calls out to her. She turns around.

"Jess?"

The young girl steps up. She has a hoodie on, obscuring part of her face. There's little light in that section of the street, but Chris can make out something's wrong from the way Jess stays in the shadows and the dark fabric covering her head.

"What happened?" Chris carefully removes a strand of hair that partly hides Jess's face. A black eye. Swollen cheek.

Chris's heart sinks. She kneels down to the teenager's level. "Who did this to you, Jess?"

"Dennis. My stepdad." Her voice is low as a whisper.

Chris gazes at Jess's small face, making her seem so vulnerable right now. "Jess, we need to report this. He's hurt you bad, honey. Shall we go to see Rosie?"

"No, I don't want to see her." She blinks a few times.

"Why not?" Chris touches Jess's hair. It's damp and messy from her wait in the light rain.

"They'll take me away. I want my mum." Jess's eyes are shining with tears.

"Where is she?"

"She's still at work."

Chris glances around to consider what she should do. "Let me take you to a café and we'll talk about this, okay? Would you like a hot chocolate to warm up?" She suspects Jess has been waiting a while for her.

Jess hesitates, but eventually she agrees.

In the nearby café, Chris sits Jess in a corner and orders the drinks at the counter. Away from the other few customers, Chris asks, "Is there anywhere else he's hurt you?"

Chris doesn't want to imagine other kinds of abuse that Jess might have suffered. She can't bear to think about it but she has to ask.

Jess pulls back her hoodie and then puts her hair behind the left ear. Chris shields her from the rest of the coffee shop with her body and inspects the gash there. It's a couple of inches long and blood has congealed like a nasty dark red brush mark.

"We should go to the club, so Rosie and I can clean you up." Chris sips from her cup of chocolate.

Jess nurses the warm mug in her hands. "I don't want to see anyone." She lowers her head, her lashes obscuring the brown of her eyes. Chris remembers all those times when she was a kid, and she knew what some men were thinking when they looked at her. Her heart sinks.

"Jess, did he? Dennis…did he touch you? Has he ever touched you sexually?"

Jess slowly shakes her head. "He only shouts at me cuz I want to be a girl. He doesn't like boys. He calls me a poof and he says he'd cut off my willy himself."

Chris closes her eyes. A small mercy, but what a fucking bastard. Her familiar anger surges inside of her.

They take a sip of their drinks and are quiet for a while. Chris is at a loss what to do if Jess refuses to see Rosie.

"Where do you live?" Jess asks, her voice trembling a little.

"Haringey."

"Do you live there on your own?"

"No. I… I live with my boyfriend Alex."

"Is he nice?" Jess's eyes are wide with curiosity. She idolises Chris. Chris can understand why she wants to know what kind of life she leads.

"Yes, he is. He's a wonderful man." Chris doesn't want to make Jess feel like she's not loved, though. "Your mum will worry about you. Let me talk to Rosie."

"I want to stay with you. I can't go home. Mum's got the worst taste in men. Dennis hates me. He refuses to call me Jess. I hate being called James."

"Oh, sweetheart. I'd love for you to visit but… My mum's the same, Jess. She brought the most dreadful boyfriends home." And the rest.

Chris smiles at the memory, though. The physical abuse she has witnessed could have happened to her too. Annette had always protected her that way, except that one time when young Chris stood between Annette and her attacker.

"Oh, I'm sorry." Jess's voice seems even softer.

"It's okay. The only thing my mum was ever good at was… She didn't allow them to touch me or beat me up." Chris gazes intently at Jess. "I don't want to nag you, but you need to tell someone about this. Where was your mum when this happened?"

Jess's eyes are full of unshed tears once more. "She was at work. I'd hidden it from her so far, but I can't go home now because she will see these."

She waves her hand in the air to indicate her bruises. So, it's not the first time. It's as if Dennis isn't only hurting Jess but Chris, too, reminding her of the previous assaults on her body. Chris is livid.

"I want to go back home with you. I can meet your bloke." The hope on Jess's face makes her look so innocent.

Chris takes a deep breath before she forces a smile. "I'm sure Alex would love to meet you. But, you see, when your mum starts to look for you and can't find you, she'll call the police. We will be in trouble."

Jess shakes her head. At that moment, she seems every bit a barely teen—young, lost, confused and sad. The mirror image breaks Chris's heart.

"If you let me speak to Rosie, we may find a solution. She is very clever like that. Don't you think?" Chris needs Rosie's support, and she wants to clean up Jess's face and the bloody mess behind her ear.

Jess bites her lip and considers the suggestion. She slowly nods.

Chris glances around the café. They're quite far away from the next occupied table. She turns on the speaker, but keeps the volume down. She places the phone on the table.

"Chris, are you not coming in tonight?"

Chris hunches over the table. "I'm with Jess." She looks to Jess to gain her consent and Jess nods. "Her stepdad has beaten her up, but she doesn't want to report him or go home. Yet."

Rosie inhales. "Jeez. How bad was it?"

Jess chirps in, "It's okay, Rosie. I mean…I want to go home with Chris."

Rosie is silent for a few seconds. "Jess, you need to report him. Where are you? I'll come to get you."

Jess pleads to Chris with her eyes and shakes her head. "Mum's not back till late. I don't want to go home in case he's still there."

Rosie insists, "You won't need to go home yet, but—"

Jess closes her eyes. "I don't want to be taken away. I want my mum."

Rosie is right, of course. Jess should report Dennis to the police.

"Rosie, is it all right if I take Jess home with me for now? I'll clean her up and make her some dinner. You can come after the youth club and talk to her and help her report the assault? Will that be okay?" Chris wants to protect Jess, who has become like a little sister to her.

Jess gazes at the phone hopefully as if she can see Rosie. After a few beats, Rosie exhales. "Okay. I'll come right up—after nine."

Chris gives her the address to save her looking up her details and finishes the call.

Jess breathes a sigh of relief. "What's Rosie going to do?"

Chris shakes her head. "I'm sorry, sweetheart. I have no idea. But let's get you home, yeah?"

Chris calls for a taxi. They put on their jackets and wait outside the café.

When they arrive at the block of flats, Chris takes Jess up the first floor. The three-storey building is a conversion from a large Victorian house. It's homely if a little untidy and old. The white walls in the hall and stairwell have seen better days but at least the place is clean enough. There are only two flats on each floor. As soon as the door opens, the musty scent is replaced by the whiff of toasted bread and Jess's stomach growls.

"Someone's hungry," Chris comments.

"I've not eaten anything since school lunch. I sat at the corner of the dining room because these boys are always calling me names."

"That's dreadful."

"They'd been shouting in my face, saying things like 'What's with the long hair, JESSICA?'"

Jess has already told Chris about how she feels excluded since starting secondary school. She has tried to tone it down in her presentation. Her mum has asked the school to let her use Jessica as her name.

"School bullies are so cruel!" Chris wants to protect Jess so badly.

"Hey, you're back early! I'm about to heat up the oven for pie and chips—"

Alex turns to see Chris bringing the young girl into the small sitting room.

"Oh." He wipes his large hands on a tea towel. Alex was home first today after his day shift. He usually plans their dinner in time for Chris when she finishes at the youth club.

"Alex, this is Jess." Chris puts her arm around Jess's shoulder. "Jess. This is Alex."

She's put the hood up again, but the black eye wouldn't have escaped Alex's attention. At just over five feet, Jess looks tiny indeed compared to Alex, so he stoops down and holds out his hand.

"Nice to meet you."

Jess turns shy all of a sudden even though earlier she was so curious to know what kind of boyfriend Chris has. Jess stands back with apprehension as she faces the rather intimidating-looking man. She tentatively shakes Alex's hand. "I'm...I'm Jess."

"Hey, are you staying for dinner? I'll make more and eat a little less myself!" Alex is trying to be jovial about it. He and Chris make eye contact over the teenager's head, trading an understanding look.

"Damn right you will. Rosie will be coming in a couple of hours to fetch Jess."

Alex and Chris exchange a quick kiss. Alex ruffles Chris's hair as a sign of support.

Jess watches the couple. Chris wonders if she's thinking about her mum and stepdad.

To distract Jess, Chris steers her to sit down on the sofa. "Shall I put the TV on?"

Jess agrees. Chris clicks on the remote control and finds an innocuous game show. Then she leaves her to search for a flannel, warm water, and some saline lotion and gauze. Luckily, they bought a small first-aid kit when they moved in on account that Alex can be clumsy around delicate things.

Alex puts the food in the oven, then goes into their bedroom, giving Chris and Jess space. Chris returns to the sitting room and cleans up Jess's face and the back of her ear while Jess watches TV. If the ministrations hurt, she isn't complaining.

After Chris cleans Jess up well, they sit side by side on the sofa. A sitcom has come on after the game show; they find themselves giggling occasionally. If only real life was like this, joke after joke and interspersed with a feel-good storyline. When the kitchen timer goes off, Alex reappears to serve up dinner.

They sit at the small table and tuck into the pie and chips. Alex has improved at cooking after getting together with Chris, but he's burned the food slightly again.

Chris smiles. "You're supposed to turn the chips halfway through. Lucky for you we're hungry!" She jabs her fork at Alex's beefy biceps.

Alex pretends to be hurt. "Ouch!"

But he proceeds to stuff his face with a big pile of food and speaks with his mouth quite full. "Not everyone's like a master chef contestant in the kitchen."

Chris giggles. "I like your backhanded compliment, but that's a bit of an exaggeration as always."

Alex laughs, making no apologies for idealising Chris. Chris worries that Jess will find it hard to be comfortable with a stranger, a big threatening-looking one. She seems relaxed enough given the circumstances.

Jess's wide eyes show that she is comfortable there even though she doesn't get their in-joke. She probably trusts Alex, too, because of her admiration for Chris.

"Do you like the youth club?" Alex asks.

"It's okay, I guess." She shrugs.

"But you must like some things to keep going back?" Alex tries to draw her out.

Jess spears a few chips with her fork and watches Chris sidelong. "Rosie and Chris are nice."

Chris beams. "That's the right answer."

Jess smiles, too, pleased to be able to join in the chitchat. "And the pizzas are good."

"Pizzas?" Alex is surprised. "You never told me that's on offer. No wonder you don't have much appetite when you come home!" He points his fork at Chris.

Chris chuckles again. "I don't eat them there. Even if I wanted to, I'm not fast enough to get a slice with this lot." She gazes at Jess with affection.

Jess joins her in giggling. "Yeah, you have to beat the others to get to them if you want some. We all love pizza. I don't mind fighting with the other people for them, though. At home, Dennis always orders them with salami and pineapple and I *hate* it with fruit."

"I hate pineapple on pizza, too!" Alex says.

They pass the time, finishing their evening meal, chatting and joking. Jess doesn't seem to be able to stop smiling. As they take the dishes into the kitchen and Alex starts washing up, Chris tells Jess they should talk before Rosie arrives. The kitchen stands to one side of the sitting room in an alcove, so Alex keeps his back to them as he cleans.

As soon as they sit back on the sofa, Jess tells Chris, "I don't want to go home, especially if Dennis is still there."

"I know. But your mum will want you back, I'm sure." Chris takes Jess's hand in hers.

"I know what will happen. They'll send me away and I won't be with my mum anymore." Jess's voice is low, trembling. "I can't pretend to be a boy just to please him." The tears fall. "He's big, not like your Alex, but big enough for me."

Chris hugs her and gently pats her back. "I understand."

They stay like that until Jess stops crying.

"We'll speak to Rosie, okay? She's a qualified youth worker. She'll know what to do." Chris hopes she does.

By the time the doorbell rings, Jess is a bit more reassured. Alex retreats to the bedroom to let Rosie, Chris and Jess talk.

Rosie inspects Jess's face and the wound on the back of her ear. "I will take you to report this to the police. We need to stop Dennis from doing this to you, okay?"

Jess frowns with uncertainty. "But he's living at home. Can I stay with Chris? They treat me like a friend."

Rosie gazes over at Chris who smiles in encouragement, but it's not a possibility.

"The police will probably make Dennis go away for a while until he promises not to hurt you again. He will not be allowed to stay with you."

"Really?" Jess asks, her eyes filled with tears once more, then straightens up. "What about my mum? Will they take her away too?"

Rosie shakes her head. "Has she ever hurt you?"

"No. She doesn't know because I've been hiding the bruises. It's the first time he's hit my face."

Rosie states firmly, "Then there's no need for you to worry. She'll have to work with the social workers, though, so we can all stop your stepdad from repeating this."

Jess looks to Chris to ask whether she should go with Rosie's plan.

"Jess, I'm sure everyone will want to take care of you. It will all work out. You should go with Rosie to the police station."

"Okay. Can I come to see you and Alex again? I want to have a boyfriend like you have when I grow up. A boyfriend who will accept me as a girl." Jess flashes her big puppy eyes at Chris.

Chris gives her a peck on her forehead. "Of course. You can ask your mum to call me if it's okay with her. Yeah? And we'll arrange something."

Tears well up in Chris's eyes, as she watches Jess leave with Rosie.

"Hey, you're crying." Alex has emerged from the bedroom at some point and now cups the back of Chris's head and rests it against his thick neck.

Chris sobs and laughs at the same time. "Very observant, Alex. Seeing Jess…it's like watching myself when I was her age."

"Hmm."

"I used to cope with so much shit. Annette, working, macho boys at school. Not being able to read and the teachers looking down on me. My gender. I used to skive a lot even when I wasn't working. And I would pretend to be ill. Annette didn't help at all. She let me stay home. She never encouraged me to do anything, other than earning money. I hated my fucking life!"

"I know, sweetheart," Alex murmurs.

Chris shivers despite herself. "And being attacked."

"Oh, Chris." Alex swallows hard.

In Alex's strong arms, Chris stops crying eventually.

"You're really good with Jess. Do you think you may want to work with teenagers instead of babies and toddlers?"

Chris pulls away so she can see Alex. "If I'm going to get this emotional with one teenager, I'll be better off with preschool kids. Don't you think?"

Alex grins. "Maybe. Either way, I think you are brilliant. You're kind of a role model for someone like Jess. I can see why she admires you."

"You're kidding, right? Me? A model queer!" Chris laughs while the tears dry on her face.

Alex smiles back. "You are open and honest about who you are. You don't take no shit from anybody. That's exactly what the kids need."

Chris kisses Alex. She will never have enough of the big man and his faith in her.

CHAPTER 18
INDIGO

CHANGE.

Alex sits Chris down at their dining table one night. His expressive hands lay flat on the surface.

"I got the job at the warehouse. It's an eight-to-six gig. Five days a week, with occasional Saturday or Sunday shifts if it gets busy. I can finally say 'fuck you' to Mike. I'll be home at night. Regular hours will be better for my depression and sleep pattern as well," he says steadily.

Chris agrees. They've talked about this, trying to spend more time together, and the shift work as a security guard gets Alex down. Chris being next to him has already helped him sleep, but it's not enough. He still suffers from insomnia and sometimes the same nightmares, though it's easier when he can reach out and know Chris is there. Alex has grown to love Chris's low snore when he is in a deep sleep, a soft hum soothing his disturbed mind.

"I'll ask Liam about the bouncer job at the club in Soho. He told me they might have some weekend shifts going." He reaches out and laces his fingers through Chris's.

Chris swallows. "And you're going to be at the boxing club too?"

"Yeah. I don't want to give that up. Coach is managing for now, but I can't take it all on because the pay is shit."

He's coaching an adult class, which Dex pays him for. The free kids' session on Tuesday is his passion. Alex enjoys the club, especially teaching the young boxers. Devan is showing great promise. Boxing remains and will always be part of Alex because the sport has been his lifeline for over twenty years.

"You'll be—"

Alex touches his finger to Chris's lips.

Exhausted, working to the bone.

Alex knows how much he's taking on. "I haven't finished. We'll go and open a joint account tomorrow. I want you to take care of our finances. We have my savings too. You work when you have to. All right? No questions asked."

Chris stares at Alex, recognising what he is offering to do so Chris doesn't have to work as much. Tears threaten to fall. He exhales.

"You'll be working a seventy-hour week, Alex. I wish I had more skills and career options."

Alex nods. "I've thought long and hard about this. At the moment, this is the only way. It's what we have to do and I'm happy, okay? We're good, aren't we? And that's all that matters."

Chris bites his tongue between his teeth, but he can't quite stop the feelings bubbling up inside of him. "I'll look for other work. Rosie mentioned that they might be able to afford an assistant at the youth club as a part-time position. It won't pay much, but…"

Alex leans across and kisses Chris. "Then, you'll apply for it, right?"

"Right." Chris smiles through the tears.

~~~

Chris is visiting Southend with Alex. He has never been to Essex, despite the fact that it's an hour or so from London. He's a Londoner through and through, so outside of the M25 ring road is *terra incognita*. They've ridden the Tube to Barking, and from there the train takes about forty minutes. Dagenham, Hornchurch, Basildon. Places merge into one another like an extended suburb of London, except for the green spaces and flat fields.

"Will I actually see the sea?" Chris asks, his face dreamy as he contemplates the landscape flying past through the train window.

He doodles on it using the condensation drops, a childish habit he's maintained.

Alex smiles. "Yes. It's called Southend-on-Sea for a reason."

Chris's eyes widen like a kid who has never seen the ocean. "Will you take me there? I'm twenty-seven but I can count the number of times I've seen the sea on one hand. Annette was not one to take me on trips."

Alex touches his lips to Chris's short hair. "Sure. There's the Pleasure Beach, but it's out of season now so there won't be much going on. We can walk along the promenade. I'll even buy you an ice cream. How's that?" There's a hint of glee in his voice.

Chris glances at Alex sideways. "That'll be dandy!"

"There's always the indoor rides and the amusement arcade if you're inclined." Alex smiles.

"Wow, you're really spoiling me, Alexander." Chris pouts.

Alex's eyes twinkle as he shakes his head. "Let's see how you feel after meeting my folks. You'll think we're all tossers and want to go back to the Big Smoke right away."

Chris gazes at the cloudy sky again, as though he's hoping to catch something interesting. "I have a very low expectation of blood families. I might find something I like among yours." He gives Alex a toothy smile, flashing his dimples. Alex laughs in response. "Is there a carousel at the fair?"

"Like a merry-go-round?"

Chris nods.

Alex can't stop the giggles. "I guess so. It's been years since I've gone to the pier."

Chris takes Alex's hand. "I've never been on a carousel. Will you take me, even if we're going to look ridiculous?"

"I don't remember ever riding one either," Alex admits. "And you never look ridiculous, no matter how much you try, especially in the morning when your hair's standing up and you have sleep marks on your face. You're kinda cute."

Chris touches his hair to make sure it's not too messy for Alex's parents. "Leave my face alone. A seven-year-old might be cute. A cute twenty-seven-year-old is an embarrassment."

Chris stares out of the train window for the rest of the journey, marvelling at the countryside that he rarely sees, while Alex shuts his eyes for a rest.

~~~

They arrive at Southend Central and take a taxi from outside the station. Alex's parents finally decided to sell their seaside palace since they couldn't afford to maintain it. They made enough profit in the sale to buy a modest townhouse. Alex gave them half of his savings, twenty-five thousand, to help with the move. He would've liked to keep all his money for himself and some kind of future with Chris, but it was the least he could do to support his parents. At least this way he knows they are not living in a money pit. Gary folded his last business and started working as a mechanic for a friend's small repair shop. He finally realised that Alex was no longer a cash cow.

Alex feels all tingly about bringing Chris to meet his family. He told his mum he was bringing a friend but didn't specify who.

In the taxi from the station, Chris clings to Alex's hand, his palm clammy. "No one has ever taken me home to meet their parents. I feel really grown up to be in a real relationship! But scared at the same time."

Alex grins. "Well, I've warned you about my parents and brother. Don't be nervous."

Chris has toned it down today. No make-up, a simple button-down shirt and tight black jeans. He's left his silver studs in his right ear and nose. He looks almost 'masculine'.

"Do I look okay?"

"Was that why you were in the bathroom for ages this morning?"

Chris giggles. "I practised my 'manly' voice. 'You're talking to me? You're talking to me?' Y'know, Robert de Niro in *Taxi Driver*."

Alex only laughs. "You sound hilarious—more like de Niro in a bad comedy."

"I'm trying to make your coming out less shocking for your family. I thought I'd pass for a few hours." Chris hits Alex on the side of the head.

"Ouch. Sorry! And thank you for doing this, for coming with me." Alex kisses him. "You're important to me."

"That's more like it. You ungrateful sod." Chris beams.

Alex and Chris stand in front of the three-bedroom terrace house. It's nothing special but at least it seems tidy and well-maintained. Chris steals a quick cigarette. Alex puts his arm around Chris's narrow waist. "All right? Are you ready?"

"Yeah."

They kiss briefly and take a collective deep breath.

Codes.

Alex's mum opens the door. She appears healthy enough today; her face isn't puffy with drunkenness. She hugs Alex and her eyes roam over to Chris.

"This is Chris. My mum."

Chris reaches out and gives her a hug too. She's a big woman, solid like Alex and only half a head shorter than Chris. Alex has her dark brown eyes and hair.

"Come through." She ushers them in.

The short hallway leads to an open sitting and dining room. Alex's mum heads to the kitchen at the back to continue with lunch preparation. Gary and Alex's dad are already drinking beer and smoking, with the ubiquitous sports programme playing on the large plasma screen TV.

Alex's dad turns his attention to Chris, but Gary's eyes are glued to the television.

"This is Chris. My dad."

Chris hurries over to shake the older man's hand.

"Sit. You want a beer?" Alex's dad asks.

Chris shakes his head. "No, I'm good. Thanks."

"And my brother, Gary."

Gary takes notice now and stands up to shake Chris's hand too. Otherwise, both father and son show little interest.

"Let's see what Mum's doing." Alex tugs at Chris's elbow and leads him to the back of the house.

The kitchen is big enough in this kind of townhouse. The roast smells delicious, though Alex's mum's cooking usually ends up a disappointment. She's preparing carrots; two pots of water bubble away.

She glances back. "Hey, you two go and sit down. It's too small in here."

Alex and Chris's eyes lock. Alex says, "We'll keep you company."

"Can I help you, Mrs. Whale?" Chris offers.

She regards Chris once more; her eyes run up and down his full height quickly. "That's great. Why don't you help chop the carrots?"

Alex's mum puts some potatoes in the pot to boil, then turns to Chris. "Are you Alex's flatmate?"

Alex and Chris exchange a quick glance. It is Alex's call to tell his parents about their relationship, so Chris replies, "Yes."

As Alex's mum turns away, Alex takes Chris's hand, squeezes and releases it. Chris beams at the tiny gesture.

Alex's mum looks over her shoulder. "When you said a 'friend', I thought you were bringing a girlfriend home, Alex. It's okay. Sam's been gone for a long time."

Alex and Chris trade another gaze behind. "I haven't got a new girlfriend, Ma." Semantic. Alex has a new queerfriend.

"I know it's hard for you after everything that's gone on. It's been what? Nearly six years. There must be lots of women up in London."

Alex scratches his head. "Yeah, I guess so."

"Even Gary's got someone now. This receptionist at the garage he works. Poor girl!"

She's making an effort. Alex has noticed that since they had to sell the house, she has finally accepted Alex is no longer able to provide for them like he used to. She has stopped drinking as much. Gary has also settled down, apparently. The only one who hasn't changed much is Alex's dad. Alex should have stopped helping his family years ago.

Decision. Life. You can only work with what you have.

Chris finishes the carrots and puts them in another pan to cook.

By the time they sit down for lunch, Alex is more than anxious, but Chris's small touches and smiles reassure him that whatever happens, he'll be all right.

They dish up. Alex's mum piles food on Chris's plate. "You look like you could do with some meat. You're like one of them size-zero models. Here."

"Thanks! That's plenty." Chris tries to stop her after the third slice of roast.

"And he's not drinking." Alex's dad says as if it's Chris's personality flaw.

They all tuck in. After a few minutes, Alex clears his throat and belatedly responds to his dad, "Chris is not drinking because I've stopped."

His dad frowns. "Why's that a reason for 'im not drinking?"

Alex puts his knife and fork down, gazes at Chris one more time and inhales. Chris squeezes Alex's hand in encouragement.

"Because he cares enough to help me stay sober. We're seeing each other."

Gary stares at his brother.

Alex's mum watches Alex and Chris, incomprehension giving way to understanding.

Alex's dad chokes mid-chew. "What the fuck do you mean?"

Alex breathes in again. "I am his boyfriend."

Gary shakes his head. "You can't be serious, Alex. It's not funny."

Alex's mum looks from Chris to Alex and back once more and says to her older son, "Your brother's not kidding, Gary. As soon as they came in today, I could see it. Don't know why, but—"

"That's bullshit. How can you go out with a bloke? I don't get it." Alex's dad crosses his meaty arms in front of his chest and regards Alex and Chris with alarm.

"There's nothing to get," Alex says calmly. "I didn't tell you all the details when I beat Ryan up. He tried to shoot me and Chris blocked him and saved my life. It's not why we are together, but...I'm trying to tell you Chris is important to me. Okay?"

Chris puts his hand over Alex's on the table.

More quietly, Alex declares, "I love him."

His dad still looks as perplexed as ever. "Did something happen in prison?"

"Prison? No. I've liked both men and women for a long time."

Alex's dad's eyes shift between the two, but he's too stunned by Alex's declaration.

Gary tuts. "He's girly, anyway. Look at his nail varnish."

All eyes descend on Chris's blue nails. He has forgotten to take the varnish off in his attempt to be more 'manly'. He holds his hands up to admire them; the minute silvery specks of glitter shine in the light. "Yeah, I had them done two days ago. Don't you like the colour?" he asks no one in particular. Chris chuckles, joined by Alex and his mum, breaking the inquisition for a moment.

She comments, "They're okay, Chris. You need to grow them out a bit, though."

"Do I?" Chris grins at Gary and his dad, whose frown deepens between his brows.

Lunch continues. Alex's family have a hundred questions for Chris but are afraid to ask, and silence stretches, masking the awkwardness. After a while, Chris puts his cutlery down and makes to stand. "That was delish, Mrs. Whale. I think I'll have a smoke outside."

Alex's mum smiles again. "You're welcome. Call me Pat, and his dad's Colin."

Colin glares at his wife.

"Okay. Thank you, Pat." Chris stands and excuses himself before sashaying out to the backyard.

As soon as he's out of the door, Alex's dad lays into Alex again. "How can you be gay? You're a fucking boxer."

"The correct term is bisexual. You may also find that all kinds of people can be attracted to more than one gender." Alex doesn't know where his boldness comes from. Being with Chris has been an eye-opener for him. Now he has to convince his family that this is no joke.

Beer foam gracing Gary's upper lip, he considers his brother's face again. "You must admit it's weird."

"Not if that's who I am. Chris came along, and I…fell for him," Alex says steadily. He wasn't sure what would happen when he came out, but interrogation by his dad and Gary is proving a bit much. He feels this warmth in his belly, though—pride and elation, like winning a match.

"Leave him alone," his mum interjects. "The man seems to make him happy."

Alex's dad tuts again when Chris walks back in and sits down.

"Alex is taking me to the fair after," Chris announces nonchalantly, ignoring the obvious tension at the dining table.

"See? He's like a fucking girl!" Gary seems to think that Alex only likes Chris because he appears androgynous despite his effort of being more masculine today for Alex's family.

Chris flashes his full set of white teeth at Gary. "I take that as a compliment."

It breaks the tension and makes Alex smile again. For now. He has always admired Chris's in-your-face attitude about his gender and sexuality. His family will just have to accept them.

Pat smiles. "The outdoor rides won't be open at this time of the year but there's the arcade. You go and have a good time."

Chris's broad grin melts Alex's heart, but his dad puts his knife and fork down as though he's given up. He pushes his chair back with a loud squeak and stands up.

"I've had enough." Alex wonders if he means the conversation or lunch.

Chris and Alex are ready to leave soon after the meal. Alex's dad ignores them, though Gary waves goodbye. Pat comes to the door and hugs them one after the other. "Love you," she tells

Alex. "And Chris, you're welcome anytime. Okay? Try put some meat on them bones."

"Okay. Thanks for the feed again, Pat."

In the taxi back to the pier, Chris starts laughing and he can't stop. It's infectious, and they both giggle and hold hands.

A trip to the fair.

Alex takes Chris to the carousel. They sit on adjacent horses. The staff operator regards Alex warily because he looks as though he might break the mechanical animal with his weight. She seems to be waiting for more customers but eventually, she starts the carousel with only four people on it. Hardly any kids are around as it's out of season.

The tinny music begins. Chris laughs and hoots when his wooden horse flies through the air. Alex joins him as the ridiculously mushy scene evolves around them. The artificial gaudy lights of the arcade blur into lines and patches of colours, cheering them up. Alex can't take his eyes off Chris as the feeling of being carefree is clearly written on his face.

The carousel fills a gap for what they have both missed as children. Chris has told Alex how he was never treated like a child by Annette. Alex spent most of his teenage years boxing, and before that his parents had rarely taken him anywhere, both busy working or drinking.

Afterwards, they walk out of the indoor amusement park, Alex's arm around Chris's shoulder, and stroll to the Esplanade. Chris is pensive, seemingly mesmerised by the bright yellow buoys bobbing up and down in the green-blue sea. The sun has come out for them, colouring the peaks of the waves brilliant silver.

Chris draws Alex close and rests his head on Alex's shoulder. "In the summer, we need to come back and play in the sand and walk in the waves," he says softly.

Alex grins. "I'd like that."

~~~

On the train back to London, the sky has already darkened and the fields are nothing but an inky mass.

Chris kisses Alex. "You came out to your family. Congrats!"

"Yeah. I did. I didn't plan how to do it, but it's happened now. I wasn't going to lie about who you are to me. It's a relief. I'm sorry about my family."

Chris smiles. "They're all right. Your mum's pretty sweet. They asked questions. I like it when people ask me questions because they're interested."

Alex is quiet for a moment. "But you don't talk about yourself, Chris."

Chris frowns. "Talking about myself is plain vulgar. I've always dealt with my shit my way. I don't discuss it with strangers."

The seriousness on Chris's face is rare.

Alex thinks about that before replying, "Okay. I get it. Thank you for sharing with me."

"You're stuck with me and my life story now, Alex Whale."

"I love you and your life story," Alex says. "My dad and Gary are missing out."

"Maybe I'll tell them about me being gender-fluid next time."

"Ha! Gary kept saying you're girly. He's going to have a hard time getting his head around queerness."

Chris giggles. "Then, I will talk to him about gender binary."

Alex gazes at Chris's dimples, one of the many parts of Chris that he loves. "I can't wait."

The relief and euphoria of coming out and being able to call Chris his partner outweigh the unpleasantness of his dad's and brother's reactions. They will have to get used to the idea of Alex being with Chris and that's all there is to it.

~~~

Jess wears a pretty floral dress, all in purple, blue and pink. Chris smiles and pecks the teenager's cheeks. Alex has gone out earlier to travel to the competition with Coach and Devan and a few other kids from the club.

Jess's stepdad and mum are currently separated, and a social worker is working with the family. Jess receives some counselling and support. She still struggles a little with school. She continues to go to the youth club and she bonds with Chris, who carries on her voluntary work after starting college. Chris absolutely loves her voluntary work. Jess's mum lets her go to see Chris and Alex every now and then. They've been to the cinema and gone for a walk. Sometimes Chris cooks a simple dinner at home when the teenager visits and they watch TV or a film afterwards.

The community hall is packed with friends and families of the competitors, all aspirant boxers from different London clubs. It's Devan's first big match and he's understandably nervous. Alex and Dex have intensified his training in the last few weeks until they are sure that Devan is in his best possible shape. This is a test for the whole club as though the matches will be a testament to both Devan's skills and Alex's training.

Jess and Chris don't know what to expect but they're excited by the exhilarating atmosphere.

"Is someone going to bleed to death?" Jess asks Chris.

Chris smiles. "I hope not. These are boxers not Roman gladiators. No, they won't let them get to that stage. The referee will separate the boys if they get too heated and dangerous to each other. There are *rules!*"

Jess grins, pleased to hear it.

The boxers have already been through the initial rounds of selection, so Devan's first match is the quarter-final. He's against a kid who's about the same size and build, but Alex recognises straightaway that Devan's opponent is not as technically accomplished. Devan's footwork is excellent, and his hooks and punches spot on, all thanks to his trainer. Devan soon dispatches the other teenager. Chris almost feels sorry for the kid who lost. The other teams are throwing glances at them, envious of Devan's famous coach.

Devan comes from a single-parent family. His mum and three younger siblings are all there to cheer him on. After Devan's first win, Jess and Chris and Devan's family all hug as though they've known each other forever.

The semi-final excites the crowd just as much. After the previous match, Devan's confidence comes in leaps and bounds. Three rounds to determine the winner. Devan makes good use of the short time and knocks the opponent down twice, completely dominating the fight.

Devan's final is more of a challenge since his opponent is a bigger and older boy. Alex calmly prepares Devan for the fight and reassures him as he talks to the youngster by the ring, whispering into his ear. Alex and Coach put the head guard on Devan and ensure his gloves are worn properly. Chris has seen boxing matches on the television, though it's not something that she paid attention to before. Jess is nervous and excited at the same time. She is so invested in Devan's fight that, when he gets hit during an early round of the final, she winces and hides behind Chris, too afraid to see what's going on. But after a few seconds, she comes out again because she *has* to see the rest of the match.

Devan soon regains the upper hand. After more pep talk by Alex, he changes from being defensive to attacking. His quick footwork serves him well. He soon starts to strike out, using his powerful right hook with purpose and strategy to beat his older and more experienced opponent. His entire family jump up and down as though he has won the world championship.

Alex has told Chris a little about Devan. Like many other kids who go to the free classes at the club, Devan's mum is poor. She works part-time and has to feed four children, so it's not easy. Being the oldest, Devan is most aware of the family's financial situation. The teenager is truly grateful for Dex and Alex who have supported him through the training, showing how they believe in him.

Alex has always said that training the kids is part of giving back. When Devan wins, he must enjoy the sensation of triumph, too.

A total of nine minutes to decide between the two junior boxers. Chris thinks there's something wonderfully simple in the game of boxing, a little like Alex Blue himself.

~~~

Why has Annette asked her to meet up in Hackney? The area is not her usual hangout. Chris rushes over in a taxi in case it's an emergency. The café sits in the middle of a line of run-down shops: a corner store, mobile repairs and a small beauty salon. She walks in, braced for her mother's usual antics.

Chris does a double-take, almost doesn't recognise her mum. Annette is immaculately made up but the pale pink blouse and pencil skirt are so conservative that Chris wonders for a moment if she's looking at the wrong person.

She pecks Annette's face and slides into the opposite bench in the booth. "What's up?"

Chris considers Annette intently again. *Whoa.* She seems ten years younger and looks much better for it. Annette had her young, so she's about forty-seven or eight. It says something that Chris doesn't know her mother's birth year.

"I should ask you the same. Have you shacked up with Alex Whale and forgotten all about your old mum?"

If Chris had been drinking, she would have spluttered. *Mum?* Annette hasn't used the word in years. Or ever. *Old mum?*

"Did something drastic happen?"

Annette laughs. Her tongue is as acidic as Chris's. "Fuck you, Chris. I found a job. That's what."

Chris's eyes widen. "Like a proper job?" There's hope for humanity if an ex-porn star and glamour model like Annette can find work.

The waitress comes along and Chris orders a coffee. One kind. No choice of sizes, flavours and foams. It seems that gentrification has escaped some small corners of London after all. Chris smirks.

Annette clears her throat. "I'm the receptionist next door: Molly's Hair and Beauty." A modicum of pride appears on her face.

There really is hope for humanity. Chris stares at Annette with wide eyes.

"Molly's a friend and I'm on trial. I won't mess up, though. I'm not taking anything or drinking, either. I've been going to AA and that 'twelve steps' programme since my stomach pump." She sips tea from a mug, swallows and gazes at Chris, who waits for her to continue.

"When you were at the hospital, I realised I could lose you, and you'd lose me. The two of us. It's always been that, hasn't it? Men come and go, but you've been there for me all along despite everything. I can see it now. I'm a useless bitch but I'm going to try. I really am." Annette has her hands on the Formica surface and she stares at them rather than looks at her child.

Chris glances away, aghast. She's been waiting for this apology for a long time.

Now that she's started, Annette seems determined to get it all out. "Your face when you were in the hospital bed and we told you Alex wasn't there. It jolted me out of my misery. I've never seen you like that. You learned to be cold and heartless, Chris, and it was all my fault. The desperation on your face showed that you well and truly love Alex. You deserve to be loved. You're fearless, Chris. All those times when you got roughed up and you just bounced back. My gorgeous, pretty, funny, incredible kid."

Annette stops, choked by her tears. She finds a piece of tissue and dabs at her eyes.

"The only thing you were good at was you never questioned my gender or sexuality." Chris's voice is throaty, too, overcome by the emotive bubbles rising up. She was only bullied and misunderstood at school, but Annette always accepted her. "The rest of it, you fucking sucked."

Annette nods. "I know. Deep down, you're beautiful, whoever you are."

With tears falling down her face, too, Chris mumbles, "Your make-up will run like that. Hope you get staff discount."

Chris has a little blue eye make-up on, but she's too raw to worry about a small detail like smudged eyeliner.

Annette smiles and shakes her head. "So, are you going to tell me what you've been up to? You two moved, right?"

Chris tells her about their new apartment, smiling widely whenever she mentions Alex's name. She talks about college and the youth club.

By the time Annette has to get back to work, Chris has come to accept the fact that she is close to her mother. They are two positives. No wonder they always fight because they are too similar in so many ways.

"Are you still taking clients?" Annette asks her.

"Yeah, mostly regulars when I have to. Alex is working three jobs. I worry about him doing too much."

Chris finds her packet of cigarettes, takes one out, ready for a smoke outside. She pays the waitress for their drinks.

Annette considers Chris's face again before speaking. "One of the reasons I asked you to come today—I don't want you to transfer the five hundred to me every month anymore. I should be ashamed of myself, of living off you for the past twenty years. When Jimmy left me, he paid for the house and it's mine now. So, I don't want you to worry about me. I want you to have a new life with your man. Try not to sell yourself if you can. I've got a couple of thousands in savings. You can have it, too. It's not much. Get that qualification and get out while you're still young."

More tears are threatening to surge, so Chris closes her eyes to control herself. She opens them again when she's calm enough. "We'll be okay, Alex and me. We'll look after each other. But I'm your kid. I won't quit you, either, no matter how much you fucked me over."

Annette grimaces. "I know. I'm sorry. I'll be all right too. Promise. That's why I want you to think about yourself and be happy. That'll make me happy, okay?"

She reaches out and shakes Chris's loose fist across the table. Chris looks away to hide her feelings.

"You can come to see our flat if you like," Chris offers outside the café before they part ways. "When you happen by, doing your shopping or whatever. Don't trouble yourself."

Annette says, cutting through Chris's bullshit. "I'll come by. I'd love to visit."

~~~

Alex remembers the smell of the hospital when he was last here. He was so scared that Chris wasn't going to make it. Two partners would have died because of him. The shock of the events with Ryan Taylor stays with him, immersed into his nightmares. When he got the phone call today, his stomach sank. How many more times will he be visiting hospitals and be scared to death for his loved ones?

Once they find Dex's bed, the entire area seems too small because of the sizes and heights of Alex and Chris. Some of Dex's numerous relatives drift off to leave, to give them some space, leaving Coach's wife Paula and their oldest son Dael.

Dex tries to sit up by himself but Paula rushes forward to help him. He eyes Alex and Chris. "What's this? I'm not fucking dying."

Alex shrugs. "Can't we come to see you unless you're on the way out?"

Dex laughs; his face has gathered more lines overnight. Alex glances over to Chris and frowns.

"I saw that," Dex complains. "I had a little funny turn. There's nothing to worry about."

Dael tuts rather loudly. "Mum found you unconscious in the flower bed. I wouldn't call that nothing, Dad!"

"What did the doctors say?" Alex asks.

Dex grimaces. "They've run some tests. Pre-cautionary. They said it's my blood pressure. I don't think they'll need to keep me in for too much longer."

Paula interjects, "Let the doctors decide on that, shall we?" She exchanges one of those looks with Dex—the kind that shows a private understanding between long-term partners. She regards Dael, too, for a moment.

Coach clears his throat. Chris instinctively grabs Alex's hand and squeezes.

"I need to leave the club to you, Alex. This lot's been telling me to retire for the past five years. I don't want to, but I can't die on the job."

Dael hoots. "About bloody time."

Alex swallows and gazes at Chris, who gives him a thumb up. Alex owes Dex and the children. He will make it work with Chris's support.

Alex promises. "Sure, I'll take it on. I'll take on the world if you ask me, Coach."

~~~

Chris steps into the sunshine after their class. They are itching to have a cigarette but they desist.

It's not good to have traces of tobacco around babies and toddlers. Fuck's sake, the sacrifices for my career.

Willpower, that's what they need. As they're pondering about a new life if they ever get through the course, a shadow appears in front of them blocking out the slanting sun.

Chris glances up, their dirty blonde hair turns a shade lighter.

"I've come to meet my boyfriend." Alex's beam spreads, so deep in affection it makes Chris shudder.

"Who's your boyfriend?" Chris switches their messenger bag to their other shoulder and takes off walking. Their facial muscles strain from trying not to smile. They push up their black-framed glasses, a new addition to help them read. They make Chris's eyes seem even bigger.

Alex follows Chris and, with his long gaits, catches up in no time. "You're not my girlfriend today. Shall I call you the *person* I shack up with?"

He presents Chris with a single black rose. Chris has forgotten all about Valentine's Day—it's not a day Chris celebrated with anyone.

Romance. Tuts.

Chris laughs. "I don't care. Boy and girl. I want to be your everything." They accept the flower and glance at Alex sideways. Their insides melt at the sight of the big man.

"Thank you. I love you, Alex."

There. Chris has never said the words before and meant them. They are walking so fast as if they are about to break into a run after that crazy announcement.

Alex clutches Chris's arm and stops them from walking. He pulls Chris into an embrace, surprising them. "You do?"

Chris turns their palms up as if to offer themself to Alex. "Yeah, this tingly feeling whenever you're around is irritating as hell. I know how fucking ridiculous I am, and how hard it is to be around me. If saying whatever I said a minute ago will make you keep me, then that's fine. If not, there's plenty of fish in the sea you could love, Alexander. It's a big world out there and everything—"

Alex interjects, "You *are* my everything, Chris. I *am* in love with you. I don't need other fish in the sea."

Chris rewards Alex with quiet laughter.

Alex kisses them. "And everything's going to be hard but I'm here. Let's do it together, yeah?"

Chris tries to suppress their smile but fails. "Yeah, all right." They tilt their face and lick Alex's lips. "And Happy Valentine's, my Big Blue!"

~~~

Alex insists that Chris can't see the design of his new tattoo until tonight. It's been twenty-four hours. When they have sex, he'll reveal it, Alex says.

Chris laughs. "You think you're going to trick me into agreeing to having sex, don't you?"

Alex shoves more pasta into his mouth—his favourite that Chris cooks at least once a week, with extra tuna for Alex.

Chris makes Alex work for it when they're in bed. "Take your top off."

Alex does, looking embarrassed for no good reason.

"Lie down on the bed," Chris commands.

Chris licks her sweet lips and regards Alex. She never ceases to marvel at the power of his body. Like a striptease without music, she takes her time shedding her top. Alex can't conceal his excitement at the sight of Chris's smooth skin and shapely nipples.

One by one, Chris unhooks the buttons of her jeans and slowly peels them off, teasing Alex with her sensuality. Her favourite black thong hardly conceals her excitement. Alex swallows.

"Are you blushing, Alex Whale?" Chris is amused.

Under Chris's gaze, Alex tries to hide from the intensity of his reactions.

Chris shimmies out of her thong slowly, freeing herself. She ghosts her fingers along Alex's stretched muscles, every inch of the big man well-defined. She scratches him with her black-lacquered nails, circulating and flirting with his body.

Chris eventually unzips Alex's trousers and releases his erection. She leans down and licks and sucks him.

When she stops teasing Alex, she asks, "So, what will you do to persuade me to fuck you tonight?"

Alex's brain freezes. After far too long, he whispers, "Anything. This tattoo…"

Chris's eyes sparkle. "Does it show how you'll do anything to make me happy?"

"Yes. I love you, and I'll do anything for you." Alex can hardly breathe under Chris's newfound power.

Chris pulls down Alex's trousers, taking them off completely, and peels off the bandage covering his left thigh.

The tattoo bursts with white and different shades of blue. Black elegant lines dance a tango through the patches of colour. Its wings raised, about to take flight. The cerulean shade bleeds like watercolour on his taut skin.

"This is beautiful." Chris traces the design etched into Alex's strong flesh like a stretched canvas.

No escape from a bond so deep.

"It's a perfect combination of you and me."

Chris's eyes take on the same indigo as the bird in flight.

A blue jay.

-- END --

ABOUT A. ZUKOWSKI

I am a London-based British writer who grew up in the gay village and red light district of Manchester, UK.

I was trained in screenwriting at the University of the Arts London; National Film & Television School and Script Factory, UK. I worked as a film journalist, wrote and produced short films. My stories are based on personal and emotional experiences, and feature strong LGBTQ-identified characters.

Connect with the Author

Twitter: @saszazukowski

Blog: http://azukowskiblog.wordpress.com

Goodreads: http://www.goodreads.com/author/show/16509569.A_Zukowski

Booklikes: http://azukowski.booklikes.com/

Tumblr: http://azukowski.tumblr.com

FB: http://www.facebook.com/aleksander.zukowski.353

OTHER BOOKS BY A. ZUKOWSKI

THE BOY WHO FELL TO EARTH

#1 London Stories

Jay Palmer is two months away from his sixteenth birthday. He doesn't realise how his life will be changed forever when a gang of thugs leaves a badly injured boy on his doorstep. The biracial boy and his white single mum Maggie nurse the stranger, sixteen-year-old Aleksander Zukowski or Sasha. Sasha ran away from care two and half years ago. He sleeps rough, is addicted to drugs and sells himself on the streets of London to fund his habit. For the first time in his life, he has a reason to change.

Sasha confirms what Jay already knows about himself but it won't be easy for Jay to come out to his macho mates in a largely black neighbourhood. Sasha has an uphill struggle to stay clean when his past threatens to throw him back into the abyss. Are the two boys strong enough to stay together against all odds?

Praise for *The Boy Who Fell to Earth:*

"I know this is one of those stories that will play on my mind long after I've stopped reading."
~Alpha Book Club

"It has a force that keeps you on the edge of the seat and a grittiness that opens your eyes and makes you think."
~Sinfully Gay Book Reviews

~~~

Leyton, London.

It happened when Ma and I were having dinner in the front room. Well, if you grew up in a poor, single-parent family in fucking East London, you were lucky to have a sitting room separate from your bedroom. Mum always said that the flat cost her half her salary, so "don't you complain". I didn't. I had a box room with a single bed, and I could never fault my mum's ability to feed me. After all, I was not even sixteen and nearly six feet tall and I ate like an elephant all the time which was down to my father's genes, apparently. My mum should have hated the way I reminded her of my dad because he walked out on her when I was only five, but she didn't.

Anyway, this night we were in the sitting room with our dinner hot on the table. It was only October, but the sky had darkened since the late afternoon. A loud squeak cut through the thick blackness outside. Mum and I looked at one another, as we sat and listened.

We could hear a car stop; tyres skidded across the road right in front of our place. Car doors opening and the voices indicated two or three men got out from the car and something heavy was thrown onto our front lawn. They shouted incomprehensibly to each other and got back in the car, slamming the doors with loud bangs. I called it our "lawn", but it was a patch of grass that was basically part of the pavement. People dumped all kinds of crap there all the time. The car sped off, its tyres screeching with the friction.

"What the fuck!" I stood up to look out, expecting to see fly tipping in our front garden again. The bastards.

"Language!" Ma never failed to remind me.

Living in our part of London, we should keep our nose out of other people's business. But, now that the men had gone, I wasn't afraid to go and investigate. I lifted the curtains and peered into the dark, my breath instantly misting up the window. I assumed they had left a bag of rubbish, a piece of old furniture, or something like that, but they hadn't. I screwed up my eyes to see in the dark, to make out the shape of the thing on the lawn, and my heart pounded. Arms and thighs shimmered oddly white in the night.

"Shit, mum. There's someone out there. They dumped a body." Perhaps I grew up watching too many crime and detective dramas. My mum loved them. But I was sure I wasn't imagining things. Around our part of London it was entirely possible it was a dead man.

"A body?" Mum was a nurse which was a good thing because she sounded curious rather than scared or panicky.

I ran out first. The man—well, he was a boy about the same age as me—lay on his side, his legs drawn up. My heart thumped when I saw that his trousers were down just below his knees; his bare arse was bloody and his balls were black, as though someone had literally kicked his nuts. The rest of him was the same, black and blue everywhere; his face was covered in blood. In the pale, yellowy lamplight he looked dead. I could make out he was pale skinned and his hair colour was light, probably blonde. My eyes were drawn back to his limp penis. I couldn't help it. I wasn't frightened or disgusted. Instead I was fascinated by the stranger as if the scene put a spell on me.

LIAM FOR HIRE

A gay novel

#2 London Stories

Liam Murphy has kicked his drug habit and now pays for the high living costs in London as an escort. His life is finally in balance. His only problem is that he obsesses about the minimum number of times he has to bend over to make ends meet. As long as he has his emotions under control, it'll be fine. That's what Liam keeps telling himself until he meets the young widower Alastair, also known as Ali, whose emerald eyes remind him of Ireland.

Featuring Liam from *The Boy Who Fell to Earth*.

This title contains material some may find objectionable or trigger-inducing: mature content, drug use, suicidal thoughts.

Praise for *Liam For Hire:*

"[Liam is] extraordinary. So is their story. And if you dare take a chance on them, I presume you'll find the same."
~ Book Unfunk

"Absolutely beautiful."

~ Love Bytes LGBTQ Book Reviews

~~~

"You don't need to lie about your age to be untruthful. I don't have anything to hide." The only thing no client will get from me is emotional attachment, as hackneyed as it sounds. It's not good for me or for them. I need to protect myself. No one else will.

He nods, as if he understands my reasoning. After finishing the joint, I light up another cigarette and take a large sip of the whisky that clouds my head. I realise I'm enjoying the conversation. Here in this little garden, I am able to relax. Living in my box room in the crowded flat isn't good for contemplation. But then, who am I to complain? I can hardly afford anything else.

As we listen to the hum of the London suburb and the distant sirens that cut through the city's streets all night, Ali's curious gaze fixes on my face as though he really wants to know the real me. "And you're Irish, right?"

My accent is unmistakable. "Yup. Born and bred in West Cork."

Ali plays with his wedding band and he takes a gulp of his whisky, almost finishing it. "So, how long have you been in London?"

"I came to London nearly four years ago." But most of the first three years were shrouded in a drug-induced fog. I'm not proud of it.

"Do you miss home? Do you ever feel nostalgic?" Ali stares dreamily at the shadows of the garden. I wonder why he's the one who seems to be pining for something.

I look intently at the dark sky as I consider his questions and finally I realise what 'home' means to me. Even with a roof over my head I'm still homeless in my heart. Bricks and mortar don't mean anything. I'm not sure if I want a real home right now, somewhere I belong. Not that one is on offer or available to someone like me. Some days, I long for the freedom of the streets, strange as it may sound to anyone who has never been homeless. My bedsit and the job are like a hamster's cage, giving me temporary shelter but making me go round and round in circles.

I reply, "I don't miss the actual places. I miss the stars and the inky nights. Sometimes I think I can smell the seaweed on damp sand and hear the sound of the waves on Inch Beach if I close my eyes. I yearn for the thunderstorms and the crystal dewdrops clinging to long grass. I want to hear the tunes played on a bodhrán and the low notes from the clarsach." I inhale deeply, then slowly breathe out, thinking about those beautiful things I once shared with someone I thought I loved and would spend the rest of my life with.

COURTING LIGHT

A novella, part of the Seasons of Love anthology

Our days were numbered but precious.

Courting Light is the story of Josie, an eighteen-year-old about to leave home to start university in London. She volunteers at a summer camp for disabled children. When Josie is paired with the autistic teenager Lucian, she faces intense experiences that are truly eye-opening. To her surprise, Lucian is not the only one who captures her attention. Over the weeks, Josie develops powerful desire evoked by the camp's enigmatic young leader with a shaved head and tattoo on her skull.

Praise for *Courting Light*:

"Poignant and moving."
~ The Lesbian Review

"A sweet story told with raw emotion, the sensitive portrayal of Autism, and an ending that will stay with me for a long time."
~ Jamie Deacon, Lambda nominated author